Debra Hurford Brown

About the Author

LOUISE WENER is the author of *The Perfect Play* and *Goodnight Steve McQueen*. She was born and raised in Ilfor, East London. In the mid-ninetics, after years of singing into hair brushes and working dead-end jobs, she found fame as lead singer of the pop band Sleeper, and went on to record three top-ten albums and eight top-forty singles. She is now a full-time author.

The HALF LIFE
of STARS

Also by Louise Wener

The Perfect Play

Goodnight Steve McQueen

The HALF LIFE of STARS

A Novel

LOUISE WENER

HARPER

NEW YORK • LONDON • TORONTO • SYDNEY

HARPER

First published in Great Britain in 2006 by Hodder and Soughton, a division of Hodder Headline.

HarperCollins books may be purchased for educational, business, or sales promotional use. For information please write: Special Markets Department, HarperCollins Publishers, 10 East 53rd Street, New York, NY 10022.

First Harper paperback published 2006.

Library of Congress Cataloging-in-Publication Data is available upon request.

ISBN-10: 0-06-084173-7
ISBN-13: 978-0-06-084173-7

06 07 08 09 10 RRD 10 9 8 7 6 5 4 3 2 1

For I.
Our little piece of stardust.

Ignition

Obviously a Major Malfunction

As Daniel yawned and climbed into his father's car that morning, he saw a poodle being dressed in a red knitted coat. Huffs of hot dog-breath sprang from the animal's mouth – white, steamy and most likely malodorous – while its owner tightened straps and fastened collars, and swaddled its shivering belly in a layer of cloth. The animal appeared resolutely unimpressed, yelping and digging its paws into the wind-whipped sand while its master tugged patiently at its neck. Even with the benefit of outdoor clothing, it still seemed unwilling to get going.

It was January in Florida and a deep, rare chill had swept the sunshine state from coast to coast. Palm trees swayed uneasily beneath a stiff crust of frost and beaches the length of the Space Coast looked like they'd been newly dusted with sugar. The freeze extended as far south as Miami and the Keys, and the crisp cold air, loaded with the prospect of rain, reminded Daniel of winters back home. In the hours before dawn only the intrepid and the insomniacs and the crazies were out on the streets and Daniel wished – like the dog – that he could have slunk back to the warmth of his bed.

It might not have brought him much comfort. Even safe in their houses, buried beneath their quilts, Floridians were having trouble sleeping. Old men lay awake worrying about their pets. Fruit growers worried about their oranges. Cuban émigrés worried about their relatives making landfall in the sub-zero cold and hoteliers fretted about lost business. And some way to the north, in the depths of a government building, the seven loneliest people in all the world tossed and turned and called out in their sleep, their minds alive with unwelcome nightmares.

As they hit the start of the turnpike, Daniel's father extinguished his breakfast cigarette. He gave an empty belch like a small cry for help and felt around in the glove compartment for a half-eaten box of Rennies. Lately he'd been guzzling antacids like a newborn baby guzzles milk, and the early start had set off a vigorous bout of indigestion. So profuse were his father's digestive juices that Daniel sometimes imagined his stomach to be awash with them: gallons of fizzing acid; pools of yellow bile; creeping up the narrow tunnel of his oesophagus until they burnt a hole right through his chest.

'Excited?' said his father, stuffing squares of chalk into his mouth. 'It's going to be pretty exciting, if it goes.'

Daniel nodded.

'Long drive again, though. Four hours at least. Should we stop off for pancakes, are you hungry?'

Daniel shook his head.

'I could eat some dry toast. Maybe we'll stop for some toast.'

Daniel knew his father wouldn't stop. The same way he hadn't stopped the day before. He'd speed without a break all the way to Titusville, then he'd buy them both a hamburger at a drive-through McDonald's. They'd eat in the car with the radio on while his father muddled himself with directions and map-books, and complained about the illogic of American road signs. They'd been living in Florida for close to a year now, but the exit signs still managed to confuse him.

'Hey, you awake? We're almost there.'

Daniel had slept most of the way. He stirred as he felt the car's engine cut out beneath him and his body snapped easily back to life. These days it took his father a full hour to escape the bounds of sleep, but Daniel was whole in mere seconds. His father examined him carefully, his pride hiding a brief spike of envy. His son the athlete: the daredevil; the championship sprinter. His son the malcontent: the back-talker; the monosyllabic mood machine.

'How's your burger?'

'It's OK.'

'Is it good, you like it?'

'It's fine.'

'Your coffee warm? Sometimes they give you a cold coffee.'

'It's OK, Dad. Stop asking me.'

Daniel's father screwed up his serviette and pointed his car eastward towards the Cape. When had his son started drinking coffee? When exactly had he made the switch from Coca-Cola? When had he decided he knew everything about the world when he really knew nothing at all?

'You think it's going to go this time? You think that teacher lady's going to make it all the way up to Mars?'

'They're not going to Mars, Dad.'

'Yeah, I know. Just testing. Just trying to put a smile on your face.'

Daniel turned to stare out of the window, embarrassed by his father's attempt at humour. How had their relationship deteriorated this far? He'd expected to be an embarrassment to his teenage son – wasn't that the fate of all fathers – but he hadn't expected to disgust him. This, then, was the purpose of their trip. Daniel's mother and sisters had stayed put in Miami Beach while the two of them drove north to repair their bonds. Already, it was turning out badly. This was the second time in two days he'd made the long drive up to Cape Canaveral and he was fighting exhaustion as well as his son's contempt. Yesterday they'd left Dade County even earlier and stood for hours in the bitter wind with the other sightseers at Jetty Park, while they'd waited for the rocket to go. His son had sneered at him when he'd called it a rocket. But what else was it? It was a rocket that came home again; big deal, it was still a rocket.

They'd called off that first launch just past noon. And for what? Some jammed door bolt that wouldn't loosen. They'd had to fetch up a portable drill to break it open, but when they'd found one its battery was dead. A billion dollars of the most sophisticated technology known to man, an entire space centre crammed with NASA's sharpest minds. And still they couldn't get the damn thing off the ground: for the want of a lousy pack of Duracell.

But he had to show willing. His son was enamoured by space. When he wasn't training or running or moping around the house he was combing the universe with his telescope. He wondered what his son was looking for. Black holes? Aliens? Some meaning? What was the point? There was enough to be confused about right here.

Recharged with food and wrapped up in heavy coats they braced themselves for another long wait. The crowd was larger than it had been the day before but the same rumours, whispers and half-baked theories circled the width of the park. It was too cold for the shuttle, too windy; there were icicles hanging from its wings. Daniel's father rubbed at his eyelids. He hated delays at the best of times and this constant indecision, this permanent state of flux, left him feeling distracted and sleepy. He tried to stay alert through the announcements – it was going, then it wasn't, then it was again – but he just wished they'd make up their mind. He wondered why people could never do that – take a decision and stick to it. And then, out of nowhere, came the go-ahead. They were positive now, it was certain. The damn fool rocket would go.

By eleven o'clock with the wind dropped to a whisper, the tedium was accelerating to an end. Daniel had a pair of binoculars glued to his eyes and all around him shone the glow of expectation. Children knelt up on their parents' shoulders, teenagers balanced on the roofs of cars; couples held tight to one another waving flags and freshly painted banners in their hands. Everyone had their radios tuned to the same frequency and the launch commentary spilled out, lubricating the crowd, from a thousand different directions.

At fifteen minutes to lift-off, the air filled with great whoops and cheers and Daniel's face drenched pink with excitement. Goose bumps spread out like a rash along his arms and he could barely stand still any longer. His father allowed himself a smile. He could drink all the coffee he wanted, be as surly as he liked, but this boy was little more than a child. As he watched him fidget in those minutes and chew nervously on his lips, he was reminded just how young his son still was. Young enough to judge him: not nearly old enough, yet, to forgive him.

'Look at it, Dad. Can you see? Here, take these. Take a look.'

Daniel's father took the binoculars and trained his eyes on the launch pad. Christ, what a bird it was up close. A wild white Moby Dick of a machine, rearing up out of the ground. That gigantic silo that it clung to, framed with rocket boosters four-teen storeys high; each juiced up with five hundred tons of rocket fuel, burning ten tons of the stuff for every second that it flew. What were they thinking of, those crazy astronauts? What was going through their heads, right now? Seven lonely souls locked into a cockpit the size of a saloon car, strapped to the back of the world's largest firework.

'How fast is she going to go?' He said, lowering the bino-culars. 'How fast will she go, after lift-off?'

Daniel squinted at his father, wondering if he might risk the chance to swear.

'Pretty fucking fast. Close to 2000 miles an hour.'

'Don't swear, Daniel, I told you . . . Jesus *Christ*. Are you sure?'

How could that be? How could that possibly feel? To tear through the earth's gravitational field, to fly like a bullet and be free. It had crept up on him, this feeling of astonishment, risen up inside of him without him even noticing. His pulse began to race, his chest began to heave and Jesus, what a show. What a *show*. They could see a bed of steam rising up off the launch pad, a billowing cloud of smoky white. It was vapour, Daniel told him. An avalanche of water sluiced out onto the launch site to cushion the violence of the acoustic shock. The sound waves generated by lift-off were so ferocious that they could shake the shuttle apart where it stood.

A thousand radio announcers interrupted them in unison at that point, blared out the same clarion call: *T minus ten seconds and counting – go for main engine start.* The crowd began to count and Daniel and his father, caught up in the excitement, began to count along with them. So this was it. After two days of waiting and twelve hours of driving back and forth, it really was about to go. All around them hungry faces strained upwards and outwards, away from their own fears and confusions towards the heady recesses of space. What hopes they levied on this fearsome machine, what great expectations it carried. What a thrill it was, just to witness it: to see it break through the boundaries of earth.

They felt the vibrations all at once and together; a faint low groan that rumbled up their bones and spread out like a tremor beneath their feet. Then came the flames, a wildly vivid fluorescent orange glow, that seemed to swallow up the base of the launch pad. And then the monster began to move. It began so carefully, so slowly, like it mightn't make it at all. They could sense how heavy it was in the air, feel every inch of the effort it was making. And everyone standing with them felt it too, and used their collective influence to will it forward.

'There she goes, Daniel. Will you look at *that*. Jesus, *look*, there she goes.'

Suddenly she was airborne. Slicing through the sky – as clear now and blue as a Glacier Mint – on a raging catapult of flame. The roar of lift-off thundered towards them, engulfing them where they stood like a living thing. Daniel and his father braced themselves, their troubles all but forgotten. What a vision this was. What optimism linked them at that moment.

It lasted just over a minute, just long enough for a father to relax and exhale and squeeze his son's shoulder. And was this true? Did he turn and mouth something to him in those final seconds? Don't worry? I'm sorry? I love you? Daniel wasn't sure. He couldn't quite remember. Because somewhere overhead, in the depths of the machinery the edifice was starting to crumble. An aching joint had sighed open, allowing a snap of rocket fuel to break lose. The giant rubber O-ring designed to guard this vital seal was splitting apart like a yell. The sub-zero temperatures had killed it; made it rigid, taut and inflexible. And though

it strained and fought and battled to do its job, it became clear
– all too late – that it couldn't.

'What the fuck is that? What the *fuck*?'

The bird had stopped dead in its tracks; it simply wasn't there
any more. The skies above the ocean filled with debris and a vast
spreading cloud ripped sideways like a storm, in the shape of a
scorpion's tail. They stood in silence for a lifetime. Was it even
possible? That this beautiful, brutal machine could all but vanish
from the sky?

It was the radio announcer who gathered up their thoughts, who
held out a hand to every one of them. In a soothing, respectful
voice – one that he had practised at home in front of the mirror
in preparation for calamitous occasions – he spoke directly to
the nation. It seemed certain that the shuttle had indeed exploded.
Recovery boats were in the field. The parachutes they could see
unfurling over the ocean were likely to be paramedics, not astronauts. His voice began to slip at that point, crumbling through
the speaker like sand. There was a break in the transmission while
he took the time to compose himself and new voice – projected
from a Tannoy in the park – appealed for the crowd to keep
calm.

And what were they thinking, those silent onlookers? Amid
the shock and the grief the overriding emotion, Daniel thought,
was one of intense betrayal. They had invested in this machine,
a part of them had travelled with it. For the brief seconds that
it flew they had felt less mortal, less earthbound, less dreary; less
bowed by their day-to-day lives. Now the crowd were in free fall;
decelerating from hope at an alarming speed, crashing headlong
into the grind. It left them feeling dazed and vulnerable. Some
began to cry, some began to swear and thump the side of their
cars. Most continued to gaze open mouthed at the sky, convinced
that if they stared upwards long enough and hard enough, the
lost white bird would reappear.

And Daniel stared along with them. He knew those seven
astronauts hadn't made it, but still he couldn't tear his eyes away.

He felt like he'd be deserting them if he lowered his gaze, that he'd be insulting them the second he turned away. It took a while for him to notice that his father was tugging fiercely at his arm. His face was white with exhaustion, his palms felt gooey with sweat.

'What a shame,' he said, breathlessly, as he dragged his son through the crowd. 'Jesus, what a god-awful shame.'

Bad Choice of Boots

Daniel hadn't wanted to leave. He hadn't wanted to climb into the car so soon after the accident and battle his way out into the murderous traffic. He hadn't realised how angry he'd become or how eager he'd been to start in on that particular argument. It wasn't the time or the place. He should have left well alone. He hadn't realised how bad his father was feeling. How could he possibly have known?

In the lengthening shadows of the disaster, Daniel's feet were starting to bleed. His tight winter boots dug hard into his toes and grated raw skin from his heels. Why had he rejected his sneakers that morning? Why had he picked out these wretched boots? He couldn't run in them properly, the soles were rigid and as heavy as bread boards. It felt like his ankles were weighted down with lead, like the shock waves that sprang from his pounding of the road were trying their hardest to snap his bones.

How far had he come? A mile? A mile and a half? He was too exhausted to tell. He had used up his body's propellant too soon and appeared to be slowing with every step. His tough sprinter's frame was deflating, unused to such fierce acceleration over distance. Cramp began to fizz in the meat of his legs and he wondered how much longer he could stave it off. As long as it took. He'd fight it off as long as it took.

The road was utterly clogged now, sticky with caravans and trailers like his father's blood was sticky with fat. Traffic spread across the freeway like a vast jammy clot, inching forward on its hands and knees. There was definitely an ambulance out here somewhere, they had overtaken one not so long ago. If only he could battle his way through this maze then sprint back to find his father's car.

Daniel redoubled his efforts and wrenched some extra speed from his legs. He passed a gas station – closed – then a billboard the size of a cinema screen that offered the way to Miami Beach. The road beyond the billboard was clear. Cars hummed forward like oil through a pipeline, streaming southwards towards the sun, towards his home. This was the road that they ought to have been on, but his father had become disorientated after leaving Jetty Park and had somehow managed to miss the vital sign. He wasn't sure how it had happened but they appeared to have double-backed on themselves and within minutes they'd found themselves trapped; caught up in the swarm of tourists and rubber-necks who were battling their way out towards the Space Centre: no way forward, no way back; no valve or artery nearly strong enough to release this sudden intense surge of pressure.

People were staring at Daniel, peering through their wind-screens at the wild, crazy boy, running down the freeway like a startled cat. The lunatic with the sweats and the tough pumping arms, the kid without a jacket or a coat. What a sound he made as he passed them. The clackety-clack-clack of heavy boots on ice-cold tarmac as he tore in and out of the traffic. The violent suck of his tongue and his throat as he ripped each gasp of oxygen from the air. In the stillness some imagined they heard a steam train passing by, or an echo of the space shuttle itself. Some climbed out of their vehicles and chased after him for a while, worried he knew something that they didn't.

From time to time his route became impassable. He'd reach a brick wall in the mass of sightseers and vehicles and have to construct a new way through. Here and there drivers had inched out onto the hard shoulder in an attempt to get ahead, but all had become stranded within just a few yards. Daniel leapt their bonnets like they were track hurdles, his knees rising quick and level to his hips. Sometimes his boots would hit the shell of their cars, sometimes he'd fly straight over the top. If he found his way blocked by a trailer or a truck he'd scramble up over the roof. He didn't stop to speak to anyone. He didn't look behind him once. He never hesitated, stuttered or paused along the way to gauge where his heavy feet might land. He ran as if he were being hunted. And in a sense, he truly was.

After another mile or more he came upon it, an ambulance with red and white paintwork, a redundant siren pinned to its roof. Through the window Daniel could see that the paramedics were eating lunch, resigned to the fact that they were stuck. One man birthed thick pink sausages straight from a can, another shared out chicken legs from a Tupperware box. They listened to their radio as they discussed the fatal crash and shook their greasy faces at one another.

'You have to help me,' Daniel said, when he got to them, his face knotted tight against his fate. 'My father. He's not well. Please, you have to help me, up ahead.'

They took an age to get going, moved agonisingly slowly when they finally did; weighed down by bags and heavy equipment, and low-slung bellies filled with hot-dog buns and meat. It took them thirty minutes to jog those three short miles back to the car. Daniel had reached them in less than fourteen.

As he retraced his route through the traffic, blood began to pool in Daniel's socks. Leather seams ground into raw heel bone, and a ligament that he'd damaged from a single misplaced jump began to pull apart beneath his kneecap. When the pain became too much, he paused and tore off his malicious boots, tossing them out onto the embankment and running the rest of the way in his stocking feet. Still he urged the medics forward – willing them to hurry, begging them not to rest, tugging them over the hoods and bonnets of the stranded cars. They panted and suffered and hugged their sides in pain but no one could say that they slacked.

The moment his father's tan-coloured car came in sight, Daniel began to fall down. His legs gave way beneath him, dissolving into the ground like strands of newly dampened gelatine, and he felt his heart break in his throat. People began to gather round. Bored of sitting in their cars and playing I-spy with their kids they came rushing out to see what all the fuss was. They had thought Daniel's father was sleeping. The traffic wasn't moving, probably wouldn't be for hours, and they had thought this man was getting a little rest.

'Is he dead?' asked someone, carrying a camera in his hand. 'I thought he was sleeping. You think he's dead?'

They seemed unable to help him. They seemed unwilling even to try. No one thumped on his father's chest with the heel of their fists; no one offered him an electric shock or thrust a shot of adrenalin into his pale arm. No one leaned over and blew air into his thin blue lips or waved a jar of foul smelling salts under his nose. After some minutes an onlooker reached for a frayed winter blanket that lay crumpled and neglected on the back seat of the car, and lowered it disconsolately over the dead man's face.

'How'd he get those marks on his cheek?'

'Fell forward onto the steering wheel, I guess.'

'Do you know, son?' said one of the paramedics, scraping Daniel off the ground. 'You got any idea how he came by these marks?'

Daniel couldn't begin to say. He didn't speak again for the next five days. It took every shred of concentration he had left in his body to erase those desperate minutes from the recording of his life, and make the answer to their question disappear.

Countdown

The Pastry Chef

The night my older brother Daniel decides to disappear, I'm right in the middle of something. This is typical of him. As long as I can remember he has always had to be the centre of attention, and on this occasion he's truly surpassed himself. I'm lying in bed with the man I might almost love and it's reached a delicate stage in the proceedings. We're newly naked – on the point of entry – and a telephone is raging on my bedside table. It rings so fiercely, stopping then starting all over again, that I've either to smash it or pick it up.

'Who is it?'

'Claire, it's Kay.'

Just what you want with your pants down; a phone call from your high and mighty sister-in-law

'Kay, uh, it's late . . . you know, I'm sort of in the middle of something.'

'God . . . I'm sorry . . . are you . . . is somebody *there*?'

Of course there's somebody here. And it's not just anyone, either. It's the man that I might almost love.

The man I might almost love is a pastry chef. In all honesty I'm not sure I can make a life with a man that comes home smelling of pastry. He has dough in his fingernails and flour on his shoulders that looks suspiciously like a coating of dandruff. At work he wears a nylon cap on his head which looks like it's made out of stocking tops and is meant to stop his hair from falling out into the cannoli batter. I imagine him wearing it when I close my eyes and kiss him; it makes him look deranged and a little cheap. But this is my weakness all over – the things that repel me are the things that attract me the most.

My sister-in-law pauses at the end of the line, composes herself and starts over.

'Claire, I'm worried about Daniel. We don't know where he is.'

'What, you mean you've lost him?'

'No, we haven't lost him, we're just not sure where he is. You haven't heard from him, have you?'

'No. Not since the weekend.'

'He didn't mention anything to you? About going to a Christmas party this week. About staying out late for some reason?'

'He phoned to talk about the loan, Kay. He wasn't in the mood for chit-chat.'

'No . . . right. Of course not.'

I shouldn't be short with her; it's not her fault I've had to borrow money off them again.

'What's up? You going to be long?'

The pastry chef is rubbing my thighs; he's kissing my belly as she speaks.

'It's just . . . he's not home yet. He never came home from work.'

I should never have invited him back to my flat.

'It's gone midnight. He hasn't even rung.'

The pastry chef and I have no future.

'I don't know what to do. Do you think I should call the police?'

He hasn't had any kind of education; not in the traditional sense.

'Claire, please, I'm worried. I've got a bad feeling about this.'

I give in. I can hear the choke of panic rising up in her throat and I clamber to the edge of the bed. The pastry chef lays there nonplussed; erection gleaming in the lamplight, a smile on his face like a lick of warm butter. My stomach flips; he is a god. He is the man that I might almost love.

'So, what do you want me to do? Do you want me to, you know . . . to come over?'

'Would you? You don't mind?'

My lover is stroking my breasts.

'No . . . no, I don't mind.'

I swing my legs wearily over the mattress and pull my underwear and skirt back on. Why did I say I'd go over there? I should have told her to call her mother. Or *my* mother. Or a friend. I should never have moved this close to them in the first place. I had a decent buffer against them all when I lived in Oxford; an hour and a half if the traffic was bad, a blissful hour and a half. But, as with everything in my life, from money to men to choosing where to live, I have the worst instincts imaginable.

The pastry chef offers to drive me to my brother's house and because he's doing me this favour and being so understanding it only seems polite that I tell you his name. He calls himself Gabe, short for Gabriel.

'Like the angel?' I said, when he told me.

'Yeah,' he said. 'Just like the angel.'

There's been a car accident on the Hammersmith flyover and all traffic has ground to a halt. Sirens are brewing in the distance – raw and urgent – and I suspect we might be stuck for some time. It makes me nervous. Everything was fine while we were moving but sitting here stranded, just the two of us – virtual strangers – neither of us knows what to say. The car fills up with awkwardness, with a silence I feel obligated to quell.

'I'm divorced,' I say, suddenly, even though he hasn't asked. 'I separated from my husband last year.'

'Well . . . that's a shame.'

'It was. We ran a business together and he was a bit rash with money . . . the whole thing, it sort of fell apart. We ended up going bankrupt.'

'I see.'

'And we . . . well *I*, lost the flat. because it was me that put down all of the deposit, and when I think about it now . . . we should never have got married in the first place. It was a total impulse sort of thing.'

Gabe's foot eases down on the accelerator and we edge forward a couple of metres.

'Forget it,' I say, sinking back into my seat. 'It's a long story, I'm sure you're not interested.'

'No . . . I am . . . what kind of business did you run?'

'A language school. I speak seven languages: Spanish, Italian, Russian, some Japanese . . . we were going to set up our own place.'

'Your husband was a linguist, too?'

'No, a jazz pianist. We were going to teach music as well.'

'But it didn't work out?'

'We never even opened. Michael, that was my husband, he sort of got carried away with the ordering.'

'The ordering?'

'He ordered a lot of pianos.'

The pastry chef smiles. I start to relax.

'So what now?' he says. 'How does a bankrupt linguist make a living?'

'Translating, mostly. It's pretty mind numbing at times, but, you know, it has its upsides. You get to meet a lot of interesting people.'

'I'm not sure I'd like it all that much.'

'Really? Why not?'

'Translating other people's words. I think I'd find that . . . stifling.'

What? Like baking wedding cakes is so rewarding. Like making tea roses out of lumps of greasy marzipan is the pinnacle of human creativity. He sees the look on my face. Quietly attempts to placate me.

'But it must be nice, though. Being able to talk to people in their own language. I'd like that. I'd like to be able to do that.'

It's taken the best part of an hour to reach my brother's house: a white-faced Edwardian villa with strands of Christmas lights burning in the windows. It is a dream house, in the sense that I can only ever dream of having one like it. Three storeys of oak floors, high ceilings and wood panelling, filled with all that is tasteful and authentic: real fires in the grate, real fruit in the fruit bowls and art from actual galleries on the picture rails. I still have posters on my walls. Occasionally I might run to a clip frame.

'Where were you? We thought you weren't coming.'

It's my mother who opens the door to us and I let out a sigh, unable to contain my disappointment.

'There was an accident on the flyover . . . what are *you* doing here?'

'We're all here, Claire. If Kay had relied on you, where would she be?'

Less than thirty seconds and she's already sticking it to me. It must be some kind of a record.

'Oh, hello, who's this, now?'

My mother sucks in her belly. She tugs at her winter kaftan, trying to fashion herself a waist, and her eyes rest squarely on Gabriel.

'This is my uh . . . my friend, Gabe. He drove me over, he's just dropping me off.'

'Hello, Gabe, nice to meet you. I hope my daughter hasn't been an inconvenience.'

'No . . . not at all.'

'It's just that we're experiencing a bit of a family crisis this evening . . . my mental son has gone missing.'

Why would she say that? Why would she say that in front of someone she's only just met?

Gabe holds up his hands, already surrendering.

'It was no trouble. I'll leave you to it.'

'Nonsense . . . you should come in and wait with us. We could all use the company, you should stay.'

He hesitates a moment too long and by the time he realises his mistake she's already reaching for his coat. It's not an obvious move – she's a master at this – but I notice her fingers graze over his buttocks as she drops his coat from his shoulders and walks away. I give her a look that says 'behave yourself' – she gives me a look that says 'screw you'.

Kay comes out to greet us: a skinny, snub-nosed woman in a tightly buttoned blouse who reminds me of an over-bred dog, a Pekinese or something like that. I find I have trouble breathing when I'm near her: she makes me feel like there's no air in the room.

'Who else is here?' I say, kissing her bony cheek. 'You didn't tell me everyone would be here.'

'I told them not to bother . . . there's really no need . . . but when I mentioned you were coming—'

'We called ourselves a taxi straight away,' my mother says. 'And Sylvie was adamant . . . she insisted we stop and pick her up.'

My sister's here too. Of course she is. She wouldn't have wanted to be outdone.

'You don't have to wait,' says Kay, awkwardly. 'Especially if . . . well, you're *busy*.'

Kay glances at Gabriel. He coughs.

'No.' I say. 'I'm here now. I'll stay.'

Kay ushers us onto one of the stiff-backed antique sofas that decorate the living room and disappears to the kitchen to make tea. My mother heads for the drinks cabinet – her second home – and it's left to her second husband, Robert, to fill us in. What a sweet man he is. He quite likes me, I think, but because he knows how to toe the party line he keeps his greeting brief and succinct. These are the facts the way he tells them.

No one has heard from my brother since he left for work this morning. He gave no indication to anyone that he was working late. His secretary said he was still in the office when she left, but that's the most anyone knows. His friends had nothing arranged. One of them – and it's only a suspicion – thinks he might have accepted an impromptu invite to a seasonal party.

It's clear that this has become the optimistic view. A client has taken him out for drinks, it's nearly Christmas; he's been invited to a club and got drunk. His phone has run down, he's stuck in a taxi queue, he'll probably be home any minute. It's not like him to come home late or forget to call his wife but who knows, he works hard, it happens. We decide that 2:00 a.m. is our cut-off point. If we haven't heard anything by then we'll start calling the hospitals.

'So . . . Gabe,' says my mother, sitting back down with her drink. 'How long have you and my daughter known each other?'

Christ, she's started. What is he going to say? How is he going to sell this? Well, Mrs Ronson, your daughter picked me up at the pastry shop where I work. She was overcome with a dose of ants in the pants for the sexy Latino boy, his beauty cruelly blighted by the net stocking on top of his head. In fact, Mrs Ronson, since you ask, we were just about to start fuc— excuse me, *making love,* when the call came. She'd known me for what? An hour by then, an hour and a half?

'Three weeks,' he says, not missing a beat.

'And you met, where? Through work?'

Go, Gabe. You're on a roll. Make something up. Something impressive.

'No. She came into my shop. I'm a chef. I make pastries.'

'Pastry?'

'Cakes, pies, biscotti. Our speciality are pasties de nata.'

'What are they?'

'Portuguese tarts filled with custard.'

The way he says this – slowly, deeply, to her face – it's nothing short of heroic.

'Oh, I love those, they're delicious. We buy them at Café Vasco in Soho before we go dancing. You can go all night on one of those things.'

This is Sylvie, my sister: twenty-three, gorgeous, as blonde as an angel, a bigger slut even than I am.

'Yes,' says Gabe. 'That's the place. It's my father's bakery, his name is Vasco.'

Sylvie uncrosses her legs and leans into him.

'And what is the secret, do you think?'

'The secret?'

'Of making good pastry.'

'Attention to detail. The art of baking is to take great care. You have to be . . . *precise*.'

Precise. The word makes her shift in her seat. She's getting it now. Inhaling it. Feeling the Gabriel buzz. Please don't let him want to fuck her. It would so piss me off if he wanted to fuck her.

The night stretches on quietly: everyone tense, everyone distracted, my mother never more than an arm's length from a gin and tonic. Kay is beginning to unravel. Creases are forming in her neatly ironed blouse and she's finding it hard to control her nerves. She grips her cup tightly in her manicured fingers, and there's a rash developing on her neck from where she keeps scratching at an itch that turns out to be nothing.

I want to tell them not to worry, to persuade them that there will be some harmless explanation. Any time now a key will turn in the lock or a phone will ring in the hallway and it'll be Daniel. He'll come belting through the door, all fretful and apologetic and regale us with some astonishing and fanciful story. He's a capable, intelligent, responsible man: the rock of our entire family. It's only a matter of time before he turns up, shakes his head, and explains about the power cut, or the flat tyre and asks us what on earth we're all doing here.

Even as the words start to form in my mouth, I know I can't say them out loud. What makes me so sure that something hasn't happened to him? How can I possibly know? It's something as weak as superstition, I think. It's just that I've come to believe over the years that the same level of misery and misfortune can't strike the same family more than once.

No Earth Tones

'How beautiful it is out here. The sea a deep, religious blue. The light as sharp as lemons.'

'Miles and miles of sunburnt flesh, and breasts the size of melons.'

'Claire, leave your brother alone. He's just trying to express himself.'

That's a good one, I thought. I'd never heard it called that before. He'd been pretending to write his stupid poem all afternoon, but he'd barely managed to complete the opening stanza. That's because he'd spent all his time ogling the Rodriguez twins in their string bikinis, and repositioning his note-pad to cover up the bulge in his nylon shorts.

'OK,' I said, turning over on my Lilo. 'You freaks can call it what you like. But just so as you know, I don't think there's a whole lot of artistry in masturbating twelve times a day and pretending to be a Russian cosmonaut.'

'I'm not pretending to be a Russian cosmonaut.'

'What are you pretending to be, then? Why do you wear a goldfish bowl on your head and make everyone call you Vasily?'

My mother gave that short snot-less sniff she did when she was irritated and readjusted the straps on her swimsuit.

'It's fine if your brother wants to experiment with his body,' she said. 'It's natural. It's normal. There's nothing dirty abou—'

I sank to the bottom of the pool. The sunlight dimmed and their faces faded out and I bathed in the calm and the silence. What it was to have enlightened, liberal parents.

The horror, the horror.

★ ★ ★

1986. North Miami Beach. A stroll along the boardwalk with old Mr Kazman.

'You left your family back at the pool again, huh?'

'Yeah, I left them there. They drive me mad.'

'Don't say that about your family. Family is the best thing a person can have.'

Change the subject. Don't get into it. Distract the old boy with the birds.

'They look a bit pre-historic, don't you think so? Don't you think they look a little weird?'

'The pelicans? Sure. Fine at catching fish, though. Look at that one go, quite the fisherman.'

We stared for a while and focused on the dive, but the pelican shuddered and came up empty.

'No luck, it looks like.'

'No, he missed again. Bad luck.'

'You want a peanut?'

'OK, why not?'

Peanuts. Mr Kazman, always had peanuts. Someone had told him it would stop him getting colon cancer if he ate a bag a day, and colon cancer was Sol Kazman's biggest worry.

'You got to eat fruit. And peanuts. You got to make sure that you keep yourself regular.'

'I'm only thirteen. I don't think I need to worry about that yet.'

'You can never start too early. My Esther, she never ate peanuts. That's how it got her.'

'The big C?'

'Yep. Yep. The big C.'

This was a typical conversation at Siesta Pines, the apartment complex where we lived. Crushed between a car lot and a fast-food outlet that stank of old coffee grounds and grease. A building, so worn out and weary it looked like it was gasping in the heat. And parked on every bench, shuffling along each walkway were an army of narcoleptic retirees: sunburnt and cranky, held up by wooden canes, like rows of runner bean plants in the sun. Christ knows how we ended up living there;

apart from the Rodriguezes there wasn't another young family for miles around. I suppose that's what happens when you pack up your life one spring morning, and flee your suburban home with indecent haste.

My father received his job offer on a Friday afternoon and the following weekend we were gone. The entire Ronson clan: me, Mum, Dad and Daniel and my oblivious little sister, Sylvie. It was so unexpected, so out of the blue, we didn't even have time to get excited. Dad had been offered work abroad from time to time over the years but Mum had always made him turn it down. On this occasion it was her that got the ball rolling. Mum that booked the plane tickets, Mum that rented out the house, Mum that packed all our clothes into tight cardboard boxes and made us wave goodbye to each one of the rooms before we left. She packed that entire place up in five days flat, to this day I've still no notion how she did it. And then she pulled off the greatest trick of all, the greatest act of faith I've ever seen. When she saw where we were going to live – the place we'd call home for the best part of a year – she stood up straight, lifted her chin and swallowed her disappointment whole.

'We're going to do fine here, I can feel it,' she said. 'I've got a good feeling about this place.'

Daniel and I stood there open mouthed and I'm pretty sure I reached out for his hand. It looked nothing like it did on the TV. It looked nothing like it did on *Miami Vice*.

'Who do you like better, Crockett or Tubbs?'
    'Neither.'
    'Come on. You have to choose one.'
    Nothing. Silence. Not even a groan or a stifled sigh.
    'Mum, is Daniel autistic?'
    'Don't be stupid, of course he's not.'
    'Can you catch autism, or are you born with it?'
    'Your mother just told you, now, eat your soup.'
    'Because if he *is* autistic, I think he should complain. He's been short changed. You're meant to have some special skill to

compensate, like adding up really fast or being able to paint all squiggly like Van Gogh.'

Still nothing; just more huffing from my father.

'I wonder if running fast counts. Hey, there you *go*. That's proof. Daniel is low level autistic and sprinting is his compensatory skill.'

'Fuck off, Claire. I *am* not.'

Hallelujah, a reaction; the slamming down of a mash-potato-covered fork.

'Why don't you talk, then?'

'Because . . . I've got nothing to *say*.'

'You had stuff to say when we lived in England.'

'So what? Now I don't, all right?'

And that was that. Discussion over.

'Mum?'

'What?'

'Why did we move to Florida?'

'You know why, for your father's work.'

'Is he making a lot of money?'

'No.'

'Is he working less hours?'

'No. He's not.'

'Can I have some of your gin and tonic?'

'Don't be an idiot. No you can't.'

'Well can I go out running with Daniel, then? There's nothing to do here, I'm bored.'

'You're not going out tonight,' said my father, piping up. 'You've both got homework to do.'

'She can come with me if she likes, what's it to you?'

'Are you going to let him speak to me like that? Are you going to let him talk that way to his father?'

'Leave Mum alone, can't you? It's not *her* fault.'

Daniel had had enough. He pushed back his chair and stormed out of the room, away from the dinner table towards his cave. To his telescope and his space manuals and his pile of worn out running shoes; to his sanctuary of weirdness and stink.

'See what you've done now?'

'What did I do? I just said he should get on with his home-work. He's wasting his life. He'll be a nothing, that kid. What does he think, he can make a living from *running*?

'He might do. Mum, tell him. Daniel's the best in the county. One day he might win the Olympic games.'

My father's eyes flickered in my direction, resting briefly on the bridge of my nose.

'Jesus,' he said, glancing away again. 'If I'd had the chances he's had, the education he's had . . .'

My mother laughed without pleasure.

'You wasted your chances, David,' she said. 'You ruined them. Every single one.'

My mother stood up from the table and the front door clicked shut behind the porch. No one heard it but me. Because I was tuned into Daniel's habits by then. I knew that he needed to escape from them – to break away from them – that he was going outside to take his run.

'You got any more questions, clever clogs?' said my father, tartly. 'Anything else you want to say to upset your mother?'

We stared at one another across the table. Grilling each other, sizing each other up. As alien as a pelican and a fish.

'No,' I said, clearing my plate away. 'I don't have any more questions.'

That was the way it went that year. Nobody filled in the gaps. Arguments reared up like stepping stones in a flow of silence that sometimes held out for months. It was like waiting for a rainy season that never came. The tension would build with the humidity until all of our clothes were sopping wet. You could hear the drip drip drip on the floor tiles as we ate, pools of tension would form at our feet. They grew so deep I imagined they had banks, that fish swam back and forth between their tides. I'd beg, yell, pray for the sky to crack and when it finally did, what intensity. The violence of that lightning, the thunderous roar, and rain that cut into your skin like pins. Words in whole sentences, emotions on sleeves, tears and accusations and spit.

And just when you thought you'd made some sense of it, drawn some lesson from it, the clouds would roll over and snuff it out. Dad shrinking and distant and full of self-loathing; Mum frozen, eccentric and adrift. He began working longer hours, she began smoking more pot, and she started to dress oddly too – going without a bra, wearing too much make-up, gardening in those short, short shorts.

When Sol Kazman had his stoke they all said it was on account of those endless bags of fatty peanuts that he ate, but I knew better than that. I knew it was down to my mother's wacky fashion sense, to her hot pants and her unfettered breasts. When she went outside to water the ficus tree each morning after breakfast there were always a crowd of old men waiting: cloudy eyes out on stalks, wooden canes tight in their hands, lined up neatly along the bench.

Frustrated and grouchy I left my father at the dinner table and started on a postcard to my friends. What a time I was having, how great it was out here; the sun, the sea, the fabulous views. But the weather was humid and the sea was often rough and the views from our apartment at the rear of the building were of alleyways and *Honest Murray's Autos*. I gave up. I threw away the card and went looking for little Sylvie, playing in the den with her building bricks. Three years old, as bright as a copper penny, the family tonic to all of us. And because I'm an optimist or a fool, or a little of both, I convinced myself things would get better. Mum and Dad would settle in here eventually, and Daniel's mood swings would calm down soon enough. Any time now we'd be friends again, mates again, two fine compadres against the world. I had to think things could improve over time, that life could fix itself and heal over. Instead of this, the world chose to rupture.

Me and Julio

'Hey kid, don't cry. It's a bad day for all of us. A real bad day for America.'

I didn't care about America, I just wanted to go home.

'Come on now, you're not alone. The whole country's grieving today.'

For my dad?

'For those astronauts, poor souls. What a thing to have happened.'

I wasn't alone with my tears that afternoon, the whole of the hospital was in shock. I lost count of the number of people who said they knew how I felt, who sat down beside me and offered me a shoulder or a dampened tissue. They cried for something bold and intangible. I cried for something that was real. A person I knew. A person I cared about. Not a hero, not even someone good. Someone wasteful, imperfect and begrudging: someone complicated and difficult to love.

I'd been strolling on the sand when it happened, collecting seashells and seaweed and boys. Sylvie and Mum were watching the shuttle launch back at the apartment and I'd snuck out without saying where I was going. I was sulking because I hadn't been allowed to go up to Cape Canaveral with Dad and Daniel and because I'd been told off for making a fuss. Sylvie wasn't making a fuss. Sylvie didn't mind staying home with Mummy and making cakes. Sylvie didn't mind if Mummy smoked a little pot. It didn't make any kind of sense. I wasn't a space nut like Daniel, but they knew I would have loved to have gone along. When the launch got delayed and they drove all the way home,

I felt sure they would take me with them on that second day.
But they didn't. So I was pissed off. So I was AWOL with the
pelicans beside the sea.

It was a beautiful morning: frigid, cold and icy with a freshness that seemed to spring clean the entire beach. The wind blew
sand through the palm trees polishing their fronds and making
them shine, and the sea coughed straight from its belly spitting
globs of black seaweed onto the beach. I did star jumps on the
sand to keep myself warm and skimmed handfuls of shells into
the choppy waves. And then I spotted someone that I recognised, a person who wasn't sick or cross or old. Julio Rodriguez,
my next-door neighbour; the boy in my school that I loved the
most; the boy whose name I drew on my notebooks in felt-tip
pen, whose face was engraved on my eyelids. There we were,
just the two of us. Out in the cold, away from prying eyes,
puberty's merry cocktail of hormones fizzing unchecked through
our veins.

I greeted Julio coolly. He asked how I was, and I tried hard
not to seem smitten.

'I'm fine,' I said, in Spanish. 'How are you?'

'My family are crazy, my twin sisters do my head in.'

'I know how you feel,' I said. 'Sometimes it's good to get out
on your own.'

He smiled at me. He understood. That was the instant I fell
in love.

'Your Spanish is getting better.'

'Really, is it?'

'Yeah, it is. You learn fast.'

What a delightful thing this was. Simply by concentrating, by
paying attention, by bending and furrowing your tongue a certain
way, it seemed you could understand the entire world.

I suggested we went to get pizza, but Julio turned up his nose.
This was the kind of boy who liked to do things; he wasn't the
kind of boy to sit around. In no time at all he was pulling off
his shirt and insisting we went for a swim. Our skinny bodies
shivering like whippets, we ran across the beach towards the sea.

Julio told me that we had to dive deep under the waves, that once we were past our shoulders it would be warm. It was true. The sea temperature hadn't had time to drop yet, and the contrast to the bite of the cold winter air made it feel like we'd jumped into a bathtub.

The pair of us swam about like seals that afternoon, jumping in and out of the seaweed until we were exhausted and out of breath. At some point our naked legs rubbed up against one another and a look of acknowledgement passed between us. Julio swam up beside me and without asking if he could, began to tug away at my thin underwear. We began to kiss, awkwardly, roughly, and I felt his fingers rub up inside my pants. It felt nice. He moved slowly and calmly, not frantically like a boy – at least he did to begin with. And some minutes later, I don't recall how many, I realised that he must be entering me. I felt the ache, the stretch, the thin shot of pain, but I needed tangible proof. Something to take away, a souvenir of some kind, something to mark the occasion. Suddenly, there it was: a tiny puff of blood, reddening the foam at the top of the waves and spreading out through the warm salty water.

Daniel had blood spots on his bandages. He lay completely still on that hospital bed, his eyes fixed unsteadily on the ceiling. His mouth was bolted shut. No matter what we said, no matter how tight we clung to him, his lips refused to ease apart. I couldn't stand the way he looked: so fragile and scared and wired and fucked up, his feet all broken and swollen.

The facts of the matter were brutal. Even after they'd managed to reach my father's car, the traffic hadn't moved again for another hour. They couldn't carry his body away through the stranded vehicles, so he'd had to stay exactly where he was: slumped in the front seat with his arms folded over his exploded chest, a blanket pulled up over his face. Daniel had sat on that embankment the whole time: utterly alone, knowing what he knew, giving up on words, giving up on language, giving up on childish explanations.

We tried for a good long time to get him to talk but eventually he closed his eyes and went to sleep. It was amazing how he managed to do this; with us hugging him and harassing him and telling him that we loved him and promising him that he'd done his very best. Somehow he managed to shut us out. For the whole of that day and for four days after that, he managed to shut out the entire world.

They took Mum to identify my father's body while Sylvie and I waited outside in the corridor. The stink of disinfectant made me want to throw up but Sylvie didn't seem to mind it all that much. I wondered if she knew what was going on, if she could sense the heartbreak that was all around her. I didn't know what to say when my mother came out. She hadn't spoken to me the whole way up in the police car, she'd just sat there and stared out of the window, plaiting and replaiting Sylvie's hair.

'Where have you been?'

That was the last thing she said to me. When I turned up from the beach with my clothes in a knot and the last of Julio's semen spilling out into my sea-soaked underwear. I looked almost as frightened as Daniel. I'd seen the police car parked outside the apartment block and though I knew it wasn't true, I half suspected that they'd come to arrest me. Mum was crying. A policewoman had her arms round her shoulders and a policemen tried to take hold of my hand.

'I didn't do anything wrong,' I said, backing away. 'It wasn't my fault, it was Julio's.'

'It's not important now,' said the officer, bending down. 'Claire, something very bad has happened.'

'I know,' I said. 'I heard it on the radio. I already know about that.'

'No, sweetheart. It's about your dad. He had a heart attack.'

'Is he . . . OK?'

'No. I'm sorry. He's not.'

I didn't feel anything. I didn't feel anything at all. Tears ran down my cheeks and stung my wind-chapped lips, but I couldn't begin to take it in. And Mum just stared at me. In one searing glance she saw right through me, determined just exactly where I'd been and what I'd done.

'What about my brother? What's happened to Daniel?'

'He's gonna be fine. He's a hero as a matter of fact.'

This was a strange turn of events. My father stone cold dead and Daniel at the same time a hero. There was something in the police officer's voice that suggested there was something to be happy about in all this. I didn't feel it. I didn't feel anything at all. I thought about Julio's mouth pressing hard onto mine, and about our bodies wrapped up tight in the salty waves. I thought about the tiny rush of pain as he'd entered my body for the very first time and tried to remember exactly how it had felt. I thought about it all the way up to Cocoa Beach. All the way along the coast, past the cities and the swamps, to the hospital where they'd taken my father and brother.

She walked out of that morgue like she was made of cardboard. The tears had rubbed her make-up to distant corners of her face and a crust of salt and orange coloured lipstick had settled heavily into the lines around her mouth. It looked to me like her face was rusting, like my mother had begun to corrode. I wanted to go up and hug her – I desperately wanted her to hug me – but Sylvie got to her first. She marched straight towards her, put her arms around Mum's legs and sweetly, dutifully, began to cry.

'Hush Sylvie,' she said, gathering her up in her arms. 'Don't cry now, it'll all be all right. You were there when Mummy needed you, you're a wonderful girl. You were always there for your Mummy.'

Born Free

It's gone 3:00 a.m., Daniel still isn't home, and we've run out of logical excuses. No one has called, his mobile remains un-answered, no one has knocked on the door. We've tried all the hospitals, woken all his friends, dragged his boss and his colleagues from their beds. Nobody has any more suggestions. Nobody has anything more to say. Kay decides that she's going to call the police, and the pastry chef seizes on the momentary distraction to make his overdue escape and bolt for the door.

I might be mistaken but I think I see him raise his hands to the sky and offer a silent prayer as he sprints down the path towards his car. What a story to tell his friends. How he got invited back to some crazy woman's flat for a quickie shag and ended up in the centre of a family crisis. How he was goosed by the semi-drunk mother, seduced by the sexy sister and confronted with the mystery of the missing brother by the immaculately groomed wife. I stand in the porch and watch him drive away (make a mental note to avoid walking home past the Café Vasco for the rest of my life) and head back inside. Another one down. Another vision of awkwardness and embarrassment, drifts away into the night.

Back in the house, Kay is just off the phone and my mother is giving her the third degree.

'What good is *tomorrow*? Why can't they send someone now?'

'It's too early. They said we'd have to wait . . . at least until morning.'

'Well, what are we meant to do? We can't just sit here. Give me the phone, I'll call them back.'

Kay shakes her head, she looks pale. The mere act of dialling 999 has visibly dented her.

'If he was younger, or vulnerable . . . they could do something now. But a grown man staying out late . . . we'll have to sit tight. They said a missing adult usually turns up within twenty-four hours.'

'Well, that's good then,' says Sylvie, weakly. 'I mean, in a way . . . he's probably just . . .' She fades out.

'Did you tell them it wasn't like him? Did you tell them it's completely out of character?'

'Of *course* I did. You just heard me.'

'Well, what about his phone? Did you say he wasn't answering his phone?'

My sister-in-law checks herself. I sense her battling to stay calm.

'They said we should try not to panic. That he's probably held up somewhere. If he's not back by tomorrow . . . we can fill in a missing person's report.'

Kay lifts her hands to her ears, partly to compose herself, partly to shut out my mother. She's wondering if the police might be right; if she's missed something; if there's some small chance she might be overreacting.

'They asked if he could be staying at a hotel,' she says, quietly. 'They wanted to know if we'd had a fight.'

'Did you?'

She shakes her head, no.

'Maybe he crashed out at a friend's house,' says Robert. 'Perhaps he just flaked out after too much wine.'

'We've tried them all, Robert. I've tried *everyone* I can think of. I don't know who else I can call.'

'Perhaps he's with someone you don't know.' says Robert, trying to be helpful. 'Could that be possible . . . do you think?'

'What are you suggesting?'

Robert shrugs his shoulders. He's not suggesting anything.

'Might he have met someone? Could he have run into someone and gone home with them?'

'A *woman*?'

'No . . . God, no. I meant someone from school . . . an old schoolfriend, something like that.'

We shift uncomfortably in our seats. He didn't mean to imply it, but this would make some kind of sense. Kay and Daniel have had a row of some kind. He went to spend the night in a hotel. Could he be cheating on her? *Could* he? She picks up on our betrayal immediately, feels us all slipping away.

'Daniel and I are fine,' she says, turning to my mother. 'There've been no arguments. *None*.'

My mother stares hard at her drink. Kay sits down next to the phone.

'They said I should call again later,' she says, dejectedly. 'I'm supposed to let them know . . . if he turns up.'

'He will,' I say. 'Don't worry, Kay. He will.'

The Snow Queen

What a stark week it's been. It snowed yesterday. Great grey clouds of the stuff came swirling through the air, like a ton of duck down shaken from some giant wintry pillow. People were so excited to see a heavy snowfall in central London that they came tearing out of their houses just to watch it. They were laughing. They seemed to like it. They immediately began scooping up frozen clumps from the ground and stuffing it down one another's jumpers. I gave them a disapproving look as I walked by, like I was an old person or something.

Snow makes me a little uneasy, always has. I hate the way everything goes so deathly quiet after a snowstorm. You can't hear the comforting hiss of the traffic any more and your feet make no reassuring echo when they hit the ground. Everything's muffled and silent and cloaked, like the world's been shut up in a freaky padded cell. I want the world to be noisy, vibrant, active and alert. Especially today. Especially now.

'Where are you? Where the *fuck* are you, Daniel? You bastard, you'd better come home.'

I say this to no one in particular. Stood in the road outside my mother's house, ankle deep in the snow.

'This isn't funny any more, do you *hear* me? You can't leave me alone with them, we had a pact. Whatever you've done, whatever went wrong. No one bloody cares about it. *No* one!'

Daniel never made it home that Friday night. He isn't home still, he's disappeared. There's a manila file sitting on a desk at our local police station with his name written on it in bold black letters. My brother is officially missing. He's been gone for over a week.

We've barely slept since the night he disappeared, we look like ghouls, the lot of us. Every hour we can muster has been spent glued to the phone or out pacing the streets, desperately trying to find some living trace of him. In the past seven days I've spoken to relatives I didn't even know I had: great-aunts, great-uncles, fourth cousins twice removed, people from the phone book that just happen to share the same surname. Between us we've probably spoken to everyone Daniel's had more than a fleeting relationship with in his entire life: long-forgotten friends from college, kids he went on outward-bound courses with when he was a teenager, kids from his junior running club that haven't heard from him since he was seven years old. And still there's nothing. No leads, no evidence, no documents, no sight nor sound of him of any kind.

Actually, that's not strictly true. There is some footage of him leaving his office building last Friday night that was caught on his firm's security camera. I've watched that footage maybe a hundred or so times in the last week and every time I look at it I try to pick out something new. Something in the way that he turns his head or swings his arms; something, *anything*, in the 10 short paces he takes to cross the screen that indicates an intention of some kind. Is he walking too quickly, is he anxious? No, it doesn't appear so. Does he have his head bowed, is he depressed or forlorn? No, he's looking straight ahead. Purposefully? It's hard to tell. It lasts exactly 8.79 seconds this piece of film, just long enough for him to pass through the marble foyer of his building and make his way out onto the forecourt. How does he move? Not determinedly, not casually, not care-fully, just, well, *normally*, I suppose. Which is an exceptional thing to say, because after he left the building at 7:00 p.m., no one has the least idea where he went.

And so it went on. The next day and the day after that. Not a call, not a text, not a sighting, not a conclusive piece of infor-mation that we could use. He never got into his car, he didn't visit a cash point, his passport is still safely tucked away in his drawer at home. He didn't rent a car. He didn't turn up at any hospitals or police stations or homeless hostels, he didn't answer or make a call on his mobile phone. He wasn't there when I spent ten hours pounding the streets last Tuesday night clutching his picture in my hand. He wasn't at the soup kitchens or the train stations or the bus shelters, or camped out in the woods near his home. No one has seen him. No one. Which is odd, because somebody clearly must have.

Somebody hears me shouting in the snow. My voice builds fiercely through the static and the gloom, and hits them with a suddenness that makes them start. It's a woman, weighed down against the cold in her winter armour: a coat and a heavy poncho, and a brightly coloured hat with a fluffy bobble. I take particular exception to that bobble. If I had a pair of scissors on me now, I'd go directly over there and snip it off.

The woman gives me an indecipherable look as she passes by. Does she think I'm crazy? Probably. Does she wish I'd keep my voice down, learn to respect the claustrophobia of this miserable weather? Maybe. More likely it's because she recognises me. I can tell by the way she turns her head away so fast, even though it's obvious that she wants to keep on staring. This has happened to me a lot in the last three days – people averting their eyes when I get off the bus; grown adults whispering about me behind my back when I stop off to buy a pack of chewing gum from the local shop. I'm famous now, so I suppose I should expect it. I'm a celebrity. I've been on TV.

Four days after Daniel failed to return home from work, the police persuaded us to make a TV appeal. We were ushered into a tiny interview room, sat down at a worn trestle table and directed towards a bank of cameras and microphones. The fact that we were even doing it, the singular absurdity of it, seemed to bring it all home to us: how desperate it was, how serious it was, how bleak it was turning out to be. The recording was delayed a few minutes while my mother went to fetch a picture of Julian, Daniel's baby son; the police thought it would be a good idea for Kay to hold his photo up to the camera while she was talking.

You know what I was thinking while they went to look for that picture? I was thinking that Julian's a pretty odd name for a toddler to have. That when you look at him in his cot – all sleepy and angelic or yowling like a cat – he always seems a tad perplexed. Maybe he thinks he ought to have been given a better name. Maybe he's pissed off that he has a moniker better suited to an estate agent than an eighteen-month-old. Daniel sometimes calls him 'Stinky Jools' which I think is cute, but Kay always insists on using his given name.

This is the kind of stupid thing I think about. That this baby – this gorgeous, rosy child – might have to grow up with a mother who doesn't believe in nicknames. That he might never know the gentleness or the sweet irreverence of his own father. He won't experience it, so he won't inherit it. He'll grow up officious and a little pedantic, like Kay, and I won't like him quite as much as I would have.

This is the direction my head was going in while I waited to talk to the British public. To ask them, as kindly as I could, if they'd mind keeping an eye out for my older brother. Maybe they'd spotted him already: walking through a shopping centre, hiding out in a cheap hotel, or wandering through the streets like a bewildered amnesiac asking passers-by if they knew the way to Stinky Jools.

I didn't have to say much of anything, in the end. I just stood there while the police officer who was running the investigation read out a statement and introduced Kay to the world. Sylvie stared at the floor the whole time, while Mum and Robert clung tightly to her hand, and Kay – quite reasonably – cried her eyes out. She tried so hard to get the words out without faltering but you could see exactly how crushed she was to be doing it. It meant we got upgraded from local bulletin to the national news and that her face was splashed all over the next morning's tabloids. 'Blonde mother, 36, weeps in anguish over missing husband this Christmas.' Mystery of the pretty blonde and her vanished love. It made her physically ill. The indignity of it made her throw up.

My picture didn't appear in the papers but people always recognise me from the TV broadcast. That's because I spent the whole time staring directly into the camera like I was some kind of a demented person. I was trying my hardest to communicate with my brother. I was trying to tell him that I understood; that if he wanted to escape the flack or had something to confess, it was me that he should come to first. I wouldn't judge him, I'd cover him. I'd make any kind of arrangements that were necessary. I was letting him know that I was there for him, no matter what. Under any kind of circumstances, whatsoever. All this I was trying to communicate with a single gnawing look. It stayed with people, I suppose; it's always me that they recognise first.

'Hey . . . excuse me. I just wanted to say how sorry I am . . . about your brother. I hope they find him. I hope he's OK.'

I nod at the bobble-hat woman and say a muted thanks, and head along the driveway to my mother's house. Damn this snow; it makes people think they can stop and talk to one another.

My mother is wobbly from alcohol. Her head bobs about on the end of her neck as clumsy and rootless as a helium balloon. I have to be careful of her now. Her skin is as thin as a sheet of clingfilm when she's in this state and a single misplaced word or ill-judged look is liable to provoke a sudden tear in its surface, releasing a bitter stream of effluent.

'What kind of a coat is that?' she says, slurring her words together. 'A *fur*?'

'Mum, you know it is. I've had it ages.'

'You don't care that animals died to keep you warm . . . you don't care about the suffering you cause?'

'It's second hand, it's old. The killing was already done.'

This is not a fair argument, I know it, but I love this coat. My ex-husband bought it for me at a winter market when we took a trip to Moscow a couple of years ago and it's the warmest thing I've ever owned.

'I don't want you to wear it to Kay's lunch, do you hear me?

I don't want you to upset me on Christmas day. I want you to make an effort, I want you to look decent for a change.'

I had all but forgotten about Christmas; it seems like such an odd thing to care about. Is she really expecting us to keep up with the winter rituals under these circumstances? Is she really expecting that we all go out and buy presents and pull crackers round a tree in two days' time? My eyes wander off course for a moment and I make the elementary mistake of glancing too long at her hands. And there it is. The steady rip in my mother's fragile mood. A small but significant puncture.

'What are you looking at?' she says, goading me.

'Nothing.'

'My drink? You're looking at my *drink*?'

'No Mum, forget it. I wasn't looking at your drink.'

'Come on, don't bottle it up. You think your mother's drinking too much? *Say* so. You think I should feel ashamed because I'm drinking in the afternoon? *Say* it.'

I don't say it.

'Daniel could be lying dead in a gutter somewhere. Did you think of that? *Did* you?'

It's pretty much all I'm thinking about.

'It helps me sleep. It helps me get through it. I'm sixty years old, what does it matter to you if I have a couple of drinks to help me cope?'

'It doesn't, it's none of my business. But it won't make you feel any better, it never does.'

'How do *you* know how I feel?'

'I don't . . . but we all need to be thinking straight. To be there if . . . *when* Daniel needs us.'

She gives her trademark sniff, but mis-times it ever so slightly, sending a trickle of tonic water spilling down her nose.

'*This* from the responsible one,' she says, holding up her glass in triumph. '*This* from the girl who threw away her husband and her savings and her home. This from the one who's never there, who's always off fucking some filthy boy when her family needs her.'

There it is. There's the quality invective I was waiting for.

Predictably she's worn herself out with this tirade and she attempts to make a grand exit from the room. She stumbles to the bathroom – to throw up or compose herself, I'm not sure which, and I sit down opposite Robert.

'You want one?' he says, holding up the gin bottle.

'Yes,' I say. 'Absolutely.'

As he makes the drinks – great boats of gin and tonic with rings of lime floating on the surface like life preservers – it strikes me that I know too much about him for us to hang out comfortably one to one. Among other things, I know that he and my mother have no sex life any more; that they haven't had one for quite some time. I know that Robert's prostate is enlarged, that he's mildly incontinent and that these days he finds it near impossible to maintain an erection.

I know this because my mother told me. And Sylvie, and Daniel and Kay and Stinky Jools, and just about anyone else in the distant recesses of our family that cared to listen. The same way she still tells people that I was busy losing my virginity on the afternoon that my father suffered his fatal heart attack. The same way she sometimes refers to Daniel as her 'mental son' when she's drunk, because of his infamous five-day silence. It's her lack of respect that's so fearful. The way she delves into everyone's wounds like a maggot, irritating the core of the infection instead of allowing it to stiffen and heal. It means people keep her in the dark. No one tells her anything unless they're forced to.

'She doesn't mean it,' says Robert, handing me my drink and attempting a smile. 'There have been more crank calls today, it's wearing her down.'

'Haven't you changed the number yet?'

'She won't do it, in case he phones.'

Mum comes tottering out of the bathroom and collapses back onto the sofa like someone's emptied her out of a carrier bag.

She's all weepy now – and contrite – and she slips her arm gratefully through Robert's.

'Did Robert tell you,' she says, dabbing at her mouth with a tissue. 'Some woman phoned to tell me Daniel was dead. Said she was a psychic, that she knew where my dead son was buried.'

'Mum, *please*. Change the number. You can't put up with that. It's just cruel.'

'Do you think she knew something? Should I have listened to her? Robert made me put down the phone.'

'No Mum, you did the right thing. These people are sick, they don't know anything. They're just doing it for attention.'

'What do *you* think?' says my mother, leaning towards me. 'What do you think has happened to my beautiful son?'

He belongs to her, right now. He only belongs to her.

'I don't know. I just . . . I think he's OK.'

'Alive?'

'Yes,' I say. 'I'm sure he is.'

'Why?' she says falling back into the sofa. 'Are *you* a psychic now too?'

She doesn't really want my answers to these questions, she just wants to make me feel worse. And what am I meant to say? That I think Daniel's alive because I *know* him, because we're close. Because I think I would be able to feel it in my bones if something dreadful had happened to him?

'It's early days, that's what the police said. There's no point in us thinking the worst.'

She seems comforted for a moment and relaxes long enough to take a sip from her glass of water.

'Have you spoken to your sister today?'

'No . . . not since the broadcast.'

'Would you look in on her for me?'

'Me? Why?'

'She hasn't called. I've been leaving messages for her . . . she hasn't called me back.'

'I'm sure she's fine. She's probably just busy studying.'

'You'll go and see her?'

'Yes,' I say, reluctantly. 'I'll go round and check on her tomorrow.'

'She's such a sensitive soul, Sylvie. I've no idea how she's coping.'

'She's OK, Mum, she's getting through it. Just like the rest of us are.'

Pussy Talk

'Do you want to lick my pussy?
   '. . .'
   'Yes, yes, u-huh, that's so good. Ooh, amazing you're so hard.'
   '. . .'
   'Ooh . . . you're so big. Mnnng . . . I don't think I can take it.
You might have to try it in my ar—'

My sister is bent over her feet, digging toe-jam out of her nails
with a pair of scissors. She's wearing lose sweatpants and a grubby
sweatshirt and has a slick of hot oil conditioner spread through
her hair. A brown sludgy face pack is smeared across her cheeks
and an episode of *Friends* plays dimly in the corner. She slips her
free hand over the mouthpiece of the phone and whispers to me,
'*Wait, I won't be long.*'
   I don't hang around. I head for the kitchen and turn on the
kettle so I can't hear the rest of what she's saying. I like to think
that I'm pretty open minded, but listening to my twenty-three-
year-old sister describing her pussy to pervert strangers over the
phone is pushing it, even for me.
   'What are you so bothered about?' she says, sloping in after
me.
   'Nothing. I'm not bothered. At all.'
   'So come and sit down, then. Have a drink or something. Take
off your coat.'
   'In the living room?'
   'Yes, in the living room.'
   'Is . . . uh . . . is the phone likely to go again?'
   'It might do, Claire. Why do you ask?'

'No reason. It's just . . . well if there's going to be more, you know . . . pussy talk . . . maybe I should come back another time.'

'Don't be so uptight,' she says, making cracks in her face pack. 'It pays my course fees, it's easy work, I don't even hear what I'm saying any more. I know the entire script off by heart.'

'You say the same things every time?'

'Pretty much.'

'And a stranger masturbates at the end of the phone while you say it?'

'Yes, that's the general idea.'

'And you're OK with that?'

'I'm fine with it.'

'You're sure?'

'It's a job, Claire. I'm the only one on my course who's not in serious debt.'

'Right . . . well, sure. I understand.'

Sylvie goes to the bathroom to wash off her mud pack and rinse her hair and when she comes back she looks about sixteen years old: fresh faced and perfect and pretty, like a Victorian porcelain doll. Not like the medical student who dissects cadavers once a month and moans about the human grease getting stuck under her fingernails. Nothing like the girl who spends hours on the phone muttering a stream of profanities to total strangers.

No one ever thinks that we're sisters at first. When you tell someone we're related – nine times out of ten – they rise up on the balls of their feet and say *really*? Her hair fine and blonde like my mother's, her eyes big and brown like my dad's. People do nice things for Sylvie. Usually for no apparent reason. Most people in the world have to jump up and down and wave their hands from side to side just to get decent service in a restaurant: Sylvie just sits there looking vacant and dewy and the whole world flocks right to her feet.

★   ★   ★

'So,' she says. 'I take it there's still no news?'

'No. I've just been with Kay, still nothing.'

'How is she?'

'She's numb. The doctor gave her more sleeping pills but she won't take them.'

'She must be distraught.'

'We're all distraught, Sylvie. This is fucking desperate.'

'You think I don't *know* that?'

'You haven't phoned anyone. You haven't spoken to Kay since the appeal. You haven't called Mum back, she's worried. It's not like you . . . that's all.'

Sylvie seems to have disengaged. All her life she's been told she's the caring sharing intuitive one, but there's never been an occasion to test it. Now something's happened that requires her to step up to the plate and I'm not sure she even knows how to behave. I've seen Mum every day since Daniel disappeared, put up with her rages and her drunkenness because I know that it's part of the deal. Still all I hear from Mum is Sylvie. How must this be effecting poor Sylvie? How is she ever going to cope? Maybe I should tape a bit of pussy talk and play that back to her; that would show them all what's what.

'I have to study, you know,' she says, miserably, 'There's so much to do, it's the only thing keeping me sane.'

'I know, I understand. Just give them both a call, OK? They just need to know that you're all right.'

She nods; I assume this means she will.

'I can't believe it's been ten days, it feels like forever already.'

'Yeah,' I say. 'It really does.'

'Did you see the newspapers this morning?'

'Yeah, I saw them.'

'It's all bullshit,' she says, quietly. 'I don't think Daniel was in trouble. I don't think he's been kidnapped or hurt.'

'No one's saying that, Sylvie.'

'So why are the police spending time on this idiot, then? Just because some guy who worked in his building was dealing coke, I don't see what it's got to do with Daniel.'

'The man said he'd been threatened. He looks similar to Daniel, they're just making sure. They have to check every lead they can.'

'It's a waste of time, that's all I'm saying. It's just a waste of everyone's time.'

She's probably right; it feels like they're clutching at straws now. But what else is there to go on? His bank accounts still haven't been touched, his passport wasn't used, there's no evidence that he tried to board a flight or ride a ferry. The news-paper story is most likely garbage but the truth is we're lucky to get the coverage. Daniel is white, wealthy and middle class. He has an attractive, articulate wife and a cute, photogenic baby. It's Christmas, there's not much other news, it means we're getting far more attention than we reasonably deserve.

In some respects this actually makes things worse. Half the country probably knows my brother's story by now but still no one has come up with a concrete sighting of him. If he was hiding out in a hotel or renting a room, someone would have spotted him by now, surely? He has to get money, he has to eat; someone must have sold him something or served him some food. It can't last much longer, this media interest. We've probably got until new year's day before it dies down for good. And then what? Another curious story that people half remember; another file growing dusty on a police station shelf.

Sylvie is shivering now. Her shoulders are twitching under her dressing-gown and her lips are pursed into a silent growl.

'You know,' she says, suddenly, 'you might want to think about your part in all of this. Did you ever think about that?'

'*My* part?'

'Yes. If you hadn't kept borrowing money off them all the time; giving Daniel extra stuff to worry about.'

'What was he worried about? Kay swears everything was fine.'

'Why was he on antidepressants, then? Have you thought to ask Kay about that?'

'What are you talking about?'

'I saw them in the bathroom cabinet, a half-dozen packs of Ceroxil.'

'Are you sure they were his?'

'They had his name on them. So he didn't need you coming to him with your problems. He didn't need the extra worry.'

'It was only a few hundred pounds, Sylvie. It was only a few hundred pounds.'

'But it all mounts up. And you're always doing it. You've been a drain on everyone in this family since your divorce.'

She takes my breath away. Sometimes she just takes my breath away.

'I should leave,' I say, standing up. 'I'll talk to Kay about the tablets. I'll let you know what she says.'

'He didn't approve, you know,' she says, as I walk towards the door.

'Of what?'

'You two separating. He said you two ought to have worked it out.'

'He said that?'

'Yeah, he said it all the time. He said you two gave up too easily.'

'I didn't love him any more, Sylvie. Michael didn't love me.'

'Yeah, well, so what? He didn't deserve what you did to him.'

'What did I *do* to him? It was Michael that lost us the flat.'

'Christ knows,' she says, turning up the TV. 'But Daniel said you must have done something.'

I have to keep reminding myself how young she is. She's hurting; she's just lashing out.

'Is this about you and Sam?' I say, trying to make sense of her outburst. 'Have you two been having more problems?'

She rolls her eyes.

'Jesus, Claire. We split up ages ago, that's all done with. And, no . . . it's got fuck all to do with this.'

I wonder what she means by ages – in my sister's language that could mean a matter of hours.

'Well, you never said anything. I didn't know.'

She laughs.

'Yeah, that's right, you don't know *anything*. And it doesn't matter now, anyway. I'm already going out with someone new.'

'*Already?* With all this going on?'

'I have to get out. I have to see my friends. It's the only thing keeping me sane.'

'Who is it? Someone from the hospital, another doctor?'

'No. It's that pastry guy . . . Gabriel. We went out a couple of times. I've been seeing him.'

Jin Itchi

When I'm feeling this negative and down on the world I like to have something good to eat. A Portuguese cake, a bar of the cheapest kind of chocolate, or a thick slice of freshly buttered toast. Right now I'm craving something savoury, something rich raw and slippery, like fish. And if it's going to be sushi at midnight on Christmas Eve then there's only one place it can be – ladies and gentlemen I give you, the Jin Itchi Sushi Bar and Restaurant.

I've been coming to this place – off and on – for the last eight months, and it's definitely something of an acquired taste. Ordering food here is a minefield. The menu is seven pages long with letters the size of rice grains, and only half the items have an English translation next to them. The pages are grubby and sticky to the touch, and whatever you decide to eat, the waitress always acts like you've chosen spectacularly badly.

'I'd like the mackerel sashimi.'

'Bad idea. Stupid lady.'

'Did you just call me stupid?'

'No.'

'Well, what about the mixed tempura? I'd like that. How about the mixed tempura?'

'Foolish. *Foolish.*'

'The sea urchin?'

'No.'

'The sushi set?'

'Uh uh.'

'Well, is there something that you could recommend?'

'Hold it. I see what we got left over in the kitchen.'

★   ★   ★

On balance, you might think this is the type of dining establishment that's best avoided, but in the months since I split up with Michael I've made a special effort to seek it out. Jin Itchi is not the kind of place you could happen upon casually; it's hidden away in a low-rent basement room in China Town and you need a detailed set of directions in order to find it. There's no sign on the door, no gaudy pictures on the steamed-up windows, no two-for-one buffets to reel in the hoards of bargain-hungry tourists. Just a narrow set of steps – perilous when it's wet – leading down to a battered, smoky vestibule.

It seems like there have been a few attempts to brighten the place up over the years but none of them have made it look any more cheerful. There's a poster of Mount Fuji on the back wall, its edges stained black from the constant breeze of passing nicotine; a couple of paper lanterns tied loosely to the ceiling, their thin folds choked up with fish grease and dust; and over in the corner an ancient TV set plays silently for no one, its speaker long since blown from overuse.

When they're not serving gourmet sushi or insulting their nervous customers, the waiters sometimes feed tapes to a worn-out video machine. Japanese soap operas and quiz shows broadcast on a loop – bizarre, garish, soundless – but no one pays them much attention. Occasionally you might glance up to see a midget hitting an old woman with a rubber truncheon or a topless girl chasing after a bus, but the programmes are mostly there for decoration. It all adds to the general sense of otherworldliness, to the feeling that you could be anywhere other than central London.

The customers here are mostly locals – Chinese shopkeepers, Asian businessmen, the odd language student chain-smoking cigarettes and reading Manga comics – and most lunchtimes you'd be hard pressed to hear an English voice. From time to time a lost shopper takes a wrong turn and heads down the steps in the hope of sustenance, but they almost always leave without taking a seat. The noise and the heat and the general ill will hits them, and they quickly scamper back from whence they came.

And that's the way I like it. When I was breaking up with Michael, this place always felt like the perfect balm and it still feels comforting to me now. I know I won't bump into anyone that I recognise here, and even in the midst of all this craziness with my brother I'm unlikely to come across a nosy soul who will recognise me. It's quiet and calm and I can practise my Japanese, and if you can tolerate the insults and the décor, it's an excellent place to sit and think. The other great thing about Jin Itchi is that it was Daniel who first recommended it to me.

When I say recommended what I mean is, that I once asked Daniel if he knew of anywhere near his office that I could eat a good lunch for less than five pounds, and Jin Itchi was the best he could come up with. It was April this year, I'd just moved back to London and I was as broke as I'd ever been in my life. Daniel was loaning me some money to see me through the ruins of my marriage break-up and he'd seemed almost confused by the question. A cheap restaurant? A place you could eat lunch for less than five pounds? Who knew of such a place? He seemed a little embarrassed that he could actually come up with an answer.

'So, remember,' said Daniel, writing out my loan cheque, with his Mont Blanc pen. 'Whatever you do, don't order the sushi.'

'No, OK. I won't.'

'It's great, but it's too pricey for your budget.'

'OK, I get it. I understand.'

'Stick to the noodle soup. £4.50 a bowl, it's pretty good.'

'The soup. I hear you.'

'And the waiters can be a little rude, so don't take any shit from them.'

'I won't.'

'It's not the most salubrious place in the world, but if you want to eat that cheaply . . . it's the best I can do.'

'Daniel?'

'What?'

'Why don't you come with me?'

'I can't, I'm busy this afternoon.'

I frowned at him.

'Daniel?'

'What?'

'You're a *partner*.'

'So?'

'So, live a bit. Take some time off.'

My brother smiled at me; a firm polite smile that said it was never going to happen; a signal that said it was time for me to leave . . .

'Well . . . look, I'd better go. And thanks again . . . for the money.'

'That's OK. No problem.'

'I'll pay you back as soon as I can.'

'No hurry. I know things are difficult, take your time.'

'I'll see you soon, then?'

'Yep . . . uh-huh . . . absolutely.'

He'd already turned back to his files. He was already lost somewhere else.

I walked out of my brother's office that spring afternoon with his cheque burning a hole in my pocket; I didn't even know how much it was for. Daniel was too embarrassed to ask me how much I needed and I was too humiliated to take it out and look at how much he'd given me. I felt awful, to tell you the truth. I wanted to hang out with my brother in a different way to this. I wanted us to be able to relax and have a laugh and chat honestly and openly about our lives. I wanted to ask him how he'd been getting along these days, I'm never entirely sure. Whenever you ask Daniel how he's doing he always says he's doing great, then he immediately begins on a story about Kay, or the baby, or the business.

Is that about getting older? I suppose it is. He has his own family now, a life that's utterly separate from mine. We share not a single friend nor acquaintance in common – we haven't done for years – and we rarely see each other one to one even now that I've moved back to London. We generally meet up at family gatherings, or horribly choreographed dinner parties where Kay tries to fix me up with someone 'suitable'. Failing that I visit him at his office every six months or so to ask him if he'll bail me out – yet again.

It took me a good while to locate Jin Itchi that first afternoon and when I'd finally navigated my way down the series of back roads and blind alleys, I remember being shocked by how low key it was. It was so unlike the kind of place I'd expect Daniel to know about. I couldn't resist it. The idea of seeing my brother stripped bare in these surroundings was too good an opportunity to miss. I decided to call him back and harangue him some more.

'Daniel, just get yourself down here.'

'I can't, I told you.'

'You can, come on. The waitress is already being rude to me and taking the piss out of my Japanese. Come down here and look expensive so she'll like me more and won't spit up in my food.'

'I can't . . . *really.*'

'Daniel . . . come on. It's my treat.'

'Did you look at it yet?'

'The cheque? . . . No, I didn't look.'

'Do me a favour, then, don't. Not until after we've eaten.'

'You'll *come*?'

He hesitated for a moment.

'Yeah . . . I'm a partner. Why not?'

We had the best afternoon. We drank too much sake, ate too much raw fish; talked about my marriage, my divorce and my lousy taste in men, and my consistently woeful financial acumen. We even talked a little about the old days. There were certain things we skirted over (there always were) but we connected in a way we hadn't done for years.

'So, how are you?' I said, not knowing exactly why I was asking.

'How am I?' he said, loosening his tie. 'You know . . . I'm fine, I'm good.'

'Really?'

'Yeah. The job is going great, Kay's enjoying the baby . . .'

I frowned and bristled at him slightly.

'No. Not Kay, not the business, *you*. How are you, Daniel? Are you happy?'

He looked almost bemused at the question. And then I just blurted it out.

'You ever miss the running? You ever sorry you gave it up?'

I shouldn't have said that; it's on the list of things we're not meant to talk about.

'You know what?' he said, wiping his mouth. 'I do miss it. Sometimes I miss it a lot.'

He looked like a different person as he said it. His cheekbones almost seemed to change shape. It was as if he'd been training his muscles to hold his face a certain way all these years and for a moment they'd given up on the effort. He looked the way he might have if his life had been altogether different, if he'd chosen an entirely different course.

'Hey,' I said, giving his arm a squeeze. 'Maybe you should take it up again, for fun. Keep yourself fit, stop your arteries furring up from all those rich dinners your wealthy clients keep treating you to.'

He laughed for a second and smiled this delightful, youthful smile.

'Maybe,' he said. 'Maybe.'

I stayed a long while after he left. I drank a cup of coffee and ordered a bowl of cherry-blossom ice cream that still stands as one of the most delicious things I've ever eaten. It tasted floral and sugary, like a bowl of frozen jam, and it took me an age to get through it. I savoured every mouthful, rubbing my finger round the bowl to collect the pools of melted cream, and tapping the sugary droplets into my mouth. I put off opening that cheque for as long as I possibly could and when I eventually did, it made me gasp. A cheque for five thousand pounds. It would cover my debt, pay the solicitor's fees, and put me properly back on my feet. I couldn't believe it. I was overwhelmed, actually. Too over-whelmed to call him up immediately and tell him how much I'd enjoyed our meal together. Too overwhelmed to call and let him know what an exceptional brother he was and to assure him that this was the last time I'd ever have to borrow money from him.

When I tried to reach him later that evening he'd gone out somewhere with Kay and I didn't manage to speak to him again until the following afternoon. By then his whole tone had altered. He'd closed up again, pulled away; become reserved, efficient and polite. And I let things slide, like I always do. I paid back the money bit by bit, went back to the melodramas of my own dysfunctional existence and neglected to delve any further into his.

So what if Sylvie is right? What if there was something going on in Daniel's life that I didn't know about; that I managed to ignore or exacerbate? What if he'd become depressed and despondent and I'd missed it because I was too caught up with my own problems? What if it turns out that I failed him, if it turns out to be too late?

'Hey, waitress . . . I was wondering. Have you got any of that cherry-blossom ice cream in the fridge?'

'Do you see it written on the menu?'

'Well, no.'

'So, what do you think? I'm gonna go find a tree, cut down some cherries and make a special bowl all for *you*.'

'Look, I was only asking.'

She takes pity on me and brings me a bowl of tinned lychees instead.

'You look tired,' she says, setting down the bowl of fruit. 'Tomorrow is Christmas. You don't look very Christmassy to me.'

'Yeah, well, it's been a bad week.'

'What happened?' she says, nonchalantly. 'You broken up with a boy?'

'Sort of. Among other things.'

'Another woman?'

'It's not important . . . he wasn't my boyfriend. Not really.'

'But you liked him?'

I shrug.

'And now he's with some other tarty bitch?'

'It's my sister, actually,' I tell her. 'He's started seeing my sister.'

Her mouth falls open and she giggles.

'Ah, rubbish . . . you're only joking.'

'No, really. It's true.'

'It's real? How old is she? *Younger?*'

'Yeah, a lot younger. Twenty-three.'

She takes this in for a moment. She lets out a hoot of contempt.

'Twenty-three, *pah*. What the point in that? She barely got hair on her fanny yet.'

I laugh. Despite it all I start to laugh. I like it that this woman doesn't look sorry for me. She doesn't dip her head to one side or avert her eyes from mine, she just shrugs her shoulders as if to emphasise the chaotic ups and downs of life, and pours out a little extra green tea.

'Lot of people with problems come in here,' she says. 'Down here is a good place to hide from your problems.'

'Yes,' I say. 'I think you're right.'

'My name is Yori, by the way.'

'Claire,' I say, holding out my hand.

'You been in here a few times before now, right? This week you been in here a lot.'

'This week I've had a lot of problems.'

I say this last part in my best Japanese and she smiles and raises her eyebrows.

'Not bad,' she says, collecting up my plate. 'Pronunciation bit loopy, but not too bad.'

She doesn't ask any more questions. She disappears behind the sushi counter for a couple of minutes, returns with an unlabelled video tape, and slips it into the ancient machine. Without asking if it's OK, she sits down at my table and folds her slim arms around her knees. The customers are almost all gone now and she's ready to relax and take a break.

'You like to watch the TV?'

'Sure,' I say. 'Why not?'

'The sound is broken.'

'I know,' I say. 'Has been for a while.'

'One day we'll fix. Maybe next year . . . but I like the pictures. I like this programme. This programme very good.'

'What's it called?'

'*Yonigeya*,' she says, darkly. 'Very thrilling and mysterious.'

She concentrates hard on the television screen and it feels like an imposition to ask her any more. So we sit for a while, just the two of us. Two strangers in an empty sushi bar on the loneliest evening of the year: sipping tea, eating lychees and watching pictures of a distant Asian city flicker gently back and forth on the screen in front of us. As calm and empty as a silent movie.

The Other End of the Telescope

For Christmas day lunch at my brother's house I wear an outfit that declares war on the world of gloom: a lemon-coloured skirt, a pale green wrap-around cardigan and a T-shirt that says *Aloha Hawaii* on the front. Everyone else is decked out in their Sunday best, in funereal shades of black and grey. I keep my cardigan tightly fastened so they don't see the Hawaii logo or notice the screen-printed rainbow that joins the two dots above the i's, but I fear that the damage has already been done.

'Nice outfit, *sis*. Good one.'

I hadn't fully realised it yet, but we are a family in mourning. The chains of multicoloured fairy lights have been removed from the windows and the porch, and replaced with tall white candles. Muted flames dance unhappily in the living room grate – careful not to burn too high or crackle too enthusiastically – and even the paper used to wrap up Julian's presents is a subdued and tasteful shade of navy blue.

'Is that your Hawaii T-shirt under your cardigan?'

'No, Sylvie. It's not.'

'It looks like it to me.'

'Well . . . I'm sorry. I just thought that if we were going to do this today, I should make an effort.'

This is typical of me. Somehow I always manage to get it wrong; to interpret things in a way that isn't appropriate. How did Sylvie know to wear a charcoal coloured trouser suit today and tie her hair back into a stiff blond bun? How did Kay know to match her demure woollen dress to my mother's, and who put Robert in that undertaker's suit? Did they all discuss it before hand? Was there some pre-arranged signal that was shared between everyone but me?

Kay goes upstairs to change Julian's nappy and I tag along with her; partly to avoid Sylvie, partly in an effort to make the peace.

'Don't listen to them,' she says, not quite meaning it. 'You look cheerful. It's nice . . . for Julian.'

'Really?'

'Of course, who cares what you wear?'

'Hello, Stinky,' I say, patting Julian's nappy. 'Did you get any lovely presents?'

My nephew wriggles on his changing mat.

'Do you think he understands that his daddy is missing?' I say, cleaning him up.

'No,' says Kay, taking a deep breath. 'I don't think he does.'

'It's better that way. With a bit of luck, he won't ever have to know about it.'

She looks at me, wondering what I mean.

'I'm just saying that he needn't know this happened. When Daniel comes back . . . afterwards. Julian will be too young to remember.'

'You think he's coming back?' she says, quietly.

'Yes . . . of course I do. Don't you?'

She looks at the floor, she can't answer. She thinks it's time we made a start on lunch.

All of us chip in to prepare the food and make the meal, and at 2:00 p.m. on the dot the Ronson family sits down with the rest of the country to eat a traditional Christmas lunch. The table is perfectly laid. Each place setting has a napkin and a cracker and a china plate, and a crystal glass filled up with wine. It seems faintly perverse to be eating a meal like this now, but in truth its preparation has given us all something to concentrate on. We haven't had to talk about anything awkward for the last couple of hours. We've boiled and baked and grilled in a frenzy with no talk of psychics or police officers or mysterious coke deals, or sisters sharing one another's one-night stands.

Sylvie has kept away from me all morning, amusing Julian with his new toys in front of the fire. Robert has busied himself making a starter for our meal and even my mother has helped prepare the vegetables and managed to lay off the alcohol. All of us have kept our ears wide open for the phone; our eyes happily diverted from one another and trained furtively on the windows and the door. We are all hoping for – perhaps expecting – the very same thing. It's Christmas day, he knows we're all together, if he's out there somewhere, *anywhere*, now would be the time for him to ring.

But, there's nothing. No call as we sit down to the bland tomato soup that Robert has made. No grand entrance as we force down powdery slices of meat from a turkey that still managed to dry out like a bone, despite our vigilantly over-attending to it.

'Should we light the pudding?' Robert says, breaking the silence. 'Is there some brandy we can use?'

Nobody wants to light the pudding, but my mother would quite like a glass of brandy. The party is over. It's done with. The honoured guest has failed to arrive. We've acted out our play, draped a veneer of normality over the day as best we could, and still we failed to entice him back.

We can't wait to clear up the detritus of the meal. It seems to be mocking us: the livid green sprouts, the roast potatoes barely touched, the Christmas pudding still swimming in its gravy of discoloured cream. The crackers are tossed un-pulled into the bin and the last of the wine is recorked and refrigerated before it sours. With everything cleared away and cleaned there's nothing left to occupy us and nothing useful we can think of to say. In the silence we can hear the walls breathing and floorboards creaking, and our own minds spinning uselessly around. As if to express all the pent up emotion that we can't, Julian begins to wail.

'I'll take him,' I say, gratefully. 'He's probably tired. I'll see if I can get him off to sleep.'

Julian falls asleep almost immediately, his small chest rising and falling in his cot as I stroke the side of his face. He's exhausted.

We've passed him between us like a parcel all day long, demanding that he distract us from ourselves. He's done his job; he's worked as hard as he possibly could.

'Is he down yet?'

'He went out like a light.'

Kay is standing in the doorway. She comes over to check that I've lain Julian on his back the way she told me to, and the two of us sit for a while, watching him sleep.

'Should we leave? I don't want to wake him.'

'No, he's fine when he's like this. Nothing will disturb him now.'

'Right. Well. That's good.'

'Claire . . . I meant to say, Sylvie told me.'

'About what?

She looks uncomfortable.

'About *Gabriel*? Great, does Mum know?'

She nods.

'Well, that must have cheered her up a bit. What did she say?'

She pauses for a moment, wondering whether to tell me or not.

'She said it made sense. That he wasn't really . . . your type.'

'She said he was too good-looking for me, right? That Sylvie and him made a better match?'

'Well, you know your mother, I'm not sure she thinks a pastry chef is much of a match for anyone . . . but, yes. She thought Sylvie was more in his league.'

'God . . . that woman is harsh.'

'Yes,' says Kay. 'She really is.'

We both exchange grudging smiles and in the spirit of frankness I decide now's a good time to ask her about the pills.

'Look, it's nothing,' she says, coolly. 'I already explained it all to Sylvie.'

'Sylvie *spoke* to you about this?'

'When she found the boxes. She wanted to know what they were.'

I rub my eyes. It's impossible to work out who knows what around here.

'I would have said something,' she says, uneasily. 'But he never took them. He was better, he was fine. And you know what doctors are like, they hand out antidepressants like sweets these days.'

'Do they?'

'He was feeling under the weather. He was working too hard. We were arguing a little after Julian was born but it wasn't . . . anything serious.'

'You're sure?'

'He's my husband, Claire. You might not have known what was going on with him day to day, but that doesn't mean that I didn't.'

'No . . . I'm not saying that. But I think you should have told us . . . it's important. We should have informed the police.'

'And let it get into the *papers*?'

I don't know what to say to that. The fact that she cares how things look to the outside world strikes me as astonishing.

'It might help, that's all. If they knew Daniel was depressed, having problems.'

'He wasn't having problems, he was fine. He wasn't about to do something crazy . . . he wasn't *suicidal*.'

'I didn't say that. I'm just saying he might have needed some time.'

'For what?'

'I don't know for what, Kay. That's why I'm asking.'

She's getting angry now; she's finding it hard to look at me.

'Might he have wanted to get away for a while?' I say, pushing her. 'Might he have needed some time alone?'

'This is ridiculous.'

'Is it?'

'What am I supposed to think? That he just walked out on me and Julian? That he hated us *so* much, cared for us *so* little that he didn't care to let us know if he's alive or dead. Daniel's had some selfish moments in his life, but he wouldn't do something like this. To me, to *you*. To his family.'

'Well, not normally, no. But what about the medication? It can cause side effects can't it? I've heard it can make you worse sometimes.'

'She already told you, Claire. He didn't take them. They're still up there in the medicine cabinet. Go take a look.'

Sylvie is stood on the landing looking fierce. She struts into the bedroom, sits down on the bed and lays a protective arm around Kay's shoulder. This is her tactic, then, it seems – to play people off against one another. To turn up just in time to mop up the emotional damage that she's provoked and fulfil her leading role as this family's carer.

The warmth of Sylvie's embrace seems to break Kay's resolve and she begins to crumple and cry. The stress, the ridiculousness, the dreadful sadness of the day overwhelms her. As the tears run over her cheeks Sylvie hugs her even tighter, scowling at me as if I've purposefully hurt them both.

'Men like Daniel don't walk away from their lives,' Kay says, almost to herself, her voice battling hard against the words. 'He had everything he wanted. *Everything.* He had no reason to leave us.'

'Of course not,' says Sylvie, offering her a tissue. 'He loves you. He loves all of us.'

'But, what if he was in trouble?' I say, refusing to let it go. 'Could he have been in some kind of trouble?'

'He would have told me about it. I would have known.'

'Maybe it was something . . . he couldn't talk about.'

Kay swallows hard and scrubs at her face with the tissue.

'Something criminal, is that what you mean?'

I don't answer. I don't know what I mean.

'He wouldn't abandon us, Claire. Not Julian, he just . . . he couldn't do it.'

I lower my head, unable to bear the force – the accusation – of her stare. She has to be right. He would never have walked away from all this voluntarily, not if he and Kay were genuinely happy. He had it all, the life most people dream about. The money, the status, the home, the loyal wife, the baby, the successful career. He had exactly the life my father would have wanted for him, planned for him; a life that would have made him supremely proud.

'So?' I murmur. 'If you don't think he left . . . what *do* you think?'

'Honestly?'

I nod.

'Don't make me say it, Claire. For Christ's sake, don't make me say it out loud.'

Sylvie takes Kay downstairs and I wait until I hear the living room door click shut behind them before I make a start on my search. I can't help myself. I go to the bathroom unlock the medicine cabinet and root around for the boxes. They're still there, just like Sylvie said: six months' supply, still sleek in their cellophane wrappers, none of them opened or used. I turn them over in my hand, weighing them, touching them, sniffing them, searching out a clue of some kind. He didn't open them but he *kept* them, he didn't throw them away. Perhaps he thought he might still need them. Perhaps the mere fact of them being there, locked away on the other side of the landing, was enough of a comfort to get him through it.

To get him through what? A rocky patch in his marriage? The pressures of becoming a first-time parent? The stress of making partner in his law firm? I'm not buying it. Daniel's not the type of person to request antidepressants on a whim, I can barely remember him taking anything stronger than an aspirin. I don't know if it's intentional or not but I suspect that Kay is holding something back.

I examine the date on the packets, wondering if it'll spark some ideas. The prescription was first issued back in February this year, a couple of months before we had our sushi lunch at Jin Itchi. I was lost in the depths of my marriage break-up, I hadn't spoken to Daniel – to any of the family – for several weeks. I hadn't dared tell them about it. I couldn't face letting them know how badly I'd screwed up; how short sighted and rash I had been. It's unfortunate timing. Nothing makes you more inward looking than your own fuck-ups.

For some reason I decide that I want to hold on to the tablets. I shove the boxes deep into the pockets of my cardigan, rearrange the corn plasters and the Savlon so you can't see that anything's missing, and make my way across the landing to Daniel's study. It's immaculate, as always. Files neatly stored, papers carefully stowed, pens lined up neatly on a leatherbound blotter. There's a picture of Julian on the polished oak desk alongside a pair of wedding photos in smart silver frames: Daniel smiling in a grey morning suit and top hat, Kay in acres of satin and vintage lace looking like something out of a magazine. Michael and I got married in a registry office. We both wore T-shirts and jeans.

Beyond the study there's a small balcony where Daniel still keeps a telescope, and I brave the Christmas chill and go outside. He always complains that it's too bright in London to see the constellations properly so he doesn't use it as much as he used to. When he was a kid he used to spend hours – whole nights sometimes – staring at the sky, especially in the months before we left to go to Florida. In the summer he'd sometimes camp out in the garden so he could wake up in the small hours of the morning to view a predicted meteor shower, or spot a particular comet that he'd read about in one of his library of astronomy books. I used to tease him about it mercilessly, I used to call him 'the boffin'. In those days Daniel was the one they worried about. The moody one. The dreamer. The drifter. The kid who only ever showed singularity of purpose when he was training or racing or stargazing.

The way he transformed himself after Dad died surprised all of us. He gave up athletics completely and went from academic underdog to top of the class in under a year. He won a place at Cambridge, secured a first-class degree, then went on to finish in the top two per cent in the whole country in his law exams. I was so proud of him. We all were. In those few months before and after he left home, we never stopped telling him how well he'd done.

I pull my cardigan tightly round me, wondering if I'll ever feel warm again. The idea of my brave, clever brother being hurt or dead sucks the marrow out of my bones. Is that what Kay is saying? Are we waiting for a body to turn up? Are we waiting on the end of some fearful, savage story, the details of which we might never fully understand? I don't dare contemplate it. I'm worried that if I acknowledge it openly, there's a chance that it'll come true.

I stand out on the balcony blowing warm air onto my frozen fingertips, staring through the telescopic lens. I imagine the viewfinder is exactly where Daniel last trained it, on this vast patch of diamond-lit cosmos. It's a clear night and despite the London haze, the sky is pulsating with energy: radiation from planets a million light years away; faint beams of light from ancient galaxies and moons, and stars that died before our sun ever existed. I remember when Daniel told me that some of the stars we could see through this telescope weren't really there any more. It took him a while to convince me. What we see are their echoes, their traces, he said; minute particles of their being. Posted like cosmic letters from the long-distant past and only just reaching us now. They exist as an illusion, he told me. On the surface they shine and dim and dance just as they should, but they are stars with a secret, half alive.

I stare outwards for a long time; watching the dying light from distant solar systems, turning the cardboard pill boxes over in my hands.

'Where are you, Daniel?' I say, to the stars. 'Where in heaven's name did you go?'

Return To Sender

'It's a love letter.'

'No shit, genius.'

'OK . . . OK. Don't take it out on *me*. It's not my fault.'

It *is* his fault. He looks too good. He looks better than I do after an entire afternoon spent getting ready and I have to confess, it pisses me off. It's not his clothes – Michael always dresses like a scruff – it's the fact that he makes zero effort and still manages to look so content with himself. He has this savvy, worn-out, beat-up quality that he carries off like a stray alley cat. He looks like he might smell bad, but he doesn't. He looks like he's tired, but he's not. In daylight he looks way older than his thirty-seven years, but in this dull pub lighting with a candle illuminating his face, he looks mischievous, cute, almost youthful. It brings out the maternal instinct in women, this wide-eyed look; they immediately want to nurture and mother him. And here's the kick. Michael doesn't need any looking after, he's not the gentle, affable bloke they first think he is.

'Who else have you shown it to?' he says, toying with the slip of paper I've just given him.

'No one,' I say. 'Not even my mother.'

'Are you going to?'

'I don't know, Michael. I don't know what to do. I haven't spoken to anyone for a couple of days.'

My family have retreated to their various islands. Sylvie has taken up residence above the pastry shop with Gabe. Kay is having trouble sleeping alone in the house, so she and Julian are staying nearby with a friend. Mum and Robert have hidden away with their gin bottles and their torment, and Daniel remains invisible, like a ghost. And me? I've been rattling round my flat since that awful Christmas lunch, wondering what on earth to make of this. A slip of note paper that I found by chance, buried deep inside one of the pill packets. A love letter from a woman to a ghost.

My Darling,

I hope you'll never realise how much I'm going to miss you. I love you. I love you. And you mustn't forget it for as long as you live. I have to accept this decision that you've made, but I won't lessen all you're meant to me these past years by debating it with you any longer. I've gone as far as I can, cried as much as I can stand, and I accept that I must move on now and let you go.

I wish you such happiness and luck, and I know how much you wish the same for me. I'd ask you to write, and I'm sure that you would do it, but I'm certain it won't do us any good. So goodbye, my dear, sweet man. All my love goes ever with you. In another time, in another life . . .

With glorious fondness, forever and always,
Annie x

'Wow.'

'I know.'

'That's pretty stern stuff.'

'Stern?'

'I mean she's sticking it to him a little, don't you think? Saying she's not going to debate it any more.'

'What choice does she have? He's made his decision. I think she's showing incredible dignity.'

Michael shrugs.

'Well, I'm not sure the ice-queen will see it like that. Are you even going to tell her?'

What am I meant to do? Tell Kay it looks like Daniel had been having an affair since before Julian was even born? Let her know that he was taking the antidepressants behind her back?

'I don't know Michael, I think . . . it would break her.'

He grimaces. He sees how desperate it is.

'You're sure the pills had all been taken?'

'He'd opened and resealed all the packets. Every one of them was empty inside. I was fidgeting with one of the boxes that I took and the cellophane just split apart in my hand.'

'This was the only letter you found?'

'Yes. He'd removed the information leaflet and replaced it with this.'

Michael scratches his face. He has a rash of stubble just breaking through his chin that's grey and tatty at the edges, and I suddenly want to reach out and touch it. How strange that I'd want to do that. We greeted each other like embarrassed cousins just now, and it felt so awkward and strange. I used to part-own his body. He used to have part-ownership of mine. Where does it go to, all that history? All the comfort, the joy, the familiarity.

'So, who's Annie?' Michael says, stuffing crisps into his mouth. 'You think she's his secretary or something?'

'If I knew that, I'd be talking to *her*. I wouldn't be sat here with you, watching you stuff your beardy face full of chip-sticks.'

'Hey, hold on a minute. I didn't ask you to call me. It wasn't *me* that got back in touch.'

Of course it wasn't. Even with all this awful shit going on, Michael didn't call me up once to find out how I was. OK, that's not strictly true. He did call me up last week from a jazz club in Prague, but he didn't leave a number where I could call him back.

'I *called* you. Don't say I never called.'

'You left a message. You didn't tell me where you *were*.'

'I thought you knew.'

'Michael, why would I know?'

'It was in the papers. There was a review in the *Sunday Times*. It listed all my tour dates, didn't you read it?'

I lower my head into my hands. Fear of being alone on new year's eve has forced me to this humiliating low point. It was fear that made me dial up his number on a whim and ask him to come and meet me in this pub. There were other invites – friends back in Oxford, some new work contacts here – but I wasn't in the mood to get drunk or go travelling or join a party. I wanted to be with someone who understood me, who knew my family's politics inside out. Someone who could help bear the weight of this secret I'm carrying round, welded to my back like a turtle's shell. And I'm lonely tonight. There, I said it. It's new year's eve and I'm lonely as hell.

'Hey, look. I didn't think you'd *want* to hear from me. It all ended so . . .'

'Badly, selfishly, *meanly* . . . ?'

'Claire, I am . . . so sorry.'

'I'm still paying it off now, Michael. Do you even know that? I had to borrow money from Daniel just to get by.'

'You know I'll help you out when I can. I haven't had many gigs this year, but it's picking up now. I'm getting some recognition, better reviews. And you know what I'm like, I had to go for it. That music school set up . . . it was never really *me*.'

'It was your *idea*.'

'I know . . . I know. I know.'

He puts down his drink.

'I didn't mean to ruin everything,' he says, touching my hand. 'It wasn't always so bad with us, was it?'

He's incredible. What does he want? A pat on the arm, a bat of the eyelids, for me to tell him that he's a lovely man really.

'You're a selfish fucking shit-bag,' I say, taking away his crisps. 'Didn't you even care a little bit?'

'About you . . . the marriage? How can you even ask, you *know* I did.'

'No, not just me. You were part of my family for almost three years, don't you care at all about what might have happened to my brother?'

'Of course I do.'

'We were on TV. Did you even see us? Did you once think to yourself . . . poor Claire, how fucking awful. I should maybe fucking think to give her a ring.'

'I did ring.'

'From *Prague*.'

Michael runs his hands through his straggly blond fringe, then pats it self-consciously back into place. His mood is fading fast; it always does when things get difficult.

'Look, this is fucking depressing. Do you mind if we go and get something to eat?'

I nod. I'm too worn out to fight.

'Somewhere quick, though,' he says, edgily, pushing back his chair. 'I have to be somewhere by midnight.'

'Right . . . of course.'

'I can't stay, Claire. I'd like to . . . but there's somewhere else I have to be.'

'It's fine, really,' I say, trying not to look fussed. 'And don't worry, I know the perfect place.'

I'm not sure at which point it happens but somewhere in the warren of Soho's murky streets I realise that my ex-husband is holding my hand. I don't remember him reaching for it, I'm just suddenly conscious that it's there.

'Been a bad couple of weeks huh, Shorty?'

Shorty, that's what he used to call me. Not because I'm small – that's the joke – but because I'm almost as tall as he is.

'It's been hard,' I say, wondering whether to pull my hand away or not. 'Everyone's taking it hard.'

'Seeing much of your mum?'

'As much as I can stand, she's pretty fragile.'

'Giving you a tough time?'

I don't say anything; he already knows the answer to this.

'I suppose I didn't help,' he says, slowing down and slipping his fingers between mine. 'The whole investment thing, the divorce, it must have fulfilled all their expectations.'

'Well, you know my mum . . . her favourite phrase is *I told you so*.'

He turns and smiles at me. And it hurts.

'You've still got your fur coat?' he says.

'Yeah . . . still wearing it, it keeps me warm.'

'That was a great trip, wasn't it? We had a good time, the two of us.'

'Yeah,' I say. 'We really did.'

'Remember that rollercoaster we went on in Gorky Park? Jesus . . . I thought we were going to die.'

I close my eyes. It was one hell of a rollercoaster. The kind that hurls you around, lurching and tumbling and compressing your insides, and feels like it might break free of its crooked rails at any second. It puffed up the gradient like it was being drawn by a fun-fair donkey, threatening to send us plummeting back into the rusty balustrades at any second. We howled all the way down – from fear, from relief, from pure exhilaration – convinced that our time had come. The moment we'd got our breath back and stilled our shaking legs, we went hurtling into a nearby bar for shots of ice-cold lemon vodka that we couldn't finish. The ride was wonderful but it had left us both nauseous: neither one of us wanted to go on it a second time.

I open my eyes. Michael is staring right at me.

'Claire . . . I'm an arse,' he says, putting his hands on my shoulders. 'You know . . . I just sort of freaked out towards the end. I couldn't handle it all. I panicked, I totally screwed things up.'

I don't say anything. I'm not sure how to respond. He's about to say something more when suddenly – like a beacon – a door opens up and the light from Jin Itchi's basement fills the street.

'This is it,' I say, breaking off and pointing down the narrow flight of steps. 'This is the place I thought we should eat.'

It's warm inside, like it always is, and tonight it's bustling and noisy. Yori, the waitress, nods from the other side of the room and strolls over with a pair of sticky menus.

'You in here again?' she says, grinning at me. 'What's wrong, you got no place else to go?'

'Yeah, you know. I just can't seem to stay away.'

'It's loud tonight, hey?'

'Yeah . . . you're right. It really is.'

'You know why? Can you work it out?'

I shake my head.

'Look,' she says, delightedly. 'The TV, finally fix. Just in time for new year's, do you notice?'

'Of course. Wow. After all this time.'

'I can put that same video on if you like, the one I show you the other night. Quieter than these stupid cartoons.'

'Great . . . sure, that'll be nice.'

'You remember?' she says, narrowing her eyes at me. 'Very thrilling and mysterious.'

Yori rushes off – taking our menus with her – before we've had a chance to order food. Michael calls after her, gruffly. He's a terrible complainer in restaurants and he looks like he's ready for an argument.

'Relax,' I say, trying to calm him down. 'There's no point in ordering, you never get what you ask for. She likes me, she'll bring us whatever's good.'

He's not listening. He wants to order something different, something strange; something that he's never tried before. As he marches over to harangue her, the video machine begins to click and whir. Michael and Yori argue over the menu but I quickly lose track of what they're saying. I'm drawn right into the programme, like a noodle being sucked through a straw.

'I'm getting octopus beak and raw liver,' says Michael, triumphantly. 'What do you think about that?'

'I didn't know octopuses had beaks.'

'Shit. You think she's winding me up?'

I don't know. I don't care. My eyes are still glued to the TV set.

'Good programme?'

'Yes. It is.'

'What's it about?'

'The Yonigeya.'

'What's that?'

'A secret agency. In Tokyo. They call themselves the fly-by-night arrangers.'

'What's that supposed to mean?'

'The guy in the red jacket, he's in trouble with the Yakuza, the Japanese mafia. He's in debt, if he can't find what he owes them, he'll be killed.'

'Right. I see.'

'And the guy in the black suit, the one with the scar, he's going to help him run away. Give him a new identity, arrange a new job. Supply him with a brand new life, for money.'

'Just like that?'

'Yeah, just like that.'

'What about the guy's family?'

'He's leaving them behind. He turns up for work OK, but somewhere around noon, his colleagues begin to realise that he's missing. No one sees him leave. Nobody knows where he went. And nobody that knows him can work it out. How can a person do that? Walk away without a trace, without a trail. Leave his family and his friends and just . . . disappear.'

I take a sip of green tea but find it hard to swallow. Michael is beginning to look uneasy.

'You know who recommended this restaurant to me?' I say, putting down my cup.

'No,' says Michael. 'I don't.'

'Have a guess.'

'I don't know, Claire . . . are you saying it was Daniel?'

I nod.

'Well, what makes you think he even saw this? The waitress said the TV's been broken for months. It's a coincidence, that's all. It doesn't mean anything.'

'Doesn't it?'

I put down my cup and take a breath.

'Yori? Can I talk to you a minute.'

'What now? I'm busy lady, can't you see?'

'Please . . . I need to ask you a question.'

'Cherries ice cream again?'

'No. Not Cherries. Not this time.'

The Girl Who Fell in Love
With Otoro

'Yes, yes, I recognise this nice man. He used to come in here a lot.

'Did he watch this programme? Of course, of course, it was his favourite. Many time he used to ask me about it. One time I translate whole episode for him.

'No, no, he came in here most often *before* the sound got broken. When it busted up he don't come by so much. Rich man, I think. Very well dress. Always he order otoro sushi. Blue fin tuna, very special fatty cut. Come from top of the tender belly near the . . . OK, OK, so you're not so interested in the sushi. What exactly is it you want to know?

'Where do people go to after they disappear? Hmmn . . . it depend. Sometime another city, sometime another country altogether. Maybe they get new passport so is OK to leave, but if they can't get one so quickly they leave by ship.

'Ship . . . you know. How do you say it? Stow away. They sometime smuggle away on board a ship.

'Is it real . . . yes, of course is real. Is not just a drama, let me tell you. This Yonigeya, it really exist.

'In Tokyo mostly; maybe all over Japan. People fed up with suicide. Very high suicide rate in Japan. Now some people think is maybe better to disappear, but I'm not sure really is so easy.

'Why go? For lot of reason. Maybe in debt, maybe have problem. Maybe on the run from the mafia. Some people take whole family with them. The Yonigeya very clever, they can disappear a whole family in the night. They pretend to be pest control but really they packing up the client house. Take care not to alert anybody. Take care to act normal. Many people that disappear are being watched.

'Yes. Yes, is true. Most people disappear alone. Maybe have bad marriage or maybe they are sick or have affair. Perhaps they want walk away from marriage without causing too much dishonour. Sometime the reason is sad. Sometime the reason enchanting. I hear about one woman, very romantic story. You want that I tell about her?

'OK, well, this lady – very beautiful, so they say – her life's ambition is to be sushi master. Very long training, very important job, but nobody want her to do this. They say woman high temperature will ruin fish. You know, when she has her . . . yes, menstruation, that's right. Anyway, she is very special girl, has dreamt of cutting fish all her life. When she is eleven year old her father take her to the docks in Fukuoka where she live and she see a blue fin just landed from the boat; a gigantic and fabulous beast. This fish can weigh as much as eighteen hundred pounds. This fish can swim up to fifty-six miles an hour. This fish have acute hearing and magnetic sensors in its skin that act as extraordinary compass. Can navigate all the way from California to Japan. But the special thing about this fish, the *truly* amazing thing, is that it has to keep swimming all its life. Always moving. Always searching. It is a feature of this fish that it can never slow down or come to rest. If it does, it will suffocate.

'So, this young lady she is very respectful. When she meets this creature eye to eye she is humbled. She feel that she owe it to this fish to cut its flesh with special care and she swears a solemn oath to regard its spirit. She devote her life to becoming the best sushi chef in all Japan and it turns out, at least this is what I *hear*, she has supernatural flair.

'No. Still none of the sushi schools decide to take her, so she study in secret for seven year. She is the best cutter, the best shaper, the finest, most dexterous girl you have ever seen. She can know a fish – its sweetness, its freshness, its texture, it's absorbency, the way it will fall on a plate – just with a blink of her eye. Her palette so trained, so sensitive that if you cook her a bowl of rice she can tell you which exact river the water that steamed it come from. Maybe it will taste of fresh melt water from the mountains, maybe a leaf of cherry blossom will have fallen into water as it meander its way through valley. If so, she will immediately sense it.

'Still, nobody will take a chance to employ her. So she get sad and marry a man she doesn't love. Not a cruel man, just a boring man. Drink too much, work too hard. Want his breakfast and his dinner and his shirts and his shoes and his woman and his life just so. This girl she want to divorce him but she know her husband will never allow it. Family very strict. Family say she must stay.

'This woman so sad in her marriage and her life, she sometime think she might die. But one day she hear about Yonigeya. She take her small savings and a dish of otoro that she has prepare especially for him. The Yonigeya is so amazed, so thrilled at the taste and the skill of this young lady, that he agree to help her right away. He arrange for her to escape and not charge her too much money. When she set up her own restaurant abroad and make her fortune, then she can send Yonigeya what she owes.

'One month later her husband awake and there is nobody there to fix his breakfast. Husband furious. When he realise his young wife is set free and escape, he bangs his fist through treasured rice paper screen. To this day no one knows where she go to. Some say Australia. Some say Toronto. Some clever people think London.

'No. No . . . ha ha, is not me. This not even my place. No, the Yonigeya not here. I don't think there are any in London.

'No. I am not one. Of course not. Is too much trouble . . . for a simple waitress.

'Really? This man disappear?

'No. I don't see it in the papers.

'No. I don't see it on TV. TV was broken, remember?

'Where do you think he go to, this man?

'Sorry, sorry. Your brother.

'No, I don't know either. He never say anything to me. Just one day I tell him the story of the sushi girl and he seemed to like it a lot.

'No, I didn't help him, why you say this?

'OK, I accept your apology. But this programme is very romantic. Is also a little dangerous, I think. Who in this world hasn't wondered for a moment what it would feel like to start their life over. To begin again sweet and crisp, like a new spring plum, freshly cut from the tree. No blemish, just perfect and ripe like a newborn, with a life to start over afresh. No mistake, no hang up, no problems. Erasing every one of your wrong turn. How light it would make a person feel. How better to fight his mortality than to give a person a second chance at life. So you see, I don't have to do anything. I don't even put the idea in people's head. The idea already there, snoozing like fat dog with an empty belly. Is there in all minds at some time or another; with this man, maybe was time his dog woke up.

'No, there's nothing else I can help you with.

'No, there is nothing more I can say. If you know him well enough you will guess where he went. They say the sushi lady kept postcards of London bus under her bed, but still the lady family not work it out. Or maybe they not want to know the truth. That she was right and they were wrong. Sometimes is so hard for people to change the way they see a loved one, they prefer not to see them at all.

'How do I like London? Very nice. Very open. Very green. But the water not so good. Give a funny taste to the rice. They say it go through seven people before it get to tap. Sometime, I think I taste every one.

'Am I good sushi chef? Of course. How you can ask? I am spectacular chef. A true master.'

It Helps to Have a Plan

My family looks utterly flabbergasted. At my suggestion? At my detective skills? At my logic? Or at the fact that I'm sat here with Michael? They're staring at me like I'm insane: Mum, Robert, Sylvie, Kay and even – I suspect – Stinky Jools.

'This is your big idea?' Sylvie says. 'That's why you dragged us all over here, to tell us about a soap opera in a Japanese restaurant?'

'I think it's too much of a coincidence, that's all. The waitress said Daniel went there all the time.'

Kay looks confused. Distressed.

'Daniel doesn't like Japanese food,' she says, quietly. 'He hates sushi, I know he does.'

'Well, I don't know what to tell you. I showed his picture to the waitress and she said he was in there a lot.'

'Watching this programme?'

'Yes.'

'And she thinks there are Yonigas . . . whatever you called them, operating here in London.'

'No. She thinks not. But it's more the idea of it. She was very persuasive. I think this programme might have influenced Daniel.'

'He wouldn't eat in a basement,' Kay says. 'Daniel hates anywhere cramped.'

'Yeah,' says Michael, helpfully. 'It was a really shabby place. Not the kind of place you'd expect Daniel to go.'

'Look,' I say, glaring at him. 'That's exactly my point. It wasn't his usual kind of place but he liked it; he actively sought it out. Who knows how he first stumbled upon it. Perhaps one of his clients took him there. The food is really authentic. They do this amazing tuna sushi . . . otoro, it comes from the belly of—'

'*Claire*, we don't need to know the entire menu.'

'Daniel hates tuna . . . he does. He'd never so much as have it in a sandwich '

I wipe my eyes. I take a deep breath and try again.

'Listen to me a minute. What if this programme was on when he first went in there? What if it somehow caught his eye. Maybe he went back from time to time because he found the restaurant quaint or unusual. And when he became depressed, this programme, this waitress, her story . . . perhaps he found it intriguing, maybe it began to make some sense to him.'

'He wasn't depressed. How many times do I have to say it?'

'Is this what you think, Claire? Honestly? That Daniel ran away because of a TV show?'

'I don't know, Sylvie. I'm not sure. I'm just thinking we should tell the police.'

'Tell them what? That Daniel got fed up of eating in expensive restaurants. That he sometimes liked to eat somewhere cheap? That some bored waitress likes to make-up tall stories to keep her customers amused? She's probably seen you on the TV. She's probably read about us in the papers. She's taking you for a fool. This is her idea of fun.'

They sigh with disappointment and pain, every one of them. And why shouldn't they? It's new year's eve, I've called an emergency meeting at my mother's house, promised them something significant and delivered nothing. I could back things up by telling them about the letter, but not with Kay here, I don't want to hurt her. And I can't very easily tell them about the pills: not without admitting that I stole them; not without making Kay look foolish. I should have worked all this out before rushing over here. I should have made some kind of plan.

'Well, it seems like you've had quite an evening,' my mother says. 'It seems your imagination has run riot. And what a pleasure to see *you* again, Michael. You were always a great influence on my daughter. You always gave such wonderful . . . support.'

There's nothing left to say, no new evidence left to dig through, so everyone gets ready to go. Kay's heading back to her friend's house with Julian, and Sylvie is seeing in the new year with Gabe. I stand up to leave along with them but my mother is looking at me strangely. I know what this means; she wants me to wait behind for a moment so she can give me a proper telling off.

'Not so fast,' she says, icily. 'Sit down and talk to me. Not you, Michael, you can wait outside.'

'In the cold?'

'You have a coat don't you?'

'Yep . . . yep. I have a coat.'

'Pity.'

'Come with me, Michael,' says Robert, gently. 'We'll leave the girls to it. I have some hot coffee in the kitchen.'

The good news is she hasn't had a drink yet; the bad news is, she's just about to start. She twists open a fresh bottle of gin and waits for its tight seal to snap apart. It's clear from her face, she half relishes this process, half loathes it: loves what it will do for her, hates that she's under its control.

'What else do you know?' she says, simply.

'Nothing,' I say. 'What do you mean?'

She glares at me.

'Come on, I'm not an idiot. I know you have more than you're letting on.'

She has this knack with me, this odd mind-reading arrangement. If only I had it with her.

'What is it?' she says, stiffly. 'Was he sleeping with this waitress, is that it? Has my son turned into one of *those* men?'

'I think, well . . . not with the waitress.'

'Someone else, then?'

'I don't know. It's just . . . a suspicion.'

I gaze at the floor. I don't want to show her the letter. I know what she's like; she'll be drunk by the time I'm gone and the first thing she'll do is call up Kay.

'Do you want a drink?'

'No. no. You're OK.'

'Mind if I have one?'

I shake my head.

She raises the glass to her lips but doesn't drink from it, then slowly, purposefully, she sets it down. It seems like such an effort, such a trial, that I feel like I ought to reward her.

'But you're right,' I say, 'there is something else. Those anti-depressants that Daniel had in the bathroom. Kay says he never took them, but he did.'

'You *know* this?'

'Yes . . . I opened them. It was an accident really . . . but all of the tablets were gone.'

She sits down and rubs her hand over her face.

'When was it?'

'When what?'

'Think, Claire. When did he start taking them?'

She's making me nervous; I can't think straight.

'I don't remember . . . no, wait, it was February. It was back while I was breaking up with Michael.'

She looks crestfallen. At what exactly? Is she worried at the effect this medication has had on Daniel? Is she displaying some long overdue sympathy for my broken marriage?

'Look,' I say, 'I don't want you to worry . . . we're just catching up. For old times. There's nothing going on between the two of us.'

She snorts. Her fingers go to her glass, but she pulls them back.

'What difference does it make?' she snaps, crossly. 'Michael, Gabriel, some other low-life that you've plucked off the street. How many has it been now? In the last year? In the last six months? None of them do you any good.'

I don't even have time to take this in. She's motoring, she's already moved on.

'I want you to go and see Tom tomorrow.'

'Daniel's partner? Why?'

'See what he knows. Ask him about the restaurant. See if they went there together. He'll know if Daniel was . . . if he was seeing someone else.'

'I don't know, Mum . . . I'm not sure.'

She leans in to me and reaches for my arm.

'Do this for me, please, Claire, it's important. I think you're the best one to do it.'

This trust, this kindness, this sudden softness in her voice, it leaves me a little disorientated. I wonder if I'm not imagining it, if she's not fooling or tricking me in some way.

'Of course, I'd ask Sylvie to go, but she's busy. Sylvie would have been my first choice.'

Cinderella

Outside in the cold, in the remnants of last week's snow, the city is singing off key. Drunks skid along the road on thin layers of ice and piles of cinnamon slush obstruct the pavements. People squeeze, bristle and churn through the streets, all in a hurry to get somewhere. The end of an old year, the beginning of the new, some still seem to think it worth celebrating.

'Don't you have to be somewhere by midnight?'

'I did . . . yeah,' says Michael, glancing at his watch. 'But it's probably too late to get there now.'

'Sorry. I didn't mean to spoil your evening.'

'It's fine, really. Don't worry about it.'

'Thanks for coming with me. It helped.'

'You think so?'

I shrug, I'm not sure it did.

'She hates me, doesn't she? I could tell?'

'Mum? Yeah . . . a little bit.'

'And you? Do you still hate me, Claire? Is that how it is?'

He's so transparent, so easy to read; Michael can't stand to feel rejected by anyone. He's seeking absolution, some reassurance, like a kid waking up from a nasty dream. I can tell, right now, that he wants to sleep with me. The idea's just popped into his head. He's blown out his date, he's ruined his night and he's wondering how far he can push it. He's testing himself, daring himself; wondering if I'll be fool enough to bite. But that's the comforting thing about Michael: everything about him is on the surface.

'No, Michael, I don't. I don't hate you.'

'Well, good. Good. That's good to know.'

We walk off in the direction of his car; Michael quiet and wondering how to play it.

'So,' he says, fiddling with his car keys. 'Do you want to come back to my flat?'

Do I? I'm not sure. I just know that I don't want to go home alone.

Sometimes it's not about love. Sometimes, not even desire. In difficult circumstances, in moments such as these, the fact that someone knows you well can be enough. It's comfortable with us. It's easy with us. We still know where everything fits. If it wasn't new year's eve, if Gabe wasn't screwing Sylvie, if my family didn't make me feel as lonely as a stranger sometimes, then maybe, well, who knows? But sometimes I just want someone to be nice to me: to hold me right, to touch my skin a certain way, and to not have to say too much of anything.

'You want me to stay over with you, don't you?' I say.

'Yeah, Shorty,' Michael says. 'Of course I do.'

And when he leans in to kiss me, it's not special, it's not exciting, but it's enough.

It's good waking up in someone else's flat. It's nice having them make you coffee and stale toast. It's nice not having to ask them what they do for a living or to have to admit that you don't remember their last (or first) name. I like it that I know this man's habits. I like it that I know how he ticks. This man still has two sugars in his coffee. He still waits for his toast to go cold before he butters it. And he just rubbed my neck as he walked past me: he always used to rub my neck.

'So, what does this mean?' he says, sitting down with his food. 'Does it mean we're back together? Is it important? Do we even *have* to define it?'

Rhetorical questions, every one.

'I had a great time last night, don't get me wrong. But I think we should just see where it goes. No pressure, no expectation. That's what killed it the first time round.'

Right. *That's* what killed it. The pressure.

'And I don't know how you feel . . . but I was wondering. If you'd *like* to, if you think it's OK. Maybe we should go on a couple of dates.'

Translation: he'd like to have sex with me from time to time.

'Because you're vulnerable at the moment, and I don't know where I'm at . . . and I'd hate for you, you know, to *expect* too much.'

He narrows his eyes as he says this, he actually sticks out his lip. But I don't expect anything. I know what this is. I smile and let him off the hook.

'Cool . . . cool,' he says. 'That's great.'

He leans in and squeezes my arm: pleased with himself, content with himself, relieved that he has it all worked out. There's no emotional complexity with Michael; it's only ever about how he feels at a given moment.

'I'll come over to Tom's house with you later, if you like. Would you like me to come over there with you?'

Of course he'll come, I remember this of old. Sex makes Michael briefly doting.

'And here, while you're eating, you might like to take a look at this.'

'What is it?'

'That *Sunday Times* review I was telling you about. I'll fix you another coffee while you read it.'

My brother's partner opens the door to us dressed in a pair of silk pyjamas; a little bit dozy and bleary eyed. He clearly had a time of it last night. He looks tired, sluggish, guilty.

'Claire . . . happy new . . . I mean, come in.'

'It's OK. You can still wish me a happy new year.'

'Sure, sure. I'm sorry.'

'You remember Michael, don't you?'

'Michael, yes . . . uh, of course.'

Tom welcomes us into his home. His place is a lot like my brother's: plush, expensive, well kept, but a little more arty and relaxed. There's modern art on the walls instead of landscapes and gloomy oils, and everything is brighter and warmer. The kitchen is in a bit of a state: empty champagne bottles strewn across the marble countertops and ashtrays stuffed full of cigar butts and ash.

'Bit of a party last night,' Tom says, apologetically. 'Not a big one, just a couple of close friends.'

'Really, it's fine. Why shouldn't you celebrate?'

'Well . . . I don't know. With everything that's going on.'

'Yes,' says, Michael, earnestly. 'It's a tough time for us right now. Not much celebrating for *us*.'

'No,' says Tom, lifting his eyebrows. 'I expect not.'

Michael helps himself to a left-over prawn canapé while Tom and I get down to business.

'So, why the early visit? Is there news?'

'No. No. Nothing really.'

Michael coughs. I'm not sure if this means he's got a flake of filo pastry stuck in his throat or if this is his attempt to urge me on.

'Tom,' I say, quietly, 'this is difficult. I know you've spoken to the police already . . . and that Chloe had a long talk with Kay, but was there something, anything . . . that you didn't mention?'

'Like what?'

'Well, did Daniel seem OK to you before this happened? Did he seem distracted, unhappy, depressed?'

'He was busy . . . he was working very hard.'

'Did my brother ever talk to you about his marriage? Did he ever mention that he and Kay might be having problems?'

'Not really, but he wasn't the type. You know Daniel, he's very private.'

'What about a woman named Annie?' says Michael, piping up. 'Do you know anybody called Annie?'

'*Michael?*'

'Well, what's the point in being coy? We have to ask.'

Tom shakes his head.

'No . . . I don't think so. Is she important, was something going on?'

'We don't know. We don't know who this woman is. But it seems like Daniel had been having an affair.'

'Claire, I thought I recognised your voice. How are you, is there any news?'

Chloe, Tom's wife, has come into the kitchen; she looks like she's just got out of bed. Her hair is messed up and there are creases in her cheeks, but she still looks effortless and pretty. She paints the murals that decorate this townhouse: splashes of pigment and startling colour, that sing out from the monochrome walls.

'They think Daniel was having an affair,' says Tom, crisply. 'They want to know if we knew anything about it?'

'Claire, is that true?'

I nod.

Chloe reaches for the coffee pot. She must have one hell of a hangover because the jug seems unsteady in her hand.

'I found a letter among Daniel's things,' I say, pulling the note out of my bag. 'It's not much to go on. I just thought if I could find out who this Annie woman was, she might know something.'

'Do you mind if I take a look?'

I hand the note over to Chloe. She takes an age to read through it.

'Well,' she says, quietly, running her eyes over the words. 'It seems like your brother was . . . in love.'

'Can I take a look?'

She hesitates. She passes the letter to Tom.

'Right, I see . . . does Kay know anything about this?'

'No, she doesn't . . . and I don't want her to. Not yet.'

'Of course,' says Chloe. 'It wouldn't do her any good. But we don't know any Annies, do we Tom?'

'No. I'm sorry.'

Michael studies their faces intently; he thinks he's being subtle but he's not.

'Do either of you like Japanese food?' he says, suddenly. 'Is sushi the kind of thing you like to eat?'

'Me, no, can't stand the stuff. Chloe likes it though, don't you Chloe?'

'Well, it's good for you. It's healthy.'

'She's into all that healthy stuff. I prefer a good steak and chips myself.'

Michael strokes his chin.

'So the pair of you have contrasting taste in food stuffs. Interesting, very, very interesting. Now, did either of you ever go to a restaurant called Jin Itchi in Soho? Did either of you ever go there with Daniel?'

What is he doing? Why does he have his thumb pressed into his cheekbone like that? Why is he narrowing his eyes at them? He thinks he's Columbo or something, he does. I bet he's thinking about buying himself a trench coat.

'Not me, never heard of it. Chloe?'

'No . . . no, I haven't. Why do you ask?'

'Well, it seems like Daniel went there a lot. Last winter, he was in there at least a couple of times a week.'

'And this is important, because?'

I distract Michael with another filo parcel and fill them in on the waitress and the Yonigeya. Tom and Chloe politely nod along.

'It's an interesting story, I'll grant you. But just a coincidence, surely?'

'I don't know, Tom, it's difficult,' I say. 'Right now it seems coincidence is all we've got.'

We pick at a croissant and drink some more coffee but it's obvious that we've outstayed our welcome. We chat a little longer, begin our goodbyes then Tom ushers us both to the door.

'If I think of anything else,' he says, 'I'll call you. And I'll see what I can dig up on this Annie woman.'

'Please. I'd appreciate it. And in the meantime . . .'

'Don't worry, we wouldn't dream of it. We won't breathe a word of this to Kay.'

'Well, that was odd, wasn't it?'

'Was it?'

'They seemed shifty the two of them, don't you think?'

'I think they were embarrassed. We'd probably caught them in the middle of something.'

'You think they'd been having sex?'

'I don't know, possibly.'

Michael thinks about this. For quite a long time.

'Well, I bet you a million quid that Tom knows exactly who this Annie woman is. It's obvious, I could see it in his face.'

'Why wouldn't he tell us, if he knew?'

'He's probably seeing her friend. I'll bet Tom was having a bit of extra curricular as well.'

'Tom, no, I don't think so. He doesn't seem the type.'

'Of course, that's *it*. I bet they're swingers.'

'Who?'

'Tom, Chloe, Daniel, Kay. I bet it's all key parties and orgies and porn nights and basement dungeons round their house.'

'Seriously? This is what you think?'

'Claire, you'd be surprised what goes on,' he says, know-ledgeably. 'Not sure about Daniel, he's a bit too uptight, but Kay would definitely be up for it. Those glacial women, those cool, icy blondes. They're always the most uninhibited when it comes down to it.'

And I know what this is all about with Michael. It's purely a case of wishful thinking.

The two of us agree to meet up later for a meal – our first new 'date' – and I head on back to my flat. I've left it in a bit of a mess. The floor is littered with clothes, record sleeves, damp towels and pizza boxes, all evidence that I've not been looking after myself properly. I've not been taking care of anything. Bills remain unpaid, emails remain unanswered and there's a stack of paperwork piled up on my makeshift desk. It's easy enough work – some museum pamphlets that need translating – maybe I should bite the bullet and get down to it.

I take off my coat, light the gasfire and get into a rhythm pretty quickly: English to German, German to French, French to Italian, then back to English. It's all to do with the way that the brain works. I don't translate the words as such, I'm able to think in the language that I'm using. It feels good, actually; relaxing. It's the same when I'm translating face to face. It's easy for me. I can understand people this way, people that other people can't. Some like to call this interpreting, but I don't interpret. I *translate.* That's the whole point. It's already there, on the page or in the mouth of some other person, all I have to do is pull it out. It's easy. Clear. Uncomplicated. People tend to say what they mean in these circumstances. There's hardly any margin for error.

My work keeps me focused and occupied and it must be at least half an hour before I notice the blinking light. There's a message waiting on my answer-phone and its discovery makes my cheeks flush and tighten. I can't help hoping it's good news; I can't help thinking it might be Daniel.

'Claire . . . are you home yet? It's Tom. Look, it might not be much, but give me a call when you can, I just thought of something.'

Standing on the Dock at Southampton

'I was right, wasn't I? About the orgies. That's what he called you up to talk about? He wants to invite us down to their secret dungeon?'

'Yeah, Michael, that's right. That's exactly what it was.'

Michael smirks and fold his arms.

'So where are we going, then, Shorty? I thought we were going out to eat.'

'We are.'

'Where? Out of town?'

'The docks.'

Michael twists his head and stares out of the window, struggling for a moment to get his bearings.

'Docklands? Are you serious? You know it'll be way overpriced . . . full of bankers and city trader arseholes and . . . *hey*, this isn't the way to docklands.'

'I didn't say dock-*lands*. I said the docks. Southampton to be precise.'

We are both of us freezing out here. Standing on the quayside beneath the cranes and the creaking derricks, with the wind sawing skin off our faces. It's late now, gone eleven, and the whole place appears to be deserted. Ships tower over us, ten storeys high, their giant hulls scabbed with flakes of rust. In the distance metal clangs hard on metal, an eerie, otherworldly sound. Proof there is life out there somewhere. Proof that the two of us are not alone.

The man we've come to meet is Alexi Resel: a sailor, a Russian, a convict; a long-forgotten name that Tom plucked from an old appointment book. Daniel's law firm is strictly legitimate. On occasion, it turns out, it's not.

'I don't know about this, Claire. I don't think this guy's going to show. We don't know who he is, we don't know what he did, we're not even sure how he knows your brother.'

We've been waiting here almost twenty minutes, but there's no way I'm letting Michael make us leave. I'll be a block of ice before he moves me. I'll be the weeds that grow out of the asphalt blocks. Tom thinks this man has information that I need and besides, it's already too late. I suspect that gaunt figure is him.

He approaches from the north of the ship yard: hands in deep pockets, head stuffed in hat, body stooped low against the wind. It's hard to determine his age, difficult to say exactly where he came from. The harbour entrance is in the opposite direction, so I'm guessing he must have stepped off a boat. He is lopsided, slim and slow moving; his skin so raw and weather-beaten it looks like a strip of tree bark. He wears a polo neck, waterproofs and a heavy black coat, an outfit that swamps his narrow frame. None of this makes him look any less threatening, in some ways his weaselly shape makes things worse. It feels like he's playing a trick on us, masking his strength with an elaborate ruse.

'Thomas said you know Russian?'

This is the first thing he says to me. I try hard to smile; my facial muscles weak against the wind.

'Yes,' I say. 'I do.'

He nods. From now on we'll speak only in Russian.

'I'm not meant to say anything. To anyone. I don't think I should have come.'

He says these things simply. They are facts. He doesn't look anxious in the least.

'Mr Resel, please, I'm his sister. I didn't know where else to go for help. On the phone you told Tom you might help me. You said if I came in person you might help.'

Alexi sighs hard and spits. He has a pouch of tobacco lodged deep in his ravaged cheek that's turned his saliva dark brown. He coughs and sniffs and gathers a thick glob of it between his lips. It spittoons from his mouth, high and with some speed, and lands shuddering on the dockside like the skin of a tiny chocolate custard. Michael is fascinated, disgusted, a little awed: all the more so because he can't understand what we're saying.

'This is your husband? This man?'

'No, not my husband. A friend.'

'You trust this man? I can trust him?'

'Yes, he's OK. You can trust him.'

Alexi stares at Michael, so intently it makes Michael shrink.

'I don't think I can trust this man. I don't think I have anything to say. I think you have journey for nothing.'

He turns up his collar and motions to leave, and against my better instincts I reach out and grab for his arm. I'm scared. I am. I don't know where to begin with this man and it unnerves me. I have no point of understanding; no insight into his life. I try not to think too much, to *fret* too much. Translating his words will get me through it.

'This is not something you should be involved with,' he says, crossly, pushing my hand away. 'This is not the place for you to be.'

Michael says 'hey' and steps forward; thinks better of it, and retreats.

'I know that,' I say. 'But I'm lost here. I don't know who else I can ask.'

'If people find me talking to you, I am in trouble. Do you understand that, city girl? In your thick fur coat? Worried about your big rich brother.'

He speaks to me like I should be ashamed. I swallow hard and try again.

'My brother helped you once, didn't he? Tom said that he helped you in some way.'

'Yes,' he says, staring at me. 'He saved my life.'

'Maybe you could tell me about that?' I say, gently.

'Maybe you don't want to know.'

It's galling how little you can know a person. Unimaginable that my brother should know a man like this. Daniel so upright and proper and prim, friends with a man like Alexi Resel. Maybe friendship is pushing it too far. These are simply two men that came across one other. Alexi when he needed a lawyer, my brother pulled in to do a favour for a friend. Tom doesn't even know the full story. All that he told me, all that he knows, is that Alexi was once accused of murder.

'Tom says it wasn't your fault . . . the man who died. He says that it was a shipping accident.'

'You think so, city girl? Is that what you heard? How do you know it wasn't my fault? When the winch flew out and cracked his skull in two, how do you know it was not on purpose? When his brains fell out onto the dock. When they shrank and puckered and cooked from the salt, perhaps I planned for this to happen to this man.'

'Did you?'

He bristles hard and sneers at me.

'Enough,' he says. 'Too many questions.'

I feel my heart thumping in the quiet. It beats hard and firm, in contrast to my breathing which seems erratic. Michael is shrinking further inside of himself. He can't even bring himself to look at us. He wants us to go, but there's no chance of it now. It would take one of those giant cranes to lift me. Alexi can sense this, I think. He knows he won't shake me off easily.

'Let's just say your brother knew the truth,' he says. 'That he was a good man. That he kept me out of jail.'

'He defended you?'

'Not himself, no. He arranged it. And when I was free he helped get me transferred to another shipping line.'

'You were innocent, then? You must have been. Daniel wouldn't have helped you otherwise.'

'Innocent?' he shrugs. 'What is innocence? It all depends from which side you are looking.'

I can't believe I'm having this conversation. Standing here in this place, amid the jetties and the wharfs talking to a stranger about life and death. I feel like I've reached the start of some elaborate and dangerous trail. I'm wondering where on earth Daniel will take me next.

'But the truth, since you ask,' says Alexi, 'this man that died, Kowlosjz, was a pig. I'm happy, in fact, that this man die. But it wasn't my doing, and I swear this. It wasn't my intention to kill him. Not that time.'

This last part 'kill him' he says in English and I sense he's doing it just to scare Michael. It does the job. Michael jumps and lets out a small squeal.

'Your friend is a coward.' Alexi says.

'No, not a coward. He's just afraid.'

'You're not?'

I hesitate. I don't feel that I can lie to this man.

'I'm a little scared, yes.'

Alexi chews on his tobacco and makes another elaborate spit. This time the phlegm, as thick as treacle, lands menacingly close to Michael's feet.

'Your brother liked the stars,' Alexi says, lifting his head skyward. 'He liked to look at the planets.'

'It's a big universe out there,' I say, looking upwards. 'A person could easily get lost.'

'Sometimes a person wants to stay lost. Perhaps it is better that way.'

'Not for Daniel. He has a family. A wife and a child.'

Alexi pulls a hip flask from his pocket, unscrews the cap and takes a hit.

'This waitress, the one Thomas mentioned. She told you people sometimes leave by ship?'

'She said a person might be smuggled out, if they weren't able to arrange a counterfeit passport. I thought you might know something about this. Tom said it was something . . . you had knowledge of.'

'It happens, of course. But I couldn't begin to say if this is what happened with your brother.'

He's lying. The metre of his speech seems tight now and clipped, he's using his words as a screen. When you work with foreign language every day of your life, you become exquisitely tuned to its rhythms.

'Did you ever have a conversation with Daniel?' I say, pressing him. 'Did you ever talk about how a person might stow away?'

He shakes his head.

'You really think it is better if he's found?' he says, sceptically. 'Not for *you*, city girl, but for him?'

'Yes, I believe that. Absolutely.'

He growls and lifts his flask to his lips again. Shuffles uneasily from side to side.

'Then we may have talked about it once or twice,' he says. 'In relation to me, you understand, not to him. If a person were tempted to stow away, there is a tramp ship they call the *Grunhilde*. A person might think to try this.'

'Where does it go to, this ship?'

'Anywhere it's needed. It doesn't have a set routing, no permanent itinerary. This is what makes it useful to a person like Daniel. A tramp ship is like a scavenger, always on the move. Can pick up whatever needs relocating. Collect any cargo that is spare: loose grain, coal, mineral ores; sometimes, perhaps, even people.'

'And where is it now, the *Grunhilde*? Could I talk to the captain? Would there be a way for me to do that?'

Alexi shrugs.

'Who knows where she is? But you're bright, city girl. You want it enough you'll find out.'

He turns his head sharply and I think that's going to be the end of it, but it seems he has one last thing to say.

'City girl, just promise me one thing. If you should come across your brother, and he should want to stay lost, promise me now that you'll leave him be.'

What can I do? In the circumstances, I have to say yes.

The Lady and the Tramp

Why is it that people always seem so keen on having sex in hotel rooms? I get it that you don't have to tidy anything up. I get it that it's nice to be away from the stresses and strains of home. But all I can think of is the thousand other couples who've had sex on this mattress before me. Their fat and thin bodies squelching about on the long deadened springs; their dead, bored and passionate eyes, staring up at this same yellowed ceiling. Their skin is in the fabric, their breath is in the sheets, their semen is spilt on the pink and orange piping that runs along the edge of this flowery valance. Right in the centre of that daisy. There on the corner of that rose. The sex of sailors and prostitutes, of travelling salesmen, and of bored hotel staff who simply couldn't wait. These rooms always feel crowded to me; filled with the imprint of all the other guests who have stayed there before me.

Thankfully, I don't get round to thinking about all this until long after Michael and I have finished. He's quiet now, with the sheets and the blanket pulled tightly round him, sleeping off the strangeness of the day. And I'm wide awake, cursing my insomnia and wondering who last slept in this bed: a tourist, a businessman, some overexcited newlyweds, or a couple scraping the last dying remnants from a doomed and illicit affair.

All these queer lives swirling round us: going on, being lived, going under. And how do you know you're living the right one? The choices we make, the turns that we take, so often seem abstract and arbitrary. I met Michael at a gig I wasn't meant to go to; studied languages merely because my first love spoke Spanish. I got married, why? Was I really in love? Was Michael the man I wanted to spend the rest of my life with? Sometimes I think I did it because the sun was out that day; because this man had dared to ask me and a part of me, a shred of me, had thought that no one else ever would. And he'd bought me a ring. A stupid, extravagant, square cut, diamond ring, that made us both laugh when we looked at it. This was a man who didn't care for the consequences of things, a man whose emotions I could read. A boy who'd spend the very last coin in his pocket (and mine), just to put a smile on my face. I was lost. I was done for. It felt like love.

I've made so many poor decisions in my life up to now, I barely trust my own instincts. Sylvie believes in fate but that's lazy, I think. It's also unbearably arrogant. What does it mean? That if good things happen to you, you deserved them? That if bad things happen then you invited them in some way? Fate absolves us from responsibility; cures us of any need to change. Everything happens for a reason. Was there ever a more dishonest phrase?

In the sixties we were supposed to tune in and drop out, in the seventies we were meant to run off and 'find ourselves'. Do people even do that any more? Or are we all too busy, achieving, competing, comparing and pill popping to ask ourselves the questions any more. We are all of us defined so early on. By the place, the position of our birth. By the desires and the quirks our parents press on us. The loud twin and the quiet twin, the sporty son and the smart son, the good and the bad, awkward daughter. I wonder, if I had been home that afternoon when my father died, would things be different for me now? If it had been me comforting my mother instead of Sylvie, if she'd still been sleeping in her cot. Would I love better, know better, judge better, be closer to my family than I am? Can a single event, a simple twist of fate, dictate the way we go on to live our lives?

What if I could start all over again? What if I could wipe the slate clean? If I were allowed to live the life of the guest that was here before me, would I do better than them? Worse? Is there something intrinsic that makes me, well, *me*? Or is it simply a question of circumstance? If Daniel has left, if Alexi's notion is correct, is he, in fact, becoming a different Daniel? Was his plan to run away, not from here, not from *us*, but to somehow escape from himself? Did he wake up that morning, see the sky full of snow clouds and decide for some reason that his world was utterly wrong for him? That it fitted him like another man's suit. That no matter how hard he tried to squeeze his limbs inside the sleeves, there would never be enough cloth to cover him?

This is the reason I'm wide awake. I'm haunted by the imprint of the guest list in this room and by the idea that my brother could actually have done this. I am amazed by him. At turns a little jealous, then appalled. I wonder if he's on that ship now, and where? I wonder if he's taken Annie with him. This woman that he loved; this woman, it seems, he forbade himself. And just the merest possibility of this, the slightest hint that it might be true, makes me relax enough to close my eyes. Wherever he is now, whatever he's becoming, I feel, for a moment, that he's safe.

'I joined the navy, to see the *world*! And what did I see? I saw the SEA! I saw the Atlantic and the Pacific, and the Pacific wasn't terrific, and the Atlantic wasn't all it's cracked up to *BEEE!!*'

Michael is singing in the shower; a sea shanty of some sort, I believe. He's in fine spirits this morning, suffused with a sense of adventure. The adrenalin of last night – the risk of last night – has left him as thrilled as a child. It took us two whiskies, maybe three, to calm down after we checked in here last night, but even the dire state of this hotel couldn't dull his mood: the wallpaper, stained; the bathroom, unheated; the trouser press and kettle, both broken. He slept exceptionally well on this hard, narrow bed. Made love on it pretty well, too.

'You managed to get it working, yet?' he says, towelling himself down. 'You had any luck with it, yet?'

I have finally managed to get my laptop working; fussed about with the odd connections in these thin, hollow walls and fought for a line to the outside world. I am searching for the names of a shipping line, tracking down the name of a particular ship.

'I've found a number. An agency that books passengers onto freighter ships. You can take these things right around the world.'

'What are you waiting for?' he says, excitedly. 'Are you going to call them? Do you want me to?'

'I'm on it,' I say. 'It's already ringing.'

The phone rings fifteen, maybe twenty times or more, before anyone picks up the receiver. I'm not hopeful. It's the second of January, the year's barely begun, I'll be lucky to find a useful person there.

'Ja?'

A German voice. Good, I can do this.

I'd like to travel on a tramp ship, I say. I'd like to book a passage, would that be possible? Of course, he says, no problem. Where exactly is it that I'd like to go? These ships, they are slow, do I realise? They stop in many ports, but usually just for one night. Not much chance for sightseeing trips. Nothing is organised, no tour guides at the other end; no fancy taxis waiting to collect me on the dock. Am I the kind of girl who's used to taking care of herself? Good, then, yes, it would suit me. It is cheap? Fairly. But I have to be aware, there is no entertainment on these ships. Windows? Of course. A sea view? Perhaps. But just as likely, the view of a giant metal container. I can have my own room but I should bring lots of books, there is nothing much to do but sit and think.

I can take a slow boat to China. Really? I can? Or a banana boat all the way to South America. Well, I'm highly self-sufficient, this sounds fascinating, but China, it's not really me. The thing is, I've heard of one particular ship that takes my fancy. Yes, I know that sounds strange, but the boat is more important that the destination. I am keen on a ship called the *Grunhilde*, operated, I believe, by the Olan line. Are you familiar with this ship? Is she sailing any time soon?

Some minutes pass while he looks at his timetables, then he tells me that he's sorry, but it won't be possible. The *Grunhilde*, it seems, is far away. A small tramp anyway, run down, not too comfortable, old cabins, not even a tiny pool. Only room for two paying customers, the German officers and a small Filipino crew.

Where is she now? Why do I care so much? OK, well, Belize then, he thinks. When did the ship last dock in England? He doesn't know. Again, he'll have to check. Ah, yes, not long before Christmas. She was docked for two nights in Southampton. Southampton, *really*? Yes, that's what he said. Am I deaf?

Where did she go to? Does he have her itinerary? Does he know the exact details of her onward route?

I can hardly manage to get this last part out. I squeak it, it peals from my throat. Waiting for the answer makes the seconds stretch and bow, and Michael is asking me if I'm all right. The German is back to the telephone. He's lifting it. He's clearing his throat.

'On the 14th of December, in the night time, she sailed first for Lisbon.'

My heart turns over. The 14th. That's the night Daniel left.

'And then where?' I say. 'And *then*? Do you know?'

On to Cadiz, and then Gibraltar he suspects, and yes, then onwards to Tenerife.

Tenerife. No, I can't see it – Daniel sunburnt on a beach, downing pints of luke warm lager, wearing a sun hat tied from a spotted hankie.

'Of course, then she crossed the Atlantic,' he says. 'Landed, first, in the Bahamas.'

The Bahamas. This I could contemplate. This I could actually see.

'And where then . . . where after that?'

'Well, let me check. Yes, she headed out into the Gulf of Mexico.'

Mexico. Could Daniel be there?

'No, wait, pardon my mistake. She made one more stop before that. She docked for one night in the port of Miami.'

'Miami?'

'Yes.'

'In Florida?'

'Yes.'

'Are you *sure*?'

The German is sure.

I'm lying on the bed next to Michael, staring back at this same yellowed ceiling. Michael is rubbing his hand across mine, slipping his fingers in between my knuckles. It feels nice. Safe. Reassuring. I can sense myself getting used to it.

'What a place to choose,' says Michael, squeezing my palm. 'I mean, you hated it, right? When you were kids. It's not the kind of place you'd want to go back to?'

'No,' I say. 'Not in a million years.'

'Why go, then? What was he thinking?'

I don't know. I can't imagine. But he must have had a good reason.

'Still,' says Michael, sitting up, 'Miami's pretty fashionable these days, isn't it? I mean, from what I hear. People tell me . . . you know . . . that it's cool. Great music scene. Loads going on.'

'Michael, he ran *away*. He's not gone on holiday. He hasn't gone there to get off with Gloria Estefan.'

'Of course not. You're absolutely right.'

My ex-husband is finished with questions, an idea is rupturing in his head. He wants to impress me, he wants to make amends; he wants a stake in the latest strand of this adventure. He's sitting up now, reaching for the phone, getting a number for the airlines.

'Two seats. No, not business, economy. Actually, is there anything *cheaper* than economy? Right, right, well sure . . . I understand. No, not Orlando. Miami. Yeah. As soon as we can. You're kidding? From Heathrow?'

Michael sits beside me with the phone in his hand, waiting patiently for my answer. It's a busy time of year, there's been a lucky cancellation, if we don't fly today we'll have to wait the best part of a week. I'm not sure what to do, it's impossible to know, my brain feels like it's choked up with sludge.

'You'll come with me?'

He nods.

'You'll help me look?'

He says he will.

'You're *sure*?'

He swears that he is.

'I owe you this, Claire,' he says, squeezing my arm. 'I won't let you do this on your own.'

'But won't it be—?'

'Awkward between us? No . . . I don't think it will.'

I sit up and take a deep breath. Michael takes hold of my hand.

'Book it.'

'You're sure?

I nod my head.

'Great,' he says, excitedly. 'It's the right thing to do. Shorty, what's your credit card number?'

The morning dissolves with the rush of it. We race back to London, grab spare underwear and passports and I call up my family from the airport. My mother's not in. I leave a message. A woeful, inadequate message. Sylvie is home and she's furious. This is bullshit, she says. You can't do this, she says. This is typical of you, to walk away. She doesn't buy the story. She thinks I've lost my mind. I should have discussed it with all of them first. Why am I in such a rush? Why can't it wait a couple more days? The trail's still warm, what does that mean?

And to top it all off – most important of all – if anyone's going to look for him, it should be *her*. I'm selfish, she tells me. I'm in cloud cuckoo land. It's cruel of me to raise everybody's hopes like this. I'm just doing it for attention. Do I realise that? Am I even aware of what I'm doing?

I don't get into it with her. I let her cold, flinty voice steam down the telephone line, and tune it out as best I can.

'I need Kay's number,' I say, when she pauses for a breath. 'The friend that she's staying with. I forgot my mobile phone, I left it back at the flat. I don't know her number off by heart.'

Sylvie is adamant. She won't give it to me. Fine, I say. I'll get
it from Mum. Mum's gone up to Scotland for a few days, to
rest. The stress of it all, the pain of new year; they've both gone
to stay with Robert's brother. You're lying, I tell her. Mum
wouldn't leave, not now. But it seems that she would and she
has.

'What will you tell them?' I say, weakly. 'Where will you say
that I've gone?'

A snort, disarmingly like my mother's.

'Easy, I'll tell them you've gone mad.'

She seems to think they'll believe this. She has no problem
with this.

'I'll say you've got back with Michael, that he's taken you away.
Who knows what your latest crazy plans are.'

My latest crazy plans. Perhaps she's right. I can feel every
atom in my body twisting. This is the moment I almost crumble.
Half of me knows the story I've just told Sylvie is true, but half
of me thinks I made it up. The waitress, the Russian, the tramp
ship; the mysterious, unproven affair. I want so badly to walk
out of here, past the ticket lines and the check-in queues and
the hyped up holidaymakers, and take a taxi back to my flat. I
want this all to be over. Because *I* can't do this, I'm not capable
or responsible enough. At some vital stage, in some small but
crushing way, I am duty bound to screw this up.

Michael is hovering behind me, frowning and tapping at his
watch. He has our bag slung over his shoulder: a faded brown
carry-all with a creased paper label and a broken zip, held
together with a grungy strip of duct tape. For some reason
the idea of our clothes being packed together in that same
suitcase makes me sad. It's all wrong. It's dated. It's out of
time. His pants and my knickers, his shaving foam and my
make-up, his jazz CDs and my pulpy Russian novels. But he
smiles at me and holds out his hand, encouraging me, beck-
oning me forward. I give in to the simplicity of Michael. He
doesn't have questions, he doesn't have doubts; he's certain
what we're doing is right.

A voice, thick and nasal, calls our flight number. I wonder if Sylvie hears it too.

'Aren't you going to wish me luck?' I ask her, quietly.

She lays down the phone and it clicks. She just can't bring herself to do it.

Blast off

If I Were Ever in a Coma

American airports smell of cheap coffee. It's the first thing that hits you when you step off the plane; burnt coffee grounds, bitter and thin, with all of the perfume knocked out of them.

'Coffee, I need a cup of coffee. Fuck, I can hardly stay awake. How much longer is it going to be, now? It's been hours already. It feels like hours.'

The queue at immigration is growing restless. Rows fifty deep, exhausted and fierce, all vying for their turn at the desk. I hang back. I'm in no hurry to get to the front; I have no idea what I'm going to say. What are you doing in Miami? How long are you staying? What is your business in the city? Everyone seems to know the answer but me.

'Have you filled in your form right? Check that it's right. They send you to the back if you get any of it wrong.'

'It's fine, Michael. My form's all OK.'

'Check it, Claire. *Check* it. I'm not queuing up all over again.'

Michael is grouchy from the flight and just to calm him down, I go through the pretence of checking through my form. I'm in better shape than he is. Unusually for me, I managed to grab a few hours' sleep on the plane, I even managed to dream. I dreamt of pelicans and peanuts and old Mr Kazman, and a beach covered over with snow. I was walking on the frozen sand with someone that I knew. Daniel? Michael? Sylvie? Dad? I had my swimming costume on. And a coat.

'This is us,' says Michael, anxiously. 'We're up next. But we shouldn't go through together. You go first.'

The officer barely looks at me while he stamps my passport but he seems to be taking his time with Michael: asking him questions, listening to answers, flicking back and forth through his travel documents. I cast my eyes around the arrivals hall while I wait for him. I don't recognise it, not exactly, but it all feels weirdly familiar. Perhaps we queued up at that same desk on the way in all those years ago. Perhaps we walked down these same corridors going out. Just the four of us. A family with a missing limb, a missing heartbeat; a family diminished and altered.

'Was there a problem?'

'No. Uh . . . no problem. He was giving me a hard time, that's all. I told him I was a musician, he was worried I was coming out here to work.'

After baggage claim and a cup of the bitter coffee, Michael seems a little cheered up.

'So,' he says, rubbing my neck. 'I have this idea. Did I tell you my idea, yet?'

I shake my head.

'OK, the thing is, we *could* check into a hotel, but that would be expensive, right? We don't know how long we're going to be here. Could be a week, could be a month, maybe longer. We should try to save as much money as we can.'

'What are we meant to do, sleep on the street?'

'No, see, I have this friend, an acquaintance really. There's someone I know in Miami.'

'You didn't say anything.'

'Didn't I? No. Well, his name is Huey.'

'Where did you two meet? Are you in contact? Did you tell him about us coming out here?'

'No. But he'll be cool with it, though. We hooked up at a jazz festival in New York a couple of years ago. He has an apartment out on South Beach. He said if I was ever in Miami . . .'

'You should stop by?'

'Exactly.'

'Michael, people *say* things like that all the time, but they don't actually mean it. We can't just drop in on him out of the blue.'

'You're right, you're probably right. But what the hell, it's worth a try.'

Michael gets out his diary and heads for the payphone. He shrugs his shoulders while he dials. I would never have the guts to do something like this, to impose on someone like this.

'We're all sorted,' he says, rubbing his hands together. 'He's going to meet us at his apartment in an hour.'

'You're sure?'

'Absolutely, Huey's cool. He's very easy going, you'll like him.'

There are a dozen more questions I want to ask, but I'm wilting now, I want to lie down. A bed, a floor, a mattress in someone's flat. Really, how bad can it be?

'So, you're OK with this? You're sure you don't mind?'

'No, Michael,' I say, 'I don't mind.'

It's early evening in Miami, but it's still hot and sticky outside. A mini winter heatwave has gripped the city pushing temperatures up into the nineties. The dense humidity takes hold of me as we exit the terminal, making me feel nauseous and sick. We climb into a taxi, Michael stowing our luggage safely on his lap, me clinging hard to my stomach. I clutch it tighter as we move out onto the Dolphin Expressway. Six lanes of traffic, cram-packed with cars, it makes me feel anxious, claustrophobic. Everywhere I look the picture seems wrong to me and I can't seem to make any sense of it. The billboards advertising cheap legal services and plastic surgery, the bikini-clad girls on the back of Harleys. I'm over-whelmed by the smells, the look, the style of this place, even Michael's face seems wrong out here. His cheeks rough and pasty, his blond hair in wisps, his skin drained of colour in this sunlight.

'Are you all right?'

'Yeah. Uh-huh.'

'Are you sure?'

I nod. Michael peers at me closer.

'Uh, Claire?'

'What?'

'You might want to do something about that.'

'About what?'

'Right there. On your lip.'

'What, *what* on my lip?'

'*Moustache.*'

He says this all hushed, all quiet, the way my grandparents used to say the word *cancer*. I've been in such turmoil the last few days, the last few weeks, the last thing I've thought to do was wax my lip. It must have taken seed on the plane. I have dark body hair, on my legs, on my face; Jewish girl's hair, from my father. I am mortified that Michael would mention it. Right here. Right now. Just as we're driving past Star Island.

'It's not too much,' he whispers. 'Just a little bit. Should I not have said anything?'

I can't answer. Can't speak.

'It's just that . . . you know . . . *remember*?'

'Yeah. Oh God, I remember.'

This was just before we got married. The moment I realised the two of us might have a real chance. A personal thing, an intimate thing. Michael catching me in the bathroom with a tub of hot wax.

'What are you doing?'

'Nothing,' I said.

'Shit, what's that goo on your face?'

I confessed to him, I had to, and we laughed. He swore blind to me that he'd never noticed it. Not once.

'So you'll be the one, then?' I said, afterwards.

'What one?' he said, all confused.

'I can rely on you?'

'To do what?'

'To tend to my moustache, if I'm ever in a coma.'

'What coma?'

'You know. If I got ill. If I was . . . I don't know, brain dead or something. I mean, it would just keep on growing, it could easily get out of hand.'

'Well . . . what about the nurses? Wouldn't they take care of it for you?'

'No. I mean, you couldn't be sure they'd get round to it. There'd be so much else for them to do.'

Michael grinned and patted my hand.

'You've thought about this a lot, haven't you, Shorty?'

Yes. I had to confess, I had.

'OK, then. I swear.'

'You *promise*?'

'No question about it.'

'Cross your heart?'

'Absolutely. If you should get hit by a truck and end up a cabbage, I promise that I'll personally . . . that I'll, uh, get the nurses to keep your moustache in good order.'

He said it with a completely straight face. It was the nicest thing anyone had ever said to me.

As we cross the Macarthur Causeway towards the beaches I get my first glimpse of the port. Crisp, white cruise ships fill the basin, their fairy lights glinting off the water. Beyond them, in the distance, sit the jetties and the piers where the freighters empty out their precious loads: iron, maize, tin, ore; silicone, golf clubs, people. And away to the right sits downtown, glowing in the apricot sun. It looks like someone has thrown fertiliser over this city; it's grown so big, so impossibly tall. I remember the first time I saw it from the back of the rental car my dad was driving. Sylvie was fast asleep on Daniel's lap and the pair of us – brother and sister – were staring out of opposite windows. Daniel moody, grumbling and quiet; me overcome with excitement. I was carried away with the difference of it all. After the leafy green suburbs and terraced houses we'd left behind, Miami seemed to me like an alien landscape: hot, breathless and arrogant, a city with its arms folded across its chest.

There were cruise ships on the water that day too, and I remember being awed by the size of them. This was a time in my life when size impressed me, when taking a cruise seemed like the best of all possible holidays. A floating hotel, a different country every day, and a kids club where they could stow my sister, Sylvie. I think of her now, back in London. I think of my mum and of Kay. Already it feels like they're a world away and I begin to feel calmer and quieter. I begin to enjoy the stickiness, the heat on my skin. I begin to relish the absence of winter. The city's arms are unfolding; embracing us, pulling us in.

There's an ocean and palm trees outside our taxi window now, and a street lined with pavement cafés. Art deco palaces in chalky pinks and blues; sea colours, sky colours, instant summer. The ice cream coloured buildings cast long shadows over the dunes, sunbathers twist their toes in warm sand. Beautiful boys cruise the sea front in vintage cars; pretty girls drive cherry-red Lamborghinis. There is sadness in this part of the city, there must be, but at the beginning you just can't see it. It's so new, so shiny, so pleased with itself; the way rediscovered venues always are.

We turn off the beach, away from the sparkle, and head to where the streets are coarser and shabbier: past the clubs, the discount pharmacies and the T-shirt shops and the needle buzz from the dingy tattoo parlours. We come to a stop a few blocks to the west, at the corner of Washington Avenue and Espanola Way. Our new home. Our new host. Our first staging post in this segment of our journey. As we drag our bags from the taxi I notice the stars are coming out, peppering the inky sky with dots of light. I stare up at them for a moment: wondering if I'm the only person doing it, wondering if someone I know is doing it too. It's a brief moment of reverie, a heady moment of optimism, quickly shattered by the rumpus on the street.

There's No One Quite Like Huey

'Sell me your hair.'

'My hair?'

'Yeah, man. I want to buy your hair.'

'How much you gonna give me for it?'

'How much do you want?'

'A thousand dollars.'

'A *thousand*? Are you crazy?'

'This is nice hair that I've got. Very thick. A nice curl. When it's clean it comes up pretty nice.'

'Christ, Christ, it's so unfair. This is *so* unfair. You're a bum. Why do you even need hair?'

The bum shrugs.

'You live on the streets. You pee in your own damn pants. What are you? Sixty, sixty-five? Fuck . . . this universe, man, it's so . . . *unjust*. You have the finest head of hair I've *ever* seen.'

'Thanks.'

'I'm not complimenting you, man. I'm cursing you. Don't you get that? I'm cursing you.'

'Not complimenting me?'

'No.'

'Well. That's not very nice. I don't think I want to sell you my hair no more. What you gonna do with it, anyhow?'

'I'm an actor. I need it. I've been in movies. *Actual* movies. Do you even know what that means?'

'That you're rich?'

'No, idiot, I'm not rich, I can't get cast any more.'

'Why not?'

'Because I'm *bald*!'

'You can't even get the character parts?'

'The *character* parts? Jesus, no. That's not what I want. You should have seen me when I had hair, man. I was the hero, the love interest, the *lead*. Now all they want me for is, like, villains and stuff.'

'And that's no good to you, huh?'

'No, man, it's not. I don't have a villainous nature.'

'I thought you said you were an actor.'

'I *am*. But I don't like to play against type.'

'So get plugs, then. Why don't'cha get plugs? . . . Hey, hey, don't kick me. That hurts. Jesus Christ, ain't my life bad enough?'

I stare at the actor and the bum. Michael stares at them too, his face broken wide open by a smile.

'Well, there he is, Claire, that's Huey.'

'That *man*?'

'Yeah.'

'With the head like a hard-boiled egg.'

'Yep.'

'Kicking that homeless guy in the shins?'

'What did I tell you? There's no one quite like Huey. That Huey, he's a real one off.'

Huey, to his credit, is quickly overcome with something approaching guilt. He apologises for losing his temper with the bum, and offers him a compensatory cheque for fifty dollars on the condition that the bum doesn't sue him for assault. The bum wants to know what he's meant to do with a cheque. Huey says some people are never grateful. The bum says he'd prefer cash. Or a bottle of Thunderbird. Or a vegetarian happy meal with extra fries. Huey wants to know how long the bum's been vegetarian. The bum says he likes to keep up with his daily quota of fruit and vegetables. Huey says the bum should think about going organic. The bum says organic produce is way overpriced.

It seems like this argument could go on all evening, and it would have, I'm almost sure, if Huey hadn't turned round, suddenly and spotted us.

'Michael. Wow, man. How *are* you? I can't believe you're finally here. How long has it been, now? How long have I been trying to get you to come out here?'

'Too long, Huey. Too long.'

The two of them embrace.

'Well, you finally made it. You look great, really great. And I'm sorry, you know . . . for the argument here, but I've had kind of a stressful day already. I mislaid my favourite hat this morning.'

'Shit, that's rough, man. I'm sorry.'

'Pure alpaca wool. Blue. A real nice blue. You couldn't find another hat like that if you tried.'

I loiter on the pavement with our bags, wondering if either of them are ever going to acknowledge to me. It seems that they're not, so I cough. Loudly.

'God, *sorry*. Huey, this is Claire . . . the woman I told you about.'

Huey holds out his arms, insists that I give him a hug.

'Claire, it's great to meet you. I heard all about your problems. You're the girl with the runaway brother, right?'

I nod.

'That's rough. That's totally rough. Here's me all worked up about my missing hat and you've lost a member of your actual family. You must be feeling what I'm feeling times a hundred. A thousand. A *million* even.'

I don't know what to say to the egg-headed man who's comparing my missing brother to a hat. I have no idea how to respond. Are you on drugs? That's what I should say. But instead I just smile politely.

'I know what you're thinking,' he says, picking up my bags. 'You're thinking why does he need a hat in this heat, right? What does a guy who lives in Miami need with an alpaca woollen hat?'

I don't say anything.

'Thing is, Claire – and Michael can vouch for this – I feel the cold really badly. Ever since I lost all my hair.'

'Uh . . . when did you lose it? If you don't mind me asking?'

'Three years ago,' he says, gravely. 'A month after I starred in my first feature. I woke up one morning sort of achy in the head, and all my hair had fallen out onto the pillow. Just like that. Every single strand. Doc said it was stress related, that it'd all grow back. But . . . it never did.'

'Right . . . well. That's a shame.'

'You have no idea,' he says, raising his eyebrows. '*No* idea. And the worst thing about it is, the toughest thing of all, is that it left me feeling permanently cold. As if ruining my movie career wasn't bad enough, now I have to be chilly all the time, too. I thought moving down south from New York would do the trick. Those Brooklyn winters were rough, let me tell you. But I still get the shivers, even now. Even on a hot day like this. A person loses thirty per cent of his body heat through his head. Did you know that?'

'No . . . no, I didn't know that.'

'Well, there you go, then. That's a fact.'

Huey unlocks a flaky wooden door and leads us up three flights of narrow stairs to his apartment. It's shabby, run down, dreary, but clean and comfortable enough. Two closet-sized bedrooms, a tiny kitchen and a shower room, and enough bongs, pipes, Rizla papers and smoking paraphernalia to open up a small market stall in Camden Town. In the centre of the living room is a worn red sofa, shaped like a pair of smiling lips. A petite bug-eyed woman with beads tied in her hair is sat on it, cross legged, watching TV. She gives us a little wave as we come in but she doesn't look up from the screen. She's watching a programme called *Extreme Makeovers*.

'I love this bit, don't you love this bit?' she says. 'When they finally get them up there on the table. It's like magic, what they do to them. They take these fat, ugly people and transform them, make them all thin and good-looking.'

'That's Tess.' says Huey, gruffly. 'Don't mind her, she's just leaving.'

'Yeah. Don't mind me, I'm just leaving.'

Tess doesn't look like she's going anywhere. She has no shoes on her feet, a glass of wine in her hand and she's eating stuffed olives from a tin; picking out the tiny pieces of pimento with her elaborately painted fingernails and depositing them neatly back into the oil.

'Olive?'

'No. No thank you.'

'Sure,' says Michael. 'I'll take one.'

'Smoke?'

'Joint? Yeah, why not.'

'Can you roll? My fingers are oily.'

Michael sits down next to Tess, and we stare at the TV while he rolls. A pretty young woman – a primary school teacher – is having her left breast sliced open by a plastic surgeon. Tess is visibly moved.

'Go girl, pump it up. Get that saline *in*. God, I am desperate for a boob job. Do you think I need a boob job, uh . . . ?'

'Michael.'

'Right, Michael. Do you think I'd look better with bigger breasts?'

Tess lifts up her tank top so Michael can have a closer inspection. Her breasts are high and tanned – as good as perfect – supported by a skimpy, see-through bra.

'I'm saving up for the operation,' she says, weighing her breasts in each hand. 'I want to go from a B cup, to double D. I'm gonna get a nose job, some lipo and a chin implant at the same time. I have enough money for the boob job already, but my surgeon thinks it's better if I get it all done in one go.'

'Put them away, Tess. Come on now, be nice. Can't you see, we've got guests.'

'But I'm just getting Michael's opinion.'

'Give the guy a break, he just got off a plane. I'm sure he's not interested in your tits.'

'What about you . . . uh, miss?'

'Claire. My name is Claire.'

'Right. Well, what about you, Claire? What do you think?'

'I wouldn't have plastic surgery.'

'Really?' she says, astonished. 'Why not?'

'Well, you seem to have a nice body already. I don't see why you'd want to change it.'

'I'm a singer,' she says, as if that explains it. 'I'm trying to get a record deal. I'm managed by a friend of Lenny Kravitz's hairdresser.'

'I see.'

'My manager says I need to get bigger tits. Bigger tits, bigger deal, that's what he says.'

'Right. Well. That makes sense, then.'

Tess lowers her tank top, takes the freshly rolled joint from Michael and the two of them set about smoking it. Amid the puffs and the giggles and scratch of the surgeon's scalpel I notice another noise in the room; something fast, repetitive and twitchy, like a bird hitting its beak on a branch. It's a couple of minutes before I work out what it is, it's the sound of Huey's teeth chattering.

'So, what do you do for a living, Claire?' says Tess, offering me the joint. 'Are you in entertainment, too?'

'No,' I say, taking a shallow toke. 'I'm a translator.'

'Excuse me. What? You do *transplants*?'

'No. *Languages*. I translate foreign languages.'

Tess nods but I'm not sure she gets it.

'So I guess it doesn't matter what you look like, then. For that kind of a job, am I right?'

'Well, you know. It's not so important.'

'That's great,' she says, beaming at me. 'That really is. I actually admire you actually.'

'Do you?'

'Yes,' she says, eagerly. 'You're happy with yourself. That's such a rare quality these days. I mean, I think you're sort of brave. I don't think I could go out with that on my face.'

'What on her face?' Huey says.

'*Moustache*,' whispers Tess, pointing at me then tapping her upper lip.

'I mean, I think it's great that you don't care about it, but just in case, you should know, I have some spare hot wax in the bathroom. I know girls are all hairy in Europe – you don't shave your armpits, right? Or douche, am I right? But this is Miami. You might want to think about . . . you know, getting rid of it. *Just* while you're here.'

Michael seems to think this is hysterical; high and sleep-deprived he's practically convulsing on the floor. I decide to cut my losses and go to bed, and Huey does the decent thing by confiscating Tess's tin of olives and showing me into the spare bedroom. I walk in, close the door and collapse. The mattress is thin and smells of mildew, it's gooey and lumpy all at the same time. Michael is still out there: laughing, chatting, getting stoned, getting drunk, trying on some of Huey's spare hats. I turn out the light and fall asleep like a brick. I dream I've been committed to a nut house.

God's Waiting Room

'Morning, Claire. You sleep OK?'

I wasn't expecting anyone to be up yet, but Tess is already making pancakes in the kitchen.

'I love pancakes, don't you? They're the best. I could eat this entire stack if you let me. Here, let me fix you some coffee.'

I don't say anything. It's just her and me. I sit down.

'Sorry about last night,' she says, sweetly. 'I can be a bit full-on when you first meet me. I know it doesn't seem like it, but I'm actually a very shy type of person. I'm hoping the breast augmentation will help out with that. You know, showcase the true inner me.'

She smiles, hands me a cracked mug of coffee.

'Well, that's OK.,' I say. 'Don't worry. And thanks, you know, for . . .'

'. . . the hot wax?'

I nod.

'Sure, no problem. Did it hurt?'

'Yeah, it did. A little bit.'

She grins. She has some advice.

'So, you might want to think about taking a Valium the next time. Just ask me. Whenever. I've got plenty. When I get my bikini line waxed I always make sure to take a couple of Valium before they start. You have to try it, it's fantastic. They could whip off both your eyebrows and all your ass hair while they were at it. You'd barely feel a thing.'

Tess piles half a dozen sweet smelling pancakes on to my plate, loads me up with blueberries and a generous slug of maple syrup, and sprinkles the dish with sugar and cinnamon. She watches me intently, she's keen to know what I think.

'They're delicious,' I say, meaning it. 'Really, they're very, very good.'

'I know,' she says, contentedly. 'I'm a great cook. It's part of what Huey loves so much about me. It's weird, though, him and me,' she says fixing herself a plate. 'The two of us are always arguing with each other. We're always splitting up and getting back together again. Once a month at least, sometimes twice. Huey says I annoy him, which is rich, you know what I'm saying? Because *he's* the one that annoys me.'

'The bald thing?'

'No.'

'The hat thing?'

'No.'

'The noise? The chattering teeth?'

'No, not so much.'

She narrows her eyes.

'I'd have to say, if I had to pick one thing, it's more the way that he likes to do anal all of the time. In all of my years, of *all* the men I've slept with, I've never met a guy so into anal.'

'Right, uh . . . I see.'

'Then, of course, there's his taste in music. He's crazy for modern jazz, like Michael is, right? And I can't stand the stuff, never could. Why not have a tune? Would it kill them? Would it kill them to put the notes into some kind of an agreeable order?'

I shake my head. I don't think it would.

'Anyway,' she says, popping a blueberry into her mouth, 'despite all of that, the jazz and the anal and the coupons and everything . . .'

'The coupons?'

'Huey collects coupons. He has a drawer full of them. Money off of soup, soap, foot spray, sanitary towels . . . there's nothing you can think of to buy, that Huey won't have a coupon for it somewhere. I can hardly stand to go shopping with him any more. It takes him so long to sort through them.'

'Wow, that must be . . .'

'Annoying, right? It's annoying. But I still happen to think that we're soul mates. I still happen to think we're meant to be. Must be the same with you and Michael. I mean, divorcing and getting back together all over again. You must have something special, the two of you, like Elizabeth Taylor and . . . ?'

'Richard Burton?'

'Yeah, *right*. Richard Burton. I loved him in *The Godfather*, didn't you? He was *so* good-looking when he was younger. It's such a shame he let himself get fat. He was gross, right? Totally gross.'

Tess sighs hard and lays down her fork. Apart from the blueberry and a dab of syrup that she's licked off her index finger, she's barely taken a bite. She rubs her stomach, indicating that she's full and throws her uneaten pancakes into the bin. She immediately sets about making fresh batter: for Huey, for Michael, for me if I'm still hungry, for the pleasure of stirring and frying. Her own reward, it turns out, is entirely confined to the preparation.

'So,' she says, cracking another egg into the bowl, 'I've been thinking some about you and your runaway brother, Michael told us the whole story last night. It's so sad, and also a little weird if you don't mind me saying so.'

Weird. She thinks *my* life is weird.

'Anyway,' she says, getting busy with the whisk. 'I've been thinking that there's someone you ought to go see.'

'Really, who?'

'My psychic, Madam Orla. She does my cards for me every couple of months. She's so tuned in, it's actually frightening. For example, she told me that Huey and I would end up getting back together last year, and we did. And this was when we were going through a really rough patch, so no one could really have predicted it.'

'I see.'

'And another time she told me my career was about to take off. And the very next day *who* should I bump into?'

'The friend of Lenny Kravitz's hairdresser?'

'*Exactly*. How'd you guess? Don't you think that's impressive? Don't you think that's spot on? You have to let her read your tarot cards, Claire. She has a long wait list these days but I'm a regular. If I call her up now I can probably get us an appointment for this afternoon.

'Tess . . . I don't know. I'm not sure.'

'Trust me, you'll love her. I can tell you two would really hit it off. And she's got like this sixth . . . no, *wait*, it's more like a *seventh* sense or something. I bet she'll have a good idea where your brother's at.'

I let Tess down as gently as I can. I realise she's trying to do a nice thing but frankly, I don't have time to waste on some cheap, back-room psychic and the musings of an anorexic dope head. I tell her that I have a lot of things to do today. I have to visit the port and talk to the harbour master, and I want to visit the apartment block where my family used to live. Tess is pretty nice about it all. She says we can see Madam Orla another time. She thinks she'll call her up anyway, just to check. She thinks Miami Beach must have changed a fair bit since I was last here. I tell her that it has.

'More hotels, right? More high rise? And not so many old people. You'll notice that right away when you go out today, there's far less retirees down here now. You know what they used to call Miami Beach in the old days?' she says, 'before it got itself all spruced up and rejuvenated?'

'No,' I say. 'I don't know.'

'God's waiting room, that's what they called it. Don't you think that's kind of creepy? Doesn't that sort of creep you out? I mean I like old people well enough, the cute ones, but I don't like the idea of the whole island filled up with them. I mean you've got to admire this place, right? For reinventing itself like it has. Twenty years ago it was all decrepit and dangerous and full of old folk, and now it's shiny and hip and full of models. And all it took was a TV programme and a lick of paint. Don't you think that's amazing? You see how easily it can happen, right?'

I nod. I tell her that I do.

'Michael says your dad worked in construction,' she says. 'When you lived over here. Is that right?'

'Sort of. He was overseeing the refurbishment of one of the big hotels on Ocean Drive. It was a total wreck before they started.'

'How come he ended up here?' she says, quizzically. 'I'm guessing art deco was his thing, right?'

'Not really, not that I know of. It all happened pretty quickly, us coming out here. I'm not even sure how he got the job.'

'See,' says Tess, slapping her hands together. 'That's what's so *great* about Miami. It's such a welcoming kind of place. There's so many different types of people living down here, all different types of persuasions and nationalities. What do you call that? When you've got a totally interesting mix of different peoples?'

'Diversity?'

'*Exactly.* You got it in one. That's what I like the best, the diversity. For instance, you can go get yourself a table at a restaurant and you'll just as likely find yourself sitting next to De Niro or Stallone as you would find yourself sitting next to me and Huey. You can be anything you like in Miami. It's a real equal opportunities kind of place. It just helps, you know, if you're beautiful and rich, but that's like anywhere, right?'

I don't have time to offer up an answer. There's a sudden piercing scream from down the hall that sounds like it's coming from the bathroom. It's followed by a frantic, high-pitched whine.

'Jesus, no,' says Tess. 'Not again. *Huey!* Go check on the snake.'

'Come on, it's not *that* bad, is it?

'Michael, they're freaks, they've got no boundaries. He's weird, he's neurotic, she's nosey, she doesn't eat. She makes a living letting tourists pose with her pet boa constrictor.'

'You want to go to a hotel? Fine then, we'll go to a hotel.'

'It could have killed you. It could have squeezed you to death.'

'It only got as far as my leg. It looked a lot worse than it was.'

'That's why you screamed so loudly is it? That's why you were trying to poke its eye out with your toothbrush?'

'Look, I'll check out some prices, but it's not going to be cheap.

We're right in the middle of high season.'

'And he's sexually deviant, did you know that?'

'The *snake*?'

'No, not the snake, Michael, *Huey*. Tess says he only does anal sex.'

'Well . . . strictly speaking, that's not . . . *deviant*, exactly. I mean, if that's what he's into . . .'

We're stood on the corner of Collin's Avenue in the baking heat, waiting for our rental car to be delivered. I'm having something approaching a mild panic attack. It could be the jet-lag or the effects of last night's joint, but I suspect that it's something far worse. My palms are sweating and my lungs are seizing up and my words feel tight in my throat. I'm hopelessly out of my depth here. Marooned in this strange city, with all of its bad memories, my brain feels under attack. I just can't seem to get my bearings. It all looks so much different than it did. I'm not sure I know how to do this. I'm not sure I know how to start. I feel like I'm sliding down the insides of a giant greasy pipe that's about to deposit me into the ocean.

'Come on,' says, Michael, gently. 'The car will be here in a minute, you'll feel much better when we're mobile. And we have a plan don't we, the two of us?'

I nod, he strokes the back of my neck.

'We'll visit the port first, then we'll go to your old apartment building . . . and tomorrow we'll find the hotel where your dad worked.'

I stare into my ex-husband's face. Concentrate hard on his mouth and his lips. On his eager, uncomplicated eyes.

'Better now?'

I think so. A little bit.

'*Hey*, here it comes, that's our car?'

Low. Shiny. Black. Topless. Delivered by a man in silver shades.

'What is it?'

'Mustang.'

'Convertible?'

'Of course.'

'Isn't that going to cost me a lot more money?'

'Look, I know it's a bit more expensive than we talked about. But we're in Miami. It's the law. We're duty bound to drive a soft top.'

The World Has Turned

They come here from all over the world: Guatemala, Honduras, El Salvador, Panama; Cyprus, Bangladesh and Brazil. They come weekly from Melbourne and Darwin, bi-monthly from Yokohama and Hong Kong. Every nine days they sail in from Casablanca; every eleven, from Santa Cruz. Cargo ships, tramp ships, freighters, tankers, and mail boats eager with parcels. Twenty metres, thirty metres, one hundred metres long; capacity fifty thousand metric tons. The *Marie*, the *Mathilde*, the *Columbine*, the *Quetzal*; the *Delight*, the *Deluxe* and the *Ever Decent*. Hulking containers, piled high like Lego bricks, stowed neat and tidy on their bows. Red cranes, black hulls, blue-painted railings; their great engines wheezing in the sun. The world flows through this place every hour of every day, it is an axis on which the earth turns. But we can't get close to them, these adventures, these vessels. We can't get anywhere near.

Michael and I wait at the visitor's desk. There are documents to be queued for, appointments to be made and ID cards to be handed out. It could take all day, but you're from England, they say. Well in that case, it could take all week. There is no one here with time spare to talk to us and we're getting in their way, we can feel it: the indolent slowing down the industrious. But if we want to, if we need to, there's another office we can visit, a place where we can check out the current shipping schedules. And this, I think, is all I really need. To know this ship arrived and departed, just like the German said it did: to know for certain that it was here.

The *Grunhilde* docked in Miami on Christmas Eve, she stayed in port less than twenty-four hours. No one will talk to us about stowaways. It's a sensitive issue – drug smuggling, immigration – and security here is brisk and tight. But it's clear that this thing could be done, couldn't it? One man? In a trunk, in a case, in a crate? If he had the money and the time and the sheer determination, an individual, a person, could have done this?

What person? What man? If we think a crime's been committed in the Port of Miami, then they'd like to know all about it. Forget it, we laugh. It's purely hypothetical. In truth, we were only wondering – you know, just the two of us – if such a thing were even possible. They'd like us to wait where we are. They have time to speak to us, now. But we can't hang around, we must be going. Didn't we say, we're running late. For what? For something. A swim, a meal, a drink; a sudden burning desire to visit Mickey and the gang at Magic Kingdom. We're tourists, we're dumb, we don't want to be causing any trouble, and the last thing we'd want to do is upset the authorities.

We retreat as fast as we can; the cruise ships honking and bellowing behind us, warning them not to let us go. But it's too late now, we're back on the road, heading out towards the golden beaches. I'm wondering if Daniel left this same way. In a truck? In the boot of a car? And where would he have gone to, that first night, that first hour? Where exactly would he have ended up?

'Where to, Shorty?' says Michael. 'Where do you want to head next?'

'North,' I say. 'Let's go further north. All the way up to Sunny Isles.'

Michael puts his foot down and accelerates, and the hot air blasts hard against our faces. I have black sunglasses on and a scarf around my head, I look like Grace Kelly's mutant sister. We look to all the world like we're enjoying ourselves – the soft top down, the radio on – but deep down I'm overcome with nerves. The apartment building where my teenage self lived seems almost mythical to me now. I sometimes wonder if the five of us were ever there. The open plan rooms, the rough concrete balcony, the air conditioning unit with the furred up vents that coughed like a consumptive in the night. My mothers tights drip-drying in the bathroom. My brother's socks stinking up the hall. My father with his feet up and a beercan in his hand flicking through the weather channels like a man possessed. He liked to watch CNN in the evenings because you could find out what the weather was doing back at home. He dearly liked to keep track of it. If it was raining in London, he'd say, don't you miss the rain? If it was sunny he'd say don't you miss the English summer?

My mother didn't seem to miss any of it. At least, she never joined in with any of his lamentations. She just kept quiet and got on with things: waxing her legs, poisoning the cockroaches, making sure the five of us were halfway presentable; Sylvie's long hair brushed and bunched, Daniel's sports kit neatly folded and half ironed. These memories seem wilted to me somehow, and I dearly want them to shine. As different as it is now, this city, this place, a piece of our history is etched into it. It's the last place we lived as a complete family.

Beyond the gaudy splendours of South Beach, the island begins to exhale, sagging like a new year's eve Christmas tree, weighed down with one too many baubles. You travel through time as you travel south to north, from the art deco thirties to the beige-coloured seventies, then back round again to the fifties. The buildings are tired up here; sloppy, run down. Why make the effort, who'd be coming up here to see them? They are your middle-aged uncle in his favourite pyjamas surprised when you come round to visit unannounced. They are the pot luck dinner that you pull from the fridge, cold ham and chicken with leftovers. Beyond the golf courses and the high rises and the last good restaurant, beyond the slick of Golden Beach and Bal Harbour. The bulldozers have their eye on these low rise condos and cheap motels, but the original buildings are blessedly plain here. They are scruffy and worn, and I like them.

'This part more like you remember it?' says Michael, noticing my smile.

'Yeah,' I say. 'I think I recognise some of it.'

'Think your building will still be here?'

I don't know. I can't say. New development is everywhere, but I dearly hope so.

Siesta Pines has been spruced up. By this I mean its exterior has been painted a mixture of almond pink and key-lime green. The European-style shutters – they are fake, they don't open or close – are sickly and bright, and the plaster walls are muted and salt stained. I stare at the building like I would at a ghost, but it was here all along, always has been. It simply carried on its life without us. The disaster, *our* disaster didn't touch it. Michael takes my hand and we walk round the scrubby gardens to the pool. There's a locked gate there now, there didn't use to be, and we have to wait for someone to leave before we can make our way inside. The chairs around the sun deck take my breath away. Some are new – white, with candy striped fabric seats – but a few are scratched and old and bottle green. Hard moulded plastic that makes your bottom ache, whose surface sticks to your skin when you perspire.

'Stop making that noise, do you have to make that noise?'

'It isn't me, Mum, it's the *seat*.'

The pool, was it always this colour, this washed out and grimy grey-blue? I remember it being clearer and brighter. The tiles that line it are exactly the same, though – that flirty mermaid still swimming on the bottom, her blond curls spilling down her narrow back. I spent hours in this swimming pool staring at her through my goggles: eye to eye, nose to nose, face to face. I'd poke my tongue out and pull all kind of faces but she never did anything but smile back at me. I liked it that she smiled, I appreciated it. I valued her blessed lack of moods.

At the rear of the building the old awnings have all been torn down. They used to flap around like flags when it was windy, and if ever there was a strong and sudden gust in the night, the noise would wake me out of my sleep. Three flights up is our apartment. I can see it, right now: our front door, our old window frames, our same brass knocker, our doorbell. And I feel . . . what exactly? Crushingly, overwhelmingly homesick.

'You want to go and ask if we can look around? You want to knock on the door?'

It turns out that I do.

There's no answer – there's nobody home – so we rise up on tiptoes and peer through the sheer net curtains. Whoever lives here now has shocking taste. Swirly gold carpets, a mess of florals and pastels, and sofas still dressed in their tough plastic covers. The layout is exactly the same as it was when we lived here: over to the right, the tiny kitchen where we'd all crowd together to eat our breakfast; down to the left, along the hallway, my parents' room with its little en suite shower room. How happy was my mother to see that? To have a place to wash and dress and put on make-up that wasn't blighted by the mess and dirt of her children.

'Hey, what is it? Are you crying?'

I don't know, I hadn't realised that I was. But over to the left is another narrow doorway, it used to say *Claire's room – Stay out!* I remember how relieved I was when I stepped inside this flat, how pleased I'd felt about getting my own place to sleep. Daniel and I had been forced to share a bedroom after Sylvie came along and I couldn't wait to have my privacy back. What surprised me, what shocked me, what I didn't expect, was that I found it hard to sleep alone. The truth was – and I'd never have admitted this to Daniel – that for the first month or so, I sort of missed him. There were nights in the old house back in London when I'd been all too glad to have him around.

Late One Evening in a Car

Most of all I remember the sound that it made, the click of the front door closing. He didn't slam it, he just pulled it gently shut. I imagine he did this so he wouldn't wake us up, but already it was far too late. We had stirred, Daniel and I, an hour earlier, alerted to the sound of our parents' shouts: my mother's voice high pitched and shrill as a fish wife's, by father's lungs rumbling like a bull's. The walls were thick enough in the ramshackle house where we lived that we couldn't quite pick out the words, so we had to make do with just the rhythms. Up and down their voices went, rising and falling as they crisscrossed the room, all good detail soaked up by the heavy curtains. If I closed my eyes it sounded like a rock song about love, alternately soft and pleading, then wild and stern.

'What are they arguing about?'

'How should I know?'

'Shall we fetch a glass?'

'What for?'

'We can put it to the wall. If we put it to the wall and lay our ears to it, we'll be able to hear what they're saying.'

My brother wouldn't have it, he wasn't interested. He switched on his pocket torch, picked out one of his astronomy magazines and began to flick idly through the pages.

'You're going to *read*?'

'Yes.'

'*Now?*'

'Why not?'

'How can you read at a time like this?'

Daniel didn't bother to answer. He yawned so wide I could

see the fillings in his teeth, and concentrated harder on his magazine. I watched him squint in the half light but I could tell he wasn't actually reading it, he was too agitated to absorb the words. His toes tapped back and forth under the covers and his index finger kept returning to the exact same spot on the page. Every so often he'd catch me frowning at him, at which point he'd cough or clear his throat and turn the magazine to a fresh article.

'Interesting, is it?'

'It's OK.'

'What's it about?'

'Black holes.'

'What are they?'

'They're what's left after a star collapses and dies. If you got caught up inside of one you'd be crushed as thin as a strand of spaghetti. Everything that enters it gets trapped inside.'

I thought about this for a while. A hole you couldn't get out of. Me as thin as spaghetti.

'You're sure I wouldn't be able to get out again?'

'No, you wouldn't. Not ever.'

'Why not? If I really wanted to I'm sure I could do it. I'm better at climbing than you.'

'Nope, not a chance. That's the power of gravity, keeps you exactly where you're put.'

·'I see.'

'No, Fats, I don't think you do.'

Clever clogs. Swot pants. Show off. Taking the piss out of my puppy fat.

'They're not bothering you, then? Mum and Dad?'

He gave a shrug.

'You don't mind the noise?'

'No, not really.'

'You don't care that they hate each other, then?'

'They don't *hate* each other, Claire, it's complicated. You're too young, you wouldn't understand.'

Damn it. I didn't like it when he did that. When had that started, exactly? When had he got so much bigger than me? The second he'd reached his teens he'd seemed to roar away from me like a rocket. It happened so fast; it was as much as I could do to keep up with him.

Some quiet now. A moment of stillness. No more raised voices from down the hall. Daniel and I glanced at one another and crossed our fingers, offering up all kinds of secret pacts to God. I promised to do my homework if they would stop shouting for good. I promised to hang up my clothes and brush my teeth and be nice to the girl in my school with the lazy eye. It looked in two directions at once, it was creepy; her eyelashes were always covered in a sticky yellow crust. All of these promises to no avail. A brief slip of silence – a minute, a minute and a half – then they started it up all over again.

The argument crackled on like a bonfire. Every time you thought they'd reached the end of it, the whole thing would spontaneously reignite, as surely as if someone had opened a door and poured oxygen onto the dying embers. I began to feel a little uneasy. It seemed this disagreement had a life of its own and that my parents were losing their battle to control it. It was louder, more intense than it had been, with a deep and forbidding undertow. I closed my eyes tightly, put my fingers in my ears, but still I could hear their vibrations: muffled, woolly and soupy, reaching in and pulling me under.

'Hey, fat-face. Come on, let's get up.'

Daniel had climbed out of his bed. He was standing right next to me in his pyjamas, shining his torch under his chin so he looked like a ghost. In ordinary circumstances this might have made me jump, but I knew he wasn't doing it to scare me.

'You've got bum fluff,' I said.

'No, I haven't.'

'You have, on your cheeks. Mum said what it was and it's bum fluff.'

He should have given me a dead leg or dead arm at that point – he usually would have – but this time he decided not to bother.

'We'll go downstairs,' he said. 'To the back room. We won't be able to hear them down there, not if we put the TV on.'

This seemed to me to be a mixed blessing. I liked the idea of not being able to hear them, but I was a little afraid to leave them both alone. What if something happened? What if they set about one another with a hair brush or a torn-off chair leg? One of them might need us; they might need the two of us to intervene. On top of all that, most worrying of all, if we went downstairs we'd have to negotiate the haunted landing. There was no light on out there, not even from the bathroom, and we couldn't risk the chance of putting one on in case my parents saw us.

'Claire, are you coming down, or not?'

Decisions, decisions. Daniel was already on his way. I had no option but to follow him.

I held on tight to my big brother's hand as he guided me across the landing, then on past Sylvie's room and down the stairs. Astonishingly, no ghosts appeared from the shadows and even though Daniel had said I ought to expect it, we didn't come across any giant spiders with teeth like knives. There was a moment with a rogue moth that might have caused us some problems, but even then I managed not to cry out.

'Phew.'

'Phew.'

'We made it.'

'Yes, we did.'

It was only then that I realised Daniel had been scared, too.

The house seemed larger in the darkness. It was sprawling, ill kempt and ill cared for and we'd only moved there because my father had promised to do it up. We'd been here two years already but he'd never seemed to get round to finishing it. It struck me, sitting there on the sofa in the dark, that it must have been a struggle to take care of – the dusty floors without carpets, the walls with no plaster, the half-built kitchen and the rusty, dripping taps. Dad often had to work weekends or late into the night and I imagined my mother sitting here on her own, long after we'd all gone to bed: watching the TV, reading a book; smoking a secretive and strange-smelling cigarette.

'Shall we put on the TV?' I said, to the quiet.

'Yes,' Daniel said, 'I think we should.'

Mum had told us that the TV stations stopped broadcasting at midnight, but Daniel and I had long since decided this was a lie, an elaborate ruse drummed up by our parents to make sure we stayed in our beds. When we were fast asleep we knew full well that it came back on again; all kinds of programmes, all manner of adventures: war films and weirdness and nakedness.

'It's blank.'

'Really, is it? Try tuning it to a different station, then.'

Daniel had been hoping for a Dracula film or an episode of *The Sky at Night*, I'd been hoping for an episode of Dallas. Instead there was the low shush of white noise and a screen of fizzing black and white pixels.

'It's true, then?'

'Seems so.'

'Shall we try listening to the radio instead?'

I nodded but we never switched it on. The sounds in the house had begun to warp and change shape. Upstairs, Sylvie had started bawling, they had finally woken her up. We crept to the door and listened as hard as we could, but we sensed all the shouting had stopped. Mum was comforting Sylvie now and Dad was thumping about in his wardrobe.

'Shit, be careful. He's coming down.'

My father walked towards us in his weekend clothes and we spied on him from exactly where we stood. He turned the light on in the hallway and turned it straight off again, once he could see where he was going. And then he opened the front door, so quietly, so carefully, as if this one gentle act could erase all the anguish of the night. He closed it so precisely it barely made a sound, it just sort of clicked shut and sighed. Daniel and I stood there, motionless and alert, listening to the beat of our own breathing. Had he seen us? It seemed impossible that he hadn't.

Was he cross with us for coming down? Would he punish us in some small way in the morning?

'Quick,' said Daniel, pulling me to the window, 'he's getting into the car.'

My father was sat in the front seat. He had something in his hand, he was reading. He'd turned the light on to see it better and if we peered hard enough we could just make out his face. It didn't look like my father's face any more; the stuffing had gone out of it, all the firmness. It was deflated, loose, without support. His shoulders moved up and down like he was dancing, but his chin sat heavy on his chest.

'What's he doing?' I said.

I knew the answer to this question, but I needed to have it confirmed. It was the moment I realised he was fallible; the moment I knew he wasn't strong. This man that could pick up all three of us – Daniel, Sylvie and I – in one arm. This man that smelt of brick dust and concrete.

'What's he doing?' I said, again. 'What is he doing?'

I thought I knew exactly what my brother would say but I wasn't prepared for the dreadfulness of his answer.

'It's obvious, isn't it? he said, quietly. 'He's crying. Dad's crying again.'

Killing Harvey Weinstein

Huey is more agitated than I would have liked. When we get back to the apartment – tired, hot and laid low with jet-lag – he's tearing about the kitchen in a rage. His teeth are chattering like castanets and he's repeatedly slapping his leg. The snake is on the move again, it's escaped from its tank. He has to find it in the next ten minutes (before Tess arrives home from her teeth whitening appointment) or he's a dead man.

'Jee-*suz*. Harvey, come on, man. I was only trying to stroke you. I wasn't trying to kill you or nothin'. Harvey, little *Haaaarvey*. I got some nice mice babies for you, right here. You want some mice babies? They're extra soft. Come on now, stop dickin' me around!'

A sound at the door. A click of a key. Tess is back already, she's early.

'Fuck, man, *no*. She's going to kill me. You have to do something, you *have* to help.'

'What can we do?' says Michael, looking anxious. 'None of us knows where he is.'

'He's under there.'

'The *cooker*?'

'I think so. He slithered in here a couple hours ago and I totally forgot all about him. I switched on the oven to bake some mini-pizzas just before you guys turned up, and I noticed smoke coming out from underneath it. I think I must have cooked him. Fuck, man. Oh *fuck* . . . I cooked the snake.'

Tess goes from placid to hysterical in under a second, it's the most incongruous thing. Her teeth, white as snow, smiling all by themselves; her lips all snarling and twisted. And Huey, tearing frantically at his smooth, bald head; motioning the pulling out of hair where there is none.

'I leave you alone for a second . . . *this* is what you do, you freakin' idiot. Huey, you stupid freakin' *idiot*.'

'Tess, don't get mad now . . . come on, don't get all crazy. That snake just won't stay in his friggin' tank.'

'That's because he's *afraid* of you.'

'He's a boa constrictor . . . what the fuck has he got to be afraid of?'

'He knows you hate him, he's not stupid. He's aware that you're trying to kill him.'

'I'm not trying to kill him, I *like* him. Why would he think that I hate him?'

'Why else would you give him a name like that? Why else would you name him Harvey Weinstein?'

'It suits him.'

'*Why?*'

'He's a *snake*.'

'No Huey, that's not good enough. He's a happy reptile, he's sweet. He and I, we've got a special bond. He's intuitive, you know, he's very intuitive. He knows *exactly* what you think of him . . . he does.'

'I like him.'

'*No,* no you don't. Only last year you tried to kidnap his namesake and kill him. You were going to force feed him poison.'

'It wasn't poison, Tess. It was Rogaine.'

'What's the difference? He would have grown hair on his gullet and choked. You think that's a nice way to die?'

'He wasn't going to die, come *on* now. I was never going to kill him, not really. I was just going to scare him a little bit.'

'Only because they stopped you just in *time*. Only because they took out a *restraining* order against you.'

'Well . . .'

'And had you arrested.'

'Hey, don't side with the law, Tess. You know that was a total . . . like . . . overreaction.'

'Huey, it was *not* an overreaction. You tried to poison the biggest film producer in Hollywood. You're barred from California for the rest of your *life.*'

'He ruined my *career*,' says Huey, slapping at his head. 'You think that's fair, Tess? That he totally *ruined* my career.'

'How is that the snake's fault, Huey . . . *how!*'

Tess is hitting Huey with her shopping bag, a blue and white carrier from Gap.

'If he's cooked it's your fault,' she says, laying into him. 'If he's dead, then *you're* dead too. If you've damaged a single shiny scale on his cute albino head, if any harm has come to my . . . *look!* There he is . . . Harvey *Weinstein*, behind the fridge. Come here to Mommy. Come here to Mommy, Harvey Weinstein.'

The snake sticks it's head out from behind the fridge, slowly, tentatively; it's bright red tongue darting back and forth. Nobody moves, we don't want to scare it. Tess is sobbing with joy.

'Quick, Huey. Tell him that you love him.'

'Fuck that, no. No way.'

'Get down on your knees here, and *tell* my damn snake that you love him.'

'Tess, you've gone, like, totally AWOL. There's no way in the world I'm going to do this.'

'You get down there and apologise to him, Huey. Right *now*. Or so help me God, I'll never let you near my ass again as long as you live.'

A sharp intake of breath from me and Michael. Huey sighs and gets down on his knees.

'*Closer.*'

Huey gets closer.

'Say it, we don't have all day.'

Huey looks at the snake. The snake looks at Huey.

'I, uh . . . hey, man. I uh . . . love you . . .'

'No, no, that's not right. Say the whole thing. Say it properly. Say – I love you, Harvey Weinstein.'

'You've got to be *kidding* me.'

She's not.

Huey gives Tess a pleading look but she just won't budge. She nudges his shoulder with the heel of her shoe and tells him to hurry up and be quick. Huey lets out a moan. His face contorts, his lips can barely stand to form the words.

'I love you,' he says, finally, tears of resignation in his eyes. 'I love . . . I love you, Harvey Weinstein.'

It works like a charm. The snake crawls out from underneath the fridge and sidles straight over to Tess. Huey collapses in a heap, overcome by what he's just done.

'Thanks baby,' she says, brightly, bending down to pick up the snake. 'I know how hard that must have been for you to do.'

Huey can only manage a grunt.

'I'll fix us all something to drink, how 'bout that? Soon as Harvey Weinstein's safely back in his tank. I'll fix us all a pitcher of frozen margaritas? I'll use my extra special recipe, what do you say?'

'Thanks,' says Michael. 'That would be nice.'

Tess sets the jug of lime-green liquid on the table and pours each of us a generous glass. We down the first batch pretty quickly and mix up another just as fast. Huey is recovering from his ordeal, slowly; it's taken him a while to find the strength to speak. Neither of them refer directly to what's just happened. They don't apologise or say something to the effect of, *Well, Claire, well Michael, you must think we're pretty strange, am I right? You must think we're both pretty highly strung?* This, it seems, is another regular day for them; just another raucous South Beach evening.

'So, Huey,' I say, 'if you don't mind me asking, why exactly did you . . .'

'Try to kill Harvey Weinstein?'

'Yes . . . I mean it's fine, if you don't want to talk about it.'

'No, that's OK. It's a pretty simple story, as a matter of fact. It happened just after I lost all my hair. I wore a wig for a while, you know, to go to auditions and stuff, but I still wasn't getting any work. Then, out of nowhere, when I'd just about given up hope, I landed this once-in-a-lifetime role. Would have been a total comeback for me. Would have set up my entire career.'

'Anyway,' he says, miserably, 'it was all worked out. My agent said I had the part, the director said I had the part, and I'm just about to sign the contract in front of them both – I have the pen in my actual hand – when there's a glitch. Producer calls up before I've had time to write my name, says he doesn't want me for the role any more. Says the romantic lead in a movie of this stature has got to have all his own hair. What about Bruce Willis, I say. Not important, he says. People still remember Willis with hair.'

'And then his wig starts to slip,' says Tess, bleakly.

'Yeah. And then the wig, it starts slipping. I don't notice it at first, I can't feel it. By the time I realise what's going on, the rug's slipped so far back they can all see exactly how bald I am. And, 'cos I'm so wound up – I'm practically begging for the job by now – my forehead, it's all slicked up with sweat. Then my teeth, they start chattering and the director, he says, "What the fuck is that? Is that *you?*" Up until that point I think he would have fought for me, you know? You should have seen my audition tape, man, it was immense.'

'It was awesome, you really ought to see it.'

'They ripped the part right out from under me. All because of that phone call. All because the producer had seen me in some crappy science fiction pilot playing a hairless Venetian.'

'*Venutian.*'

'Whatever. But it was all down to that one guy. Har . . . *Har* . . . well, you both know his name. You both know exactly who I mean.'

Tess hugs Huey and gives him a kiss and we nod and sip our margaritas. They're excellent, they're beginning to work. Slowly, quietly, ever so gently, everyone's starting to relax.

'So how was your day?' says Tess, brightly. 'You get any lead on your brother?'

'No, I didn't, not really.'

'That's a shame.'

'Claire went to her old building,' Michael says, licking salt off the rim of his glass. 'She got a little upset.'

'Oh, Baby, I'm so sorry,' says Tess, stroking my arm. 'I know exactly how you feel. I feel like that every time I drive past the women's penitentiary. Even though my mum isn't in there any more, it still brings the whole thing right back to me.'

'What did she . . .'

'Get imprisoned for? Cheque-book fraud. And arson, a little bit.'

'I see.'

'I guess that was the last time you were all together as a complete family, am I right? Must have been pretty hard for you to go back there. Especially with your brother missing and everything?'

She really is the strangest kind of woman; just when you think she's as mad as a fish she says something generous and perceptive.

'Huey and Harvey are my family now,' she says. 'You have to make your family where you can. I have a sister called Rita, she lives in Wyoming, farms emus, so I don't really see her all that much. Still, at least I know where she's at, right?'

Huey smiles. Michael licks up more salt.

'Hey,' says Tess, eagerly. 'I know what we should do. Let's all four of us make a list. Claire is on a mission here, we ought to get busy. We should write down everything we know, everything we can think of that might help her. Huey and I know Miami like the back of our hand, we must be able to come up with some ideas of where to look, right?'

I can feel my limbs going soft. I like the idea of everybody helping; I like the idea of everybody joining in. My cheeks ache, I'm smiling like a fool. Michael is . . . Michael is drooling.

'Everybody feeling a bit better now, huh?'

It's true, we're all feeling much better.

'Must be the jet-lag wearing off,' I say, contentedly.

'That's probably got something to do with it,' Tess says. 'But more likely it's my special recipe margaritas. Secret is to crush a little Valium in with the salt. Makes a whole heap of difference. The cocktail can taste bitter if you mix it in direct, so it's better if you just crush the pick-me-up into the salt.'

'You spiked our drinks?'

Why don't I sound angry when I say this. Why do I sound so blasé?

'Sure, but it's only a little bit. You get a mild hit every time you take a sip. Won't effect you all that much, not unless you suck up every grain.'

We take a moment. Everyone turns to look at Michael. His own glass is licked clean, and he's already making short work of mine and Huey's; his tongue is coated in granules.

'Great drinks, Tessa. Superb. Without doubt the finest, meanest, most delicious tequila based cocktail I've ever, ever tasted in my entire *life*.'

Columbia Is Lost,
There Are No Survivors

I make Michael a cup of strong coffee in an attempt to sober him up, but it's clear he's not going to be much good to anyone. The rest of us are severely relaxed, but Michael is mildly catatonic. We deposit him on the red-lip sofa and Tess fetches the rest of us pens and paper. She writes 'Claire's Search' at the top of each page and brings out a ruler and some Post-its so we can make the whole thing look much more professional.

'So,' she says, glancing round the dining table. 'What exactly do we know? We know your brother walked out of his office one evening, last month, and that somehow he never made it home. No trace of him was found – no phone calls, no paper trail, no car crash, no nothing. But your gut instinct is that he wasn't kidnapped or involved in something criminal, am I right?'

I tell her that she is.

'He didn't take his passport or pack any clothes. He didn't clear out his bank accounts either. But he's a lawyer, right? He's wealthy. He could have had some money stashed away, funds the rest of his family didn't know about.'

It's highly possible.

'Michael said your brother had been having an affair. Do you know who she is, this other woman?'

'All we have is her first name, Annie.'

'Right. Annie.'

She copies it down.

'I have the love letter she wrote to him,' I say. 'Would you like to take a look at her letter?'

'*Could I?* You sure you don't mind?'

I have it in my suitcase, I go and fetch it. Tess is close to tears by the time she's finished.

'Don't you love how she wishes him luck at the end? Even though he's broken it off with her, don't you *love* how she still wants him to be happy?'

'It's touching,' Huey says. 'It's really touching.'

Tess exhales and straightens up in her chair, signalling she's ready for us to get back down to business.

'OK,' she says. 'So, it seems like he finished it with this Annie woman. And it couldn't have been easy, a love as deep as that, it had to have been devastating for him. But he's a good guy, your brother, he decides to do right by his family. He decides he ought to stick by his wife and his kid.'

'A son. He and Kay have a baby son, Julian.'

'Julian,' she exclaims. 'What a precious name for a baby.'

She writes down Julian and Kay.

It's very important to Tess that she learns the names of all the principal players. She's creating a family tree in her head, tying down all the loose ends. She tells me she buys a lot of thrillers and mystery novels, and that she likes to make detailed notes while she reads them.

'I keep Post-its in my pocket at all times,' she says. 'Just in case I come up with a clue. I underline the best passages with a highlighter pen, then I copy them out into my clue book. I like to try and work out who did it before I get to the reveal at the end. Nine times out of ten I can usually guess.'

'Tess is meticulous,' says Huey, proudly, 'She's very good at working out this kind of stuff.'

I nod. I tell them I don't doubt it.

'OK, then,' she says, linking her fingers together and cracking her knuckles. 'So don't shout me down straight away . . . but I feel like I ought to go out on a limb here.'

We don't shout her down, we wait to hear what she'll say.

'Because a rich man like your brother, I mean, it doesn't make much sense . . . for a person like that to walk out on his life. If it was me or Huey you could understand it . . . but a man like that, a success like that . . . sorry, Claire, but someone's got to say this. The truth might be way darker then you think.'

She beckons for me and Huey to lean forward.

'Now, I'm not saying she *did* definitely do it, but I don't think we should totally rule it out. The thing is, the question we have to ask is . . . could your brother's wife have found out about the affair and gone psycho-nuts and killed him? In *Revenge of the Five Foot Cuckold* the wife kills her husband with a frozen leg of pork and buries him underneath the garden patio. Could your brother be under the patio, you think?'

'Daniel doesn't have a patio,' says Michael, from the sofa.

'What do they have then? A lawn?'

'Decking.'

'Well, then,' says Tess, turning back to me and narrowing her eyes. 'Could your brother be under the decking?'

'No. There's no way Kay could have done that.'

'She's not the violent type?'

'No . . . no. Quite the opposite.'

'Might she have hired someone?'

'A *hit* man?'

'Don't rule it out. It's not out of the question. I once knew a woman that did it. The cousin of my neighbour's manicurist back in Tampa. She hired some Colombian guy to kill her dentist.'

'Why?'

'Dunno. He messed up her veneers, or something.'

'Christ.'

'I know. My cousin said her smile was totally ruined.'

Tess shudders. Huey pulls his hat tighter over his head.

'So, where does that leave us?' Tess says, a little disheartened. 'If you don't think his wife had him smoked, then where does that leave us, exactly?'

I tell them everything else I know. All about the sushi waitress and the Japanese secret agency. All about the docks and the Russian sailor. I run through the coincidence of the shipping

schedules and the freighters and Tess listens closely, totally rapt.
She pumps me for information on the Russian. She wants to
know if he was good-looking, if he looked anything like Omar
Sharif. She's disappointed when I tell her that he didn't.

'So, you figure he came out here on a cruise ship?'

'Well, not a cruise ship exactly, more like a . . . yeah . . . exactly,
he took a cruise.'

Tess is happy with this; she writes down Russian, Miami,
cruise.

'So the big question has to be, why'd he decide to come back
here? If we can work out why he came, we can probably work
out where he is, am I right?'

I hope she is.

'We need to think of it like an acting class,' says Huey. 'We
need to get deep inside your brother's head. Was he happy when
you lived out here, when you were kids?'

I shift in my seat.

'I don't . . . it's hard to say. The whole thing . . . well, it ended
pretty badly. My father died out here, he had a heart attack.'

'I'm sorry,' says, Huey, taking his hat off. 'Really, I'm sorry to
hear that. How did it happen, exactly?'

This isn't a story that I care to tell often, but the details seem
to spill from my mouth; the Valium has made me talkative,
confessional.

'It was the day the space shuttle exploded, the Challenger,' I
say. 'Daniel and my dad had driven up to Cape Canaveral to
watch the launch . . . they saw it go down right in front of them.
He collapsed on the drive home. They got stuck in the traffic,
these terrible jams . . . they couldn't get an ambulance to him in
time. Daniel was all on his own.'

I close my eyes for a moment.

'He ended up running through the traffic to get help. He ran
until his feet bled, till he'd damaged both of his legs. And I
can't . . . I can't imagine how he felt.'

Tess and Huey look at one another.

'Jesus,' says Huey, 'poor kid.'

'So, where were you when all this happened? Were you waiting for your dad, back at home?'

'No . . . I was out. On the beach.'

'And your mom?'

'At the apartment, with my little sister. Mum says Sylvie woke up and started to cry seconds before the police knocked at our door. She thinks my sister must have sensed that something was wrong.'

'Wow,' says Huey.

'Amazing,' says Tess.

Tess writes down, Sylvie, sixth sense.

'I remember that day really well,' she says, 'the day that the Challenger blew. All of us watching it on the TV set. All the neighbours in and out of each other's houses. The look on that poor woman's face, that teacher's mother. Christ,' she shakes her head, 'I'll never forget that woman's face.'

'Where were you when the last one went down?' says Huey.

'Columbia?' says Tess. 'I'm not sure. You remember that one Claire, the Columbia?'

I do, it's at the back of my mind. I know that it happened, that it exploded on re-entry but I can't for the life of me remember when it was. This is something I should know. I wonder why I never spoke to Daniel about it? It must have been hard for him to see the pictures on the news, to read about it in the papers: it must have brought that first time right back to him.

'It was early last year,' says Huey.

'When exactly? Do either of you know which month?'

'January, I think.'

'No,' says Tess. 'It wasn't. I remember it now, it was February. Right before my first consultation with the plastic surgeon.'

'Isn't February when he started on the antidepressants?' says Michael, sleepily, shuffling over to join us.

And, of course. That's exactly when it was.

We spend the next half-hour on the Internet looking up details of the Columbia explosion. A few clicks of the mouse and suddenly the pages are full of it. Shuttle bursts into flames over Texas. Seven astronauts never had a chance. Observers report seeing two white streaks in the sky. Witnesses claim their front doors rumbled and hummed. The explosion was caused by giant lightning, some say. Nonsense, it was nothing of the sort. A small fault. Of course, just a tiny random blip, like that failed rubber washer on the Challenger. In the midst of all this clarity, this scientific excellence, a small but significant factor failed. A slice of foam broke off and tore away from the fuel tank, causing damage to an insulation tile. The shuttle was left unprotected, vulnerable to the searing heat of re-entry. There was no way out. Not for anyone. There was no possible escape.

I turn off the computer, it fizzes and dies, and Tess lays her hand on my shoulder.

'It's the worst,' she says. 'I know what that's like, when they start taking the antidepressants in secret. What was it, do you think? Was he ashamed or something?'

'I don't know,' I say, quietly. 'Daniel's hard to get close to, he's very . . .'

'Keeps it all locked inside, am I right? Doesn't share his problems with anyone?'

'No, I . . . not really.'

'You feel lousy, I bet? Wish you'd tried to get more out of him while you could?'

I don't answer. All of a sudden, I can't. It's criminal that I didn't pick up on this or notice this. I wonder if Kay did, or Mum. Why did no one speak about it? Why did no one say anything at the time? What a talented family we've become, to bury all this stuff away so neatly.

'Hey,' says Tess, noticing the look on my face. 'Don't be so hard on yourself. I mean, you're here now, aren't you? Doing the best you can to look out for him. You got on that plane right away, the second you thought he might be out here. And I'll tell you one thing for absolute certain. We're not going to let you leave until you find him. Isn't that right, Huey?'

'Yeah, man,' says Huey. 'That's totally right.'

'The best thing you can do now is relax for the night. It's been a tough month for you, tough couple of days. We should get ourselves pumped up, let off a little steam, we can start up fresh again in the morning.'

'I don't know, Tess. I'm not sure.'

'Come on now, trust me, it's exactly what you need. And we've done well tonight,' she says holding up her note-pad. 'We already found out something important. If you ask me your brother's suffering from post traumatic stress syndrome. Chances are, he's got amnesia or something like that.'

'Amnesia?'

'Yeah, amnesia. Maybe the Columbia crash set him off, sort of a delayed reaction kind of a thing. What with that and the affair and the break-up, I doubt he even knew what he was doing. I'll bet all he could remember when he left his office that night was his time as a kid out here in Miami.'

'I'm guessing this happened in a book that you read?'

'Yeah, it did. How d'you know? It's a great story, actually, *The Forget-Me-Not Bride*. I'll tell you all about it while we get changed to go out.'

'What about . . . what about Michael?'

Michael has his head on the table. He can hardly keep his eyes open any more.

'You leave Michael to me,' says Tess, mischievously. 'I have just the thing to wake him up.'

Pretty Woman

Tess fixes Michael a *special recipe* energy drink, which seems to perk him up again in seconds. I have a suspicion there's more than caffeine in the syrupy brew she makes, but the truth is, I'm too relaxed to care. On Tess's insistence I've had a touch more of the margarita salt mix in preparation for our special night out. I'm grateful not to feel anxious or worried for a while, I'm looking forward to us being outside. We're all going to change into party outfits. We're going to drink more cocktails and eat spicy Cuban food, and finish the night off at a jazz club. Michael and I didn't have time to pack much more than T-shirts and shorts before getting on the plane, so Huey and Tess are going to lend us clothes. We let our hosts get ready first. The two of them emerge hand in hand, some minutes later, looking like they're going to a film premier. Huey is decked out in a silver-grey suit with a vintage *'I ♥ cannabis'* T-shirt underneath it. The outfit is nicely topped off by a pair of crocodile-skin loafers and a khaki hunting cap with bendy ear flaps. Tess's look is marginally more traditional. She wears a short white mini-dress with sequins down the front, and gold stiletto slingbacks that make her look almost a foot taller. It's Versace, she says, giving us all a twirl. Of course it is, what else would it be?

Tess drags me into her bedroom, tottering over the lino in her narrow heels. The room is decked out like a bordello – pink satin sheets, mock velvet curtains, a red bulb in the overhead light.

'You're so lucky,' she says, watching me strip down to my underwear. 'I wish I had long legs like you. And your boobs are awesome, Claire, if you don't mind me saying so. Thirty-four C, am I right? I hope mine look that good after the operation. I want them to look natural. I don't want them to end up too tight, too rigid, you know what I mean?'

Tess takes her time choosing a dress for me. She picks out something slinky and black, not too showy, and decides to perk it up with some choice accessories. Her wardrobe is crammed tight with extras: shoes, lingerie, handbags, belts and drawer after drawer of costume jewellery.

'You'll need a necklace,' she says, narrowing her eyes. 'Definitely a necklace with that dress. Something discreet, something classy.'

Tess's idea of classy and discreet is a butterfly pendant the size of my fist, covered in multi-coloured gemstones and pale pink seed pearls.

'It's my favourite, but I'd love for you to borrow it,' she says. 'And don't worry about damaging it or nothing, it's not worth nearly as much as you'd think. The gems are totally fake.'

'Really? I'd never have guessed.'

'I know. Because they're pretty realistic, right? You want to try it?'

How can I say no? I put it on. It hangs heavily from its chain (thick and gold) and nestles in my cleavage like a bird of paradise

'That's it. That's precious on you. Now we need to do something about your make-up. You definitely need lips, and eyes.'

'I have lips and eyes.'

'Not like these, you don't. Check this out.'

Tess's make-up box is the size of my suitcase: brimming with glosses, varnishes and powders, and bottles of mysterious scents and unguents. She applies false eyelashes to my scrubby ones. She paints a thick goo on my lips. She layers on bronzer, blusher and mascara and, just to be sure, she sweeps some glittery shadow over my eyelids.

'Wow, that's quite a transformation. You look so Miami now, take a look.'

I don't dare.

'Come on,' she says, excitedly. 'Open your eyes.'

I look like someone completely different. I don't recognise the woman staring back at me. I'm a cross between Jane Seymour and Alice Cooper. I'm a ballroom dancer and a synchronised swimmer. I'm the kind of woman who'd be eliminated first in a local seaside beauty pageant; my special talent would be baton twirling or advanced dog grooming.

'You look just like J-Lo, don't you think so? That's what I was going for, that kind of a look. Your hiney looks just like J-Lo's in that dress.'

'Tess, are you saying I've got a fat arse?'

'No, not at *all*. But for Christ's sake don't point it at Huey, that's all I'm saying. He's like a dog on heat in this humidity. When we go out in a little bit, we ought to make sure that you walk behind him.'

'You're *serious*?'

'Deadly.'

'I see.'

Michael looks almost as uncomfortable as I do. My scruffy ex-husband, come boyfriend, is wearing a fringed suede jacket and leather trousers. He smells like an abattoir. He squeaks as he walks. His pupils are fixed and dilated.

'Are you OK?'

'Yeah, yeah. I'm good. My vision's a little blurry that's all. Do I look . . . I mean, is this OK?'

It's the way that he asks me – gently, a little vulnerable – it makes me reach out and stroke his face.

'Michael,' I whisper, smiling at him, 'You look . . . ridiculous.'

'Really?'

'Yeah, but we both do, it's fine.'

'I can't tell what you've got on,' he says, squinting at me. 'Is that a . . . is there something on your chest?'

'Butterfly.'

He looks confused.

'Not a duck? It looks just like a duck.'

'Oh, man, you look wild,' says Huey, coming over to join us. 'Turn around. Let's take a proper look at you in that dress.'

Tess frowns at me. She mouths *no way* with her lips.

'Uh . . . you know what, Huey? Better not. It's getting late. I think we should probably just get going.'

Huey shrugs, pulls down his ear flaps, and off we go.

The air feels warm on my skin. We parade with the other peacocks to our starting position on Ocean Drive and shimmy through the sleek, shiny bodies. I'm enjoying my clothes; I feel like I'm wearing a costume, like I've walked onto the pages of a comic book. Tess says hello to a lot of different people. She knows the cigar girls peddling fake Cubans; she knows the other snake charmers with their writhing boas. She knows the happy hour waiters in their hot pink thongs and the drag queens in their ten-dollar dresses. The flash and the trash, the camp and the curious, the college kids and the pudgy, fat-faced tourists. Tess points out two guys from a famous hip hop band that I've never heard of, Huey points out an actor from a film I've never seen. Their chatter is filled with who goes where and who stays here, and who knows anyone important. They find out who's in town from the cigar girls, they find out where the best gigs and pool parties are from the hotel concierge. Tess wants to know if any cool record producers are in town, she thinks we might hook up with her manager later. From time to time she asks if anyone's seen a love-sick English guy wandering the streets who looks like he might have amnesia. The answer is always no, but I never get the feeling that they think it's a ludicrous question.

Halfway down the street we settle in at a bar, cooled by the soft ocean breezes. We order a pitcher of Majitos and a bowl of conch fritters that we can share. From time to time a clutch of fashion models sweep past the bar on their way to some fabulous party; freakish-looking women, genetic mutants: long limbed, tanned, and blonde as fairies. Tess checks out every single one. As the rest of us dig into our greasy bar snacks, Tess calculates a beauty rating in her head for each and every woman that walks past us. In an instant she has it all down – age, attractiveness, breast size, slimness, nose shape, who has and hasn't had plastic surgery. I imagine her marking them out of ten. The low scorers seem to keep her happy, the high ones leave her reaching for her make-up compact. She dabs at her nose repeatedly – she's not powdering it exactly, it's more like she's trying to make it smaller or shapelier just by touching it.

'So,' she says, putting her mirror away for the twentieth time. 'This is some cool music, huh?'

Salsa is playing in the hotel bar next door, and beyond that, somewhere in the distance Phil Collins is singing 'Another Day in Paradise'. It has a strange effect on me, this odd musical mix. It begins to make me feel dizzy. The noise the colour, the intensity, the heat, I suddenly feel overloaded. I sit back to catch my breath, close my eyes for a while, try to focus through my Valium haze. When I open my eyes I'm looking upward, staring at the hotel behind us; a pretty white building, deco and elegant, whose façade reminds me of the bow of a ship. Deep inside the lobby, a party blossoms. Wild, chatty voices, light with expensive drink, echo off the walls of the foyer. Upstairs bright bulbs glint on and off in the guest rooms, and up in the penthouses something strange protrudes from the balconies; long, black and phallic, their ends tipped up to the night sky. It takes me a moment to work out what they are.

'Are they . . . ?'

'Telescopes? Yeah. Cute, huh?'

'What are they . . . what are they for?'

'Beats me . . . so the guests can look at the cruise ships, I guess.'

'Have they always been there, these telescopes?'

'Ever since I can remember,' says Tess. 'That hotel has always had telescopes. Only difference from when I first moved here, is that this hotel used to be bright blue.'

The Blue Hotel

'What kind of hotel are you building?'

'I'm not building it. I'm overseeing the renovation.'

'You're painting it?'

'Among other things, yes.'

'Is it as rundown as our house back at home?'

'More so, it's practically a shell.'

I thought about this for a moment. A building like a shell, brittle and empty, just a skeleton frame to hold it up.

'Can I go there one day, can I see it?'

'No.'

'But I'd like to see what it looks like.'

'It's dangerous. Things could fall on you, you might get hurt.'

'I'd wear a hat.'

'We don't have any hard hats that would fit you.'

'What about the one you give to Daniel? His head's not much bigger than mine is. He has a pin head, everybody says so.'

'I don't have a pin head . . . shut up, *Fatso*.'

'You do. And you have weird-shaped ears as well.'

'It's not going to happen, Claire, that's *final*. Stop asking, you'd only get in the way.'

I don't think he realised how harsh he sounded. I don't think he realised what he'd said. I felt myself shrinking into my chair, like I suddenly needed to take a pee. My father had one of those large, resonant voices whose volume knob only had three settings: off, regular and loud. When he was angry or peeved, like he was after I'd spent the last ten minutes badgering him, it sounded like the honk of a bassoon. And I *was* in their way, I could feel it, just by my being there in the kitchen. Mum could barely get past me to empty out the washing machine; Daniel couldn't get to the cupboard to fetch his cereal. And Dad couldn't shuffle out from behind the breakfast bar without me squeezing my stool tight into the counter top until it knocked all the air out of my stomach.

'So, that's definitely a no, then?' I said, as my father reached up for his file of blueprints.

He didn't reply. He didn't have to.

My father always left for work before the rest of us had properly woken up yet. He was dressed, showered, and halfway through his eggs before we'd had our first glass of juice, or changed out of our pyjamas. He always wore a serviette when he ate because he sometimes spilt food down his front. By the end of his breakfast his newspaper would bare a tell-tale egg stain, or a translucent butter stain, or a splash mark from the coffee he'd just gulped down to help aggravate his ulcer. Everything my father did was in a hurry. He was a man who always did things in a rush. He ate too quickly. Spoke too soon. He sometimes didn't speak to us at all. He had hair that grew out of his ears and his nose, and a thumb that was crooked from where he once hit it with a hammer. He liked Marx Brothers' films and football and fatty food, and he never forgot the punchline to a decent joke. He was an atheist. A pessimist. A mischievous cynic. I never once saw him wear a suit or tie. Nothing got him down like the winter time. Nothing cheered him up like the spring. He wasn't as bright as we thought he was. He wasn't as ignorant as he feared. He was fiercely, blindly judgemental and blunt. He was generous, affectionate and kind. Sometimes he'd pick us up and kiss our cheeks for no reason, sometimes he'd ignore us all for days. He didn't know why we didn't get him. Couldn't work out why he didn't quite get us. This was his greatest confusion, I think. Open minded as he tried so hard to be to the world, a part of him seemed ever closed to us.

★   ★   ★

'So what's it like, then?' I said to Daniel.

'It's amazing,' he said. 'It's ten storeys high and it's crumbling, they're going to paint the whole thing bright blue.'

Thanks. Don't play it down, then. Not for my sake.

'It's like somebody set fire to its insides,' he said. 'It smells damp inside, like a cave. They're taking it apart piece by piece and making it shiny and new again. Better than it ever was before.'

'Will it still be the same place?'

'How do you mean?'

'Well if they take all the pieces away and replace them with new ones, if all that's left is the façade. Will it still be the same place, or different?'

'Who knows, Fats? But Dad said I can have a say in the final design.'

'*You?*'

'Yeah. I'm going to think of something really good. I'll get to choose how big the swimming pool is, or something cool like that. Maybe they could lay a running track around it.'

What a way to bribe your teenage son; the chance to design his own running track. I'd never seen my brother look so excited.

'A running track,' I sniffed. 'That's boring. If he'd asked me I'd have chosen a waterfall, or a lake with alligators in it and tropical fish and . . .'

'And what?'

I thought for a moment.

'A giant slide.'

'Dad would never go for that.'

'How do you know?'

'I'm telling you, Fats. He just wouldn't.'

I never got to find out what it was in the end, the detail that Daniel added to the blue hotel. I didn't even know where the building was or how it looked; I never even found out what it was called. I wanted so badly to go there: to see it, to touch it, to smell this rotting cave that he was magically transforming into a palace. But If I couldn't go with them, then I didn't want to know too much about it, so I let Daniel get on with it on his own. He started going down there more often, sometimes as much as twice a week. Most times it cheered him up immensely when he went, other times it left him thoughtful and morose. On one occasion, just after the brand new bar had been fitted out, the two of them came back in the foulest mood. My dad silent and heavy, his stomach slopping with acid, Daniel as taut as a drum.

'What's wrong with you two?'

'Nothing. There's nothing wrong.'

'Daniel, what's the matter? What's going on?'

He wasn't a cry baby, my brother, you'd never see him in tears, not even when he was a tiny kid. But this time he couldn't hold it in; his whole face withered and cracked. He put his arms round my mother's neck and sobbed. Mum scowled over his shoulder at Dad and they held each other's gaze like lasers. For seconds. For minutes.

It took me a while to work out why Daniel had been so upset that afternoon, but I finally figured it out. A couple of weeks later I asked Dad if there was going to be a running track fixed around the swimming pool and he looked up at me like I was mad and shook his head. That was why Daniel had been so pissed off. That's why they'd argued, it was obvious.

'In that case,' I said. 'I mean, it's only a suggestion. But you might want to think about having a waterfall.'

'A waterfall?'

'Yes. With, you know, stepping stones and stuff like that. Or maybe, perhaps, a giant slide?'

Dad forced another Rennie past his rough chalky lips and turned straight back to his newspaper. Daniel wasn't getting his way on this matter and, it turned out, neither was I.

I lean further back in my chair. I spend a long time gazing up at those telescopes, all bent in different directions, like broken limbs. Some point out at the ocean, some of them are focused on the street. My father rejected the waterfall and the running track, but I'll bet the telescopes were another of my brother's ideas. So this must be it, the blue hotel: spruced up for a second time and painted white. This is the secret place my father came to, six days a week while we lived here. This is where he worked so hard and stressed out so much that none of us knew his heart was breaking.

I feel sick to the pit of my stomach. I am doing it all over again; letting things slide, letting things slip, letting things drift out from underneath me. Sitting here on the street, full of alcohol and pills, dolled up like a 1980s prom queen. I should be fast asleep getting rest for tomorrow. I should be out pounding the streets. I should be writing stuff down, totting things up, racking my brains for ways to look for Daniel. What if I walked right past him on Ocean Drive just now? What if I was too stoned to notice? What if he saw me and blinked once or twice at the strange girl who looked a little like his sister? I'm hiding in this outfit, in this make-up, in this bar, because my real life's too strange, too complicated. And Miami, these surroundings, this city, this street; it's all so gloriously, comfortingly shallow.

I stand up, heavily, jogging our wicker table and head for the lobby, next door. No one seems to notice me leaving and no one calls for me to stop or follows after me. I get as far as the white marble staircase before the hotel doorman bars my way with his hand. I can't go inside, it's a private party tonight; entry is only for guests of the hotel and specially invited VIPs. I raise my voice and press hard against his arm, but there's no way he's going to let me through. I'm not nearly beautiful or sober enough; my face doesn't fit, it's all wrong. I'd need to be a different kind of person to get into this place; someone famous, rich or important.

'My father restored this hotel,' I say, weakly. 'He helped to build this place where you work.'

'Is that so?' says the doorman, unimpressed. 'So, go tell him he should have built a bigger VIP room, then. It's crushed so tight in there the guests can hardly breathe.'

I turn round to leave; to give up, to walk away, but suddenly Tess is right next to me.

'Let the girl in, it's important,' she says. 'This girl, she really needs to get inside.'

The Rose Room

Tess knows the doorman, she slips him a couple of Valium, she gets all four of us inside. The VIP Rose Room is out of bounds tonight – it's crushed too tight – but we have free reign over the rest of the hotel. Hucy and Tess head outside to the pool while Michael and I queue up at the registration desk. It's a long shot, I know it, but still, it can't hurt to ask.

A second hotel employee, hip and humourless, flicks through the bookings for late December. They were sold out, he tells us; Christmas is their peak time. If my friend did stay here, then he must have made his booking some way in advance.

'Check,' I say. 'Please, can you check?'

He shakes his head, there's nothing; no room booked under the name of Daniel Ronson. What else would he have called himself? What alias could he possibly have used? I ask if I can take a look at the bookings myself, but the receptionist won't let me near the computer. I beg, plead, hustle and mope, until he agrees to read out all the names for Christmas Eve and Christmas Day. Nothing rings a bell or strikes any kind of note, so we move on from the doubles to the suites. Were any rooms booked under the name of Annie. Annie what? Annie anything at all. No Annies, he tells us, only an Andrew and an Alex.

With some effort I persuade him to give me a copy of the guest list and, with the print-out safely folded into my pocket, I look for a place to sit down. Michael and I squeeze through the crowds back to the lobby, and sink into an empty white sofa. It's the first chance I've had to look around. How elegant this place is; how tasteful, how discreet. How completely unlike my father. The floors are polished white marble, the walls are painted eggshell and cream. Original deco pillars, painstakingly restored, support the inlaid ceiling like flower stems. The round porthole windows; the wide, filmstar staircase, it feels to me like we're sitting in the ballroom of a vintage cruise liner. Nothing is too gaudy, too laden with gilt; nothing is too dressed up or over-done. It is the antidote to all the brashness, the roughness, outside; the very model of taste and restraint.

I'm guessing it's been decorated over again since the eighties but whoever restored it first had a delicate touch. And I can't imagine my father being delicate with anything; this clumsy man with egg yolk down his front. I can't imaging him fretting over ebony inlays or the quality of the walnut veneers. He was the site manager here, the project supervisor, but I can't pretend to know quite what that means. Did he stand here shouting at the archi-tects? Did he whip the decorators into shape? Was he the foreman, the leader, the playground bully, or did he contribute to the look and feel of this place? Did he etch a part of himself into it; a stamp I can't fathom or recognise? His skilful side, his artistic side; the side he took off at the doorway like a uniform, before he came home to live with us.

Why is it only as adults that we wonder what our parents did all day when we were kids? When I was young, I simply took it for granted. My father went out looking tired in the morning, he came back hours later looking measurably worse. He never spoke until he'd washed and changed out of his overalls, and we knew better than to bother him with our gossip or our grievances until he was fully a civilian again.

What exactly did he do those ten long hours he was out? How did he get covered in brick dust and pencil lines and slicks of oily, pungent-smelling paint? Was he the builder, the designer, the furtive pen pusher? Did he lay these stones and planks with his own hands? If Daniel was suggesting design details to him, then he must have held some sway in this place. He must have had an input, an influence, an eye; yet we never credited him with having talent or finesse. I knew he could draw – pencil lines, plans, detailed sketches – but we never thought this valuable or skilful. In our house the only things that seemed important to us were whether or not Dad had fixed the leaking taps. Had we enough money to pay the rate bills that month; had we enough saved up to buy new track shoes for Daniel, or to put in that proper fitted kitchen.

What a huge project this hotel must have been, it must have meant an enormous amount to him. It was his vision, his baby, a legacy of sorts, but at home in the silent apartment, it was barely mentioned.

Michael is up out of his seat. He's hovering at the lobby bar, still buzzing and high, schmoozing with a beautiful waitress.

'Yeah, I'm with the party in the Rose Room. It's too crowded in there. But I can still get free drinks from you, right?'

She eyes him suspiciously.

'So, you'll know what the party's for, then?' she says, testing him.

'Yeah . . . of course . . . a launch of some kind? An album?'

She shakes her head.

'Film, then? Is it something to do with film?'

The pretty waitress raises an eyebrow.

Michael flirts a little harder and flashes her a smile, but she still won't dish up the goods.

'This place, it's hard work,' he says, miserably, when I come over. 'No one will make me a cocktail.'

'Try paying them, Michael. Try offering one of them money.'

'I have no cash on me, it's all in my other jacket. You mind getting me something while you're up here?'

Michael goes back to the sofa to fidget and chew his cheeks, and I queue up in line and take my turn.

'That your boyfriend?'

'Yeah.'

'He's cute.'

'Uh . . . thanks.'

'Yeah, I like his accent, are you from England?'

I tell her I am.

'So,' I say, while she fixes our drinks, 'this party tonight, who *is* it for?'

'Hollywood people,' she says, looking bored. 'Some big shot director or something. They make a lot of noise, order a lot of champagne, but mostly it's just a load of hangers-on waiting to get a glimpse of someone famous. I don't even think the host is in there. He's probably up in his suite with the A-list.'

I nod, like I know how it is.

'What's it like in there, the Rose Room? Is it nice?'

'It's gorgeous,' she says, simply. 'The only place they didn't redecorate during the refit.'

'How come?'

She shrugs.

'Didn't think they could enhance it, I guess. It's old-fashioned, sort of unique. And it's, well, it's kind of romantic. You'd really need to see it for yourself.'

I balance the cocktails so as not to spill them, and make my way back over to Michael. He downs his drink in a gulp and a half, licks his lips heartily and declares it excellent.

'Better?'

'Yeah, much. Just what I needed. Let's go and find Huey and Tess.'

We take the long way round, past the ocean front and the beach, and the low white cabanas, their gauze curtains lifting in the breeze. Michael holds my hand as we walk; calmer now, more patient, his dilated eyes absorbing every detail. The garden is illuminated with candles, and hanging lanterns that throw out a soft, fat light. Palm trees sparkle under their frosting of fairy lamps, guiding us up the steps to the pool. It stretches out in front of us like a lagoon, not blue but inky and black. No running tracks here, no waterfalls to speak of, nothing tacky or cheap or fake tropical. More cosy sofas in monochrome colours and a sprinkle of ruby cushions that look like jewels. Waiters ferry drinks back and forth on silver trays to toffee-skinned girls in pale dresses. And away at the back stand Huey and Tess, gaudy and refreshingly loud.

'Where were you guys? There were free drinks out here, they just finished.'

Michael groans. He can't believe he missed them.

'It's beautiful out here, isn't it?' says Tess, admiringly. 'I mean credit where it's due. They did an awesome job.'

'On what?'

'The pool. They ripped it out last year and started all over again. Cost millions. Several. At least. The pool runs right into the underground spa, it's easily twice as big as it was.'

'What did it look like before?'

'It had this tropical vibe,' says Huey, twisting his earflaps. 'It sort of looked like Hawaii, or something.'

'Tikkii huts, thatched parasols, waitresses in hula skirts, that kind of thing.'

'Sounds tacky,' says Michael.

'You know what? It really wasn't. It all sort of fit together somehow. It had these cool stepping stones that you could—'

'*Stepping* stones?'

'Yeah. You could walk right across the pool, even at the deep end, from one side right to the other. It was sort of fun, actually.'

'I liked that swim-up bar that they used to have.'

'With the waterfall? Yeah, that was great. You had to get soaked to go through it but they made the *best* pina coladas. And you know what was over in that corner, Claire? Where the stainless steel sculpture is now?'

I take a breath before I answer.

'A giant slide?'

'Yeah, there was. How on earth did you guess? God, I *loved* that giant slide.'

Action Replay

We wander home together in the early hours: drunk, restless and a little shabby. We've eaten cheap bowls of chilli in a diner and danced for a couple of hours in a jazz club. Tess has torn the heel off her high golden sandals and my make-up has slipped down my face. We climb the stairs to Huey's apartment and head straight to bed without washing. I strip, letting my black dress fall to the floor like a rag, and stumble onto the mattress still wearing the butterfly necklace. Michael seems fascinated by it. He rubs his hand over the rough, paste jewels and strokes his fingers down to my breasts. I like the way he feels; his hands on my body, his mouth on my neck. I like the warmth and the strength.

'You're quiet,' he says.

'It's been a long night.'

'You want to . . . ?'

I do. It's exactly what I need.

We lie still and quiet on the mattress after we've made love. My breathing is quick, I have my arms round Michael's hips, his body feels clammy and hot. There's a scar on his thigh, white and hairless. I let my fingers trace its smooth edges.

'Thank you,' I say.

'What? For the sex?'

'No. For coming with me. For being here. I never really said thank you.'

'Don't be daft,' he says, rubbing my hair roughly. 'It's fine, I wanted to come.'

'It was great.'

'That I came with you?'

'No . . . the dancing. And the *sex*. I'd forgotten how . . . you know, I'd just forgotten.'

He smiles and kisses my shoulder. I wait a beat before I tell him.

'Sylvie told me something before we left.'

'About your brother?'

'No. About us.'

'Really,' he says, getting interested, 'what did she say?'

I close my eyes. I wonder if I should answer.

'She said we should have tried harder. Daniel thought . . . he said that we gave up too easily.'

My lover turns silent. For too long. This is a first for me and Michael, I'm not at all sure what he's thinking.

'What is it?' I say. 'What's wrong?'

Michael pulls his hand away and scratches it.

'Nothing. I'm a little surprised, that's all. I never thought your brother liked me all that much.'

I lie there waiting for sleep to wash over me but I can't seem to shut down the engines. It's four in the morning, there are still shouts and calls from the street: motorbikes, cars, life, arguments, hails of chatter and laughter. I wait a few more minutes, until Michael's breathing slows, then I make my way towards the kitchen and the phone. It's only eleven back in London, I doubt Sylvie will be sleeping quiet yet.

'Hey, it's me.'

'*Claire*, are you all right?'

'I'm fine . . . has there been any news?'

'No,' Sylvie says. 'There's no news.'

I'm surprised by the level of urgency in her voice, the warmth and the crisp note of worry. She seems happy to hear from me, relieved.

'I'm sorry,' I say, 'I should have called earlier . . .'

'No. No, that's all right. How is it? Are you OK? Have you . . . have you found anything?'

Maybe it's because she's an ocean away, maybe it's the last edge of the Valium. Either way I feel able to talk to her; confident that she's taking it in. I tell her about going to our old apartment. I tell her I saw the door to her old room. I remind her about the red float bands I used to fix to her arms when she was little, and about Mum telling me to make sure she had enough cream rubbed into her skin before she went outside in the sun. I describe the blue hotel: the way it looks, the way it smells, how elegant and beautiful it is. I tell her the story of Daniel's telescopes and all about the waterfall and the giant slide. *My* slide. Dad's slide. The one I never even knew existed. My sister is silent. I suddenly realise I must be gabbling.

'Are you still there?'

'. . . I'm here.'

'Are you OK?'

'I'm fine.'

I stiffen. I don't think she is.

'Did I say something? Did I say something wrong?'

She pauses and sighs.

'No, you didn't say anything wrong. It's just . . . I don't remember much of that stuff. I barely remember us being there, in Florida. I hardly . . .'

She has trouble saying it.

'I hardly even remember Dad.'

It's my turn to be silent for a moment, I'm not sure what to say next. Sylvie was so young when it happened, it's true, she really never knew him. I stutter and run out of steam. It's stilted. It's suddenly hard.

'Well . . . you loved it out here . . . you liked the water . . . you were always such a good baby. You made them feel good, Mum and Dad . . . you always made everyone feel so much better.'

'How?'

'How what?'

'How did I make people feel better?'

'I don't know . . . but you just, you always did.'

The sound of a girl shaking her head.

'So, what do you think?' she says, after a while. 'Do you really think Daniel might be out there?'

I tell her that I do. I tell her why.

'Did he ever mention it to you?' I say, when I'm done. 'The second shuttle crash? Did he ever talk to you about it?'

'He mentioned it,' she says. 'But it wasn't a big deal . . . he didn't seem upset by it or anything.'

'You're sure?'

'I don't think so . . . but . . . I don't know. I'd been working so hard. I wasn't hanging out with him all that much.'

There's a noise in the background: a man's voice.

'Sylvie, is someone there?'

'Yes,' she's says, hesitantly. 'It's Gabe.'

'Right. So how . . . how's that all going?'

'It's good. It's, you know . . . it's good. How are things with you and Michael?'

'Great,' I say, quickly. 'They're great.'

'Well . . . as long as you're sure.'

'Absolutely, he's being a rock.'

A rock? What kind of a phrase is that? In what way is Michael a rock?

'I'm pleased,' says Sylvie, kindly. 'I'm glad.'

The two of us talk a while longer. I give her my number, she gives me the numbers for Mum and Kay.

'Have they asked where I am yet?'

'No, not really. I told them you were hanging out with Michael.'

'They don't know I'm in Miami?'

'No. Should I tell them?'

I can't believe she's asking. Sylvie's never once asked me what she should do.

'I'll call them tomorrow, it's late now,' I say. 'Just tell them I'll call them both tomorrow.'

'Claire . . . *wait*. Don't hang up yet. I have to . . . I *want* to say sorry. For how I behaved when you left.'

An apology. Is this an apology?

'It was the shock, you know, of you leaving like that. It was all so sudden . . . I was upset.'

'Forget it.' I say. 'It's fine.'

'So, we're OK?'

'Yeah, Sylv. Don't worry. We're OK.'

She sounds a little happier. She wishes me good luck and I wait for the phone to click dead. Maybe it's just that she's too tired to fight, maybe it's just the late hour, but something is having a good effect on her.

On my way back to bed I realise I'm not the only one up. Away down the hallway a television plays and a bald head shines brightly in the lamp light. Huey is sat on the sofa all alone, a remote control clutched tightly in his hand. The screen flickers brightly in front of him, the sound turned down so low I can hardly make out the voices. The man on the screen is driving a police car. His face is edgy, expressive and full of life. He has wonderful hair: lush, thick and black, that gives a childish warmth to his sculpted features. I hear the chattering of teeth, then muttering under his breath, Huey says: 'Where did you go to? Was that really me? Man, where the fuck did you go?'

Call Me Madam

'I'm a little worried about Huey.'

'Why? What is it? What's wrong?'

'He's gone silent on me. Morose or something. It's not a good sign when he gets like this.'

Tess slumps on the sofa, shoves her fingers in her mouth and starts to chew down on her nails. She looks thin in her white tank top and baggy jogging pants; she doesn't look like she's slept.

'You notice anything weird about him last night?' she says, quizzing me. 'You notice anything funny while we were out?'

I tell her that I noticed he was up late, that I caught him watching himself on TV.

'Are you sure?'

'I think so. He was rewinding the same scene over and over.'

'That's how it starts,' she says, shaking her head. 'I tell you, it doesn't look so good.'

Tess chews harder on her fingers, she's clearly anxious about him.

'He can't stand it,' she says. 'He really can't. Most of the time he seems to cope OK, but some days I know it eats him up inside. He's wanted to be a star for so long. And it's not just a vanity or a money thing with Huey, because he really is a super talented actor. You can tell, right? Soon as you meet him. You can tell what kind of actor he'd be.'

I nod. I think that I can.

'I wish I knew what'd set him off so bad. He hasn't been like this for months.'

'Maybe it's because of . . . you know, uh, that thing with the snake.'

'No. No. I don't think so. I think this all has to do with your brother.'

I frown. I don't know what she means.

'He's left his life behind him, right? Thrown his whole past in the dumper. I think Huey finds that sort of attractive.'

She sits up and leans forward on her knees.

'You know what's been going through my head all night?' she says. 'You know what's been driving me crazy? I've been worrying Huey might want to run away, too. Maybe he thinks that's what he needs. To walk away from it all, to pretend like his big chance never happened. Sometimes I think he can't stand to live with it any more. He was *this* close, Claire, you know what I'm saying? He was this close to having it all.'

Tess presses her index finger into her thumb to show me just how close Huey was.

'It's serious this time . . . I'm can feel it. Something's not right . . . I'm sort of scared.'

I tell Tess she ought to go and talk to him, but she shakes her head and says it's no good. She thinks Huey stayed up all night and that he'll probably be crashed out for hours.

'Michael sleeping, too, huh?'

'Yeah, he is. He's wiped out.'

'OK then. So, I know what we should do. I need to find out where this whole thing is headed now with Huey, and there's only one person who'll know. Pass me the phone, I'm going to call Madam Orla. She'll know exactly what to do.'

Madam Orla twists, turns and fidgets like a puppy getting used to its leash. She has hoops in her ears the size of donuts, and chunky silver rings on her broad fingers. Madam Orla is a pre-op transsexual. Tess and her met at their plastic surgeon's office.

'Hola, no tits.'

'Hola, man hands, how's it hanging?'

'Still hanging, yes, but not for long.'

Madam Orla tries to make a girlish giggle, but it comes out a gruff, mannish laugh.

'They pencilled me in, did I tell you?'

'For your *surgery*, no *way*?'

'They start work on me on the sixth. Next week I lose the dick and balls and get bosoms, I'm going to look just like Selma Hayek.'

Tess and Madam Orla start to scream: one high, one low; one deep, one screechy. They stand up and embrace across the table.

'You should come in with me,' says Orla, excitedly. 'They could do the two of us together.'

'You think? But I don't know, though. I can still only afford to get tits.'

'What difference? It's a start. They can fix your ugly nose and suck out your lumpy ass fat another time.'

Tess laughs along with Madam Orla but I'm not sure either one finds it funny.

'So who's your new friend here, the one with the face like lemons?'

'This is Claire,' says Tess, introducing me. 'She's staying with me and Huey for a while; she's over from England.'

'Welcome then, English. Charmed, I'm sure.'

Pleasantries exchanged, introductions made, the three of us get down to business. Orla rolls her eyes in preparation and as she lays out her tarot cards and fiddles with her crystals, it becomes clear Tess is in awe of her psychic. She hangs on every word, stares hard into her face and visibly shivers at her predictions.

'He is suffering inside. I feel it, I feel this in my chest.'

'I know it. He is, he really is.'

'Pain, I see pain. His past is like malevolent spirit . . . draining all happiness from his heart.'

'See,' says Tess, turning to face me. 'I told you Huey was in trouble.'

'You must be strong for him now. Very strong,' Orla, says.

'What is it? What can I do?'

'If you don't want bad things to happen, then—'

'*Bad* things . . . what kind of bad things?'

'Perhaps . . . no . . . I can't see it. All is out of balance . . . but it's difficult . . . he might—'

'*Leave* me? You think Huey might leave for good?'

Madam Orla holds up her hands, she won't answer.

'Please, you have to tell me,' says Tess, getting agitated. 'I don't care how bad it is, I have to know.'

Madam Orla puts her fingers to her temples like she's struggling to pull out her thoughts.

'Maybe . . . no. Maybe . . . ah, yes. You need to do something for your lover, something to help rebuild his confidence.'

'What can I do? I'll do anything.'

'Not for me to say. I'm just a stupid woman. Only listen to the predictions of the cards.'

'Turn it, then. *Fast.* Turn the next one.'

Orla flips it over with great ceremony.

'Venus . . . card of love, right? Card of love?'

'Yes, of love, or maybe,' Orla pauses, 'card for *beauty.*'

'Is that *it*, is that what the cards are saying? That I need to be more beautiful for Huey?'

I can't take much more of this, it's upsetting. I'm feeling deeply uncomfortable.

'Copy down your operation dates and I'll see what I can do. You're right, Or, I should get my tits done now.'

'But only if you want to,' says Orla scribbling her dates down on the back of a newspaper. 'I don't want you to do this just for me.'

'No, it's the right time. The cards think . . . they *say* I should do it. Thanks Or, thank you *so* much.'

'You're welcome, Baby, and don't worry now. Huey, he's going to be OK.'

The psychic strokes Tess's face with both hands like a mother might comfort a child. Tess is emotional, she's close to tears.

'OK . . . so, you have to do Claire now,' she says, reaching into her bag for a tissue.

'No, Tess. Really . . . I'd rather not.'

'But you have to. My treat. Orla, wait till you hear this, Claire has the most amazing story.'

Madam Orla tries not to yawn. Tess blows hard into her tissue.

'I'm going to go wash my face and freshen up, but I'll be back in just a minute. Don't finish without me, you *swear*?'

We both swear.

The psychic takes her time before she speaks. She leans back in her chair, eyeing me up and knitting her thick fingers behind her head. She leans forward and shuffles her tarot cards, keeps her eyes glued to my face.

'You're not buying it, English, am I right? You don't buy into all this voodoo bullshit?'

She takes me off guard. I wasn't expecting a pre-emptive strike.

'Don't worry, you're not going to hurt my feelings. But if you don't believe in the future, then I'd just as soon not bother making something up. That OK by you?'

'It's fine by me,' I say, crisply. 'But it's cruel what you just did to Tess.'

She curls her lip.

'What did I do? She comes once a month, I spin her some new bullshit story. She gives me some money, I give her some comfort, everyone goes away happy.'

'Surgery won't make her happy.'

'She's going to do it anyway, what's the difference? This is a big operation for me, you understand? Next week I change from man into woman. Is it a crime to want a good friend like Tessa by my side? Is it bad of me to need a hand to hold? I have no family here, they are all back in Cuba, they have no control over how they live their lives. I owe it to my mother, to my father, to my brother, to live my life exactly how I should. I do what I need to get through it. If I need to take a friend . . . I'll take a friend.'

Her face creases up, heavy and lined, and I realise that she's anxious and scared.

'When I'm bandaged and bleeding who knows how I will feel?

Who knows how it will all work out for me? Fuck,' she says, dejectedly, leaning, back in her chair. 'If only I were psychic.'

'How you kids doing? Am I interrupting?'

'No, Baby, don't worry. We're almost done.'

'Orla saw a journey over water.'

'She did?'

'I saw her brother right here in Miami.'

'*Where?* Did you see him somewhere specific?'

'No, alas, he moves around too much. But he misses his sister and his family. He wishes he was with them, he wishes they were here. He thinks of them and misses them every day.'

Orla smiles wanly at Tess. This is the story we decided to tell.

'So . . . OK, well that's good news, right? At least we know he's definitely out here.'

'Yeah,' I say. 'It is. It's good to know.'

'And what about your love life, you and Michael? Did you deal up the tarot cards for that?'

Orla looks at me. I shake my head.

'Really, Tess, I don't think I want to—'

'No . . . you *must* . . . it's important. She's sort of getting back with her ex-husband,' Tess explains. 'And he's cute, it's so romantic. I mean, it has to work out between the two of them.'

Orla says she'll try to read it in my palm. She runs her fingers over my life line and my love line as if she's examining them for calluses.

'I'm sorry,' she says, finally, laying down my hand. 'I don't see a good ending for you. This man does not care for you, he treats you badly.'

'No,' says Tess. 'He doesn't. He treats her well.'

'In the future he will use you like he used you before. Your lines tell me this man is bad news for you.'

Tess looks forlorn; she'd hoped for a better ending than this.

'Thanks for the fortune,' I say, in Spanish. 'Pity you had to make up something bad.'

'No, lemon face,' says Orla, frowning at me. 'I didn't make it up, I bet I'm right. You have feelings for a man who doesn't love you, who never really loved you, am I right? This is your failing. I sense this in you, I'm the same. You love men who cannot love you back. I give you this for free, as a favour. I don't need to be psychic to see that.'

A Nice Polite Fella

I drop Tess back at the flat and go for a drive on my own. The hours have been full of other people since I've been here and I need some time for myself. I end up back at the apartment building where we used to live; it wasn't intentional, it drew me here.

I find myself staring out to sea on the old wooden boardwalk, the same spot where I used to stop and chat with Mr Kazman. The pelicans are still doing their thing, flapping back and forth along the seashore – pouches swaying – until one of them folds its wings back and dives. There's an ungainly splash as it enters the water; shallow and awkward, like a child thrown into the deep end without its arm bands. Down it goes, and up it comes, nothing in its beak but sand and salt. Its feathers are heavy and slick, and I watch as it flaps hard and burns its wing muscles, struggling to break free of the waves.

How many dives does it make in a day? How long before it strikes gold and gets to eat? Does it ever get tired, disconsolate? Does it ever wish life was easier than this? It doesn't seem so. Minutes later the same bird is ready again, its keen eyes focused on the water. It turns and dips its body, deft on the ocean breezes, harvesting the merest scent of wind. This time it stops before its belly hits the surf, aborting its dive and lurching up again. It doesn't seem the least bit disappointed, not that you'd ever know.

'You like to watch the birds?'

'The pelicans? Yes. I used to watch them here when I was a kid.'

'You born here? You don't sound to me like you were born round here.'

Tess is right. There are less pensioners in Miami Beach than there used to be, but the old people haven't all fled. The man standing next to me – knuckles stiff with arthritis, left eye ripe with milky cataracts – must be ninety if he's a day. He shifts from one foot to another in his plastic sandals and breathes in through wide open nostrils, sniffing for moisture in the air. He watches the pelicans while I stare at the ocean, scanning back and forth along the shoreline for the spot where I once swam with Julio. The slim shallow inlet where we tore off our clothes; the smooth crop of rocks where we rested. The point where I sprang from the waves filled with warmth, and collided with that cold, heavy air.

'Mint Caramel?'

'Thank you.'

'They're chewy, so watch out for your teeth. The caramel can stick round your gums if you're not careful. My gums aren't so good now, they've receded.'

'Like the beach?' I say.

'Yep,' he says. 'Just like the beach.'

The sand bar is given to erosion up here, narrow and scrappy, fighting a battle with the sea. Further down the coast they restock it with finely milled rock – soft and white – but up here, they don't seem to bother. Nature takes its course: unaffected, undaunted, unstoppable.

'Lots of people from England living here,' the old man says. 'Florida's a magnet for the English.'

'It's the weather,' I say, chewing hard on the toffee.

'Sure,' he says, 'the weather, the sunshine, and the mouse. I've never been able to make much sense of it, myself. Who'd fly four thousand miles, right around the world, just to shake hands with a plastic mouse?'

He smiles and displays his reddened gums.

'You know how big the Magic Kingdom is?' he says, spreading his hands out.

'No,' I tell him. 'I don't.'

'Forty-six square miles, all told. Twice the size of Manhattan, can you believe it? Does that seem right to you?'

I tell him it doesn't.

'People like to get away, though, I guess,' he says, turning back to the sea. 'They like a place that can take them out of themselves. And it's mostly for the kids, I suppose.'

'Yeah,' I say. 'It's mostly for the kids.'

'Which apartment building did you live at?' he says, gesturing behind him. 'Where did you live when you were here?'

'The green one, the Siesta. It's hardly changed in eighteen years, I can't believe it's still here.'

'Funny,' says the man, unwrapping another caramel. 'That's what the other fella said.'

My organs flip.

'The other fella?'

'From London. Stood right here, in this exact same spot, not more than a couple of hours ago. Amazed by how little it had changed, amazed to see the old place still standing.'

'Did he tell you his name?'

'English guy? No.'

'Can you tell me . . . do you remember what he looked like?'

The old man is intrigued.

'You know this fella? What's the story? He owe you alimony, or something?'

I explain it as best I can. I reach into my pocket for a photograph and the man – his name is Samuel – fishes into his plastic bag for his reading glasses. He takes an age to put them on and I wonder if he can see well enough to read the picture.

'Yep, that's him. Neat looking fella. Nice fella, nice and polite. Said he lived out here with his family in the eighties, went back to England when his dad passed away . . . *hey!* Will you look at that. He only went and caught one. That same pelican only caught himself a *fish*.'

I ask every question I can think of, but Samuel only knows so much. He didn't seem to notice how my brother arrived and he has no notion how he left. He could have driven up here in a rental car, he might have ridden up here on the bus. Maybe he's staying out here somewhere, boarding in one of the run-down motels.

'Did he . . . did he seem OK?'

'OK?'

'Did he look unwell?'

'Nope, I wouldn't say so. He seemed pretty chipper as a matter of fact, took himself off for a good long run. Tore off his shoes and socks, left them right where you're standing now, and took off down the beach like someone had shot him right out of a gun, it was quite something to watch. Moved in this tough way, sort of strong, sort of graceful, didn't spill up too much sand as he went. When he came back to fetch his shoes he was dripping in sweat, but he didn't seem all that out of breath. Must be good to be fit. I used to be fit like that once.'

I glow. My face starts to glow. The happiness spills off my skin.

'Did you see where he went afterwards?'

'I left him sitting right here. I offered him some candy and he took a piece and shook my hand. Like I said, he was a nice fella, nice and polite.'

I walk along the beach for an age after Samuel leaves me, tracing the steps of my brother's run. I see him with his arms chugging like they did when he was a kid, I see how steady his head is on his shoulders. I have my feet in the dents that he left in the sand and I bend down so I can touch them. They are large, these marks, my brother has big feet, but the incoming waves have no respect for them. I crouch down on the sand as the high tide laps the trail, standing guard over the imprints until they fade.

'I *see* you, Pinhead!' I shout, to the waves. 'I see you. Don't you think that I don't.'

I shout this over and over at the ocean, until I'm limp and hoarse and out of breath. It makes me feel better. For some reason it makes me feel better.

Sunburnt and fresh with adrenalin, I trudge along the board-walk – up and down, up and down – checking out our old family haunts: a coffee shop that I recognise, a run-down burger bar that Daniel and I used to go to on Saturday afternoons, and the same Jewish deli where we used to buy fresh bagels – hot and crispy – and load them up with salt beef or bright orange lox. It still has those same tubs in the window; deep wooden barrels filled up with cucumbers and outsized onions all slopping about in a malt coloured broth. The vinegar looks cloudy, like Samuels's eye, like it's been sitting here stewing since we left.

I show my brother's photograph to the customers and staff but they shake their heads, so I buy myself a sandwich and head back to the car. I pull up the soft top, roll up the windows and blast my hot body with shots of cold. I missed him, that's what I think as I eat. He was here but I missed him, I missed him.

I screw up my serviette, damp and disintegrating from the meat juices and look for something clean to wipe my hands with. Tess has left her copy of the Miami Herald behind – the newspaper Orla used to scribble down her operation dates – and I tear a sheet from the listings section. As I rub the page over my fingers and palms, depositing inky black print on my skin with every small rub at the grease, a tiny advertisement takes my eye. The Southern Cross astronomical society are meeting in Bill Sadowski Park this weekend to witness a rare meteor shower. Enthusiasts are coming from all over the county, and someone important sounding is giving a lecture. No cloud cover is predicted this weekend. The skies will be clear and the view from the park, away from the city's light pollution, should be exceptionally good. Bring a picnic, it says; bring a telescope. I flatten the paper out, smooth and straight again, and slip it tight inside the back pocket of my skirt. They are expecting ten thousand people or more to descend on this park in two day's time. I'll bet my life one of them will be a nice polite fella.

The Weather Forecast

'How's the weather?'

'It's hot.'

'God, that dreadful heat . . . I never got used to how hot it was.'

'You know where I am?'

'Miami, Sylvie told me.'

What was I thinking? Of course she did.

Mum sounds well, lucid and rested – she doesn't sound distant or drunk. I'm confused by her level of alertness, confounded by her level of support. She doesn't call me stupid or tell me to come home; she believes that I'm on the right track.

'You think this man was telling you the truth?'

'He had no reason to lie, Mum. He recognised Daniel from the picture, he was right outside our old apartment.'

She rubs her head. I sense her rubbing her head.

'And he'd been running?'

'Yes, along that same stretch of beach.'

She sounds choked up, relieved, a little shocked. Her breathing deepens and quickens.

'Well,' she says. 'Thank God, then. Thank *God*.'

I let her rest for a minute. I let the good news sink in.

'He's safe?'

'Yes, Mum . . . I think he is.'

She breaks off and calls out to Robert. I listen as she tells him, as they embrace. I hear him tell her to find out more details.

'Are there any more details,' she says, when she comes back. 'Did Daniel seem, was he . . . disturbed?'

I tell her no, that he looked fit. He was polite, asking questions,

having sane conversations. Was he eating? Yes, the man said he
ate a piece of toffee. I think I hear her smiling but I know she's
confused, the same as I am. If he's well, if he's eating, if he's
mentally fit, why hasn't he contacted us?

We go round and round it on the phone and I tell her the
same things I told Sylvie. We wonder what effect the antidepressants might have had. We think long and hard about his
behaviour all last year and I quiz her about my brother's state
of mind. I ask if she kept something secret; I want to know if
she's kept something back. She sniffs hard and swears that she
hasn't.

'When the second shuttle went down, the Columbia? Did
Daniel . . . did he speak to you about it?'

'In February,' my mother says, quickly.

'You remembered, didn't you? When I told you about the date
on the pill packets, that's what you were thinking about?'

She's biting her lip. I picture her biting her lip.

'I couldn't be sure, Claire. It wasn't anything he said, we only
spoke about it briefly. You know your brother . . . he couldn't, he
doesn't like to talk.'

'But you suspected something?'

She's silent for a time.

'I should have pressed him harder,' she says, almost to herself.
'I knew he wasn't right, a mother knows. It's difficult, isn't it? For
you to talk to me, to tell me things. All three of you children are
the same.'

I'm quiet. She takes this as a yes.

'None of us were with him that first time,' she says, simply.
'None of us knows what it was like. I thought it would do them
good to be alone, your dad and Daniel. The two of them . . .
they needed some time together.'

She pauses and wonders if it's true. For the millionth time, I
think she wonders how that day went, and whether they were
happy at any point. She wonders how the drive was, what they
ate, what they spoke about: she wonders if Dad and Daniel ever
made it up.

'I should have been with them,' she whispers. 'A wife should be with her husband. A mother should be with her child.'

I hear her sniff – slowly and deeply – not with irritation, but with sorrow. A world away from me my mother sobs.

'You know what I was doing the day your father died, while you were out on the beach? I was watching TV, making brownies; singing songs, smoking pot and getting high.'

'Mum . . . you couldn't have known.'

She laughs, the edge of malicious.

'But that doesn't stop it, that doesn't stop the guilt. I don't have to tell *you* that, surely?'

I'm quiet. Glued to the spot. Feeling like a kid again, feeling like I might need to pee.

'I'm sorry,' she says. 'Claire, I'm sorry.'

'It's OK,' I say.

But it's not.

Some silence while she orders her thoughts.

'I remember seeing it,' she whispers. 'I saw it explode. I watched it spill its guts into the sky. And I was so wasted by then, you know what I thought . . . I thought it looked *pretty*. I couldn't see the horror in it, not right away. Couldn't work out what it meant. So they punished me. Brought it home to me. Made me see what suffering was. Took away my husband, ruined my son, and still it goes on, even now. We've never been right since it happened, not one of us. Not me, not Sylvie, not Daniel and not you . . . not Claire.'

I shift from side to side, like she can see me. I want to turn my face away from the phone.

'Are you still there . . . ?'

I nod. I tell her I'm nodding. I hear Robert approaching in the background, offering her some tea, laying a hand on her shoulder.

'He never talked about it, he didn't speak to anyone. We should have got him some help, Claire . . . we should have got him some help.'

She puts her hand over the receiver. I'm quiet. I just let her cry.

'Will you let Kay know,' I say, gently, when she recovers. 'She wasn't at home, I couldn't find her.'

'Of course, of course,' she says, blowing her nose. 'I'll tell her you're there, that someone's seen him. She's going to be . . . so happy.'

She offers to send me some money. I tell her I'm doing OK. I tell her about the astronomy meeting out at the park this weekend and she thinks it's as good a place as any to look. She's coming back from Scotland tomorrow. She can't begin to say how relieved she is.

'I knew he was alive, I never doubted it,' she says. 'Not my clever Daniel, not for a second. Stay out there, Claire, with my blessing. Bring him back home to us, safely,' she says. 'I'm depending on you . . . we all are, we're depending on you to bring him back.'

'You don't think Sylvie ought to come?'

'No, I don't think so, poor Sylvie. She wouldn't know the first place to start.'

I leave the phone hanging in my hand after she's gone, playing her words over in my head. Wondering if she meant it. Wondering what she was thinking. Wondering if I heard her quite right.

'Hey.'

'Hey.'

'You're up?'

'What time is it?'

'Almost five.'

'Shit, I slept all day. What's happened?'

I look down at Michael: mouth full and wide, body naked in thin sheets, eyes low and lazy from sleep. He already has the start of a suntan, just from our one day in the sun. Freckles have broken out on the bridge of his nose and the pastiness has gone from his cheeks. He kisses me on the neck, then the lips. He pulls me into bed with him, sour and sticky from sleep. He asks me how I am, how I'm feeling. He pushes his hands under my T-shirt and strokes his hands over my breasts.

'Who were you speaking to?'

'My mum.'

He recoils, as if he's just spotted the snake.

'She on your back, Shorty? She want you to come home? Just say the word and I'll take her out.'

He puts up his hands and makes comedy fists like he's going to box her.

'No,' I say. 'Quite the opposite, she actually wants me to stay.'

A smile breaks out on Michael's face as I explain it. He hugs me. We stand up. He holds out his hands and dances me up and down on the mattress.

'Fuck . . . are you *sure*? This guy really saw him . . . I mean, there's *no* words, this is great.'

He wraps his warm fingers round my waist and offers to take me anywhere I want: a restaurant, a bar, to the ends of the earth, anywhere at all that I'd like to celebrate. I feel close to him, near to him, happy to be with him, he cares about me still: I think he does. You have to take Michael in doses; he can't be like this all the time. Other people are safer, sturdier, more supportive, but that's not the way Michael is. You wouldn't want to rely on him in a moment of crisis but when things are going well there's no one bolder; more playful, more full of life. He thinks we should spend the day dancing. He thinks we should hire a plane: one of those aircraft that fly up and down the shoreline trailing advertisements behind their wings like giant ribbons.

'We'll do our own advert for Daniel,' he says, spreading his arms out. 'A big red banner with Huey's phone number on it: *Has anyone seen Daniel Ronson?*'

I like it. I sort of want to do it. But it might scare him off and the last thing I want to do is scare him.

'Of course, you're right. You're totally right.'

Maybe it's just the elation, maybe it's just the relief, but here in this tiny, hot windowless room I feel my guard starting to drop. I reach in and kiss Michael differently: briefly, intensely, from the heart. He feels it and kisses me back.

'God . . . you're fucking great, Claire,' he says, as we start. 'Really, you're pretty fucking great.'

We collapse down onto the sheets like our bones are made out of sand. I'm already half undressed as we fall. Michael pulls me out of the rest of my clothes, stretching my arms above my head. My skirt is unzipped, my underwear is gone. I'm underneath his body and I'm lost. And really, this is the question: what does a man in gaudy earrings and a dress know about the subtleties of love?

I'm Not In Love

'He fulfils a need.'

'Sex?'

'Yes.'

'So, you're not back in love with him?'

'No, Tess. Really, I'm not.'

'It's too soon?'

'Exactly, it's too soon.'

'And the break-up was pretty ugly?'

The break-up. I don't want to think about the break-up.

'Is this because of what Orla said? Because in that case, you ought to know, Orla's good, but she's not always right.'

'No. I'm sure she isn't.'

Tess walks in circles round the kitchen: clicking her heels, swift and agitated.

'I see the look on your faces. I see how you look at each other.'

What does she want? What does she want me to say?

'And I think that you like him, I'm pretty sure.'

I am not prepared to answer. For once in my life, this is something I'm not prepared to say.

'You're happy, right?'

'Of course I'm happy. I just found out my brother's in Miami, that he's safe.'

'No, you're happy with *Michael*? You get goose bumps, right? Your stomach's all liquid when you kiss.'

'We're not teenagers, we're divorced. We're practically middle aged. We're both . . . we're just seeing where it goes.'

'But you'd get your boobs done if he wanted you to? If that's what would keep him happy, that's what you'd do?'

It all becomes clear, now; all curiosity was leading to this.

'No, Tess, I absolutely wouldn't.'

'Well that settles it, then,' she says, crisply, walking out. 'It's highly unlikely you're back in love.'

'What's up with her?'

Michael comes into the kitchen, newly showered, still looking pleased with himself.

'She's in a mood. Her and Huey . . . I don't know. She thinks Huey wants her to get her boobs done. She thinks that's the way to prove she loves him.'

'Idiot . . . as if that makes a difference.'

Good answer. Very good answer.

'What have you got there?'

I have a map spread out in front of me. I'm looking for Bill Sadowski Park.

'I thought we'd drive out tomorrow night. The meteor shower isn't expected until late, but we'll need as much time as we can get to search the crowd.'

'Saturday?'

'Yeah. But it's not far away, only half an hour or so, I think.'

'So we'd have to leave, when?'

'I don't know, around ten . . . maybe eleven?'

Michael fixes himself a bowl of cereal. He eats it quickly, he barely lifts his face from the table.

'Is that OK? You don't mind coming with me?'

'Of course not, that's what I'm here for. There's no way I'd let you go out there alone.'

He smiles. I smile. He fixes himself another bowl of cereal.

'Hey, you guys want to come to a party? You guys both ready to go again?'

Huey has emerged from his pit. He looks immaculate: cream silk jacket, pressed linen trousers, brand new Nike trainers, fresh and white. His eyes are sparkling, his smile is on full wattage, he's carrying three different brightly coloured hats. He looks ever so slightly mad.

'Where are you headed?'

'Something going on up at the Delano. Cocktail party . . . someone important. Thought we'd wander by and check it out.'

'Gate crash, you mean?'

'Exactly. So, which hat do you think?'

'The hunting cap.'

'Really? The *hunting* cap?'

'No, I think the cowboy hat looks better.'

Tess is stood in the doorway in another of her showy, low cut dresses. She wears an elaborate push-up bra underneath it, her breasts are almost jutting into her chin.

'OK, then, . . . the cowboy hat it is.'

'You want to go?' Michael asks. 'Might be a nice way to celebrate.'

'We already celebrated.'

'Yeah,' he says, grinning. 'We did.'

Tess tuts. Huey swaps hats and smirks.

I tell Michael to go ahead without me. I still have some things that I want to do. I need to make a list of all the cheap motels near Siesta Pines and I want to get a stack of photos printed. I'm going to hand out photocopies of my brother's picture with Huey's phone number on them when we get to Sadowski Park, and I want to put some up in the motel lobbies, if they'll let me.

'You don't mind if I go? You don't want me to stay here and help?'

'No. Really, I'm fine.'

Michael bends down and rubs the back of my neck, and I hold his hand still for a moment.

'I might come on later.' I say. 'Let me know if you go on somewhere else.'

It all takes much longer than I thought. I get photocopies printed, I make lists of appropriate hotels, I get tired and have to stop for food. I have to get some sleep. I've been running on adrenalin for four days straight, and at eight o'clock precisely, it runs right out. I feel like I've been slapped with a hammer; I have an overwhelming need to lie down. I trudge back to the flat, collapse on the red lip sofa, and pass out for a couple of hours with the photocopies scattered across my chest like giant confetti. I wake feeling achy and sore, my limbs stiff and bent out of shape. My body wants to go straight back to sleep again, but even laid out on the mattress in the bedroom, my mind is alert and wide awake.

I get up, it's almost midnight. I wonder where the guys are, if they're still at the same hotel, the same party. No one has phoned, at least I don't think they have: perhaps I just didn't hear it. I begin to feel lonely and low so I switch on the TV for company. Nothing, just re-runs and endless stupefying adverts: adverts before the programme starts, adverts before it ends, adverts after every single scene. It makes my eyes sore so I reach for the remote.

I didn't mean to switch the video recorder on, but somehow or another, as I press another button, Huey's feature film starts to play. I wonder if it's OK for me to watch it. I wonder if he'll mind me taking a look. The titles scroll and here comes the film's name: *The Outsiders;* starring Huey Roberts Junior. Bad name. Bad titles. Bad film. I know exactly what this is going to be like.

In the fifteen years of my fully adult life, I've not been surprised all that often. Maybe it's because I look on the black side of things, maybe it's because I don't expect too much. Things are rarely much better than you think they're going to be, the best you can hope for is that they're not measurably worse.

I let the tape crackle and roll. The film stopped just over two minutes ago but I can't bring myself to turn it off. The plot was OK, the set-ups were fine, but the lead held the whole thing together. The actor I saw on the screen was nothing at all like the man: a little bit Brando a little bit Penn and, weirdly, a little bit Monroe. Some performers imitate other human beings when they act, some simply imitate themselves. But where was Huey? I couldn't see him, hear him or feel him; his physical being was altered. None of his emotional ticks or physical mannerisms were on show, he was some person utterly other. His performance was spot on, sure-footed and real; forceful and compellingly spare. This means one of two things: either Huey has changed out of all recognition since this film was made, or Huey Roberts Junior is a genius.

The commotion starts in the early hours. In my head I'm half dreaming, half asleep and I think it's the sound of my parents arguing. I smell the perfume of my mother's hand-rolled cigarettes, I see her reading a battered copy of *The Woman's Room*. Dad says she's changed. Mum says she thought that's what he wanted. Dad says he doesn't know what he wants. Well you'd better decide. You better decide. Do it *now*.

'Decide what?'

'Are you going to bed by yourself or are we going to have to call the police?'

'You're gonna call the police, to put me to *bed*?'

'I swear, so help me God. You go to bed right this second or I'm calling the police.'

'Where's the snake? Where's that shitty snake? I'm going to strangle the shitty fucking snake.'

'Michael . . . *do* something.'

'I don't know what to do.'

'Michael, he's going for the tank.'

The sound of glass breaking; my mother throwing a plate.

'He *has* him. Oh no . . . oh no. Please Huey, please Huey. *Stop!*'

The sound of . . . what? Something being hit against a fridge? A body, an arm. A coil of snake flesh.

'Jesus Christ . . . you knocked him out . . . you actually knocked him right out.'

'Shit, I didn't mean to . . . is it dead?'

'I . . . yes. Yes, I think so.'

I stand at the kitchen door. The scene is bleak. Huey laid out on the table, blood dripping off Michael's fist. Tess's party outfit is ripped up and torn, and a dead boa constrictor is laid out on the floor, it's long body lifeless and limp; it's head bowed and half strangled off. Tess is heaving in between sobs. I think she will throw up soon. Michael looks like he's in shock. I don't know what to say, who to comfort. I don't know who it is I'm meant to hug. I feel like anything could happen. The violence might erupt again, it's there in the room; atoms of it racing to four corners of the wall that might snap back together at any second. I'm crying. I'm crying out. Tess is picking up a knife and holding it to her breasts. I shout at her to stop but she doesn't hear me.

'Hey. *Hey*. Claire, it's all right . . . you're having a bad dream . . . come on, wake up.'

I sit bolt upright on the mattress; my limbs are sticky with perspiration. I try hard to focus in the dark.

'Is it OK? Is everyone . . . are you all right?'

'I'm fine. I'm fine . . . try and relax now. I'll tell you all about it in the morning.'

'I heard . . . I thought . . . did I hear fighting?'

'Huey, he's pretty mashed. He had another go at the snake.'

'It's dead.'

'No. It isn't, it's alive. Tess calmed Huey down, he's gone to bed.'

I lay back down on the mattress. I still feel a little panicked, disorientated.

'I watched him,' I say, 'while you were out. On the video . . . I watched Huey's film.'

'Did you,' says Michael, yawning and stroking my head. 'How was it?'

'It was . . . it was good.'

Michael curls up beside me, holding me tight until my heart slows.

'I wondered where you'd got to,' I say, quietly. 'It got so late. You never called.'

'I'm here now,' he tells me. 'I'm here now.'

Guess Who That Party Was For?

Huey is sat in the living room, sorting through his drawer full of coupons: money off burgers and wine boxes, and discounts on whitening toothpaste and fungicidal sprays for athlete's foot. A visit to the Everglades; discount entry to the zoo; a free guided tour of the deco district.

'You want this?'

I shake my head.

'You sure? It's a pretty cool tour. If you want to know about the history, the architecture of this place, this tour is a good place to start.'

I thank him. I take the coupon. Huey goes back to his sorting.

'Aren't you going to throw any of them away?'

'Maybe the lice powder. I don't think I'm likely to get hair lice.'

He stops. He thinks. He runs his hand over his trousers.

'Unless I get them in my pubic hair. I might need this if I ever get them in my pubes.'

He folds the lice powder coupon neatly back into the centre of the pile. Just in case.

'So, did we wake you last night? I'm sorry about that . . . I was in an odd sort of mood when we got home.'

'That's OK. This is your place . . . it's good of you to let us stay here. You don't have to keep quiet for me.'

'You think I'm weird, though, I suppose? You heard me try to get at the snake?'

'I was half asleep. I thought . . . maybe I dreamt it?'

'No, you didn't dream it. I was wasted last night. I drank far too much at that party.'

I try hard to look sympathetic. Huey decides to change the subject.

'So, who's your favourite actor?' he says, testing me. 'In films. Who's your favourite actor of all time?'

'I don't know . . . Brando, De Niro . . . Nicholson maybe?'

Huey looks disappointed, he shakes his head.

'No, *no*. You're saying that because you think you ought to. You're saying that because somebody else told you they were good. Think for yourself. Who do *you* really like. When you see them on the screen, who really moves you?'

I try to think of a good film I've seen recently. I try to come up with a great performance. I still think I like Jack Nicholson. But nothing he's done lately. I wonder if I should tell Huey that.

'Well, I don't know, it's difficult . . . I'd need some more time to think about it.'

'You should know just like that,' says Huey, snapping his fingers. 'If they're great you should know just like that. My favourite actor is Eduardo Garcia. He's new, he's Peruvian. Peruvian cinema is up and coming.'

'Really . . . well . . .'

'You've never heard of him, right?'

I shake my head.

'Amazing. *Amazing*. This guy's got everything going on. It's like he's mainlining emotion when he's up there. He's not done all that much yet, nothing commercial anyway, but man, he's going to be huge. Integrity, that's what he's got. He's not in it for the money, not for the fame game. He's in it for the passion, for the art.'

Huey visibly relaxes in his chair; just thinking about this actor cheers him up.

'That's what Tess said about you,' I say, gently, as Huey reshuffles his coupons.

'Really?'

'Well, not in so many words, but I think that's what she meant. She said it wasn't about vanity or ego with you; she said it was all about the acting.'

'Tess doesn't know shit about acting,' he says. 'She just wants the big house and the pool. She want the position, the status, the money. Tess just wants the dresses and the tits.'

'Huey, I don't think that's fair.'

'No,' he says, softly. 'I know it's not.'

I stare right at him. He looks tired. He has no hat on this morning, and his head, when you see it naked, it sort of shocks you. Some men look OK bald, but Huey doesn't. His cranium is all out of shape. It's bumpy, rough and asymmetrical, it's hard to believe he looked so good with hair.

'I watched your film last night. I'm sorry . . . if I wasn't supposed to.'

'What did you think?' he says, not bothering to look up.

'Well . . . I mean, I don't know all that much about it . . . perhaps I'm not the best one to judge. I don't even know who my favourite actor is.'

'Don't vacillate, Claire. Give it to me straight. You're the audience, you're the real people. You're not an expert so you're the best kind of judge, man. It's all about someone like you.'

I take a breath.

'I thought you were brilliant. I thought you were bold and spare and absolutely real and I should say, before I watched it . . . I didn't think you had anything like that in you. When your wife closed the door at the end of the film and you walked away, I felt like you might die from pain.'

Huey looks floored.

'You're being honest? You're not just spinning me a line?'

'No. I promise you. I'm not.'

Huey digs to the bottom of his empty coupons bag and pulls out a creased clipping from the *LA Times*.

'It wasn't a big budget feature,' he says. 'We didn't get all that much press. But they thought I was OK, the critics that saw it. They seemed to think I did OK.'

He did more than OK, the reviewer loved him.

'I lose myself in front of the camera,' he says, rubbing his head. 'I'm like a blank canvas, or something. I don't know . . . it's hard to work out. I'm not so great at expressing myself, not in real life but it's like the camera, it gives me permission. I don't have to put on any front. I don't feel choked up or self-conscious. It's some weird fucked-up alchemy . . . it's exquisite. I just . . . I become someone else.'

He trails off. He sighs.

'Now all I get offered is these stereotyped roles. Bad man number three. Young thug with chainsaw. Unhinged psychopath with sword. Tess had all these dreams for us, you know? She had the whole thing planned right out. She wanted us to be a celebrity couple or some crap like that, she was fixing up all these inter- views for me to do. It was . . . I don't know . . . the publicity part, I always hated it. I never knew what they expected me to be. Then the hair went, then the confidence, then . . . well, you know the rest of the story. If I could just have done that film, man. If they'd only let me wear that wig. They wouldn't even have had to have paid me.'

Huey gets back to his sorting. He finds a coupon for oven- ready turkey: fifteen per cent off at Heartland supermarkets.

'Do you like turkey?'

'Not really.'

'No, me neither.'

He folds the coupon back into his pile, rubs at his temples and apologises for being so morose.

'Sorry,' he says. 'It's this hangover, it's fierce.'

'Sure . . . don't worry. I understand.'

'Great news about your brother though, huh? I meant to say something before . . . it really is great news.'

'Thanks, Huey, it is. All I have to do now is find him.'

Huey stares at his hands.

'You ever think . . . I mean, did you ever wonder? What if he doesn't want to be found?'

'It's funny, someone else said that. But that's not the point.'

'Isn't it?'

'No. It's really not. People miss him, Huey. People really miss him.'

★   ★   ★

I wake Michael up for the second time in two days. Again he pulls me down into bed.

'Where were you? I missed you.'

'I got up. I was talking to Huey.'

'Is he OK? Did he tell you?'

'Tell me what?'

'About last night.'

'He said he got drunk. He said that he tried to attack the snake again.'

Michael sniggers and stretches his legs.

'He didn't tell you about the cocktail party? He didn't tell you who was there?'

'No.'

'Guess who it was?'

'I don't know Michael, who was it?'

'Guess.'

I frown; I'm done with guessing.

'His nemesis, Shorty, that's who. The party was only thrown by Harvey Weinstein.'

'He was *there*?'

'Yes.'

'Huey saw him?'

'For a second.'

'What did he . . . what did Huey say?'

Michael smiles and yawns.

'He couldn't get over how small he was. He kept saying it over and over, while he drank. How could this man be so small?'

Portuguese Man-of-War

Today the green ocean is full of rip tides, prowling for swimmers with greedy arms. Stiff onshore breezes beat the waves into a frenzy and freshen the sticky air with blasts of sweetness. The mugginess has gone, all the heaviness. We can breathe. We can finally breathe.

Michael and I have hired sun beds and umbrellas. We're laid out next to one another in our bathing suits, surrounded by the accoutrements of coupledom: shared tubes of sun cream, shared bottled water, magazines and books that we can swap. I rub sun-block on Michael's shoulders before they burn. I offer him a pretzel before he asks. He reaches out to touch me for no reason at all, other than to make sure I'm still there.

'Your nose looks red.'

'Does it?'

'You should put something on it.'

'One of those cardboard beaks, maybe?'

Michael tears the back cover off my magazine and begins to fashion me a protective beak. It looks like a miniature wizard's hat, I put it on. I try not to sneeze or blow it off.

'It looks good.'

'Not stupid?'

'Stupid but good. I still fancy you in it.'

I get a rush. There on the beach with a ridiculous paper cone on my nose. Then a breeze comes along and whips it off.

My magazine is called the *Amateur Astronomer* and it's not an overly entertaining read. It's full of articles about far away planets and galaxies, but even though the subject matter is astounding, magical even, it still reads something like a wallpaper catalogue.

'Did you know the Milky Way is six hundred thousand light years across?'

'No.'

'That's pretty big.'

'Yes, it is.'

'Do you find that interesting?'

Michael thinks.

'It's impressive,' he says, licking the salt off a pretzel. 'But in essence it's just an abstract fact. It's hard to connect with. What exactly does it mean? What difference does it make to you and me?'

I think about this for a while.

'It makes me feel small. Insignificant.'

'And that makes you feel better, or worse?'

'Better.'

'Really?'

'No. Worse.'

We listen to the waves. We listen to the wind. Michael goes back to his book. I sit up and watch the skateboarders fighting with gravity; I watch the skinny girls dancing like cornstalks in the breeze in front of their shiny silver boom boxes. You can lose yourself so quickly in the big stuff. The small stuff; it's all in the small stuff.

'Are you thirsty? We ran out of water.'

'I dunno, I suppose. A little bit.'

'The pretzels made me thirsty. Do you think that I eat too much salt?'

'How much are you meant to eat?'

'I don't know.'

'You're probably OK then.'

'I'll get us an iced tea,' he says pulling on his trainers. 'What do you want, peach or lemon?'

'Um . . . peach.'

'Sugar or sugar free.'

'Sugar.'

'Sugar it is.'

I treasure these domestic exchanges. This is the language of love.

The *Amateur Astronomer* is all worked up about the meteor shower tonight. It's going to peak at two in the morning, eastern time, and we can expect to see as many as one hundred and fifty of them in an hour. I'm exceptionally lucky to be here; the next celestial shower of this magnitude doesn't occur until August 2008. It turns out that meteors are far smaller than I'd realised, the size of a single grain of sand. How can a particle the size of a grain of sand produce such a dazzling sight? The answer is all to do with speed. This shoddy scrap of debris from a lonely comet's tail enters the earth's atmosphere at unimaginable velocity. The Space Shuttle travels at eight miles a second, these meteors travel sixty to seventy. They burn up as they go, until there's nothing left, but for a few brief seconds they glow so bright and look so colourful we wish on them and call them shooting stars. What would I wish for? I'm not even sure. I close my eyes and try to think of a hundred and fifty different wishes.

Michael has been gone a long time. I think I must have fallen asleep because my cheek is sore and my left arm is creased and I'm feeling shivery underneath my towel. There's no peach tea getting warm in the sand and no ex-husband snoozing next to me on the sun-bed. I'd like to go for a swim but the danger flag is still fluttering on the life guard station and I can't see anyone else in the water. There's a jellyfish sign up there too, now: *Beware, Portuguese man-of-war.* What a strange name for a jellyfish to have. I wonder how it got that kind of name? You don't associate the Portuguese with warring. I don't associate the Portuguese with anything, much. Golf courses. The Algarve. Sweet custard cakes . . .

Shit. I sit up straight. The sun-lounger pings and folds over, threatening to squash me flat like a sandwich. Did he do that? Did Michael go out there and swim? It's the kind of reckless thing he would do. When we went on a winter break once, to Cornwall, he went swimming in the sea before breakfast even though the waves were six feet tall. I stood on the rocks and called for him to come back, but he just kept on swimming further out: testing himself; pushing himself; making me fretful and worried. He disappeared for a moment and I thought that he'd drowned, and a thousand thoughts went through my head. I wondered if I'd be able to save him. I wished that I knew what to do. Perhaps I should construct some kind of flotation device? From what? From my jeans? From my anorak? What if he'd been strangled by seaweed? What could I use to cut him free? I was down to my bra and my knickers. I had a sharp stone in my hand to cut away the seaweed. I was up to my knees in the water, about to dive in, when he surfaced.

'What are you standing here for?'
    'I thought you might be out there, in the sea.'
    'There are rip tides.'
    'I know.'
    'You're not supposed to go swimming when there are rip tides.'
    'You would.'
    'No, I wouldn't. It's too dangerous.'
    I'm at the edge of the beach with a towel wrapped round my shoulders, staring down at my toes. The sun has dipped behind the clouds and I'm chilly. I have goose bumps on my arms.
    'You've been gone a long time.'
    'Sorry, I lost track.'
    'Did you bring the peach tea?'
    'The tea? No, uh . . . I forgot.'
    He's dressed now, in his jeans and his sun-faded T-shirt, his clothes smell of stale tobacco.

'I spent my money on a cigar instead,' he says, sheepishly. 'But, hey, the girl swore it was Cuban. I don't know if it is . . . I mean how can you tell? But it tastes pretty good. Here, I saved some for you.'

Michael pulls the stub out of his pocket: one end damp and chewed, the other end scorched black and tarry. I light it and take a drag. It tastes rich, chocolaty, strong. It makes me cough.

'Looks like it might rain,' says Michael, putting his arm round me.

Clouds are welling up on the horizon; black, angry, bloated with droplets of rain.

'I hope it clears up by tonight,' I say, tensely. 'If it's cloudy Daniel might not bother going.'

'What makes you think he'll go there anyway, to the park? You can see the meteors from all over southern Florida. Maybe he'll just watch from the beach.'

Why will Daniel go to Bill Sadowski park tonight? He'll go because he won't feel so alone. He'll go so he can share his enthusiasm with other people; people who feel something of the same way he does. He'll feel comforted by them and reassured. Even though his family are a world away, he'll feel some connection with other human beings. When they nod and whoop, he'll nod and whoop too. When they look through their telescopes, he'll join them. He'll swap facts and figures with men and women he's never met, and they'll seem like friends for a moment. You need to share your world with other people. Otherwise, what's the point?

'The park is far enough away from the city that the sky won't be polluted with light,' I say authoritatively. 'The view will be better, that's why he'll go.'

Michael shrugs.

'If it was me, if I was into that kind of thing, I'd find my own place to watch it. The top of a hill, halfway up a mountain. Maybe out on—'

'An island?'

'Perfect. *Perfect.* An island. I'd take a boat and a bottle of whisky. Maybe a spliff and a girl.'

'A girl?'

He gives me a tight squeeze. He yawns.

'You, Shorty. You know I'd take you.'

I Said I'd Be There. I'll Be There.

The thunderstorm breaks just as we're leaving the beach, drenching our clothes as we run for cover. I've never seen anything like it: lightning in sheets, forks, balls, snarling and howling out to sea. People take shelter under the awnings: chatting, drinking, smoking, eating, but most of them aren't even watching it. I can't take my eyes off the lightning and Michael seems as transfixed as I am. We wonder what causes it. We know it's electricity, that it's to do with negative and positive charges in the air – ions or something like that – but neither of us knows the answer precisely. Daniel would know. He'd roll his eyes and spell it right out for us, wondering why we didn't take better notice.

'You don't know anything about the world around you, Claire. I think you do it on purpose.'

'I know how to speak four languages already. Let's hear you try and speak to me in Serbo-Croat.'

'What's the point?'

'How do you mean?'

'What's the point of speaking a different language?'

'Daniel, don't be so stupid.'

'No, Mum, I'm serious. It's a serious question.'

Back from university. Who does he think he is? Thinks he knows the answer to everything.

'I mean it. What use is it, really? How does one language differ from another? It's just an altered set of vocal patterns. The words will be different, depending on which nationality you're speaking to, but the sentiment is precisely the same.'

Where do you start? Where do you start with an argument like that?

'It means I can communicate, Pinhead. With *people*, with lots of different people.'

'Strangers, you mean?'

'No . . . not just strangers. It means I can visit a country and get to know it. I can dig beneath its surface, peel back its skin, find out what's really going on. You wouldn't understand it, why would you? You're a robot, you're practically mute.'

Seventeen years old. New home, new dinner table. Still calling my brother the same names. Different words. Same sentiment.

Back at the flat, after the rain, Huey and Tess have made it up again. I was expecting them to be in a state of depression or madness but everything appears to be OK. The snake is safe, the apartment is quiet, classical music plays softly from the radio. The two of them are curled up on the sofa and Huey is feeding Tess green grapes. Huey is talking about an acting class he used to take in New York City and Tess is reminiscing about her days at cookery school: she was top of her class, she was a natural, she was learning to cook cordon bleu.

'You two get wet? What about that storm, wasn't it amazing?'

'Yeah,' I say. 'It really was.'

The sky is perfectly clear now. The sun came out the second the rain stopped, and all the clouds rolled away like a heavy curtain.

'Tropical storms, that's what they're like,' Tess says. 'Sudden, short and intense. Don't you love how they clean up the atmosphere?'

'Yeah,' says Huey. 'I do.'

They're so relaxed together the two of them, they don't seem tense or anxious in the least. The shape of them, all loose and liquid, it makes me and Michael look stiff. Tess oozes out of the cushions and sits up and Huey rests his chin on her shoulder.

'So,' she coughs. 'There's something I wanted to tell you both.

I've booked myself in. This Monday. I'm going into the hospital with Orla.'

'For the surgery?'

She nods.

'Huey's right behind me, aren't you Huey?'

Huey smiles and strokes Tess's boobs.

'Well . . . if that's what you've decided.'

'I have.'

'If you think it'll make you happy?'

'I do. Plus, it'll help with my career. If you've got a singing voice as weak and screechy as I have, you need all the help you can get to be a star.'

Huey smiles. Tess gets into her stride.

'The thing with plastic surgery,' Tess says, knowingly. 'Is that you have to be sure you're doing it for the all right reasons. You can't do it to please someone else, and I'm not. I'm having this operation for *me*.'

I scowl at her. I gesture towards Huey.

'No Claire, you're wrong, I was too. I'm not doing it for Huey, any more. We talked about it, didn't we, baby? And he couldn't care less what I look like. He appreciates me just the way I am. It's just something I want to do all for myself. To make me feel more . . . um . . .'

'Confident?'

'Right, Huey, exactly. That's right.'

'You're not worried about the risks?'

'What risks?'

'They could burst, they could look bad. They could leak out from under your armpit and poison you.'

'They don't do that any more, that's all hype. And Doctor Roland is an amazing plastic surgeon.'

'Dr Roland?'

'He does sex changes mostly. But if he can make tits for a guy then he has to be able to do a good job on me, right? I already have them in place.'

'How much is it costing?'

'A thousand dollars.'

'Isn't that . . . a bit cheap?'

'Uh . . . I'm getting a deal. Through Orla. It's sort of . . . uh . . . at a discount.'

I squat down on a cushion; I don't know what to say. Tess switches her attention to someone else.

'What do you think Michael? You're awful quiet.'

'Me?' says Michael, not bothering to look at her. 'I think it will hurt.'

'I'm good with pain. I have a high tolerance threshold.'

'Well, then I'm sure you'll do OK.'

He stretches his arms above his head and begins to peel off his damp shirt.

'That's it? That's all you're going to say to her?'

'What do you want me to say? It's only a boob job. Thousands of women get boob jobs every day.'

'She doesn't need it, she's fine as she is.'

Michael holds up his hands; he doesn't want to get into it.

'So, Monday at noon,' says Tess, definitively. 'If you're wondering where we are, that's where we'll be. Huey too, he's going to come along with me.'

'That's right. On Monday. The both of us. We'll both be at the hospital. That's where we'll be.'

'You're sure about this?'

'We're sure.'

'I can't say anything to change your mind?'

'Nope. We have it all booked.'

There's nothing to be done. There's nothing more I can say. Huey and Tess go back to their grapes; Michael and I go and take a shower.

'So, do you want to grab some food before we drive out to the park?'

'Definitely, definitely. And then I need to stop off at the Wheel for an hour or so.'

'The Wheel? What's the Wheel?'

'That jazz club we ended up at, after we'd checked out your dad's hotel.'

I stop. I barely remember it. I was lost that evening, I can't even picture what it looked like.

'But it's a late place isn't it, and we'd have to be out of there by ten?'

'You said we didn't need to leave until eleven.'

'Well, at a push. But I'd rather get there early. It's . . . important.'

Michael scrubs himself down with a towel: thinking, thinking; spending a long time on his toes.

'Michael, is something wrong?'

'No. Nothing's wrong.'

'What's going on? Is there something going on?'

'I have an audition tonight.'

He says it out straight; just like that.

'It might not be anything, but it might be something. Paid work. Out here. A month or two's residency. At this club and a couple of others.'

His toes. He's still drying his toes.

'When did you . . . when was it arranged?'

'Huey introduced me to the music booker when we were down there. I just ran into him on the beach. We talked, I bought him a cigar.'

'Why didn't you say anything? You never said.'

'I'm saying it now.'

'Well . . . can't you audition for him tomorrow?'

'Can't do it . . . it has to be tonight.'

'Why?'

'Claire . . . it just does.'

His voice is terse, the beginnings of angry. He notices, he tries to calm down.

'I'm sorry,' he says. 'But this guy, he's quite important. I can't piss him off now, it's all been put in place.'

I want to ask how the music booker in a dingy Miami night club can be important to someone like Michael. I want to ask him why he arranged to audition tonight and why he can't put things off for one more day. But I don't, because he's looking at me like I shouldn't.

'So . . . how long will it take?'

'An hour, tops. I have to be in there by nine.'

It's cutting it fine. We both know it's cutting it fine.

'If it takes any longer, I'll come on and meet you later at the park. You take the car, I'll ride up later in a taxi.'

Is this what he wants? Is this what he's angling for? Does he want me to do this without him? I feel clammy from the shower and flushed from the heat. I don't want to go out to that park all alone. I don't want to be the one wandering around the grounds with the smudged photocopies tucked under my arm while everyone else has their eyes glued on the sky. It feels foolish all of a sudden. Difficult. Unlikely.

'Michael, I don't want to fuck this up.'

'You won't. Why would you fuck this up?'

'I have to bring him home.'

'You will. You *will.*'

'People are depending on me.'

'And so they should.'

He puts an arm around me. Ruffles my hair.

'Come on now. This is a long shot. It'll probably come to nothing. Who knows?'

I realise he's talking about the audition.

'So why bother going, then? It's just another club gig, you can get one of those any time.'

He frowns.

'I know it's bad timing, but it had to be tonight, and I promise I'll be as quick as I can.'

'You'll come on afterwards, if you're late?'

'Absolutely. No question. Where would be a good place to meet, do you think?'

Ten past ten, I'm sitting in a coffee shop two blocks down from the Wheel. If I'm not back by ten go without me, he said. I'll meet you by the entrance at midnight. There's going to be a lecture before the meteors start. There will probably be a stage or a lectern. Good, so we'll meet at the lectern. Or the entrance. Or the biggest telescope we can find. The central place, whatever that turns out to be. Don't worry. He'll find me. Relax.

Twenty past ten. Why can't I get up? I've finished my coffee. I should pay.

'You want a refill?'

'I . . . no.'

'You're all set?'

'Yes. I am. I'm all set.'

I could go down to the jazz club and see if he's finished, but he didn't want me in there while he auditioned; he thought that I might put him off. He needs to concentrate, to get into his performance mode; he takes on a different persona when he plays. He needs to dig down deep into the music and the rhythms. He didn't want to have to worry about the clock.

Half past ten. I climb into the car and spend a few minutes looking in the rearview mirror. Hoping. Hoping he'll show up. My breathing is tight, the air is closing in; it's getting humid again. What happened to that breeze, that blessed breeze?

Twenty to eleven. He's definitely not coming. I roll down the soft top, start up the engine and drive off the island on my own.

Nowhere to Run

It's all so much bigger than I thought it would be: a wild sweep of nature trails, picnic grounds and woods, spread out over more than thirty acres. Most of the serious astronomers have gravitated to the observatory at the southern entrance to the park, but everywhere you look, families, couples, children and slouchy teens are pouring in and setting up camp. Men hump coolers and cameras, women carry telescopes and canvas chairs; kids walk briskly – hopping and jumping – fuelled with the excitement of staying up late. Everyone wants to get a good pitch, all fifteen thousand of them.

'*Really*? You think there's that many?'

'Not yet, no. But there will be by the time the show starts. Going to be quite a thing. You ever seen one before?'

I shake my head.

'Know much about meteors per se?'

'No.'

The teenager in the yellow shorts with the yellow hair and the goofy smile makes it his mission to enlighten me. He has a book, several books, about his person, and he flicks through the heaviest, balancing its well-worn spine on his portable camping table.

'These particular meteors are called Perseid.'

'Right.'

'Perseid meteors come from the comet, Swift-Tuttle. Every 130 years, the comet swoops in from deep space, way out beyond Pluto, and plunges through the plane of our solar system, not all that far from Earth's own orbit.'

'I see.'

The boy squints.

'Astronomers used to worry that Swift-Tuttle might hit our planet one day.'

'Will it?'

'No.'

He quotes from his book.

'Recent data suggests there's no danger of a collision for at least another millennium, probably longer.'

'Phew . . . that's a relief.'

'Yeah. It is. But it doesn't mean we won't get hit by something. The chances are, I mean you'd have to say, statistically speaking, the earth's bound to get hit by a comet or a significantly sized meteor of some kind. Sooner, I'd say, rather than later.'

He smiles. He almost seems pleased about it. If he had a pair of glasses on this would be the moment that he'd push them backwards on the bridge of his nose.

'But not tonight, though?'

'Nuh-uh. Definitely not tonight.'

He shifts his weight from foot to foot. I peel off one of my photocopies.

'I was wondering . . . have you come across this man?'

'Don't think so. Is he out here somewhere? Have you lost him?'

'I hope so. And yes.'

The kid blinks.

'Might be tough to find him tonight though, in all these people. It's going to be a heck of a job.'

He's right, they're still pouring in. The crowd is so dense now it looks like a solid block, a single organism. I can barely pick out the faces any more, only the shades of hair or waterproof jacket. But, I won't be disheartened. I won't.

'How many stars are out there right now?' I say, pointing to the heavens. 'How many of them are there in this one galaxy?'

'Roughly . . . around a billion.'

'Which is your favourite?'

'I'd probably have to say Betelgeuse.'

'Can you find it?'

'Sure,' he says pointing skyward, 'it's a red giant, right there, in Orion.'

I smile. This cheers me up. The boy in the yellow shorts shakes his head.

'OK, I see what you're saying. But a person isn't anything like a star. A star stays put like it's supposed to. For millions, *billions* of years. People, they tend to move about some. With people you have to know where to look.'

But I do. I know *exactly* where to look.

'If you had three minutes to live what would you do?'

'If there was going to be a nuclear war, you mean?'

'Yeah, if they set one off. If the bomb was coming, from Russia or something, where would you hide?'

'I wouldn't.'

'Why not?'

'There'd be no point.'

'You're meant to get underneath a table. You're meant to paint yourself white to deflect the heat from the blast.'

'A table? You think that's going to help? You think a table will stop your skin from peeling off like wrapping paper? You think a table will stop your eyeballs from melting out of their sockets?'

I thought about my eyeballs melting. I didn't appreciate it, not one bit.

'Well, it's never going to happen, so *there*. I don't even know why I asked.'

'Daniel, stop it now. You're scaring your sister.'

'I'm not.'

'Yes you are. Give it a rest.'

I dug my fingernails hard into the kitchen table and ran my thumb along it's rough splintered edge where the melamine had begun to peel back. Daniel ate his cornflakes noisily, kicking his chair with his heels.

'So . . . then, where . . . ?'

'Would I go?'

I nodded.

'Same place I'd go, if a rogue comet appeared, or a giant meteor was going to hit us. I'd stand in the middle of the widest open space I could find, right in front of it. Just like that.'

'You wouldn't try to run away?'

'No.'

He shook his head.

'What's the good? There'd be nowhere to run.'

I head for the widest open space I can find; away from the swampland and the patch of scrubby mangroves; away from the observatory and the towering palms. I don't see him. No one tall and limber with a young face and a middle-aged hair cut, holding his arms out to his fate. No one lonely, wandering, depressed or confused, with dirty running shoes strapped to his outsized feet. The space shrinks and tightens as people crowd into the park and eventually I give up and move away. Past the nerds with their binoculars and their sheets of elaborate star charts, past the Christians singing bible songs round a fire.

'You like a map, miss?'

'A map?'

'Help you know what it is that you're looking for.'

I'm one step ahead of him. I already know what I'm looking for.

'This is a map of the night sky. Shows you where to look for the best shooting stars. On the back here is a list of our bible meetings. How long since you last read the bible, miss?'

'Long time.'

The man reaches into his rucksack and pulls out a pocket bible.

'What you see tonight will bring you closer to God. Remind you of His hand on the universe. God made the heavens and the stars and the earth. Seven short days. That's all it took.'

'Right, well . . . uh, fast mover.'

He smiles; that smile they have.

'I'd guess you're an evolutionist, am I right?'

I don't answer. There's no point.

'Evolution is a dangerous thing, don't you doubt it. The greatest threat there is to the modern world.'

I shudder. I start to move away.

'I'll pray for you,' he says, pressing the bible towards me. 'Remember, Jesus is with you.'

I stop. I do the decent thing. I hand him one of my flyers in return.

'Who is this?'

'A missing person. My brother. I think he's out in the crowd somewhere.'

The zealot shakes his head.

'Well, you won't find him here, ma'am; far too many people. Be a miracle if you came across him tonight.'

I frown. I walk on. Seems like I'm more open to a miracle than he is.

Back at the main entrance near to where I first came in, a man is shuffling papers on the lecture stage. He's humming to himself, he looks content. I climb up the slim wooden steps behind him and cough.

'Can I help you?'

'Probably not.'

'Did you have a question about the lecture?'

'No. I didn't see the lecture.'

He has dark brown hair; wide mouth, soft skin, smart eyes.

'So?'

'So?'

'What can I do for you?'

'Are you an astronomer?'

'In my spare time. I work as a meteorologist.'

'The weather?'

'Yes.'

'So, how's it looking?'

'It's going to be clear for the rest of the night.'

'That was quite a storm earlier.'

'The edge of a hurricane, did you enjoy it?'

'I did, it was beautiful. You don't get many storms like that at home.'

I stare at him. He stares back. I like his shirt, it's a nice colour blue.

'I'm looking for someone.'

'Boyfriend?'

'No. Brother.'

He nods. He likes me. He's definitely single, I can tell.

'My girlfriend's over there. She's volunteering with the park rangers tonight. She might be able to help you.'

The meteorologist waves his girlfriend over, her name is Ashley. She looks like Nicole Kidman only short. Serious. Immaculate. Pretty. I feel dishevelled, scruffy, too tall.

'No, I haven't come across him,' she says, sweetly. 'But I'd be happy to help you with your flyers. I could hand some out if you'd like.'

'Thank you,' I say. 'I'd appreciate it.'

The meteorologist smiles. It's a beautiful smile.

'So, where you headed now?' he says.

'I thought I'd go out to the lake.'

'Any particular reason?'

'I don't know, it's stupid really. But I thought that my brother might be fishing.'

'I'm fishing, that's what I'm doing.'

'With a stick and some *bread*? That's not going to be any good.'

'Fish *like* bread.'

'No they don't.'

'How do you know?'

I didn't. I hadn't the faintest idea.

'I think they might prefer meat. Or potatoes. I left some ham on my plate, shall I go and fetch it?'

'Yeah, come on. We'll both go.'

A fishing pond in Cromer, East Anglia; an autumn visit to my Aunty Jarvis, mum's older sister. I don't know why we called her by her surname but we always did. Perhaps it's because she was a lesbian.

'Dad says Aunty Jarvis is a lesbian. Do you know what that means?'

'Course.'

'You reckon?'

'Yep. I know for sure. It means she has sex with her dog.'

Daniel stopped in his tracks. This was something. I'd shocked him.

'Aunty Jarvis has a miniature schnauzer.' I said. 'If she's a lesbian, I imagine she has sex with *it*.'

Daniel coughed. He nearly dropped his makeshift fishing rod.

'Fats, where do you even *get* an idea like that?'

'Mum's got this book which I thought was about gardening, but it's not. It's about this woman who lets her dog lick Pedigree Chum off her' – I whispered it – 'her *you know what*.'

The book was *The Secret Garden*, by Nancy Friday: a collection of women's sexual fantasies that I'd found in the corner of my mother's sock drawer while I was hunting around for *The Joy Of Sex*.

'You shouldn't be reading that.'

'Why not?'

'You're too young. And for fuck's sake that's not what a lesbian is.'

'Maybe I should ask Aunty Jarvis.'

'No, Fats, I'm telling you. You'd better not.'

Back inside the house, away from the pond, my parents and my aunt talked about this and that. Their voices strained, their inflections clipped. They talked the way relatives talk.

'Can I have the ham that I left behind please, Aunty Jarvis?'

'What do you want it for, dear?'

'Daniel's made a fishing rod and there's a pond outside with fish in it. We've been trying to catch them with bread, but I think sliced ham will do better.'

'Sorry, dear. I just gave the last of it to Max.'
'Your miniature schnauzer?'
'Yes.'
'You gave him my ham?'
'Yes.'
'And yours?'
'Yes, dear. I did. Max likes my sliced ham. It's his favourite.'

Daniel and I fell to the floor and howled. We laughed so hard we thought we'd throw up. They didn't know what was wrong with us; we were kids, who understands kids? Who knows what nonsense sets them off? All the way home in the car, in the traffic jams, we couldn't stand to catch one another's eye. My cheeks hurt from the strain of it. They hurt so much.

Daniel isn't fishing by the lake with a rod made from a stick and some bread for bait. He isn't rolling on the floor, clutching his stomach, choked up by a joke we both made. We used to talk in those days, we used to laugh; before we came out here to Florida. It was always us and them: me and Daniel versus the world.

I stare at my reflection in the lake. I can see the whole sky, clear now and vast, glinting right above my head. I know this is the kind of place that Daniel would like. It's quiet down here, private, concealed, but still wide open to the water. This is where the serious astronomers have gathered up: people in ones and twos, chatting and charting and sharing out snippets of astronomical information. No children yelling, no Christians singing, no families setting up braziers and cooking sickly smelling burgers and buns. Perhaps I should stay here a little longer. Perhaps he hasn't arrived yet. Perhaps if I wait out here patiently and dangle my toes in the water, I'll see him trudge up the hill behind me.

'Hey Fats.'
'Hey Pinhead.'
'I'm back.'
'Where you been?'
'Here and there.'

'You want to sit down for a minute?'

'Yeah. I think I'd like to sit down.'

Some shouts from the other side of the lake. I stop daydreaming and splash water on my face. I look at my watch; it's well past midnight. I suddenly have two men to look for.

Lost in Space

'You sure you don't mind me waiting up here with you?'

'No, not at all.'

'It's just, I arranged to meet my boyfriend near the park entrance. And it's so full now, I think this will be the only place he'd spot me.'

'Really, don't worry about it. You can stay up here as long as you like.'

The meteorologist's name is Connor and I'm going to watch the light show with him from up here on the lecture stage. We sit on a couple of deckchairs, sipping beer: we have the best spot in the park.

'Where's your girlfriend?'

'Out on one of the quad bikes making sure everything goes off OK.'

'Have you two been together long?'

'About a year. You?'

'Me and Michael? Uh, about a week. But we used to be married so, all in all . . . if you count the eight and a half weeks we went out before we got hitched . . . that makes it about two and a quarter years.'

Connor rubs his head.

'You two were separated?'

'Divorced.'

'And now you're back together?'

'Yes.'

Connor blinks. He shrugs. He's not going to ask me any more about it: he thinks I'm strange.

'Do you think I'm strange?'

He laughs.

'A little bit.'

It's another hour before the first perseid meteor comes into view. It streaks across the horizon: thin, uninspiring and low, accompanied by a few muted shouts from the crowd. By that time the meteorologist's girlfriend is back from her rounds and Michael is in front of the lectern shouting up at us.

'They've *started*.'

'I see that.'

'Sorry, I'm so late. I got held up at the club.'

'How did it go?'

'Pretty good. Pretty good. Can I come up there?'

Michael scrambles up onto the stage without using the stairs; he makes a big show of turning up. He has a funny story to tell about the taxi, that's not all that funny; he has news about the jazz club that I don't find interesting.

'It was great, they really liked me. I think they're going to offer me a gig.'

'For how long?'

'I don't know, they didn't say. I told them I had a few commitments to take care of.'

'Are you a musician?'

Michael simpers and rubs his fingers through his fringe, directing all attention to the meteorologist's girlfriend.

'I'm a pianist. Classically trained, I play jazz.'

The girl smiles. Connor doesn't say a word. Michael is off on a rant: who he likes, who he loves, who he hates in the world of modern jazz. He's had a line of coke – or several – and he's keen to talk about himself. I wait. I'm patient. He'll get round to it sooner or later.

'So, Claire, what's been going on? Any news?'

I shake my head.

'There's too many people, I haven't seen him.'

Michael puts his hands on my shoulders and squeezes them a little too hard. A pop like a flashbulb makes us jump and look up. A radiant, bitter-orange coloured meteor is diving towards us, dead ahead.

'We're on,' says Connor. 'Here we go.'

Every so often nature comes up with something so beguiling, so winning, it washes your mind of all thoughts and worries. A dozen shooting stars clap their hands in the sky announcing the start of the show. They race one another – playful and athletic – cajoling us, warming us up. Larger ones follow on after them – older and wiser – painting elegant arcs on the horizon. Brilliant missiles burst apart above our heads, ripping the sky like fiery whips. I feel disorientated suddenly, and unstable, like I might tumble into the very sky I'm watching; like it might suddenly devour me in its fizzy blackness. The horizon is pulsing with light, now: twenty, thirty, fifty meteors all at once, some of them combining and crossing over and almost seeming to explode. It's not a shower, it's a storm. Something rare and beautiful and largely unexpected, even by the most experienced observers.

'Fuck, it's like fireworks,' says Michael. 'It's just like watching fireworks.'

He's wrong, it's nothing like fireworks. Fireworks are man-made and ordinary: simple cones of gunpowder, garish and noisy, lit up to make tired children gasp. This is something else altogether: ancient grains of matter slamming into the earth's atmosphere at two hundred times the speed of sound. There are so many of them, fizzing, pulsating and dancing, that at times it feels like an assault. Michael puts his arms round my waist, clumsily roughly; his voice is loud. He whoops every few seconds and cries out from deep in his lungs, and I want him to be still, to be quiet.

'Look at them go? How many is there up there? Must be hundreds, *fuck.*'

Michael starts to leap about.

'We should wish. We should *wish.* What should we wish for? Guys, we should all make a wish.'

The meteorologist holds his girlfriend's hand; he doesn't squeeze it or maul it.

'A number one album, a house by the sea. For Huey to win a best actor Oscar. How great would that be? Me with a Grammy, Huey with an Oscar, you and Tess strutting down the red carpet in your sexy dresses? . . . have you wished yet, Shorty. Did you wish?'

I watch the meterologist brush his lips up against his girlfriend's cheek.

'Yeah, Michael,' I say, staring down for a moment. 'I did. I made a couple.'

Another streak, fierce and bright, scorches the sky from east to west. It seems to last for minutes, glowing and blossoming before it dies, and the crowd falls silent, stunned by its energy and brilliance. Then comes another. Then another. Then comes the sound of heavy footfalls; someone walking up the wooden steps.

'Hey, guys, how's it going? Pretty spectacular show, huh?'

We nod with our heads tilted back at the sky; it's one of the park rangers, a friend of Ashley's.

'So, Ash. I may have spotted that guy you were asking me about.'

'Which guy?'

'The guy on the print-out, that Xerox that you gave me.'

I stand up out of my deckchair. Michael lays down on the floor. He spreads his arms out in the shape of a crucifix and asks the park ranger if he has any dope on him.

'Where did you see him?' I say.

'He was over behind the picnic grounds. He came up to speak to me, wanted to know if there was anywhere quieter he could go watch the show. Some people were lighting bonfires and shining torches, it was too bright out there, messing with the view.'

'Did you . . . did you recommend another place?'

'I told him he ought to try it out by the lake, it's a whole lot quieter down there. I didn't recognise him until after he'd gone . . . I didn't unfold the print-out until later.'

I leave Michael just where he is, laid out and giggling on the floor. He's drunk and high and irascible and he's in no fit state to come with us. Connor offers to drive me over to the lake on one of the quad bikes and I have to put my arms tight around his waist to stay on. He drives agreeably fast: taking short cuts through the mud and long grasses, and tearing up the rubber wheels on the gravel paths. The meteors shine hard above us as we go – huffing, puffing, and showing off – but by the time we reach the far side of the lake the display is beginning to die down. The streaks come every few minutes instead of every few seconds and they're fainter, shorter, less colourful. People with sore necks are rubbing their aching muscles: taking a break, eating a sandwich, fixing themselves something cold to drink.

'I think this is where he meant, do you see him?'

I climb off the bike and take a breath. My heart is racing from the drive. It is quieter out here and darker, but there are still a couple of hundred people milling around. It takes me a few seconds to be sure, but I'm certain this is the same spot I came to earlier. We walk up and down the crowd, back and forth, back and forth, until my eyes are sore from the staring. I hand out my leaflets but most people ignore them or screw them up into balls after I leave. The last person I talk to takes a leaflet from my hand and actually bothers to returns my gaze. He stares at the bleached-out picture and squints.

'Yeah, I just talked to him, he just left. Cool guy, knew a lot about meteors.'

'You're sure it was him?'

He looks closer at the photocopy.

'Yeah, I'd say so. An English guy, right?'

I seem to stumble. Connor takes over.

'When did he leave . . . did you see which way he went?'

The man shakes his head, he doesn't know. He thinks my brother moved away as soon as the meteors died down, perhaps he wanted to get away early and miss the traffic. He might have walked in the direction of the car park, he might have gone off through the woods.

'Did he say where he was headed? Maybe he mentioned where he was staying?'

'A motel, I think. He didn't say which one. Said he was travelling around a fair bit. Thinking of heading down to Mexico . . . or was it Canada . . . just waiting on a new passport, or something.'

I can't stand up any longer. Somehow, I can't seem to stand up. If he moves on from here, if he gets brand new documents; there's no way on earth that I'll find him. I'll be done for. If only I'd trusted my intuition and stayed put. If only I hadn't left to find Michael. I would have seen him. I would have *had* him. I knew he'd be out here. I *knew* it.

Connor bends down to help me up, offering me his arm.

'Are you OK?' he says, gently.

'No,' I say. 'Not really. I was here earlier, barely a few feet away. I should have stayed where I was. I should have trusted my instincts.'

'Why didn't you?'

I frown.

'Because . . . my instincts are usually lousy.'

We make one final scan of the crowd and trudge wearily back to the bike.

'Hey . . . wait up.'

The man is chasing after us.

'Hey, I forgot to say . . . I just remembered. I don't know where he's headed long term, but I *do* know where he'll be Monday afternoon. He's going out to Cape Canaveral for a rocket launch. Was pretty definite about it. A little obsessive, even. A little psyched.'

'You're sure?' says Connor.

'Yes,' says the man. 'I'm positive.'

I start to cry.

The meteors stop.

On the drive back to the observatory, Connor says little. We park up a way before the lecture stage and walk back together in the quiet. People are exiting from every direction; pushing past us with their baggage and their equipment, knowing the show is over, knowing there's nothing left to hold on to. I can see Michael up by the lectern, spread out on the wooden floorboards, possibly snoring.

'Look, this is none of my business,' Connor says, as we walk. 'But that guy, your ex . . . he seems like a bit of an asshole.'

'He is.'

'So why . . . ?'

I shrug.

'He's not like that all the time, he just drank too much . . . he has his moments.'

'Well . . . sure. I understand.'

He doesn't. I feel the need to explain.

'I know where I am with him. I don't expect too much. That way . . . he doesn't disappoint me.'

Connor stops for a moment.

'Well, I could be wrong,' he says. 'But when I look at you . . . I don't think I've ever seen anyone more disappointed.'

Foreign Bodies

Huey helps me put Michael to bed. We flop him down heavily on the mattress, shift his jelly legs from the bare lino floor, and stuff them underneath the stale covers. It's hard work, Michael is almost comatose. We could use an extra person to help us but Tess is fast asleep, storing up some rest for the operation. Huey hasn't been to bed yet. He's wide awake and stone cold sober, mulling things over in his head.

'How did you get on?'

'Good. Sort of. He was there.'

'You *saw* him?'

I shake my head. One of Michael's arms flops out of the covers and he groans as his shoulders hit the floor.

'No,' I say. 'I just missed him. But I did find someone who'd spoken to him.'

'Did they know anything? About where he is, where he's staying?'

'No, they mostly talked about meteors and comets, but this guy seemed to think . . . have you got him?'

'I've got him.'

We shift Michael's shoulders back onto the mattress.

'He seemed to think Daniel was planning a visit to Cape Canaveral to see a rocket launch. I'm going to head up there on Monday.'

'The Space Centre?'

I nod. My forehead is sweating. Michael is snoring and in position.

'Well, that's cool then,' says Huey, encouragingly. 'You're still in there, still in there with a chance.'

*   *   *

We leave Michael to sleep off his excesses and head out into the living room. It's almost dawn – that blurry half-hour before the end of night and the start of day – and all is quiet. It's a late riser this island, a heavy sleeper: a stumble-out-of-bed strip of land. The beach won't be busy for hours, which means the new day can't touch me just yet. I can't fuck things up. I'm safe for a while, I can relax. Huey rolls the both of us a fat, pungent joint and the moment it's made I take it from him. I need to feel washed away: to drift for a moment, to dream. I feel so tensed up, so defeated.

'You feel lousy that you missed him, huh?'

'I should have stayed where I was, Huey. I should have just . . . stayed put.'

'You couldn't have known,' he says, kindly. 'You can't predict that kind of stuff. If you'd stayed out there by the lake, chances are he'd have ended up going somewhere else.'

He smiles a warm smile, encouraging me to keep my chin up.

'But I mess things up, Huey, that's what I do. I'm never in the right spot when people need me. I get it wrong. I *read* it all wrong . . . I never quite . . . figure it out.'

'Well, hey, that's life, man. Who the fuck can figure it?'

The two of us giggle from the dope.

'But you're wrong, Claire, trust me.' He inhales, he exhales. 'No one could have done more than you have. Keep going, you'll get there. You'll get to your brother soon enough.'

I shrug. I hope that he's right.

'You can't spend your whole life looking backwards,' he says. 'It's no good you dwelling on your mistakes. Regret, it does you no good; that stuff can cripple you if you let it. Believe me, it can eat you right up.'

A big puff. I hold it in for hours.

'I mean it,' he says, sitting forward in his seat. 'I made a decision this weekend. I'm going to move on, take restorative action. I'm going to get out there and claim my life back.'

'Good for you . . . I mean, I'm glad. Glad to hear it.'

We laugh; we don't know why this is funny.

'It's all down to Tess, that's what it is. All of this . . . it's all because of her.'

'How come?'

He narrows his eyes, wondering how much he should say.

'We've been talking a lot . . . and we decided, the two of us . . . I don't know Claire . . . I think we're pretty messed up. Tess doesn't eat enough, I obsess about what could have been . . . and I'm angry, I'm angry at a *snake* . . . it's not healthy.'

'I guess not.'

'It's not cool.'

'So you've decided to, what? Get some therapy?'

'Sort of, you might call it that.'

'I don't understand . . . you mean the operation?'

An enigmatic smile. A shallow nod.

'The operation. Exactly. The *operation*.'

'Well, I don't think she should do it. I'm serious, Huey, you hear all kinds of stories. They could rupture, they might break. And that surgeon . . . he just sounded, so *cheap* . . .'

'It's going to be just fine, Claire, don't sweat it. I'm telling you, it's all going to be fine. End of the old Tess and Huey, start of the new Tess and Huey. We have it . . . well, we have the whole thing all worked out.'

'But you could still talk her out of it. She loves you, she'd listen to you.'

'She loves me? You think so?'

'Come on, it's obvious. She *adores* you.'

Huey reddens. He fiddles with his beer bottle, clutching for a way to change the subject.

'So . . . uh, how come he got so wasted tonight?'

'Michael? I don't know, he'd been drinking before he got out to the park.'

'How'd his audition go?'

'Good. I think it was good.'

'I knew those two would hit it off. I kept saying to him, you've *got* to come out here, this guy could totally sort out your career.'

'By giving him a gig at his club?'

'No, uh-uh, the Wheel is just a sideline for this guy. He has his own record label that he runs out of New York. Jazz is making a huge comeback, up there. And you know Michael, I mean, those concerts he does, they're fine, they're pretty cool, but he'd kill his own mother to make an album. Anyway, I'm glad it worked out between the two of them. He and Michael are totally on the same wavelength. I knew something would happen when they hooked up.'

I blink my eyes. I have to be sure I have this right.

'So, let me get this straight . . . you'd been trying to get Michael to come out here, to Florida, to meet him?'

'Yeah, for the last six months or so. He kept saying he couldn't afford to make the trip. Kept saying he was broke, that it wasn't worth it. I don't know, maybe he thought I was spinning him a line or something.'

'No,' I say. 'He really is broke. He's still in debt to me, I paid his flight.'

'You did? That's nice of you. Michael always said you were pretty generous. Hey, when you think about it . . . I mean, I know it's bad circumstances and everything, but in some ways it was pretty good timing. You having to come out here and Michael being able to travel with you, sort of kills two birds with one stone. Sort of convenient, don't you think . . . hey, are you all right? Are you choking?'

'Smoke . . . too much . . . inhaled too much smoke.'

I'm silent for a long time; Huey doesn't understand why. He tries hard to keep the conversation going.

'So what about those meteors, huh? *Huh?* Weren't they, like, *ferocious.*'

Nothing.

'Must have been even better where you were? I mean, it must have looked better out there, right? What with it being so dark.'

I don't respond. He tries again.

'So, uh . . . tell me about this meteorologist guy that you ran into. Was he handsome?'

'Handsome?'

Huey is delighted that I've answered, he hands me the joint as a reward.

'Yeah, you know . . . Michael says you've got a thing for handsome guys. He says you like them a little . . . you *know* . . . a little younger?'

My face falls even further than Huey's.

'Did I cross the line? I did, didn't I? Fuck, man, I *knew* it . . . I crossed the line. It's only, Michael was talking about it the other night when we went out . . . I figured it was all in the open.'

I rub my eyes. I'm confused. Huey tries to dig his way out.

'That's how you two kids got back together again, am I right? You were dating some hot Portuguese guy? Younger than him, better looking? Made him come over all jealous?'

'Huey . . . I don't get this. Michael told you about . . . *Gabe*?'

Huey holds up his hands.

'Hey, I don't know the dude's name, man. All I know is that your uncle told Michael about this hot stud you were dating and that it totally ate him up.'

'My *uncle*?'

'Rodney, right?'

'Robert?'

'That's *him* . . . that's the man.'

Huey grabs the joint and puffs deep with relief, then hands it right back to me.

'Fuck, I thought we'd never get there. Thank God. Anyway . . . that's what happened. That's what set him off. The fact that you'd been dating a younger guy or something . . . wow, this is really neat stuff.'

I drag one more time, deep and low into my lungs, trying to make better sense of it.

'So, what are you saying? . . . that Michael slept with me on new year's eve because he was jealous?'

'That's it. That's right. Exactly so.'

I barely have time to feel flattered.

'And because he felt sorry for you, a little bit.'

'He felt *sorry* for me?'

'Uh-huh. That shit-head moved right in on your sister after he dumped you, correct? Jesus, some people have got no scruples. Another hit?'

I take another hit.

I curl up next to Michael, watching him: the shallow breaths he takes, the twitches his shoulders make, the way he chews the insides of his cheeks. He's deep asleep, dreaming, dreaming, I have no idea about what. The fresh dawn sunlight is cruel to his face, illuminating every bag, every wrinkle: he looks worn out.

I had the motivation largely right. He wanted me that night because he knew he could have me, because he knew that my wounds were raw and fresh. He wanted me because he realised I'd been seeing someone else, because I hadn't gone to ground and mourned for him like he'd expected me to. I can see poor Robert now – dragging Michael into the kitchen on new year's eve while I was left talking to Mum. She's over you son, I imagine that's the way he would have said it. She's found herself a new man; someone good, someone younger. And he likes her, he likes her a lot.

Michael would have asked questions. Robert would have told him how it was: how I didn't mope around, how I got back on the bike, how I busied myself with lots of different men after we split up. He'd have thought he was building me up, but in swift turns it's likely that he buried me. Michael would have nodded and prodded and dug around, and pretty soon Robert would have crumpled. This latest man? Well, if you really want to know . . . yes, it's unfortunate, but they just broke up. *Why?* Think Robert, *think*: say something useful, something good. Well, I'm not sure I should say this . . . but if you really want to know, he recently switched allegiance . . . to her sister.

I stare right at him. I stroke his hair but he doesn't feel it. I kiss his lips but he doesn't respond. I trace his mouth with the edge of my thumb feeling for the heat of his breathing. I want him to love me. I do. I want him to wake up and see me and care for me, and I want to fall into the bitter slick of his sweaty skin. The smell of him, the taste of him, the sheer outright thrill of him, when he's ready to hand out the thrills.

He stirs. He senses me and reaches over, pulling me down into the safety of his sheets. Why did you come out here with me? I say. I came to be with you, he says. You thought it would be an adventure? Yes, since you ask, I think I did. And what else was there? Nothing. *Nothing.* He'd stutter; I'd have to say it for him. You almost had me, I whisper while he sleeps. Well done Michael, you almost had me.

I spread out alone in the quiet and the still, and screw my eyes up tight. I don't want to read him any more. I want a book whose pages will turn with surprises, whose subtext I don't know off by heart. I want to give myself over to a foreign body, one whose actions I can't wholly predict. One whose dialogue will take some interpreting: one whose language I don't fully comprehend.

That's Some Going

'When will you arrive?'

'The flight gets in lunchtime tomorrow.'

'I won't be here.'

'Where will you be?'

'I'm driving up to Cape Canaveral, we think Daniel's going up there to watch a rocket launch.'

I can hear Julian crying in the background. I want to be there, to give him a hug.

'Should we change our flight, then?' Kay says. 'Should we try and come in at Orlando? It's nearer to the Space Centre, isn't it?'

'Yes . . . good idea. You might try.'

Any stoicism she had seems to have vanished, she is urgent now: frantic, bowled over.

'Julian's had the flu, he's been rotten. I would have come sooner . . . I didn't think . . . but I couldn't have travelled with him like that.'

'It's OK, it wouldn't have made any difference.'

She's quiet for a moment, she clearly thinks that it would have.

'So let me get this right. You were out by the lake, exactly where he was? But you went . . . you left before he got there? If you'd stayed where you were—?'

'I would have seen him, yes. Kay, I *already* feel bad enough.'

'I just . . . I don't know why you had to move. I don't know why you had to switch around.'

There's a lull. We pause. I scratch my leg.

'So, let me know if you manage to change your flight,' I say, stiffly. 'I'm going to drive up early in the morning. I think he'll watch the launch from Jetty Park.'

'Why there? Won't he go to the Space Centre?'

'He and Dad watched the space shuttle from Jetty Park. I think . . . I think he'll go there.'

I can hear the scepticism in her breathing; she thinks she knows what kind of a judge I am.

'Well, I'll go straight to Kennedy then, that way we'll have both bases covered. And I've been given some numbers, I'll bring them.'

'For what?'

'Private detectives. If we don't find him this time, we'll have to bring in the professionals. You've done . . . well, you've done the best you can. But these people have experience and Daniel . . . he clearly needs help.'

I hate the way she says this. It's almost like she thinks of Daniel as a mental patient, like she can't wait to have him committed. Julian cries out again. Or maybe Kay?

'Kay, are you all right?'

It's her, broken down into sobs.

'Fuck him,' she says. 'Really. *Fuck* him.'

I expect that she's talking about Daniel.

'You know something?' she says. 'When she called . . . when your mother phoned to tell me he was safe . . . I didn't even know what to say. I should have been happy, that's what she kept saying to me: Kay you must be *so* happy. I wasn't. I was angry, fucking angry. I wanted to get hold of him and . . . and slap him.'

She gasps from letting it out.

'He could have said *something*. He could have told me *something* . . . I'm his *wife*. I'm his . . . wife.'

She says this last part softly, quizzically, like she no longer knows what it means.

'Did he ever talk to you about—'

'The Columbia going down? No, *no*, he barely mentioned it.'

'He didn't seem altered or changed?

'Who knows . . . I don't know. There was too much . . . there were other things going on that day.'

Should I ask her what she means? Is it right for me to ask her what she means?

'What else? What other things?'

She pauses so long I think she must have put the phone down, then weakly, wearily, she says it.

'He was seeing someone else. Sleeping with, I mean.'

'You knew about that?'

'Did *you*?'

The words just came out, I couldn't stop them. They spilt right out of my mouth.

'Kay, I'm *so* sorry . . . we just . . . we thought it better not to—'

'*We?* The whole *family* knew?'

'We didn't know whether to tell you or not. I found out by accident, when I took the pill packets—'

'*You* took them? Jesus, Claire. Why?'

'They'd all been taken. Did you know they'd all been taken?'

'Of *course* I knew,' she says, with some venom. 'I was the one that took them. That's what he'd done to me. *That's* what he'd driven me to.'

My mouth is dry like cotton: last night's dope, too little sleep and Michael looking up at me from the sofa, wondering why I'm being so off with him.

'Kay, I don't . . . I don't get it.'

'They were *my* pills, *my* prescription. My antidepressants, for *me*. I kept and resealed every packet. It made me feel like I hadn't really used them. Why does no one ask about *me*?'

'Kay, none of us—'

'I didn't want to ask for them, I didn't want it left on my medical record. Daniel didn't care, he got them for me. Are you surprised?'

I don't answer.

'He would have done anything, he felt so guilty. Poor Daniel, he felt so *bad* about it all. You should have seen how he was, Claire, how shifty and secretive he was. He used to go out into the garden to use his mobile phone, he said it never had a decent signal in the house. I had a baby, I'd *just* had a baby. He was fucking her while I was pregnant with his son.'

I hold my breath.

'And *I* had to phone her. *I* had to speak to her. *I* was the one who called her up when he went missing.'

'Why couldn't . . . why didn't you say?'

'It was over . . . she swore it was over. She didn't know a thing, hadn't spoken to him for months . . . and I was just . . . but I felt so ashamed.'

She sighs, I hear her sit down.

'Who was . . . was it someone he worked with?'

She almost laughs.

'No, not quite.'

'Her name's Annie, isn't it? That's all I know.'

'What are you talking about? No, her name isn't *Annie.*'

She's frustrated with me now, getting cross.

'Chloe, it's *Chloe.* So there, now you know. Your perfect brother was fucking his partner's wife.'

'I *told* you so.'

'No, Michael. You didn't. You said they were having orgies that's not the same.'

'I said they were swingers, close enough.'

'What does she look like?'

'*Huey?*'

'Hey, I'm only asking? Don't take it out on me.'

'Did you think he had it in him?' says Tess, pouring me a drink. 'Did you think he was capable of pulling off a stunt like this? I mean, three women at once – Kay, Annie, now Chloe. If you ask me I'd have to say—'

'Tess, she didn't *ask* you.'

'Shut up, Huey. I was only going to say . . . that's *some* going.'

Your Huey Is Out There
Somewhere

'You don't want to buy my hair from me, no more?'

'No, sorry.'

'But I cut it all off. *Look*, it's right here in this bag. It took me hours, the razor was blunt.'

'You shouldn't have used a razor, man; chances are you damaged the hair follicle.'

'So, what are you saying? That you'd have bought it from me if I'd cut it off with scissors?'

'No. Uh-uh. I wouldn't even have bought it from you then, I don't need it any more.'

'*Oh*, I get it. You decided to go for plugs. Me and my big mouth – why did I even suggest it?'

'No, man, I'm not getting plugs. I've just decided, you know, that it's time I came to terms with my hair loss. It's a big step for me, so I'd appreciate it if you'd be a little more supportive.'

'So, you don't want what I've got in this bag, here?'

'No, I don't need it.'

'You're not going to give me a thousand dollars?'

'No. Uh-uh.'

'What about five hundred? I'll do you a deal for five hundred.'

'Sorry, old man. No can do.'

'Two hundred?'

'Nope.'

'*One* hundred.'

'No.'

'Come on. Name your price, name your *price*. Think of the

wig you could knit out of this stuff. Have a heart, kid, think about how long it took me.'

Huey knows when he's beaten. He goes into the liquor store and buys the bum a litre bottle of Thunderbird. Afterwards, he pops next door to the organic grocery and buys him a sandwich of grilled vegetables and purple sprouting broccoli.

'That's *it*? That's all I get? Some cheap wine and some purple sprouting broccoli? It's not even on pumpernickel toast. I like to have my sandwiches made on pumpernickel.'

'Hey man, be grateful. That's all they had.'

The bum can't decide what to do. His hair is pilled up in a brown paper bag, scrunched up tight in his filthy hand. His scalp has bald patches from where he went too close with the razor; he looks like he's suffering from mange.

'Ah . . . *fuck* it then, give me the sandwich. But if that's how it's gonna be, I'll need some wheat grass juice to wash it down with. I heard it's good for the immune system.'

'No, man. It isn't. It just makes your farts reek.'

'Look at me, my farts already *reek*.'

'OK, man. Fair point.'

Huey heads back to the organic deli for a double shot of wheatgrass juice and offers it up to the bum. Belatedly, forlornly, the bum takes the paper cone (recycled) and hands over his prize.

'You got anything else for me, a smoke or two, maybe?'

'Smoking's no good for you, you really ought to stop. Here, wait, take some of these.'

Huey reaches into his pocket and pulls out a thick wad of coupons.

'I think I've got some money off Nicorette here somewhere.'

'Really? I could sure use some of those patches.'

'Nope. They must be back upstairs.'

The bum looks disappointed.

'Hey, what the hell though, take 'em. Why don't you take the whole lot.'

The bum fills his pockets with Huey's coupons and when

every spare recess is stuffed to the brim he pulls out a handful and flicks through them.

'Great, that's just great. Hot wax, douche and extra absorbency tampons – my life just gets better and better.'

Tess is beginning to look uneasy. She doesn't like the way this day is going; this isn't how she'd planned it, not one bit.

'You'd better be throwing that bag away, Huey.'

'No, Tess, I'm not. I'm going to keep it.'

'But it's not sanitary. It's . . . *Jesus*,' she says, sniffing the bag, 'it *stinks*. It's probably got lice and ticks and all sorts.'

'I can't throw it away, Tess, it's immoral. You can't throw away a man's *hair*.'

'Well you can't take it to the *hotel* with us. Huey, don't ruin this event for me today, this is my special goodbye lunch.'

'Tess, I'm not going to ruin it.'

'So, stuff it inside your pants pocket.'

'I can't, it'll stink up my suit.'

'*Huey*.'

'Fuck, man, this is a thousand-dollar suit.'

Tess has arranged a celebration for the four of us. It's the day before her operation, the day before I head up to Cape Canaveral, the week before they vacate the flat. Huey and Tess are planning a recuperative holiday after Tess gets out of the hospital and the two of them have decided to give up the apartment. Tess wants this day to be nice, to be special, so we're going to eat lunch at the Blue Hotel.

The doorman gives a suspicious sniff as we walk past him, but he can't quite work out where the smell is coming from. Tess has sprayed Huey's suit trousers with her perfume – most of the bottle – but there's still a high note of urine in the musky bouquet.

'You think it would be better if we ate outside by the pool?'

The restaurant manager thinks that it would.

Things pick up once we're out in the open again and the four of us settle into deep comfy sun chairs, shaded by a tall cream umbrella. Half a dozen palms tree tower over us, their long leaves fussing in the breeze. A waiter has taken our food order; another is bringing us drinks.

'It's perfect isn't it?'

I have to admit, it very nearly is.

'It's been a stressful few days, hasn't it? I hadn't realised how stressed out I was. I feel good now, though. Really good.'

'You're not nervous?'

'About the operation? Yeah, a little bit, but in a good way.'

'What time do you go in?'

'Uh . . . early, around six. I want to make sure they load me up with plenty of those premeds first.'

Huey shoots an odd wink at Tess. Tess shoots an odd wink at Huey.

'You still think we . . . I mean that *I* shouldn't go through with it.'

'Tess, I think it's your life, it's up to you.'

She looks pleased. She and Huey look happy.

'I'm *so* glad I met you guys. Really, the both of you . . . you've both meant an awful lot to me.'

'Hey, Tess, come on now. Don't go getting all emotional.'

'I mean it. I wish we could all have hung out for longer, I think the four of us would have become great friends.'

'We'll keep in touch.'

'Sure,' she says. 'Of course we will.'

'We'll meet up when you're back from your holiday. If I'm in London by then, you'll have to come over for a visit.'

'England? I'd like that, all those tiny streets, all that fog. And I could let my moustache grow out, right?'

'Yeah . . . exactly. You could.'

We smile, we both know she's joking.

'A toast, then?'

'Absolutely, a toast.'

'To old friends, to new friends, to progress.'

We raise up our glasses, we clink.

'To all of us, good luck.'

'Good luck,' we say. 'To all of us good luck.'

'Here's to Claire finding her brother and here's to me and Huey, and my new boobs.'

'To Tess's boobs.'

'And Huey's head.'

'To Huey's head.'

'To New Horizons.'

'New Horizons.'

'New plans.'

'New plans.'

'And here's to my gig at the Wheel . . .'

We stop. We seem to have run out of drink.

'Huey, why don't you take Michael to the bar for a minute, see what's happened to our champagne.'

'The waiter will bring it.'

'I know, but I'd sort of like it now.'

She nudges him until he catches on.

'Right, I get you. Come on Michael, let's give these two a minute.'

'So then?'

'So?'

'How are you?'

'I'm fine.'

'Come on, how are you, really? You've fallen out with Michael, am I right?'

I lift up my wine glass and try to squeeze some extra alcohol from its empty shell.

'You two are barely talking, what's going on?'

'Tess, it's just . . . things are difficult.'

She mulls things over, leaning back in her sun chair.

'He's cute, Claire. I'll give you that, he's cute. I wouldn't turf him out of bed, that's for sure.'

Come on glass. One more drop.

'He has this way with women, am I right? *Quite* the charmer, that boy. Charmed you right out of your heart?'

'Tess, really, I don't feel like talking about this now.'

She sits up and leans into me; she can't be bothered to play games.

'Come on, I know about what happened. Huey told me what you talked about last night. Michael came out here to audition, right? Just as much as he came out here to be with you?'

A lump in the throat; what use is a lump in the throat?

'Tess, he never made me any promises.'

'Right. Sure. Of course not.'

'It was nothing, it probably never was . . . this trip, us . . . I wasn't under any illusions.'

'But it still hurts, doesn't it?'

I nod.

'Oh Baby.' she says, reaching for my hand. 'You deserve so much better than him. That's our problem all over, we always think we can change them.'

'No, I never tried to change him.'

'So what did you think, that he's was going to change all by himself? Shit, Claire, do you have a lot to learn.'

She smiles, but her mind is ticking fast. Going over it, working it out.

'Oh, right, now I get it, you're one of *those* type of girls.'

I don't need to ask what type, it's obvious she's going to tell me.

'You didn't *want* to change him, right? You liked him just exactly how he was. Knew where you stood with him, knew how to read him, knew he'd fuck it all up eventually.'

I'm going to cry. How does she do this to me, someone like Tess? Sometimes she seems to see right through me.

'Don't get me wrong, I know how it is, I didn't get on with my family either. What with my sister and her emus, and my mum and the arson and everything. And her husbands, *fuck*, don't even get me started on her husbands. But an upbringing like that, it's sort of classic. You go for what you know, what you're familiar with. You look for love in all the wrong places. You don't think you deserve to be loved.'

I stare at the floor. I can't speak.

'So Madame Orla was right, huh?'

'Yes,' I say. 'Looks like she was.'

'What a bitch. I hate it when she's right.'

A tear trickles down onto my lip.

'Hey, *hey*,' says Tess, squeezing my hand. 'I know it doesn't feel like it now, but one day you'll find a guy who loves you the same exact way you love him. Look at me and Huey. Who the fuck else would love me as much as he does?'

I blow my nose.

'Exactly, no one. And what I mean is . . . what I'm trying to say is . . . Claire, *your* Huey, he's out there somewhere.'

'I hope so.'

'*Really?*'

'Yeah, I do.'

'Fuck, I was only trying to make you feel better. I didn't expect that you'd go for it.'

She smiles.

'I mean, he's cured of the coupons, he's better about his head. Now . . . if I could *only* get him cured of the anal.'

'I'll miss you, Tess.'

'Thanks Babe, I know. Give me a hug, I'll miss you too.'

We laze by the pool for the rest of the afternoon, until a rain shower forces us inside. We don't want it to end. One more drink, one more hour, one more story.

'What about the Rose Room? We should go and drink in there. We never got to see it. I'd like to see it.'

I'd like to see it too.

'Wow, this is nice, right? It's so romantic, so pretty.'

It's a small space, intimate and delicate, its walls lined with antiques and Venetian mirrors. The panelling on the bar is a pale shade of walnut, the marble on the floor is shot through with veins of rose-coloured quartz. Thick velvet curtains line the windows and teardrop chandeliers – Murano, crystal – sparkle from the high, painted ceilings. It could look old-fashioned, overdone but it's all so well chosen, so finely balanced.

'I love this room. I just *love* it. If I was ever going to marry, I'd get married in here. What do you think Michael, do you love it?'

'Yeah . . . I suppose so. It's OK.'

'No. It's not right, though. I don't think this place is right for you.'

'Well, it's not really my taste.'

'I know what you mean, Mike.'

No one ever calls him Mike.

'It's got history this place, it's got depth. For me, that's what *makes* a room, its depth, its complexity. That's why it lasts. That's the whole reason you stay with it.'

He shrugs. He doesn't realise that she's having a dig at him.

'Waiter, sir? Do you mind if we talk to you a second?'

The waiter comes over, an older guy.

'We love this room,' says Tess. 'We think it's got something special, a special kind of atmosphere, am I right?'

'Well, people seem to like it.'

'They kept it just the same, isn't that true? They didn't redecorate in here during the refit?'

The waiter looks round, studying the décor. He wants to be sure of his answer.

'The curtains are new, a deeper shade of red than the originals. The rest of it was largely untouched. It's all much as it was, except for the name.'

'The name?'

'It didn't used to be called the Rose Room. They named it that much later, on account of the pink quartz that runs through the marble. For the first few years they called it something different.'

'Oh? What did they call it?'

'Someone that worked on the refurbishment, a British guy, he had the owners name it after his wife. He filled it with all the things he thought that she'd like. Apparently, he had some artist from London pick out all the key pieces: the chaise, the prints. The antiques, the crystal chandeliers.'

Tess nods at me, I pipe up.

'My dad . . . he worked on this place when it was restored. He's . . . he's British.'

'Maybe it was him, then. Did your mother know he named the bar after her? Tell her, I'm sure she'd love to know.'

'What's your mum's name?' says Huey.

'Annie's Bar,' says the waiter. 'That's what they called it. Annie is your mother's name, right?'

Tess sees the look on my face.

'No,' she says, gently. 'I think you're mistaken. I really don't think that it is.'

Like Father Like Son

We walk back to the apartment along the beach. The moon is up and there's a stillness in the air. It's a sweet-smelling, beautiful night.

'Ought to be fine for the rocket launch tomorrow.'

'Yes. It ought to be good.'

'Clear skies, warm weather. Nothing . . . problematic.'

'No,' I say. 'Nothing problematic.'

Tess stops for a moment. She turns.

'Did you ever suspect it?'

It didn't even enter my head.

We rest on the sand for a moment; Huey chatting to Michael, me sitting quietly with Tess. She pulls a notebook from her pocket. She flicks through her bright yellow Post-its, underlining words and crossing some out.

'I usually guess this stuff pretty early,' she says. 'I usually work out how it is, but I had this all wrong. Annie was your father's girlfriend, not Daniel's. She wrote that letter to *him*.'

I lie backwards with my head to the surf. I like how gentle it sounds.

'My mother had affairs. All the time. Couldn't keep her coochy in her pants. Went through men like dish cloths. Every man she met fell in love with her.'

'Was she beautiful?'

'No. Not so much. But she had this essence.'

'Essence?'

'Yeah . . . that's what it was. It wasn't always good but it drew people to her. It always made me and my sister feel so plain. Men were always leaving their wives and girlfriends to be with her. Maybe Annie was like that.'

'Yes,' I say. 'Perhaps she was.'

'You feel badly for your mum? You never knew your father was cheating on her?'

'No, Tess. I didn't.'

But I should have.

'Well, maybe it wasn't for long. Maybe is was something and nothing.'

The surf's getting up. Rolling and crashing on the sand.

'Why'd you think Daniel had the letter?' she says. 'Why do you think he kept it all this time?'

I shake my head. I don't know. Tess sits upright and nods.

'I know what you're thinking.'

'What am I thinking?'

'You're thinking, like father like son.'

Huey crouches down next to Tess.

'You ready to go home?' he says, reaching for her hand. 'We ought to get some sleep. It's going to be a tough day tomorrow.'

'For all of us.'

'I guess so, for all of us.'

All four of us are ready to go home.

The Operation

'You're upset. I understand. That's no reason for you to go up there without me.'

'Michael, I want to go alone.'

'It's a long drive. Let me drive you. Come on, I know you hardly slept.'

'I'm fine. I'm going to be fine. And someone needs to look after Harvey.'

'You want me to stay behind because of the *snake*?'

I shrug.

'I told Tess you'd do it. She wanted to be sure he was looked after.'

Michael looks at the floor. He shakes his head.

'There's food under the sink. Huey left him some mice. He doesn't need many, it takes him a couple of days to digest them'

'Christ, that's . . . it's revolting.'

'Really? I thought you might get a kick out of it.'

'Come on . . . don't be like that. What am I going to do out here all on my own? What am I going to do up here all day?'

'Go and see your record producer friend. Tell him you're free to work now. No commitments.'

'Shorty, that's not fair.'

'You know what?' I say, pushing his hand away. 'Don't call me that . . . I really hate it when you call me that.'

Our scruffy suitcase is slumped in the middle of the floor, exposing its soft baggy innards: crushed short-sleeved T-shirts, creased pairs of jeans, note paper, guide books, tubes of toothpaste. I make a start on repacking it. I turf Michael's possessions from the case one by one, tossing them onto the mattress:

his socks, his underpants, his CDs; I feel like a dentist, pulling teeth.

'Should I have missed out?' he says, picking his pants up off the floor. 'Should I have passed up on this chance? I would have come *anyway*. You don't think I'd have come out here with you regardless?'

'Honestly?'

'Honestly.'

I turn round. I have his electric razor in my hand.

'I think as long as I'd paid for it, you'd have gone pretty much anywhere I'd asked you to.'

Michael snatches the razor from me and removes the rest of his belongings himself. He's furious now. He's not having it. It deteriorates. We deteriorate.

'You only *slept* with me because I'd been seeing other people.'

'You only slept with *me* because you were bored?'

'I wasn't bored . . . I was lonely.'

'Lonely, bored . . . it's the same.'

'No. It's not.'

'It was a one-night stand . . . for old times' sake. You knew it, I knew it . . . we *both knew*. And I *was* jealous . . . you're right. So what does that mean, Claire? Think about it. It means that I cared.'

'It means your *ego* cared.'

'No . . . it means that *I* cared.'

He stops. He tries to rub my shoulder.

'Come on. This isn't fair. Really, it's not. We've had some great times together . . . I loved you. Don't you think that I loved you?'

'Michael. I don't think you know how.'

He turns. He walks away. He mutters something under his breath.

'What is it?'

'Nothing.'

'Come on, what did you say?'

He stops. He boils over.

'You like it like *this*, Claire. This is what you like. It turns you on, doesn't it, the thrill? You like it that I'm open with you, you like that you can't own me. You like it that I don't hide this stuff from you. I never pretended to be something that I wasn't. You've always known exactly what I'm like. You expected this, right? If you're honest with yourself? You knew I'd have an angle. You *knew*.'

I pull on the case. Zip it shut.

'You can't blame me,' he says. 'You've always known where you stood. I never lied, I never made you any promises.'

I take a deep breath. I stare up at him.

'I want someone who'll make me promises. Promises are exactly what I want.'

Michael and I are sat alone on the bed; our legs are touching, and our arms. If I move I feel his skin rub against mine; if he breathes hard my body shifts with his.

'I'm sorry.'

'I know.'

'I'm . . . selfish.'

'I know.'

'I love you.'

'No, Michael. You don't.'

He looks like me now, like he's hurting. His face is sunken and tight.

'We could make another go of it,' he says, turning towards me. 'We'll rent somewhere, I'll try harder. If I do this recording . . . I'll have money.'

'Send me a cheque then. You still owe me the best part of seven grand.'

'Is that what this is all about . . . the *money*?'

I don't bother to shake my head. I'm sorry that I said it; it wasn't what I wanted to say.

'I didn't mean it.'

'No,' he says. 'I know you didn't.'

We sit in the quiet, breathing together, trying not to touch each other's hands. I can smell him, his skin and his hair and his warmth. I can hear his mind ticking inside his skull. If he asks me to stay one more time, I'll say yes. But I know how he is, and he won't.

'That's it, then?'

'That's it.'

'You won't let me drive you to the Cape?'

'No . . . I don't think so. I'd rather not.'

I pick up the suitcase and start for the door. He waits. He chases after me. We stop.

'Shorty . . . *Claire* . . . good luck.'

'You too, Michael. You too.'

And I turn around slowly. And I kiss him.

If I hadn't halted at that moment: to look at him, to feel him, to be with him that last second, I would never have heard the phone. And it rang like an alarm. It *rings* like an alarm. I wonder if it'll ever stop.

'I'll take it. Go, you'll be late.'

'It might be Kay.'

Michael picks up the phone. He ums and ahs and uh-huhs for what seems like minutes. Shit, he says. That's not good, he says. Jesus *Christ*.

'What is it?'

'It's for you.'

'Who is it?'

'It's Huey.'

'Is something wrong with Tess? Did something go wrong with the operation?'

'Yeah,' says, Michael strangely. 'You could say that.'

'Huey?'

'No . . . no, it's me,' says Tess.

'Are you OK?'

'No, sweetie, we're not. We're in seven heaps of shit, here. It's all gone . . . fuck, it's all gone wrong.'

A muffled sound from behind her. Someone shouting. Someone trying to shout.

'Are you at the hospital? Where are you?'

'No. We're not at the hospital.'

More muffled moans. I hear Huey talking in the background.

'OK,' he says. 'So, just calm down man. There's no need to be like that. We're not going to hurt you.'

'Grueghgh . . . *grueghghgh!*'

'I just told you didn't I? I'm not going to take the tape off your mouth until you calm down. You want me to take the tape off your mouth?'

'Gruegh.'

'OK. But you better keep quiet.'

'Tess . . . what *is* it . . . what the *hell* is going on there?'

'*Help . . . heeelp!* Help me, *help me.* He's a *maniac.*'

'No man. I'm not. I am not a maniac.'

'That's right, Huey. You *tell* him.'

It seems like Tess has put down the phone. As loud as I shout, as long as I call her, I can't seem to get her to answer. All I can do is stay put and listen.

'If it wasn't for you . . . I would have been a success.'

'*Maniac. Help me, maniac!*'

'Huey, we're going to have to shut him up. Someone might hear him.'

'What'll we do? I didn't bring any more tape.'

'You used up *all* that tape?'

'Yeah. Wrapping him up to the chair. He's a strong guy, he needed a lot of wrapping.'

'*Help meeee . . . please . . . somebody help!*'

'Should we . . . should we hit him?'

'No. No way.'

'You touch me I'll *kill* you. I swear it. I'll have the two of you fucking *killed.*'

'Hey man, you know, you're not exactly in the position to be handing out the threats here.'

'Huey. What'll we *do?*'

'Tess, quick, go fetch the bag.'

'What bag?'

'The bag that's full of the bum's hair.'

'What'll we do with it?'

'Just fetch it, Tess, it's all we have.'

'Huey . . . I don't know.'

'Tess, we don't have time, just go get it.'

A struggle, a ruffle of paper bag.

'Oh . . . no. Jesus, what *is* this . . . aghgh . . . aghghghgh . . . you're choking me . . . *you're **choking** me*. This stuff . . . what is it . . . it *stinks* . . . oh Christ it stinks of, it stinks of *shit* . . . stop . . . **STOP** . . . I'm going to throw up . . . what *is* it . . . what is *ghghghghghhg.*'

'It's hair, man. It's *hair*. Pretty ironic, wouldn't you say so?'

'Nghgh. Nghgh.'

'Keep still, man. I still got some left in the bag here. I want you to chew down on this whole bag. Stop heaving. You'll choke if you puke.'

'*Agh . . . bleghghghbleugh.*'

'One chance, that's all I wanted. Would it have killed you to have given me that one chance?'

'***Bleugh.***'

'You'd never even met me. You didn't even know how good I was. You can't do that, man, it's not right. You shouldn't go around stepping on people's lives like that. Actors are people too, man. You ought to *know* that.'

'Hey, Huey *look*. He's gone quiet.'

'You think he can breathe OK?'

'Yeah. I think so. He's breathing.'

'Maybe he's thinking.'

'He's nodding. Huey, is he nodding?'

'He's looking at the kitchenette.'

'What part of it?'

'I don't know, follow his eyes.'

'The fridge, do you think he might be hungry?'

'Maybe . . . no, wait. He's not looking at the fridge.'

'The frying pan. That's what it is. Do you think he might want some pancakes or something?'

'No, Tess. I don't think he wants pancakes. I think he means we're both going to fry.'

'Agghghh, aghhghgh, *aghgh!*'

'*Fuck.*'

'I know, man. That isn't . . . this isn't so good.'

'No, it's *Claire*. I just remembered. I left her on the phone all this time . . . *Claire?*'

'*Tess?*'

'Uh . . . things are under control here. Everything's under control.'

'What's going on . . . what have you *done?*'

'I didn't go for that boob job . . . that's what. I took your advice . . . I mean, I think you were right . . . and Orla phoned me the day we got back from that reading; she thought she might have misread the cards. She said surgery wouldn't sort out my problems, not for good . . . so we decided to spend the money . . . on something else.'

'On what? *What* did you spend it on?'

'Uh . . . duct tape, and, um, and . . . uh . . . paying for the suite next door to him. The Delano is pretty expensive.'

'Tess, the suite next to *who?*'

She doesn't need to answer. Michael has turned on the TV set. A svelte anchorwoman is narrowing her eyes and reading aloud from the newsflash on her teleprompter.

'In other news today, renowned movie mogul Harvey Weinstein has gone missing from his hotel suite in Miami Beach. The news we have is sketchy right now, but police are not ruling out the possibility of kidnap. More on that story later, now news of the largest hot dog ever broiled in Dade county.'

'Tess . . . did anybody see you? Does anyone know where you are?'

'No . . . no. I don't think so. But . . . I think . . . well, maybe we went too far. I'm not sure how we're going to get out of this. Oh Christ . . . what'll we do? Will we have to kill him? He knows what we look like, who we *are*. Claire . . . I'm worried. I'm starting to panic a little bit.'

'Where are you?'

'Should I say? Over the phone?'

'Tess . . . where the *hell* are you? I'm coming to get you.'

'Claire?'

'What now?'

'Can you bring me my Valium?'

Cat On A Hot Tin Roof

A secret location

Outside a ruined boathouse the heat is building as the sun rises higher in the sky. Waves slap hard against the rotted wooden pilings, rust clings in heavy scabs to the metal roof. Two people lean against a cracked window frame, seeking shade; smoking a much needed cigarette. Their fingers have stopped shaking, their mouths are moist, not dry; they are weirdly contented. Elated.

'It made me feel better.'

'Did it?'

'You know what? I actually think it did.'

'Closure. That's all he needed, I knew it. He just needed to tell the guy face to face.'

Huey crouches down on the ground and turns his face upwards to the sun. He's warm, he's happy. His teeth are perfectly still.

'I feel good,' he says, contentedly. 'Reborn. I feel like a whole new person.'

Tess kneels beside her boyfriend and smiles. She reaches into her duffle bag, digs around in the bottom, and pulls out a large pack of Oreos. She piles the biscuits into her mouth. One after the other, a dozen or more; she doesn't stop until the packet is all gone.

'I'm starving,' she says, merrily, between crunches. 'You know what? I'm totally starving.'

'So, what happens now?'

'I'm not sure. I guess we'll do what you said.'

'You don't have to.'

'No . . . no. We do.'

'It makes sense.'

'It does,' says Huey. 'It makes a whole lot of sense.'

We go back inside. It smells musty indoors, salty and rotting, like the innards of an old gutted fish. A man is tied to a chair on the far side of the room, bound head to toe in silver tape. His hands are tied in front of him with a line of fishing yarn and a cloud of curly black fibres spill from his mouth.

'He looks small, doesn't he?'

'Yeah. Sort of powerless, sort of sad.'

'You killed him, Huey. You did it. You actually, finally killed him.'

I know what they mean by this; they mean they've killed the demon, that they've broken the spell this man had over their lives. The man doesn't know this. He shifts from side to side, getting agitated; breathing hard and fast through his nose. His captors pick up their bags. The man's eyes dart fiercely back and forth.

'We don't know how to thank you. For being there . . .'

'When we needed you. We'll never . . .'

'We'll *never* forget it.'

'Go now. *Go*. You haven't got very much time.'

'What about you?'

'Don't worry about me. I'll be all right.'

'What about Daniel . . . *God* . . . I'm *so* sorry . . . are you're going to . . . will you make it in time?'

I haven't looked at my watch. I can't bare to look at my watch.

'Don't worry . . . just, the two of you, *please. Go!*'

Huey and Tess turn and wave. Huey runs back and hugs me one more time.

'It looks good on you, by the way. Where'd you find it?'

I'm wearing Huey's blue, alpaca hat.

'It was in the mouse cage. You'd buried it underneath a mound of mice straw.'

'Right, shit. I was trying to keep them warm. I remember that the mice looked kind of shivery. It makes a good balaclava, though, don't you think? Tess, don't you think it makes a good balaclava?'

'Huey . . . *please* . . . we have to get out of here *now*.'

'Claire . . . thank you. Thank you *so* much, man. We won't forget this, not ever.'

'And be careful,' I say. 'It's not going to be easy.'

'Don't worry,' they say, in unison. 'We will.'

I walk towards the man slowly, with the blue hat pulled low over my face. There are two holes for my eyes, one for my mouth; I must look ridiculous. Insane.

'Mr Weinstein, please don't be scared. I'm going to cut one of your hands free then I'm going to lay the knife on this table. When I leave the room you'll be able to shift the chair over here and cut yourself free. Do you understand?'

He understands.

'I'm sorry this ever happened. And I'd stay around and help you, but . . . there's somewhere else that I have to be.'

The string is cut. He's not sure what to do. He's wondering if it's some kind of trick. I lay the knife on the other side of the room with it's handle pointing outwards, towards his chair. It should take him a couple of minutes to shuffle over and reach it.

'I know you won't believe it,' I say, opening the door. 'But just for the record . . . they're actually very sweet people.'

I turn around and make for the car and I hear something as I begin to turn the key. It sounds a lot like a cat: hacking, hacking, hacking; clearing hair balls out of its throat.

Highway 61 Revisited

This drive, how is it so long? Three hours it's been now, nearly four, and no way on earth I can make it. I'd need my own jet propulsion. I'd need to take off across these cars, across this highway; I'd need to spin, spin, spin, as fast as the earth. I'm driving at eighty miles an hour; racing like an Exocet missile, trying to make it in time. I speed up. I speed up. I slow down again. I'm alternately tired and wired. I should stop. I should rest. I should concentrate. Another of us can't die on this road.

'Lot of cars on the road today.'

'Excuse me?'

'I said, that's a lot of cars out there today. How many vehicles do you think?'

They stream past us in an endless ribbon: red, blue, big, green; fast, determined, insistent. Eyes straight ahead, bonnets in line, each one committed to the road.

'Everybody in a hurry to get somewhere, these days. Everybody always in a hurry.'

I'm sat on a concrete seat outside a gas station, sipping coffee with my shoulders hunched, watching the traffic. Day trippers file in and out while I rest: couples; families; fractious, scolded children; truck drivers with skulls as tight as fists. They stop for ice cream and cigarettes and bright day-glo Slushies. They stop to pee and fight and stretch their legs. I should get going. Toss this sweet cup of coffee to the back of my throat and climb back into the driving seat. If only I could keep my eyes open. If only I could fight the urge to shut my eyes.

My new friend taps me hard on the shoulder, his fingers feel narrow and bony.

'You look like you could use some shut-eye,' he says. 'You want to be careful. It's easy to fall asleep at the wheel.'

'I know,' I say. 'I know it is.'

They say my father looked like he was sleeping, that no one suspected he was dead. I wonder if he looked peaceful or in pain, with his head slumped down heavy on his chest; with the cold black leather of the steering wheel pressing an imprint into his cheek. It's no good. I'll have to have another pick-me-up. Another sweet cup of coffee or a sandwich. I *have* to take my time. I *have* to hurry up. I'll leave now. I'll go and buy my food first. I'll leave in another ten minutes. I'll leave in another half an hour. I sit on the bench immobile, unable. I crush the damp paper cup.

My lips are greasy and warm, and I'm buzzing and shaking from caffeine. I've eaten a hamburger and mainlined two cans of syrupy energy drink but I still feel like I'm driving on autopilot. The launch counts down in less than half an hour and I'm still more than a hundred miles from the Cape. It's a Boeing Delta 4 heavy rocket on a demonstration mission for the US government. This is what I hear. This is what I'm told. I have no notion, nor any interest, in what it means. I just want it see it take off. I just want to be there before it goes.

The traffic is thickening and slowing down now; the Magic Kingdom filter system clogging up the road, drawing in the crowds with its mouse-shaped magnet. Is this where they stopped and got caught? Is this the spot that it happened? Did Daniel crouch down on that shallow embankment, his raw toes bleeding into the grass? Did he run down the middle of this same highway, veering in and out of the traffic? It's hard to imagine, this child, this boy, tearing in and out of the stranded cars: desperate to get there, hoping to do it, killing himself to make time. I was swimming. I see myself swimming with Julio. I feel the bath-warm water on my skin. I feel lips pressing hard onto my lips. I feel soft skin on my skin. The explosions, the fear, the falling, the bliss; all of us reaching out for one another. All of us so far out of reach.

I'm coming up to a crossroads. The sign says next exit Kennedy Space Center, the exit after that is Jetty Park. I haven't time to think. Four seconds. Three seconds. Two seconds. One. And I'm past it. I'm already gone. I'm an hour or more late but I know how things are. There are always delays, every time. It's too much to expect that they could launch on schedule. Not this time. *Please.* Not today.

I just have time to park the car, to switch off the ignition and climb out. The air is fresher and cooler out here by the sea, and *look*, there it is, there she goes. A dash in the sky, a punctuation mark, so high up and far away, already. A Boeing Delta 4 heavy rocket; vanishing, almost out of sight. I want to rewind it, to make it come down again; I want to reverse the shouts and cheers. I can't be too late, I *can't* be. I must find a lasso or an arrow; something to bring the vehicle down with. But it's steaming so high now and so fast; detached from the gravity of earth, breaking free from this planet and its atmosphere. There are faces tilted upwards, still watching it, still staring, but not enough people, not *enough*. Some have made their getaway already and fled away from the park to beat the crowds. I know in my bones he was one of them. I know in my heart that he's gone.

The last of the observers are making their way towards the exit and I want to push them all back inside: the tourists and the nerds and the kids and the tour parties, all filing past me, eager and chattering. What a sight it was. How wonderful it was. They are satisfied, cheery, full up. I rub my forehead with my fists and try to squeeze some concentration out of my eyes. I'm facing the wrong way, towards the launch pad not the exit. I can't take my eyes off the distant launch pad. They push past me, swerving or crashing into my shoulder. They glare at me, shout at me and swear. They all look the same, they all look so different. I don't know, I can't tell, I can't focus. He could walk past me now and I wouldn't know it.

'Is that you?'

'Yes. It's me.'

'Where've you been?'

'I've been here.'

'All this time?'

He thinks for a long while. He listens.

'Yes,' he says. 'A part of me has been here all this time.'

There's only a few dozen left now and I turn and exit along with them. Off they all go to their coaches and their cars, and off I go to the sea. It's a short walk to the beach, a thin spit of coarse sand and white polished pebbles, holding back the whole of the ocean. And I just want to dive right into it; to rip off my clothes and to swim.

It isn't as calm as I would have liked, the fat waves butting me awkwardly from side to side, making me shiver in my bra and knickers. I spread out on my back, floating, floating, while the waves break over my face. Perhaps Kay found him, perhaps he's OK, perhaps she was right and he went to Kennedy. Maybe he's with them both now, her and Julian; hugging them, holding them, beginning his small world of repairs. But Pinhead, I know you were out here. I know you stood out here in Jetty Park. It would have been just like you, you stubborn bastard. To rest on that very same spot. To look out in that self-same direction. To visit the last place you stood with your father and replay that moment in your head. I failed you. I missed you. Didn't we always? I stuttered. I looked the wrong way.

I swim farther out – head down, arms tight – until all of my muscles ache and burn. They tell me to turn back, to return to the beach, but my head just tells me to keep on going. I stop for a breath when my lungs force me up, and when I surface the shore seems very far away. I could keep on going, I *want* to keep on going; the sea feels so warm, so obliging.

I bob up and down to get my breath back while the sun beats down on my head. I feel tired and small and alone and incapable, and I want to close my eyes and go to sleep. When I open them

again – my lids sore and stinging from salt – I spot a cargo boat
sailing for the horizon, heading east; its narrow bow slung low in
the water. I don't know where it's going, where it's headed, what
it's called, but it's just – well, it might – those figures on the deck,
it could be them. It's possible I did a good thing today; there's a
chance that I made two people happy. If they did what I said, if
they called the right people; if they got there in time, then who
knows.

They can't see me waving, but still I wave. Splashing the water,
spoiling the surf, warming my muscles and my heart. Some
energy from somewhere skids through my bones and suddenly
it feels like I'm swimming. For home, for the shore.

A man has broken off from one of the Japanese tour groups that
were in the park and he's wandering towards me now, along the
beach. I'm drying myself off with my T-shirt, wondering if my
underwear is see-through, grabbing at my jeans and my shoes.
He nods, he doesn't speak good English. I ask him if he saw the
rocket launch. Yes, he liked it. It was his first and only one; he
took pictures of it on his digital camera. What happened to his
group, is he lost? Lost? He doesn't understand the word. I explain
it to him in Japanese. He smiles, he doesn't think he's lost. But
their coach is delayed. It's being held up, they don't seem to
know for how long.

'What's the problem?' I say, pulling my T-shirt over my head,
'Why can't your tour bus leave the park?'

'No point,' he says. 'The road is full of problems outside.'

I'm gone in an instant. Long before he tells me it's a traffic
jam.

A Light As Sharp as Lemons

What rage there is brewing outside this park today: the honking
and spitting and railing of horns, men and women out of their
cars. They have their arms in the air and their fists, and
their mouths are wide open, full of shouts. They curse and moan
and stand close to one another, like they might spill over into
blows. Is this what it was like when the shuttle went down? Were
people in a rage like this, that day? Or had the disaster neutered
and tempered them a while; left them thoughtful, unsettled and
perplexed. These people aren't asking any questions. There is
nothing they are fighting to comprehend. They want revenge,
pure and simple. They are all for making rash decisions.

'What is it?' I say. 'What's the hold up?'

'Man up ahead, on the road.'

'Crazy fuck. I hope they run him over. Run him down, *man*.
I need to get back to work.'

Somebody laughs and an engine revs. Another man shouts
run the fucker down. I don't think they'll do it, not on purpose,
but I do think there's a chance he might die. I hear cars swerving
and skidding up ahead. There's been one crash already, a saloon
car has rear-ended a mobile home and the exit ramp is stuffed
shut and blocked. That's where he was. That's what they tell me.
The exit ramp is where he broke onto the road. And now what?
Where is he now? Out on the main highway? It can't be possible;
there is no way on earth he could survive it.

I don't have the physical strength. I am disjointed, un-athletic,
not so tough. He always had a rhythm, what was it? Arms then
legs, legs then arms; head, neck and torso impossibly still. I force
my forearms like pistons but they still feel weak from the swim.

I dredge some adrenalin from my organs, hammer my legs into the ground. I take off onto the tarmac, directly into the line of the oncoming traffic. I'm right through the barrier. I'm flying.

'Now there's two of them . . . *shit*,' says the man on my left. 'Fuck, lady. Get off the **road!**'

I have the right shoes: my white trainers. I have the right T-shirt: canary yellow. They can see me – there's no doubt – they can all see me coming, they can hear my lungs crying for gas. I'm shouting, I think I must be shouting. Warning the traffic, warning the road, screaming for everything to stop. Slow down, can't you? Daniel, *Daniel.* Why do you have to run so fast? There is nowhere to go to, no place left to run, no possible spot he can hide. But there is, of course. If he could just go one step faster, if he could just make better time; he could twist his entire world back to front. It would shift on its axis – north to south, south to north – and turn its face up to a different set of stars. He'd make the years and the days and the minutes slip away, and somehow he'd be back where he started: back on this same stretch of tarmac, back on this very same road, and this time, *this* time, he'd make it.

Because he's trained for this moment, I know it. Every minute of every day since he got here. Out on the beach, to the north of Sunny Isles, grinding his body back into shape. Hours of it, days of it, the wrath of it, the pain of it; until he was immune to the strain. One week, two weeks, morning and evening and now he has speed over distance. His blood is thick with protein. His muscles are sinewy and strong. His lungs and his heart run in unison, and they beat together sweetly, like a clock. So how can I catch him? How will I reach him? I can't. I can't I can't.

'I need it, *please.*'

'It's brand new.'

'I'll bring it back. I promise. I'll bring it back.'

'Get on. Get up here. I'll drive you.'

The motorbike growls like an animal as the driver fights to control it; turning it quickly, redirecting its wheels towards the oncoming traffic. He's working it now and it's looser, more liquid, and look how it weaves in and out. We don't scratch the bonnets, we don't skid or fall; we sew the dense traffic like a needle. I can see something ahead of us, a body, a figure? How is he so rigid, so straight? He looks neither to the right nor the left. He takes no avoiding action at any time. He leaves it to the cars, to the drivers; he is dependent on the sheer grace of others. He runs like he doesn't begin to see them. He chews up the centre of the road. His feet come down faster and faster, powered by instinct, some ancient engine. He runs like a rocket, higher, higher. We're gaining on him now and then we're not. A truck is stopped sideways, directly in front of us, and we can't get around it. And then we can.

On the other side, I can't see him. We pull the bike up on the hard shoulder, stall and shut down its engine. My eyes scan the road, forwards, backwards; over to the right then to the left. I walk along the road with my mouth held open; slowly, awkwardly, unable to comprehend what just happened. Maybe he actually did it, the fucker. Maybe he ran so fast he went back in time.

'Did you see where he went?'

'The runner?'

'The runner.'

'Went over the embankment just there. Came to this spot and stopped dead. Went over the railing, crazy fuck.'

Over the lip of the embankment stands the body of my crazy fucking brother. He's staring at a length of road that runs below us, a tributary to the main highway. The traffic isn't slow here, it's moving along fast, and the cars are flying like bombs. He's edging towards it, to the bottom of the verge, trying to work out where it was. That's right, of *course*, it must have been down there. That's where the family car stopped. And on he goes towards it and I'm running down towards him, a hundred metres take a million seconds. I'll never get down there, my body is collapsing, stabbing me, whipping me with the effort. He's not looking, I *know* he's not looking. He'll step out onto the asphalt and he'll die.

My voice. I think he hears my voice. Daniel, I say to him.

Daniel! I scream. Nothing. Nothing. No response. *Pinhead,* you fucking pinhead. Do you hear me? His legs bend and buckle by the kerb. *Pinhead, I'm telling you to stop!* And he does. Miraculously he does. And I pull him and shove him to the ground. And for a moment, for a moment – for a moment the universe stops turning.

We are salty and smothered like newborns, both of our bodies drenched in sweat. His face is rough and unshaven, peppered with specks of white and grey. We are old and young all at once. I hold his hand like I did when we were children, except this time it's me drawing him to safety. Across the haunted landing, from the dangers of this highway, through the traffic to the gentle grassy incline. We collapse onto the knoll, our legs made of fabric, my lungs screaming louder – so much louder – than his. My heart is attacking me, beating me up: angry, affronted, alarmed. The sun shines down on us even so, feeding us filling us up.

'Are you OK?'

'I'm not.'

'I mean your legs. Are you OK to walk.'

'I'd rather stay here.'

'You don't want to move?'

'No, I don't want to move.'

We're drying from the heat, we're congealing. We can see the horizon in the distance; we can hear the faint spill of waves.

'How beautiful it is out here.' I say. 'The sea a deep religious blue . . .'

'The light as sharp as lemons.'

The Best We Can Do

As soon as he's able to stand I drag him away from the hard shoulder and down through the embankment to the trees. There are police sirens giddy on the highway and we need a place we can both sit still and hide. They can't see us, it's too dense in these mangroves; we are a couple of runaways in the gloom. We stop. We don't say much of anything. My brother's face is blood-drained and grey; cracked up, broken and tear stained. He mutters under his breath. 'I could have made it. I would have made it. I should have run, run, *run* – faster, *faster*.' This is what he thinks. This is what he says. This is most of what he says before he sleeps. I tell it to him over and over while he dreams. It wasn't you. It wasn't your fault.

All is reordered when Daniel wakes up, the traffic noise restored to a roar. No one came looking for us here, which doesn't mean they won't, but life has pushed forward without us. My brother rubs his head and asks for water. I have a packet of Juicy Fruit squashed in my pocket. I hand it to him; it's the best I can do. We sit back together against a tree stump: silent, reflective, chewing gum. Listening to the traffic. Listening for bird sounds in the trees.

'Why did you find me?'

'You mean how did I find you?'

'No.'

'That's a stupid question.'

'Is it? I wish you'd just left me, let me go.'

'Fuck you, Daniel. Stop feeling sorry for yourself.'

He blanches, hallelujah; a reaction, a response. The slamming down of a mash-potato-covered fork.

'Is that what you think, that I'm sorry for myself?'

'Aren't you?'

'No. No, I'm not.'

He lowers his head. He looks so empty.

'Hey . . . I didn't mean it. It's going to be all right, it's . . . OK.'

He tries hard to smile, but he can't.

'How did you find me?'

'You mean why?'

'No, Claire. How did you find me?'

There are a lot of answers I could give. I choose this one.

'I don't know. I was lucky. I spoke the right languages, I sniffed you out. I talked to a lot of different people. The Japanese waitress at the restaurant, some German guy at the shipping line, the Russian sailor at the docks—'

'You spoke to Alexi?'

'I met him.'

'He was rude to you?'

'Exceptionally.'

'Helpful?'

'Eventually.'

Daniel's lips twitch, half a smile.

'What was it like?'

'On the ship? I was seasick . . . I puked up a lot.'

That's all he says. He drifts off, I'm losing him and he's gone again. I desperately try to bring him back.

'And when I got out here . . . then I went to our old apartment. I went everywhere I thought you might be. I went to the port and the beach where we used to swim and I met this old man who'd seen you running, and . . . I saw the meteor shower, you were there at the park . . . I just missed you, and I ended up at the Blue Hotel. *Dad's* hotel.'

The mention of our father brings the pain flooding back and Daniel retches and clings to his stomach.

'I have an ulcer,' he says. 'Just like his.'

'Does it hurt?'

He winces. He breathes in and out.

'He thought it was heartburn, that's what he thought. He thought it was a bad dose of heartburn.'

I shake my head. I don't know what he's talking about.

'When we were out in the car,' Daniel says. 'On the way home from the launch. He thought he had indigestion, he took a Rennie. I was so fucked off with him . . . so fucked *off*.'

I put my arm round my brother's shoulder. He shakes it off.

'You never talked about it.'

'No. Well, I couldn't.'

'Was it really that bad. All this time?'

'Yes,' he says, quietly. 'It really was.'

'You couldn't have run any faster,' I say. 'You couldn't have done any more. You did all you could. You were a hero, that's what they said. No one's ever doubted what you did.'

His face. What a face. What desolation.

He says, 'None of you know what I did.'

They stood in the park with their mouths held wide open watching the shuttle debris fall to earth. Every part of my father's body ached. The flight of this rocket had excited and invigorated him in a way that he couldn't have imagined. Its wild bid for freedom had touched him, and the vivid disappointment of its failure had carved a line straight to his chest. It made him sweat and cough, until he couldn't catch his breath. It felt like the end of all dreams. Right then he wanted to go home. To his wife, to his daughters, to his family; to begin his small world of repairs. How stupid he'd been, how unsteady. How bitterly, rigorously in love.

They walked away in silence, just the two of them, pushing and shoving through the grief-stricken crowds as they forced their way back to the car. His son's face was sulky and teenage, purposefully turned away from his. Daniel shouldn't have mentioned it – he wouldn't have mentioned it – but something was snapping on his skin. A mixture of the purest kind of sorrow and exhaustion. Somehow, he couldn't keep it in.

'I can't stand you,' he said to his father.

'Daniel. Stop it. Enough.'

'You shouldn't have done this. Why did you do this? Why did you have to ruin everything?'

His father wouldn't listen or talk, it's not what his father cared to do. So Daniel kept on pressing, digging, forcing, while his father began to slide away and sweat. He missed the exit they needed and he swore.

'Stupid,' he said. 'Now I've missed it.'

'You're still in contact with her, aren't you? You're still calling her, aren't you? I know.'

'This is none of your business. Do you hear me? You don't . . . you can't understand.'

But he did, of course. He was sixteen years old, he understood the whole world.

'I *do* understand.'

'No. No, you don't.'

'You've ruined Mum's life.'

'No, I haven't.'

'She's stoned all the time. Did you know she gets stoned? You dragged us out here to this dump and you spoilt it all. You ruined all of our lives.'

His father turned round, half pleading, half choking. He took his hand off the wheel.

'And what about my life? Jesus, you ungrateful . . . what about *mine*?'

Daniel decided that was the end of it. He lurched forward as they slowed in the traffic and dealt a blow to his father with his fist. Right on the cheek, near the nose, below the eye, and the sound it made when it hit him. Like a boot on a football, like a bat on a wicket, then that moan like a cow giving birth. He slumped forward so hard on the steering wheel that the car's horn went off with a howl. Daniel reached over and stopped it. He shook his father's shoulders and his face. He put his hand to his father's mouth and felt the hot shallow breaths that crept their way over his lips. He heard rasping and saw bubbles of blood. Then he ran. And he ran. And then he ran.

*			★			★			★*

I try not to recoil, but I do. I sense myself pulling away. It only lasts a second, but he feels it, *I* feel it. I break it. I move back. I breathe.

'Do you think I killed him?'

'You think you killed him. Isn't that what you mean?'

'I punched him. I hit him and he died.'

The tree stump digs hard into my back. I'm swirling like I might faint.

'He had a heart attack, Daniel, he was terribly ill. He would have . . . he would have died anyway.'

'How do you know that? How can you *know*.'

'That's what they said . . . the coroner said so. If it hadn't happened then . . . it would have happened the next day or the next.'

My brother cries out. He starts to sob.

'I made him miss the turning. I knew he wasn't well. If I hadn't . . . we wouldn't have been trapped.'

'Daniel, please, you can't do this.'

'He might have survived.'

'Daniel, what's the *good*?'

'So I killed him? Didn't I? I *killed* him.'

I grab him by the shoulders and shake him like a rattle, until some of the pain falls out.

'Listen to me. *Listen* to me. *Stop*. You asked me how I found you and this is the reason, I found you because I knew where to look. Because I know who you are, what you are in your bones. And you have to believe me . . . I swear it. I know you did the best that you could.'

Promises, Promises

We sit in a café a mile or so from the road, our bodies are sore from the walk. Daniel sips cold Coca-Cola. I stir a weak cup of tea.

'How long had you known?'

'About Annie? I don't know, for years.'

My metal spoon clinks on the rim. This cup is chipped, it has cracks.

'He introduced me to her. They used to pick me up from school in her car.'

'You're joking?'

He shakes his head.

'Was she beautiful?'

'Yes.'

'Younger?'

'Not younger, just different. He wanted me to meet her, I think he was proud. He thought that a son would understand.'

I twist in my seat, I can't stay still.

'What was she? What did she do?'

'She was an artist of some kind, I don't think she was particularly good. Dad paid for everything, supported her. That's why we never had money.'

'How often—'

'As often as he could. He didn't take overtime, he didn't work weekends. He spent all his free time with her.'

My mother. I think of my mum.

'Why not just . . . leave us?'

Daniel sips his drink and rubs his neck.

'Maybe it suited him that way, the security of us, of Mum, of home . . . and then the excitement of her . . . I don't know, Claire, maybe he was scared. I think the indecision ate away at him. I don't think he had the strength to jump.'

'He loved her?'

Daniel reaches into his bag.

'Here,' he says, 'see for yourself.'

Daniel has more of Annie's letters: years of correspondence, kept silent and hidden, letters that he knows off by heart. He found them after Dad died and hid them from Mum, and poured over them night after night. He took them with him everywhere he went after that: from home, to university, to his first shared apartment, to the first house he furnished with Kay. He hid them in all kinds of daft places: a tin in the garden, a carton in the freezer, and one he forgot to pick up when he left, squeezed inside a resealed pill packet. I take half a dozen and read them. They are frank, sweet, passionate, dark; alternately delicate then wild. One side of a dialogue – lover to lover, woman to stranger – to a man I never knew, never met.

'God.'

'I know.'

'They're not . . . when she describes him . . . it just doesn't sound at all like Dad.'

'He had a different life when he was with her. They did things, they went out a lot. Galleries, theatres, exhibitions; they ate in nice restaurants, hung out with her friends, went to parties.'

'Dad liked to watch TV. He hardly went out of the house.'

'No, not with Mum. Not with us.'

'They're quite—'

'Physical?'

'Intimate, yes.'

I fold the letters up tight and wrap them back in their brown paper envelope. I've read too much already. I don't want to know. I'm an uninvited guest, an intruder.

'I have more.'

'That's enough, Daniel . . . really.'

'You don't want to read them?'

I shake my head. My brother leans back, he looks defeated.

'I hated him for it. I *hated* him, for what he was doing to Mum.'

'He shouldn't have involved you. You were far too young . . . it wasn't fair.'

'I didn't understand it. Why *couldn't* I understand? I thought he was pathetic, just . . . weak.'

'Mum knew?'

He nods.

'When did . . . when do you think she found out?'

'I'm not sure. She'd probably put up with it for years. But Sylvie was so small, I don't think she'd have left him, and Dad doted on her, you saw how he was. I think she hoped Sylvie might mend things, bring the two of them back together.'

But she didn't, not really.

'He laid off for a while, the year after she was born, but he didn't . . . he couldn't stay away. He used to make me cover for him. I had to say Dad was out working on a build, that he couldn't be reached, that he'd called me.'

I'm feeling uneasy and adrift. How could this all go on without me? How was it possible not to know?

'She gave him an ultimatum in the end, that's when we moved over here.'

'Why didn't you tell me . . . you could have. Why didn't you say?'

He doesn't need to answer. He thought he was doing the right thing.

'I thought it would get better. I hoped it would . . . but it just got worse.'

'He missed her?'

Daniel's fingers clench and relax.

'He built that whole place just for her, the hotel, the Rose Bar, *all* of it. And I knew what was going on, I was there when they named it, I saw the neon sign they put up. He tried to buy me off with some fucking *telescopes*, can you believe it? And Mum was left at home . . . just as worn, just as lonely; getting stoned, getting drunk, and wearing those ridiculous clothes that she'd started to wear, because she thought they made her look more . . . *attractive.'*

'She still loved him?'

'I suppose so.'

'So, that's how it was?'

'Yes, sis . . . that's how it was.'

The taxi arrives to ferry us to a hotel in Orlando.

'Are you scared?'

'I'm ashamed.'

'You shouldn't be.'

'I'm a coward.'

'No, you're not.'

'Yes, I am.'

We smile at one another, I can't believe we're smiling. Even now, we squabble like children.

'Julian will be there. Kay brought him.'

He's shocked. He crumbles. He slumps.

'Hey . . . *hey*, it's all right.'

Daniel inhales from his stomach, he can't seem to get enough air.

'Is he OK?'

'He had a cold . . . but he's fine.'

He absorbs this slowly, he does everything slowly. He looks shell-shocked, stretched, overloaded.

'I didn't know what to do . . . I just, I wanted to leave.'

'Please . . . it's OK. I'm here, I'll go with you. You'll be fine.'

'I couldn't stay.'

'I know, I understand.'

'Julian would have grown up to hate me.'

'He wouldn't. He won't.'

We ride in the taxi with the dusk folding in on us; Daniel in shreds, his head resting up against the window.

'How long?'

'My affair? About a year. There was nothing much left . . .
Kay and I . . . not for me . . . there was nothing much left.'

'She knew about it, didn't she?'

'I told her. I finished it the day the Columbia went down. I
watched it on the news and it just . . . it just *shattered* me. I couldn't
believe what I was doing to them . . . what I'd *done*. I came home
and confessed the whole thing. I'm just like him, isn't that perfect?
It turns out . . . I'm exactly the same.'

He stares out through the glass.

'I tried to put things right. I tried to go backwards . . . I
couldn't . . . I just couldn't do it. I turned into such an arse . . .
so sanctimonious. I remember telling Sylvie that you and Michael
should give it another go, can you imagine?'

'No,' I say. 'No, I can't.'

'I was jealous or something. You've always been so free with
your life, Claire. You've always gone your own way with your
life.'

My own way. Perfect. Like a blind man feeling around in the
dark.

'And Chloe, I cared for her, but I didn't . . . not like Dad loved
Annie. She was an escape route, that's all.'

'From what?'

He exhales.

'From the boredom, the job, from the marriage. It was always
so *rigid* . . . such a lie. I felt crushed . . . I always felt crushed. I
tried to make it up to him, to Dad. I did everything he wanted.
I gave myself away, gave it up. What *more* could I do for him? I
did what he asked me. I rubbed myself out. I led the life he
wanted me to lead.'

We stare at each other. We understand the depth of his mistake.

'I went the wrong way,' he says coldly. 'We took the wrong
exit. I went the wrong way with my life.'

Outside on the hotel forecourt, my brother's eyes dip down and
glaze over. I tell him he shouldn't be so hard on himself and he
laughs.

'I don't know, Claire . . . shouldn't I be dead?'

'Please . . . *please*, don't say that.'

'I planned it for months,' he says, quietly. 'It's all that kept me going. Putting money aside . . . siphoning funds . . . I felt like an actor, a ghost. I didn't deserve it, the life that I had . . . couldn't make sense of it any longer.'

'So, you took it off?'

He looks confused.

'Removed it . . . like another man's coat?'

'I just wanted . . . to start again . . . to begin my life over. I thought to come looking for my old one. I hoped it might still be here, where I buried it.'

'But it wasn't?'

He shakes his head.

'I planned to move on . . . I should have moved on from here straight away. But I still had to save him. I still had to put it all right.'

'And you couldn't?'

'I tried, Claire. I tried.'

We walk towards the hotel. It has a revolving door, the kind that never stops turning.

'How . . . how do you feel about him, now?'

'I think he was selfish, a coward just like I am. I think he turned our mother into an alcoholic.'

'But you feel sorry for him?'

He falters.

'I don't think he knew what kind of a life he was meant to lead. He had no idea how to lead it.'

'You understand him now?'

'I think I do.'

We ride up in the lift, tight like a coffin, and rest for a while outside the room. I can hear Julian playing. He's ringing a bell, squeezing a toy, I think he might be giggling. He's giggling. Daniel's face is alight. He can't wait to see him, to hold him, to kiss him; he's stuffed full of grief for his child. And then I

see him stiffen and change. He doesn't know how to open the
door.

'I don't know what to say.'

'It doesn't matter. Be yourself.'

He's confused, he wonders what this means. He starts to push
at his cheeks; pulling the skin, dragging his pores, willing his
bones to shape up. He's trying to remould himself, to be the
Daniel Kay knows, the Daniel she expects him to be. He can't
do it. He deflates. He steps back.

'And then what? What happens next? Afterwards, I just . . . I
go back?'

He's so near, he's so *close*; his damp hand is pressing on the
handle, his fingertips are touching the lock. Don't do this to me
now, it's my one good chance. Pinhead, you *have* to give me this.
I turn up with you now, I'm the hero: I go home without you,
I'm lost.

'You don't have to go anywhere,' I say finally. 'It's your life,
you can do what you like with it.'

'Can I?'

'It's yours. Take it back.'

He relaxes. He calms. Looks alive.

'I might like to stay . . . I don't know . . .'

'It's fine, whatever. You don't have to decide, yet. But right
now you ought to go in there.'

'Alone?'

'It would probably be better.'

He breathes. He squeezes my hand.

'Fats, Mum will never forgive you for this. Didn't you promise
to bring me home?'

It's true, Pinhead, I did. But I promised someone else that I
wouldn't.

My brother and I stand by the ocean looking up at the carpet
of stars. I don't ask him how it went, there's no need to; I can
read the whole story – every line, all regrets – just by feeling the
roughness of his hand.

'Is that rocket still up there?'

'Yes, it'll be in orbit now.'

'What's the point?'

'What do you mean?'

'Of going out there, into space. I don't see the point, all that emptiness.'

'Look at it, Claire. See how vast it is up there.'

'I see that. It makes me feel small.'

'That's the point.'

'Is it?'

'You have to think things could be different. It gives me . . . it's always made me hopeful.'

'Black holes, they make you feel good?'

'No Fats, not the holes.'

'What then? The giant stars, the frozen planets, the lack of atmosphere? Everything charred and uninhabitable?'

'No.'

He smiles.

'The lack of gravity. Just for a second, wouldn't you like to feel weightless?'

We spend some time jumping on the sand. No matter how hard we push our legs into the ground we still come crashing back down to earth. Daniel on his arse in the sand, me face down in the water. But it feels good to try. So we jump. We both jump for hours.

Re-entry

The Meteorologist

'Come on Julian, let's find your coat. Kay, is he going to need his coat?'

'It's winter there. Pack it, he'll need it.'

'You won't come back speaking like an Aussie will you, Jools? Grandma will still be able to understand you?'

'Yes.'

'You won't change?'

'I won't change.'

'You'll still be you?'

'Yes.'

'How will I know?'

He screws up his face.

'Don't be silly, Grandma. Me's *me*.'

'You're confusing him.'

'I wasn't trying to.'

'Well, I didn't say that . . . but you are.'

We are a family subtly shifted; uniquely altered and changed. If you're careful, if you're gracious, if you don't dig about too hard, you'd probably find us much the same. But underneath the surface, deep below the skin, our atoms have fractured and realigned. The patterns we've spent a lifetime sewing into place have slowly begun to unravel. We don't refract the light in quite the same way that we did, our centre of gravity has shifted. Where did they go to, those people we were last year? Try as I might, I can't keep hold of us.

★ ★ ★

'You'll be with your Daddy at Christmas. Are you looking forward to seeing your Daddy?'

'Yes, because Daddy lives at Disney World.'

'You spoke to him at the weekend, didn't you. Weren't you a clever boy on the phone?'

My mother has her fingers on her grandson's cheeks: squeezing them, pinching them too tight. He squirms, he doesn't like it. He can't understand she's already missing him.

'Will you miss your Grandma?'

'Yes.'

'Will you call her?'

'Mummy, will we call Grandma?'

'You should visit us,' Kay says. 'Why don't you visit? Robert, you must try and make her come out.'

Robert promises to work on her, but all of us suspect she'll never make it. The Australian outback, this is where they're headed; a sheep station in the depths of New South Wales owned by Kay's uncle and aunt. The divorce came through a couple of weeks ago and Kay decided she needed to take some time out. She deserves a break and a chance to refuel, six months away from the grind.

'I won't need these shoes. Sylvie, you're the same size as me. Do you want to take these shoes?'

'They're beautiful, they must have cost a fortune.'

'Take them . . . really. I don't want them. There's more in the trunk, take the whole box if you like.'

Kay on a farm, I can't imagine it. But look at her now, look at the way she's loosened up.

'Jools, *puppy*, come on now. Put your trousers back on.'

'Don't want to.'

'I know you don't want to, but we can't always do what we want.'

'Leave him, Kay, he's all right. It's hot in here, he's probably hot.'

She ruffles his hair. She leaves him be.

There's so much to clear out when you sell a house like this and move on. Most of it is going straight into storage but much of it will just be thrown away: papers and ornaments, pictures and baby clothes, textbooks and records and tapes; fragments of a marriage snapped in half.

'Do you want to take his telescope?'

'If that's OK?'

'I'm sure he'd like you to have it.'

'I'll take care of it, for when he comes back.'

I don't know why I said that, she hates it when I say that, but I'm certain he'll settle back in London some day. He's running in another of his marathons this week. He's competed in half a dozen since he left; always in the top fifty finishers, always in under three hours. He runs them for charity, Amnesty or Oxfam, and once or twice for the British Heart Foundation.

Daniel's travelled a lot since the breakdown. Is that what you'd call it, a breakdown? Anyway, he's been all over the world: Asia, India, South America, Alaska, Japan. He thinks he might settle down in Florida for a while now to study for a degree in astronomy but I'm not convinced that he'll do it. I'm not sure he's really all that happy. I know he misses Julian like crazy, and it will take him a while yet to admit it, but there are other parts of his old life he misses too. Last month one of his running mates dragged him off to Nevada for the Burning Man festival in the desert, some kind of annual new age retreat. He called me the second he got back.

'What was it like?'

'Ridiculous, full of hippies. You have to barter for food, there's nothing to buy. Everyone coats themselves in wild-coloured body paint, takes drugs and dances all night.'

'Right, and that was . . . ?'

'I don't know, Claire it was OK . . . an experience, you know. I mean, it's supposed to be a place where everyone can be themselves. But, fuck it . . . it wasn't really me.'

So he's getting to know what he is now. He's getting to know where he stands. The last time we spoke he confessed he missed practising law, that he was good at it, better than he thought.

The marathons are wearing away the cartilage in his knees and he's not sure he can face going back to university at his age. There's a piece of him that liked the big house he had in London: the status, the cars, the security. Perhaps he chose more of it than he realised. And maybe Dad was right after all; you can't make a living from running.

'Some of these things should go to a charity shop. Daniel's suits. Kay, you *can't* throw away Daniel's suits.'

'I haven't got time. I think we'll just have to dump them.'

'I'll do it, I'll take them next week.'

My mother's face tightens.

'No . . . Claire, you'll forget. Sylvie, will you take these things for Kay?'

Sylvie knows better than to answer a question like that these days. Gabriel squeezes her hand.

'Mum, I won't forget, I'll take care of it.'

She takes a moment.

'You'll remember to wrap them up in cellophane?'

'Yes.'

'They'll get moths in them otherwise. They're wool, you ought to remember to use moth balls.'

'I said I'll take care of it. I'll take care of it.'

'Well, I suppose . . . if you're sure?'

Mum lifts a glass of juice to her lips – orange, or mango, I can't tell which. She doesn't drink alcohol at all any more, she's a recent disciple of AA. She spent so many years being absent from herself but when Daniel left, it forced her to be present. So we shifted. So we turned. So she drew the rest of us towards her. We're still drifting, still separate, still speaking in code – but we're progressing. Occasionally, we even speak the same language.

'I was angry with you,' she said to me last year.

'I know you were.'

'For not realising. For not being there. Your father was . . . it was always . . . hard for me.'

'You could have told me . . . you could have said something.'
But she couldn't, of course. She really couldn't.
'I was protecting you. I didn't mean to punish . . . to *confuse* you.'
'I would have helped.'
'Sweetheart, I know that you would.'

'I think we should all drink a toast.'
'Christ . . . must I have orange juice again? Robert, I'm so sick
of orange juice.'
'Elderflower cordial?'
'Disgusting . . . have you tried it? Sylvie, don't make me have
it, it's revolting.'
Sylvie hands the champagne bottle to Gabe and he twists off
the cork with a flourish. Still strong, still stupidly handsome, and
newly engaged to my sister.
'To the wedding, next year. Let's hope we can all be . . .' My
sister falters, she trails off.
'To the wedding.'
'And to Sylvie. Her results.'
Sylvie passed the first stage of her medical exams this month
and I've never seen her look quite so happy. She's fulfilled her
own destiny. She finally has a purpose. She's becoming the person
everyone always said she was; she's the girl who makes people
feel better. We met Gabe's family last week at her graduation,
his father baked a beautiful cake. You should have seen his mother,
his two sisters. They're stunning, outrageous, they almost make
Sylvie seem plain. Gabe's a boy grown immune to the value of
beauty, that's part of why she loves him so much. I wonder if
she's still doing phone sex? In secret, on Thursdays, when Gabriel
works late nights at the bakery. I don't know what it is, but there's
something about her. I wouldn't be at all surprised.
'So, Claire. How's it going with the meteorologist?'
'He . . . yeah, it's OK.'
'Meteorologist? I didn't know there was a meteorologist.'
'He's someone I met in Florida. We've been writing to each
other. He's over here on sabbatical.'

'She likes him.'

'Sylvie.'

'OK, OK . . . I'm just saying.'

'So, tell me about him. What's he like?'

We laugh a lot. He makes me laugh. He's layered, soulful and generous, and beguilingly difficult to read. He's wild like Michael, kind like Huey. He is the man that I might almost love.

'Come on, don't be so secretive. Tell me, what is he *like?*'

'It's early days, Mum. It's early days.'

'Shit . . . it's late. I ought to get going.'

'You're going to the restaurant, *now?*'

'I have to, Robert, it's a busy night.'

'That place . . . it's always so busy.'

'She's turned that place around. New staff, new look. That place has turned around since she bought the lease.'

It seemed like a good thing to do. A good way to use Michael's money.

'He paid her back extra, with interest. About time he did. The little sod.'

'Did you see his new album in the shops?'

'Yeah, I did. I saw it.'

'It had a snake on the front cover. Why a snake?'

'I couldn't tell you. I haven't the foggiest idea.'

Gabriel hands out the glasses, refilled and fizzing. Overflowing.

'Another toast,' he says, proudly.

'Another toast.'

'To family,' he says.

'To family.'

We embrace and clink our glasses together. It took an outsider to say it.

The Best Pancakes You Ever
Tasted in Your Life

Yori waves from the corner of the restaurant.

'OK, partner?'

'Yeah, partner. I'm good.'

She's deep in conversation with someone, the first hungry customer of the day. I have some papers to look through so I head for the office, next to the old TV set. A video is playing but, with the door left ajar, I can still hear most of what they're saying.

'Why do you ask me this question? I say to you already, is bad idea. A difficult journey. So hard for a person to come back.

'Yes, I understand, you unhappy. Yes, so you say, nasty wife. But I'm certain in my bones that it wouldn't suit you.

'Is it real . . . yes, of course it is real. Is not just a TV show, let me tell you. This Yonigeya, it really exist.

'In Tokyo mostly. Maybe all over Japan. People fed up with suicide. Very high suicide rate in Japan. Now some people think is maybe better to disappear. But like I say, like I *said* . . . I'm not sure it really is so easy.

'Why not? Pah . . . you have no imagination. Perhaps this why your wife decide to leave you.

'OK, OK. So sorry. She left you for ski instructor. I remember. But think for a moment. Open your heart. Imagine what it is that you plan to do. How empty it would make a man feel. To dispose of everything he is. How rotten and bruised like soft autumnal fruit dropped prematurely from the tree. Everything he has become, discarded like a bowl of dirty rice water. If a person is to leave on such a journey he must die a little inside. He must walk along riverbank and look into water and be content to see no reflection.

'You don't think it is so difficult? You don't think really *is* so sad? Pay attention, stupid man, I'm telling you. Don't underestimate your life. All your short time on this earth – good or bad, sad or happy – whatever it is, have special value. All you are now depend on every piece that went before you. What a dense and fabulous web a man weaves; how beautiful, how complex is his life. All mistakes are like scars. Tough. Thick. Make web even stronger than before. Every time he take turn in wrong direction just make the web even bigger.

'No my friend, spider's web not ugly. You are wrong, you don't look at it right. Get up to it close, with your nose and your eyes: see how ingenious it is. And every time it breaks, in the wind, in the storm, every time it is torn by some rude insect – the spider makes it over again. Mending it. Always trying to mend it. Maybe is only perfect for a second. Maybe only complete for one short hour. But happiness is like that. It breaks. It splits. You mend it. It breaks all over again. It comes in short bursts. Only moments.

'Yes. Yes. I see how you feel. You mend your web so many times, you prefer to start again and throw away. But you *must* understand, it is very drastic action. To wrap old life up in a suitcase and to never open suitcase again. To leave all you love, your home and your family, to put all you are in the bin.

'Yes, I promise you. This type of action only for exceptional people. Only for people in special trouble. I hear about one lovely couple who do this and succeed. You want that I tell you about them?

'OK, so these two special characters they are deeply in love but in their hearts they are sad. This poor bald man – talented actor so they say – is sucked dry like prune and unfulfilled. His career, through circumstances unforeseen, lie in ruins. The woman can't make this man happy so she feel ugly sometimes, and often afraid that he might leave her. This gentle man is the whole world to her. He is her family.

'One day they involve themselves in incredible escapade. They kidnap very famous person. Person knows who they are and sees their face. They are very much in trouble, is no way they can go back to their old lives.

'Lucky for them, they have one special friend who comes to rescue. Loyal friend who is there at *precise* moment when they need her, most capable and reliable person. This is her first ever job of this kind, but she pulls it off with big style. She sends them away on a . . . how do you say it?

'Yes, how do you guess? She smuggle them away on board a ship. She put them in contact with lovely woman that she knows in England, very beautiful and talented chef. Talented chef helps them with next part of their journey. Give them brand new life, new identity.

'Where they end up? Me, I don't know. Some say Australia, some say Atlanta, some clever person says Peru. Very interesting film industry in Peru, so they say. Very fine actors. Up and coming. For this man is nourishment for his soul just to act in small production in small theatre, he doesn't care for fame or for money. And his wife . . .

'Yes, that's right. Didn't I tell you? These two, they get marry. I hear they have child now. She has one little girl and I see in the pictures . . . I mean, I *hear* from some people, that she gets a little fat. Some people say she runs a karaoke bar. Some say she runs a special restaurant a little like this one. The best in whole town. Peruvians love it, she make pancake. The best pancake you ever tasted in your life. This woman very famous for her pancake. Her husband most admired for his astonishing acting. Everyone who come to see him at the theatre leave in tears; especially one extra special Peruvian film star. Maybe they plan to work together one day. This man also admired for his thick head of hair. Plugs very cheap in Peru.

'Are they happy? Yes. This is what I hear. Both are especially happy. And all arranged for them by one very special girl. Speak many languages, seven I think, and have the best contacts for escaping. Most intriguing and talented lady. These days, so they tell me, she is one of the finest fly-by-night arrangers in all the world. Very fine instincts, a true escape artist. Can get to heart of problem just like that. For a long time this lady believed her instincts were poor, for a long time she believed she was most unreliable person. In the house where she grew up the walls were funny shape, for a long time she can't get her bearings. But this girl is sharp, let me tell you. No one read a situation better than her. No one give better solution to a problem. No one give better service than she.

'Ah, Cherries Lady, there you are. This man, so insistent. I try to shake him off, but he has one question for you.'

He asks me. I listen. I answer.

'No,' I say, gently. 'I'm afraid you're mistaken. There are no Yonigeya in London.'

BOOKS BY LOUISE WENER

THE PERFECT PLAY
A Novel

ISBN 0-06-058548-X (paperback)

With extraordinary perception
and emotional insight, Wener
captures the comedy, pathos
and drama that mark each of
our lives in this compelling
page-turner that exposes the
dark underworld of real Las
Vegas poker.

"Abandonment issues have
never been so funny. . . .
Wener's prose is bright; her
humor, as the Brits would say,
is brilliant." —USA Today

GOODNIGHT
STEVE MCQUEEN
A Novel

ISBN 0-06-072563-X (paperback)

A charmingly romantic—
yet very edgy—novel set in the
music industry about friendship,
love, growing up, and always
following your dreams.

"Drawing on her own
experiences in the music
industry, Wener tells [a]
thoroughly enjoyable story. . . .
It is a sweet and funny read."
—Booklist